Praise for #1 *New York Times* bestselling author

NORA ROBERTS

"Roberts...is at the top of her game."

—*People* magazine

"Roberts has a warm feel for her characters and an eye for the evocative detail."

—*Chicago Tribune*

"When Roberts puts her expert fingers on the pulse of romance, legions of fans feel the heartbeat."

—*Publishers Weekly*

"You can't bottle wish fulfillment, but Nora Roberts certainly knows how to put it on the page."

—*New York Times*

"A superb author...Ms. Roberts is an enormously gifted writer whose incredible range and intensity guarantee the very best of reading."

—*Rave Reviews*

"America's favorite writer."

—*New Yorker*

Dear Reader,

Passionate, proud and hopelessly romantic, the Stanislaskis are a family you won't soon forget! We here at Silhouette Books are delighted to bring you this captivating six-book family saga by romance master Nora Roberts. We hope you'll enjoy collecting all three volumes in the series, beginning with *Catch My Heart*, which includes books one and two: *Taming Natasha* and *Luring a Lady*.

In *Taming Natasha*, beautiful, tempestuous Natasha Stanislaski catches the eye—and steals the heart—of single dad Spencer Kimball. But secrets in her past have caused Natasha to keep her own heart closely guarded. Could sexy Spence be the one man to break through the wall she's built around herself?

Luring a Lady features Natasha's handsome, artistic oldest brother, Mikhail, whose work-hardened hands aren't what wealthy ice princess Sydney Hayward is accustomed to. But the classy real estate heiress has to admit she finds the earthy stranger strangely…irresistible.

We hope you fall head over heels for this fascinating Ukrainian American family!

Until next time,

The Editors
Silhouette Books

NORA ROBERTS

CATCH MY HEART

Includes *Taming Natasha* & *Luring a Lady*

Silhouette Books

SILHOUETTE™

Catch My Heart

ISBN-13: 978-1-335-23097-3

Copyright © 2021 by Harlequin Books S.A.

Taming Natasha
First published in 1990. This edition published in 2021.
Copyright © 1990 by Nora Roberts

Luring a Lady
First published in 1991. This edition published in 2021.
Copyright © 1991 by Nora Roberts

Recycling programs for this product may not exist in your area.

For questions and comments about the quality of this book, please contact us at CustomerService@Harlequin.com.

Silhouette
22 Adelaide St. West, 40th Floor
Toronto, Ontario M5H 4E3, Canada
www.Harlequin.com

Printed in Lithuania

MIX
Paper from responsible sources
FSC® C021394

CONTENTS

TAMING NATASHA

For Gayle Link
Welcome to the fold

Chapter 1

"Why is it that all the really great-looking men are married?"

"Is that a trick question?" Natasha arranged a velvet-gowned doll in a child-sized bentwood rocker before she turned to her assistant. "Okay, Annie, what great-looking man are we talking about in particular?"

"The tall, blond and gorgeous one who's standing outside the shop window with his nifty-looking wife and beautiful little girl." Annie tucked a wad of gum into her cheek and heaved a gusty sigh. "They look like an ad for *Perfect Family Digest*."

"Then perhaps they'll come in and buy the perfect toy."

Natasha stepped back from her grouping of Victorian dolls and accessories with a nod of approval. It looked exactly as she wanted—appealing, elegant and old-fashioned. She checked everything down to the tasseled fan in a tiny, china hand.

The toy store wasn't just her business, it was her greatest pleasure. Everything from the smallest rattle to the biggest stuffed bear was chosen by her with the same eye for detail and quality. She insisted on the best for her shop and her customers, whether it was a five-hundred-dollar doll with its own fur wrap or a two-dollar, palm-sized race car. When the match was right, she was pleased to ring up either sale.

In the three years since she had opened her jingling front door, Natasha had made The Fun House one of the most thriving concerns in the small college town on the West Virginia border. It had taken drive and persistence, but her success was more a direct result of her innate understanding of children. She didn't want her clients to walk out with a toy. She wanted them to walk out with the right toy.

Deciding to make a few adjustments, Natasha moved over to a display of miniature cars.

"I think they're going to come in," Annie was saying as she smoothed down her short crop of auburn hair. "The little girl's practically bouncing out of her Mary Janes. Want me to open up?"

Always precise, Natasha glanced at the grinning clown clock overhead. "We have five minutes yet."

"What's five minutes? Tash, I'm telling you this guy is incredible." Wanting a closer look, Annie edged down an aisle to restack board games. "Oh, yes. Six foot two, a hundred and sixty pounds. The best shoulders I've ever seen fill out a suit jacket. Oh Lord, it's tweed. I didn't know a guy in tweed could make me salivate."

"A man in cardboard can make you salivate."

"Most of the guys I know *are* cardboard." A dimple winked at the corner of Annie's mouth. She peeked around the counter of wooden toys to see if he was still at the window. "He must have spent some time at the beach this summer. His hair's sun-streaked and he's got a fabulous tan. Oh, God, he smiled at the little girl. I think I'm in love."

Choreographing a scaled-down traffic jam, Natasha smiled. "You always think you're in love."

"I know." Annie sighed. "I wish I could see the color of his eyes. He's got one of those wonderfully lean and bony faces. I'm sure he's incredibly intelligent and has suffered horribly."

Natasha shot a quick, amused look over her shoulder. Annie, with her tall, skinny build had a heart as soft as marshmallow cream. "I'm sure his wife would be fascinated with your fantasy."

"It's a woman's privilege—no, her obligation—to weave fantasies over men like that."

Though she couldn't have disagreed more, Natasha let Annie have her way. "All right then. Go ahead and open up."

"One doll," Spence said, giving his daughter's ear a tug. "I might have thought twice about moving into that house, if I'd realized there was a toy store a half mile away."

"You'd buy her the bloody toy store if you had your way."

He spared one glance for the woman beside him. "Don't start, Nina."

The slender blonde shrugged her shoulders, rippling the trim, rose linen jacket of her suit, then looked at the little girl. "I just meant your daddy tends to spoil you because he loves you so much. Besides, you deserve a present for being so good about the move."

Little Frederica Kimball's bottom lip pouted. "I like my new house." She slipped her hand into her father's, automatically aligning herself with him and against the world. "I have a yard and a swing set all of my own."

Nina looked them over, the tall, rangy man and the fairy-sized young girl. They had identical stubborn chins. As far as she could remember, she'd never won an argument with either one.

"I suppose I'm the only one who doesn't see that as an advantage over living in New York." Nina's tone warmed slightly as she stroked the girl's hair. "I can't help worrying about you a little bit. I really only want you to be happy, darling. You and your daddy."

"We are." To break the tension, Spence swung Freddie into his arms. "Aren't we, funny face?"

"She's about to be that much happier." Relenting, Nina gave Spence's hand a squeeze. "They're opening."

"Good morning." They were gray, Annie noted, biting back a long, dreamy, "Ahh." A glorious gray. She tucked her little fantasy into the back of her mind and ushered in the first customers of the day. "May I help you?"

"My daughter's interested in a doll." Spence set Freddie on her feet again.

"Well, you've come to the right place." Annie dutifully switched her attention to the child. She really was a cute little thing, with her father's gray eyes and pale, flyaway blond hair. "What kind of doll would you like?"

"A pretty one," Freddie answered immediately. "A pretty one with red hair and blue eyes."

"I'm sure we have just what you want." She offered a hand. "Would you like to look around?"

After a glance at her father for approval, Freddie linked hands with Annie and wandered off.

"Damn it." Spence found himself wincing.

Nina squeezed his hand for the second time. "Spence—"

"I delude myself thinking that it doesn't matter, that she doesn't even remember."

"Just because she wanted a doll with red hair and blue eyes doesn't mean anything."

"Red hair and blue eyes," he repeated; the frustration welled up once more. "Just like Angela's. She remembers, Nina. And it does matter." Stuffing his hands into his pockets he walked away.

Three years, he thought. It had been nearly three years now. Freddie had still been in diapers. But she remembered Angela—beautiful, careless Angela. Not even the most liberal critic would have considered Angela a mother. She had never cuddled or crooned, never rocked or soothed.

He studied a small, porcelain-faced doll dressed in pale, angelic blue. Tiny, tapering fingers, huge, dreamy eyes. Angela had been like that, he remembered. Ethereally beautiful. And cold as glass.

He had loved her as a man might love a piece of art— distantly admiring the perfection of form, and constantly searching for the meaning beneath it. Between them they had somehow created a warm, gorgeous child who had managed to find her way through the first years of her life almost without help from her parents.

But he would make it up to her. Spence shut his eyes for a moment. He intended to do everything in his power to give his daughter the love, the structure and the security she deserved. The realness. The word seemed trite, but it was the only one he could find that described what he wanted for his daughter—the real, the solid bond of family.

She loved him. He felt some of the tension ease from his shoulders as he thought of the way Freddie's big eyes would shine when he tucked her in at night, at the way her arms would wrap tightly around him when he held her. Perhaps he would never fully forgive himself for being so involved with his own problems, his own life during her infancy, but things had changed. Even this move had been made with her welfare in mind.

He heard her laugh, and the rest of the tension dissolved on a wave of pure pleasure. There was no sweeter music than his little girl's laugh. An entire symphony could be written around it. He wouldn't disturb her yet, Spence thought. Let her indulge herself with the bright and beautiful dolls, before he had to remind her that only one could be hers.

Relaxed again, he began to pay attention to the shop. Like the dolls he'd imagined for his daughter, it was bright and beautiful. Though small, it was packed from wall to wall with everything a child might covet. A big golden giraffe and a sad-eyed purple dog hung from the ceiling. Wooden trains, cars and planes, all painted in bold colors, jockeyed for position on a long display table with elegant miniature furniture. An old-fashioned jack-in-the-box sat beside an intricate scale model of a futuristic space station. There were dolls, some beautiful, some charmingly homely, erector sets and tea sets.

The lack of studied arrangement made the result all the more appealing. This was a place to pretend and to wish, a crowded Aladdin's cave designed to make children's eyes light in wonder. To make them laugh, as his daughter was laughing now. He could already foresee that he'd be hard-pressed to keep Freddie from making regular visits.

That was one of the reasons he'd made the move to a small town. He wanted his daughter to be able to reap the pleasures of local shops, where the merchants would know her name. She would be able to walk from one end of town to the other without those big-city worries about muggings, abductions and drugs. There would be no need for dead bolts and security systems, for "white noise" machines to block out the surge and grind of traffic. Even a girl as little as his Freddie wouldn't be swallowed up here.

And perhaps, without the pace and the pressure, he would make peace with himself.

Idly he picked up a music box. It was of delicately crafted porcelain, graced with a figure of a raven-haired Gypsy woman in a flounced red dress. In her ears were tiny gold loops, and in her hands a tambourine with colored streamers. He was certain he wouldn't have found anything more skillfully made on Fifth Avenue.

He wondered how the owner could leave it out where small, curious fingers might reach and break. Intrigued, he turned the key and watched the figure revolve around the tiny, china campfire.

Tchaikovsky. He recognized the movement instantly, and his skilled ear approved the quality of tone. A moody, even passionate piece, he thought, finding it strange to come across such exquisite workmanship in a toy store. Then he glanced up and saw Natasha.

He stared. He couldn't help it. She was standing a few feet away, her head up, slightly tilted as she watched him. Her hair was as dark as the dancer's and corkscrewed around her face in a wild disarray that flowed beyond her shoulders. Her skin was a dark, rich gold that was set off by the simple red dress she wore.

But this woman was not fragile, he thought. Though she was small, he got the impression of power. Perhaps it was her face, with its full, unpainted mouth and high, slashing cheekbones. Her eyes were almost as dark as her hair, heavy-lidded and thickly lashed. Even from a distance of ten feet he sensed it. Strong, undiluted sex. It surrounded her as other women surrounded themselves with perfumes.

For the first time in years he felt the muscle-numbing heat of pure desire.

Natasha saw it, then recognized and resented it. What kind of man, she wondered, walked into a room with his wife and daughter, then looked at another woman with naked hunger in his eyes?

Not her kind.

Determined to ignore the look as she had ignored it from others in the past, she crossed to him. "Do you need some help?"

Help? Spence thought blankly. He needed oxygen. He hadn't known it was literally possible for a woman to take a man's breath away. "Who are you?"

"Natasha Stanislaski." She offered her coolest smile. "I own the store."

Her voice seemed to hang in the air, husky, vital, with a trace of her Slavic origins adding eroticism as truly as the music still playing behind him. She smelled of soap, nothing more, yet the fragrance completely seduced him.

When he didn't speak, she lifted a brow. It might have been amusing to knock a man off his feet, but she was busy at the moment, and the man was married. "Your daughter has her selection down to three dolls. Perhaps you'd like to help her with her final choice."

"In a minute. Your accent—is it Russian?"

"Yes." She wondered if she should tell him his wife was standing near the front door, bored and impatient.

"How long have you been in America?"

"Since I was six." She aimed a deliberately cold glance. "About the same age as your little girl. Excuse me—"

He had his hand on her arm before he could stop himself. Even though he knew the move was a bad one, the venom in her eyes surprised him. "Sorry. I was going to ask you about this music box."

Natasha shifted her gaze to it as the music began to wind down. "It's one of our best, handcrafted here in the States. Are you interested in buying it?"

"I haven't decided, but I thought you might not have realized it was sitting out on that shelf."

"Why?"

"It's not the kind of merchandise one expects to find in a toy store. It could easily be broken."

Natasha took it and placed it farther back on the shelf. "And it can be mended." She made a quick, clearly habitual movement with her shoulders. It spoke of arrogance rather than carelessness. "I believe children should be allowed the pleasures of music, don't you?"

"Yes." For the first time a smile flickered over his face. It was, as Annie had noted, a particularly effective one, Natasha had to admit. Through her annoyance she felt the trickle of attraction, and strangely, kinship. Then he said, "As a matter of fact, I believe that quite strongly. Perhaps we could discuss it over dinner."

Holding herself rigid, Natasha battled back fury. It was difficult for one with her hot, often turbulent nature, but she reminded herself that the man had not only his wife, but his young daughter in the store.

The angry insults that rose to her throat were swallowed, but not before Spence saw them reflected in her eyes.

"No," was all she said as she turned.

"Miss—" Spence began, then Freddie whirled down the aisle, carrying a big, floppy Raggedy Ann.

"Daddy, isn't she nice?" Eyes shining, she held out the doll for his approval.

It was redheaded, Spence thought. But it was anything

but beautiful. Nor, to his relief, was it a symbol of Angela. Because he knew Freddie expected it, he took his time examining her choice. "This is," he said after a moment, "the very best doll I've seen today."

"Really?"

He crouched until he was eye to eye with his daughter. "Absolutely. You have excellent taste, funny face."

Freddie reached out, crushing the doll between them as she hugged her father. "I can have her?"

"I thought she was for me." As Freddie giggled, he picked up the pair of them.

"I'll be happy to wrap her for you." Natasha's tone was warmer, she knew. He might be a jerk, but he loved his daughter.

"I can carry her." Freddie squeezed her new friend close.

"All right. Then I'll just give you a ribbon for her hair. Would you like that?"

"A blue one."

"A blue one it is." Natasha led the way to the cash register.

Nina took one look at the doll and rolled her eyes. "Darling, is that the best you could do?"

"Daddy likes her," Freddie murmured, ducking her head.

"Yes, I do. Very much," he added with a telling look for Nina. Setting Freddie on her feet again, he fished out his wallet.

The mother was certainly no prize, Natasha decided. Though that didn't give the man a right to come on to a clerk in a toy store. She made change and handed over the receipt, then took out a length of blue ribbon.

"Thank you," she said to Freddie. "I think she's going to like her new home with you very much."

"I'll take good care of her," Freddie promised, while she

struggled to tie the ribbon through the yarn mop of hair. "Can people come in to look at the toys, or do they have to buy one?"

Natasha smiled, then taking another ribbon, tied a quick, sassy bow in the child's hair. "You can come in and look anytime you like."

"Spence, we really must be going." Nina stood holding the door open.

"Right." He hesitated. It was a small town, he reminded himself. And if Freddie could come in and look, so could he. "It was nice meeting you, Miss Stanislaski."

"Goodbye." She waited until the door jingled and closed, then let out a muttered stream of curses.

Annie peeked around a tower of building blocks. "Excuse me?"

"That man."

"Yes." With a little sigh, Annie waltzed down the aisle. "That man."

"He brings his wife and child into a place like this, then looks at me as if he wants to nibble on my toes."

"Tash." Her expression pained, Annie pressed a hand to her heart. "Please don't excite me."

"I find it insulting." She skirted around the checkout counter and swung a fist at a punching bag. "He asked me to dinner."

"He *what*?" Delight showed in Annie's eyes, before a look from Natasha dampened it. "You're right. It is insulting, seeing as he's a married man—even though his wife seemed like a cold fish."

"His marital problems are no concern of mine."

"No...." Practicality warred with fantasy. "I guess you turned him down."

A choked sound caught in Natasha's throat as she turned. "Of course I turned him down."

"I mean, of course," Annie put in quickly.

"The man has a nerve," Natasha said; her fingers itched to hit something. "Coming into my place of business and propositioning me."

"He didn't!" Scandalized and thrilled, Annie grabbed Natasha's arm. "Tash, he didn't really proposition you? Right here?"

"With his eyes he did. The message was clear." It infuriated her how often men looked at her and only saw the physical. Only wanted to see the physical, she thought in disgust. She had tolerated suggestions, propositions and proposals since before she had fully understood what they meant. But she understood now and tolerated nothing.

"If he hadn't had that sweet little girl with him, I would have slapped his face." Because the image pleased her so much, she let loose on the hapless punching bag again.

Annie had seen her employer's temper fly often enough to know how to cool it. "She was sweet, wasn't she? Her name's Freddie. Isn't that cute?"

Natasha took a long, steadying breath even as she rubbed her fisted hand in her other palm. "Yes."

"She told me they had just moved to Shepherdstown from New York. The doll was going to be her first new friend."

"Poor little thing." Natasha knew too well the fears and anxieties of being a child in a strange place. Forget the father, she told herself with a toss of her head. "She looks to be about the same age as JoBeth Riley." Annoyance forgotten, Natasha went behind the counter again and picked up the phone. It wouldn't hurt to give Mrs. Riley a call.

* * *

Spence stood at the music-room window and stared out at a bed of summer flowers. Having flowers outside the window and a bumpy slope of lawn that would need tending was a new experience. He'd never cut grass in his life. Smiling to himself, he wondered how soon he could try his hand at it.

There was a big, spreading maple, its leaves a dark, dark green. In a few weeks, he imagined they would grow red and vibrant before they tumbled from the branches. He had enjoyed the view from his condo on Central Park West, watching the seasons come and go with the changing trees. But not like this, he realized.

Here the grass, the trees, the flowers he saw belonged to him. They were for him to enjoy and to care for. Here he could let Freddie take out her dolls for an afternoon tea party and not have to worry every second she was out of his sight. They would make a good life here, a solid life for both of them. He'd felt it when he'd flown down to discuss his position with the dean—and again when he'd walked through this big, rambling house with the anxious real-estate agent dogging his heels.

She hadn't had to sell it, Spence thought. He'd been sold the moment he'd walked in the front door.

As he watched, a hummingbird swooped to hover at the cup of a bright red petunia. In that instant he was more convinced than ever that his decision to leave the city had been the right one.

Having a brief fling with rural living. Nina's words rolled through his mind as he watched the sun flash on the bird's iridescent wings. It was difficult to blame her for saying it, for believing it when he had always chosen to live in the middle of things. He couldn't deny he had enjoyed those glittery parties that had lasted until dawn, or the elegant midnight suppers after a symphony or ballet.

He had been born into a world of glamour and wealth and prestige. He had lived all of his life in a place where only the best was acceptable. And he had relished it, Spence admitted. Summering in Monte Carlo, wintering in Nice or Cannes. Weekends in Aruba or Cancun.

He wouldn't wish those experiences away, but he could wish, and did, that he had accepted the responsibilities of his life sooner.

He accepted them now. Spence watched the humming-bird streak away like a sapphire bullet. And as much to his own surprise as to that of people who knew him, he was enjoying those responsibilities. Freddie made the difference. All the difference.

He thought of her and she came running across the back lawn, her new rag doll tucked under her arm. She made a beeline, as he expected, to the swing set. It was so new that the blue and white paint gleamed in the sunlight, and the hard plastic seats were shiny as leather. With the doll in her lap, she pushed off, her face lifted skyward, her tiny mouth moving to some private song.

Love rammed into him with a velvet fist, solid and painful. In all of his life he had never known anything as consuming or as basic as the emotion she brought to him simply by being.

As she glided back and forth, she cuddled the doll, bringing her close to whisper secrets into her ear. It pleased him to see Freddie so taken with the cloth and cotton doll. She could have chosen china or velvet, but had picked something that looked as though it needed love.

She'd spoken of the toy store throughout the morning, and was wishing, Spence knew, for a return trip. Oh, she wouldn't ask for anything, he thought. Not directly. She would use her eyes. It both amused and baffled him that at five, his little girl had already mastered that peculiar and effective feminine trick.

He'd thought of the toy store himself, and its owner. No feminine tricks there, just pure womanly disdain. It made him wince again to remember how clumsy he'd been. Out of practice, he reminded himself with a self-deprecating smile and rubbed a hand over the back of his neck. What was more, he couldn't remember ever experiencing that strong a sexual punch. It was like being hit by lightning, he decided. A man was entitled to fumble a bit after being electrified.

But her reaction… Frowning, Spence replayed the scene in his mind. She'd been furious. She'd damn near been quivering with fury before he'd opened his mouth—and put his foot in it.

She hadn't even attempted to be polite in her refusal. Just no—a single hard syllable crusted with frost at the edges. It wasn't as if he'd asked her to go to bed with him.

But he'd wanted to. From the first instant he had been able to imagine carrying her off to some dark, remote spot in the woods, where the ground was springy with moss and the trees blocked out the sky. There he could take the heat of those full, sulky lips. There he could indulge in the wild passion her face promised. Wild, mindless sex, heedless of time or place, of right or wrong.

Good God. Amazed, he pulled himself back. He was thinking like a teenager. No, Spence admitted, thrusting his hands into his pockets again. He was thinking like a man—one who had gone four years without a woman. He wasn't certain if he wanted to thank Natasha Stanislaski for unlocking all those needs again, or throttle her.

But he was certain he was going to see her again.

"I'm all packed." Nina paused in the doorway. She gave a little sigh; Spence was clearly absorbed in his own thoughts again. "Spencer," she said, raising her voice as she crossed the room. "I said I'm all packed."

"What? Oh." He managed a distracted smile and forced his shoulders to relax. "We'll miss you, Nina."

"You'll be glad to see the back of me," she corrected, then gave him a quick peck on the cheek.

"No." His smile came easier now, she saw, dutifully wiping the faint trace of lipstick from his skin. "I appreciate all you've done to help us settle in. I know how tight your schedule is."

"I could hardly let my brother tackle the wilds of West Virginia alone." She took his hand in a rare show of genuine agitation. "Oh, Spence, are you sure? Forget everything I've said before and think, really think it through. It's such a big change, for both of you. What will you possibly do here in your free time?"

"Cut the grass." Now he grinned at her expression. "Sit on the porch. Maybe I'll even write music again."

"You could write in New York."

"I haven't written two bars in almost four years," he reminded her.

"All right." She walked to the piano and waved a hand. "But if you wanted a change, you could have found a place on Long Island or even in Connecticut."

"I like it here, Nina. Believe me, this is the best thing I could do for Freddie, and myself."

"I hope you're right." Because she loved him, she smiled again. "I still say you'll be back in New York within six months. In the meantime, as that child's only aunt, I expect to be kept apprised of her progress." She glanced down, annoyed to see a chip in her nail polish. "The idea of her attending public school—"

"Nina."

"Never mind." She held up a hand. "There's no use starting this argument when I have a plane to catch. And I'm quite aware she's your child."

"Yes, she is."

Nina tapped a finger on the glossy surface of the baby grand. "Spence, I know you're still carrying around guilt because of Angela. I don't like to see it."

His easy smile vanished. "Some mistakes take a long time to be erased."

"She made you miserable," Nina said flatly. "There were problems within the first year of your marriage. Oh, you weren't forthcoming with information," she added when he didn't respond. "But there were others all too eager to pass it along to me or anyone else who would listen. It was no secret that she didn't want the child."

"And how much better was I, wanting the baby only because I thought it would fill the gaps in my marriage? That's a large burden to hand a child."

"You made mistakes. You recognized them and you rectified them. Angela never suffered a pang of guilt in her life. If she hadn't died, you would have divorced her and taken custody of Freddie. The result's the same. I know that sounds cold. The truth often is. I don't like to think that you're making this move, changing your life this dramatically because you're trying to make up for something that's long over."

"Maybe that's part of it. But there's more." He held out a hand, waiting until Nina came to him. "Look at her."

He pointed out the window to where Freddie continued to swing high, free as the hummingbird. "She's happy. And so am I."

Chapter 2

"**I**'m not scared."

"Of course you're not." Spence looked at his daughter's brave reflection in the mirror while he carefully braided her hair. He didn't need the quaver in her voice to tell him she was terrified. There was a rock in the pit of his own stomach the size of a fist.

"Some of the kids might cry." Her big eyes were already misted. "But I won't."

"You're going to have fun." He wasn't any more certain of that than his nervous daughter. The trouble with being a parent, he thought, was that you were supposed to sound sure of everything. "The first day of school's always a little scary, but once you get there and meet everyone, you'll have a great time."

She fixed him with a steady, owlish stare. "Really?"

"You liked kindergarten, didn't you?" It was evasive,

he admitted to himself, but he couldn't make promises he might not be able to keep.

"Mostly." She lowered her eyes, poking at the yellow, sea horse-shaped comb on her dresser. "But Amy and Pam won't be there."

"You'll make new friends. You've already met JoBeth." He thought of the pixieish brunette who had strolled by the house with her mother a couple of days before.

"I guess, and JoBeth is nice, but…" How could she explain that JoBeth already knew all of the other girls? "Maybe I should wait till tomorrow."

Their eyes met in the mirror again; he rested his chin on her shoulder. She smelled of the pale green soap she loved because it was shaped like a dinosaur. Her face was so much like his own, yet softer, finer, and to him infinitely beautiful.

"You could, but then tomorrow would be your first day of school. You'd still have butterflies."

"Butterflies?"

"Right here." He patted her tummy. "Doesn't it feel like butterflies dancing in there?"

That made her giggle. "Kind of."

"I've got them, too."

"Really?" Her eyes opened wide.

"Really. I've got to go to school this morning, just like you."

She fiddled with the pink ribbons he'd tied on the ends of her pigtails. She knew it wasn't the same for him, but didn't say so because she was afraid he'd get that worried look. Freddie had heard him talking to Aunt Nina once, and remembered how impatient he had sounded when she'd complained that he was uprooting *her niece* during her formative years.

Freddie wasn't sure exactly what formative years were, but she knew her daddy had been upset, and that even when Aunt Nina had gone again, he'd still had that worried look. She didn't want to make him worried, or to make him think Aunt Nina was right. If they went back to New York, the only swing sets were in the park.

Besides, she liked the big house and her new room. Even better, her father's new job was so close, he would be home every night long before dinner. Remembering not to pout, Freddie decided that since she wanted to stay, she'd have to go to school.

"Will you be here when I get home?"

"I think so. But if I'm not, Vera will be," he said, thinking of their longtime housekeeper. "You can tell me everything that happened." After kissing the top of her head, he set her on her feet. She looked achingly small in her pink and white playsuit. Her gray eyes were solemn, her bottom lip trembling. He fought back the urge to gather her up and promise that she'd never have to go to school or anywhere else that frightened her. "Let's go see what Vera packed in your new lunch box."

Twenty minutes later he was standing on the curb, holding Freddie's hand in his own. With almost as much dread as his daughter he saw the big yellow school bus lumbering over the hill.

He should have driven her to school, he thought in sudden panic—at least for the first few days. He should take her himself, instead of putting her onto that bus with strangers. Yet it had seemed better to make the whole event normal, to let her ease into the group and become one of them from the outset.

How could he let her go? She was just a baby. *His baby.* What if he was wrong? This wasn't just a matter of picking out the wrong color dress for her. Simply because it was the designated day and time, he was going to tell his daughter to get onto that bus, then walk away.

What if the driver was careless and drove off a cliff? How could he be sure someone would make certain Freddie got back onto the right bus that afternoon?

The bus rumbled to a halt and his fingers tightened instinctively on hers. When the door clattered open, he was almost ready to make a run for it.

"Hi, there." The driver, a large woman with a wide smile, nodded at him. Behind her, children were yelling and bouncing on the seats. "You must be Professor Kimball."

"Yes." He had excuses for not putting Freddie on the bus on the tip of his tongue.

"I'm Dorothy Mansfield. The kids just call me Miss D. And you must be Frederica."

"Yes, ma'am." She bit her bottom lip to keep from turning away and hiding her face against her father's side. "It's Freddie."

"Whew." Miss D gave another big grin. "I'm glad to hear that. Frederica sure is a mouthful. Well, hop aboard, Freddie girl. This is the big day. John Harman, you give that book back to Mikey, less'n you want to sit behind me in the hot seat the rest of the week."

Eyes swimming, Freddie put one foot onto the first step. Swallowing, she climbed the second.

"Why don't you take a seat with JoBeth and Lisa there?" Miss D suggested kindly. She turned back to Spence with a wink and a wave. "Don't worry about a thing, Professor. We'll take good care of her."

The door closed on a puff of air, then the bus rumbled ahead. Spence could only stand on the curb and watch it take his little girl away.

* * *

He wasn't exactly idle. Spence's time was eaten up almost from the moment he walked into the college. He had his own schedule to study, associates to meet, instruments and sheet music to pore over. There was a faculty meeting, a hurried lunch in the lounge, and there were papers, dozens of papers to read and digest. It was a familiar routine, one that he had begun three years before when he'd taken a post at the Juilliard School. But like Freddie, he was the new kid in town, and it was up to him to make the adjustments.

He worried about her. At lunchtime he imagined her sitting in the school cafeteria, a room that smelled of peanut butter and waxy cartons of milk. She would be huddled at the end of a table scattered with crumbs, alone, miserable, while other children laughed and joked with their friends. He could see her at recess, standing apart and looking on longingly, while the others raced and shouted and climbed like spiders on jungle gyms. The trauma would leave her insecure and unhappy for the rest of her life.

All because he'd put her onto that damn yellow bus.

By the end of the day he was feeling as guilty as a child abuser, certain his little girl would come home in tears, devastated by the rigors of the first day of school. More than once he asked himself if Nina had been right all along. Perhaps he should have left well enough alone and stayed in New York, where at least Freddie had had friends and the familiar.

With his briefcase in one hand and his jacket slung over his shoulder, he started for home. It was hardly more than a mile, and the weather remained unseasonably warm. Until winter hit, he would take advantage of it and walk to and from campus.

He had already fallen in love with the town. There were

pretty shops and rambling old houses all along the tree-lined main street. It was a college town and proud of it, but it was equally proud of its age and dignity. The street climbed, and here and there the sidewalk showed cracks where tree roots had undermined it. Though there were cars passing, it was quiet enough to hear the bark of a dog or the music from a radio. A woman weeding marigolds along her walkway looked up and waved at him. Cheered, Spence waved back.

She didn't even know him, he thought. But she had waved. He looked forward to seeing her again, planting bulbs perhaps, or sweeping snow from her porch. He could smell chrysanthemums. For some reason that alone gave him a shot of pleasure.

No, he hadn't made a mistake. He and Freddie belonged here. In less than a week it had become home.

He stopped on the curb to wait for a laboring sedan to pass, and glancing across the street saw the sign for The Fun House. It was perfect, Spence thought. The perfect name. It conjured up laughter and surprises, just as the window display with its building blocks, chubby-cheeked dolls and shiny red cars promised a childhood treasure trove. At the moment he could think of nothing he wanted more than to find something that would bring a smile to his daughter's face.

You spoil her.

He could hear Nina's voice clearly in his ears.

So what? Glancing quickly up and down the street, he crossed to the opposite curb. His little girl had walked onto the school bus as bravely as any soldier marching into battle. There was no harm in buying her a small medal.

The door jingled as he entered. There was a scent, as cheerful as the sound of the bells. Peppermint, he thought and smiled. It delighted him to hear the tinny strains of "The Merry-Go-Round Broke Down," coming from the rear of the shop.

"I'll be right with you."

He had forgotten, Spence realized, how that voice could cruise along the air.

He wouldn't make a fool of himself again. This time he was prepared for what she looked like, sounded like, smelled like. He had come in to buy a present for his daughter, not to flirt with the proprietor. Then he grinned into the face of a forlorn panda. There didn't seem to be any law against doing both.

"I'm sure Bonnie will love it," Natasha said as she carried the miniature carousel for her customer. "It's a beautiful birthday present."

"She saw it in here a few weeks ago and hasn't been able to talk about anything else." Bonnie's grandmother tried not to grimace at the price. "I guess she's old enough to take care of it."

"Bonnie's a very responsible girl," Natasha went on, then spotted Spence at the counter. "I'll be right with you." The temperature of her voice dropped a cool twenty degrees.

"Take your time." It annoyed him that his reaction to her should be so strong, while hers played tug-of-war at the opposite end of the spectrum. It was obvious she'd decided to dislike him. It might be interesting, Spence thought, while he watched her slender, capable hands wrap the carousel, to find out her reasons.

And change her mind.

"That's 55.27, Mrs. Mortimer."

"Oh no, dear, the price tag said 67."

Natasha, who knew Mrs. Mortimer juggled expenses

on a fixed income, only smiled. "I'm sorry. Didn't I tell you it was on sale?"

"No." Mrs. Mortimer let out a little breath of relief as she counted out bills. "Well, this must be my lucky day."

"And Bonnie's." Natasha topped the gift with a pretty, celebratory pink bow, remembering it was Bonnie's favorite color. "Be sure to tell her happy birthday."

"I will." The proud grandmother lifted her package. "I can't wait to see her face when she opens this. Bye, Natasha."

Natasha waited until the door closed. "May I help you with something?"

"That was a very nice thing to do."

She lifted a brow. "What do you mean?"

"You know what I mean." He had the absurd urge to take her hand and kiss it. It was incredible, he thought. He was almost thirty-five and tumbling into puppy love with a woman he barely knew. "I'd meant to come in before."

"Oh? Was your daughter dissatisfied with her doll?"

"No, she loves it. It was just that I…" Good God, he was nearly stuttering. Five minutes with her, and he felt as awkward as a teenager at his first dance. He steadied himself with an effort. "I felt we'd gotten off on the wrong foot before. Should I apologize?"

"If you like." Just because he looked appealing and a little awkward was no reason to go easy on him. "Did you come in only for that?"

"No." His eyes darkened, just slightly. Noting it, Natasha wondered if she'd erred in her initial impression. Perhaps he wasn't harmless, after all. There was something deeper in those eyes, stronger and more dangerous. What surprised her further was that she found it exciting.

Disgusted with herself, she gave him a polite smile. "Was there something else?"

"I wanted something for my daughter." The hell with the gorgeous Russian princess, he thought. He had more important things to tend to.

"What was it you wanted for her?"

"I don't know." That was true enough. Setting down his briefcase, he glanced around the shop.

Unbending a little, Natasha came around the counter. "Is it her birthday?"

"No." Feeling foolish, he shrugged. "It's the first day of school, and she looked so…brave getting on the bus this morning."

This time Natasha's smile was spontaneous and full of warmth. It nearly stopped his heart. "You shouldn't worry. When she comes home, she'll be full of stories about everything and everyone. The first day is much harder, I think, on the parent than on the child."

"It's been the longest day of my life."

She laughed, a rich smoky sound that seemed impossibly erotic in a room full of clowns and stuffed bears. "It sounds like you both deserve a present. You were looking at a music box before. I have another you might like."

So saying, she led the way to the back of the shop. Spence did his best to ignore the subtle sway of her hips and the soft, fresh-scrubbed flavor of her scent. The box she chose was carved of wood, its pedestal topped with a cat and a fiddle, a cow and a quarter moon. As it turned to "Stardust," he saw the laughing dog and the dish with the spoon.

"It's charming."

"It's one of my favorites." She'd decided that any man who adored his daughter so blatantly couldn't be all bad.

So she smiled again. "I think it would be a lovely memento, something she could play on her first day of college and remember her father was thinking of her."

"If he survives first grade." He shifted slightly to look at her. "Thank you. It's perfect."

It was the oddest thing—his body had hardly brushed hers, but she'd felt a jolt. For an instant she forgot he was a customer, a father, a husband, and thought of him only as a man. His eyes were the color of the river at dusk. His lips, as they formed the barest hint of a smile, were impossibly attractive, alluring. Involuntarily she wondered what it would be like to feel them against her own—to watch his face as mouth met mouth, and see herself reflected in his eyes.

Appalled, she stepped back and her voice grew colder. "I'll box it for you."

Intrigued by the sudden change in tone, he took his time following her back to the counter. Hadn't he seen something in those fabulous eyes of hers? Or was it wishful thinking? It had gone quickly enough, heat smothered in frost. For the life of him he could find no reason for either.

"Natasha." He laid a hand on hers as she began to pack the music box.

Slowly she lifted her eyes. She was already hating herself for noticing that his hands were beautiful, wide-palmed, long-fingered. There was also a note of patience in his voice that stretched her already frayed nerves.

"Yes?"

"Why do I keep getting the feeling you'd like to boil me in oil?"

"You're mistaken," she said evenly. "I don't think I'd like that."

"You don't sound convinced." He felt her hand flex under his, soft and strong. The image of steel-lined velvet seemed particularly apt. "I'm having some trouble figuring out exactly what I've done to annoy you."

"Then you'll have to think about it. Cash or charge?"

He'd had little practice with rejection. Like a wasp it stung the ego. No matter how beautiful she was, he had no desire to continue to ram his head against the same brick wall.

"Cash." The door jangled open behind them and he released her hand. Three children, fresh from school, came in giggling. A young boy with red hair and a face bursting with freckles stood on his toes in front of the counter.

"I have three dollars," he announced.

Natasha fought back a grin. "You're very rich today, Mr. Jensen."

He flashed her a smile that revealed his latest missing tooth. "I've been saving up. I want the race car."

Natasha only lifted a brow as she counted out Spence's change. "Does your mother know you're here spending your life savings?" Her new customer remained silent. "Scott?"

He shifted from one foot to the other. "She didn't say I couldn't."

"And she didn't say you could," Natasha surmised. She leaned over to tug at his cowlick. "Go and ask her, then you come back. The race car will still be here."

"But, Tash—"

"You wouldn't want your mother to be mad at me, would you?"

Scott looked thoughtful for a moment, and Natasha could tell it was a tough choice. "I guess not."

"Then go ask her, and I'll hold one for you."

Hope blossomed. "Promise?"

Natasha put a hand on her heart. "Solemnly." She looked

back at Spence, and the amusement faded from her eyes. "I hope Freddie enjoys her present."

"I'm sure she will." He walked out, annoyed with himself for wishing he were a ten-year-old boy with a missing tooth.

Natasha locked the shop at six. The sun was still bright, the air still steamy. It made her think of picnics under a shady tree. A nicer fantasy than the microwave meal on her agenda, she mused, but at the moment impractical.

As she walked home, she watched a couple stroll hand in hand into the restaurant across the street. Someone hailed her from a passing car, and she waved in response. She could have stopped in the local pub and whiled away an hour over a glass of wine with any number of people she knew. Finding a dinner companion was as simple as sticking her head through one of a dozen doors and making the suggestion.

She wasn't in the mood for company. Not even her own.

It was the heat, she told herself as she turned the corner, the heat that had hung mercilessly in the air throughout the summer and showed no sign of yielding to autumn. It made her restless. It made her remember.

It had been summer when her life had changed so irrevocably.

Even now, years later, sometimes when she saw the roses in full bloom or heard the drunken buzz of bees she would ache. And wonder what might have happened. What would her life be like now, if…? She detested herself for playing those wishing games.

There were roses now, fragile pink ones that thrived despite the heat and lack of rain. She had planted them herself in the little patch of grass outside her apartment. Tending them brought her pleasure *and* pain. And what was life, she asked herself as she ran a fingertip over a petal, without them both? The warm scent of the roses followed her up the walkway.

Her rooms were quiet. She had thought about getting a kitten or a pup, so that there would be something there to greet her in the evening, something that loved and depended on her. But then she realized how unfair it would be to leave it alone while she was at the shop.

So she turned to music, flicking on the stereo as she stepped out of her shoes. Even that was a test. Tchaikovsky's *Romeo and Juliet*. She could see herself dancing to those haunting, romantic strains, the hot lights surrounding her, the music beating like her blood, her movements fluid, controlled without looking it. A triple pirouette, showing grace without effort.

That was past, Natasha reminded herself. Regrets were for the weak.

She moved out of habit, changing her work clothes for a loose, sleeveless jumpsuit, hanging up her skirt and blouse neatly as she had been taught. It was habit again rather than necessity that had her checking the cotton skirt for wear.

There was iced tea in the refrigerator and one of those packaged meals for the microwave that she both depended on and detested. She laughed at herself as she pushed the buttons to heat it.

She was getting like an old woman, Natasha decided, cranky and cross from the heat. Sighing, she rubbed the cold glass over her forehead.

That man had started her off, she thought. For a few moments in the shop today she had actually started to like him. He'd been so sweet, worrying about his little girl, wanting to reward her for being brave enough to face that momentous first day in school. She'd liked the way his voice had sounded, the way his eyes had smiled. For those few moments he had seemed like someone she could laugh with, talk with.

Then that had changed. A part of it was surely her fault, she admitted. But that didn't diminish his blame. She had felt something she hadn't felt, hadn't chosen to feel in a long, long time. That frisson of excitement. That tug of need. It made her angry and ashamed of herself. It made her furious with him.

The nerve, she thought, as she yanked her dish out of the microwave. Flirting with her as if she were some naive fool, before he went home to his wife and daughter.

Have dinner with him, indeed. She jammed her fork into the steaming seafood pasta. That kind of man expected payment in full for a meal. The candlelight and wine type, she thought with a sneer. Soft voice, patient eyes, clever hands. And no heart.

Just like Anthony. Impatient, she set the dish aside and picked up the glass that was already dripping with moisture. But she was wiser now than she had been at eighteen. Much wiser. Much stronger. She was no longer a woman who could be lured by charm and smooth words. Not that this man was smooth, she remembered with a quick smile. He—Lord, she didn't even know his name and she already detested him—he was a little clumsy, a little awkward. That was a charm of its own.

But he was, she thought, very much like Anthony. Tall and blond with those oh, so American good looks. Looks that concealed a lack of morals and a carelessly deceitful heart.

What Anthony had cost her could never be tallied. Since

that time, Natasha had made very, very certain no man would ever cost her so dearly again.

But she had survived. She lifted her glass in a self-toast. Not only had she survived, but except for times when memories crowded in on her, she was happy. She loved the shop, and the chance it gave her to be around children and make them happy. In her three years there she had watched them grow. She had a wonderful, funny friend in Annie, books that stayed in the black and a home that suited her.

She heard a thump over her head and smiled. The Jorgensons were getting ready for the evening meal. She imagined Don was fussing around Marilyn, who was carrying their first child. Natasha liked knowing they were there, just above her, happy, in love and full of hope.

That was family to her, what she had had in her youth, what she had expected as an adult. She could still see Papa fretting over Mama when she neared her time. Every time, Natasha remembered, thinking of her three younger siblings. How he had wept with happiness when his wife and babies were safe and well. He adored his Nadia. Even now Natasha knew he still brought flowers home to the little house in Brooklyn. When he came home after a day's work, he kissed his wife, not with an absent peck on the cheek, but robustly, joyfully. A man wildly in love after almost thirty years.

It was her father who had kept her from shoveling all men into the pit Anthony had dug for her. Seeing her father and mother together had kept that small, secret hope alight that someday she would find someone who would love her as much and as honestly.

Someday, she thought with a shrug. But for now she had her own business, her own home and her own life. No man, no matter how beautiful his hands or how clear his eyes, was going to rock her boat. Secretly she hoped her newest customer's wife gave him nothing but grief.

"One more story. Please, Daddy." Freddie, her eyes heavy, her face shiny from her bath, used her most persuasive smile. She was nestled against Spence in her big, white canopy bed.

"You're already asleep."

"No, I'm not." She peeked up at him, fighting to keep her eyes open. It had been the very best day of her life, and she didn't want it to end. "Did I tell you that JoBeth's cat had kittens? Six of them."

"Twice." Spence flicked a finger down her nose. He knew a hint when he heard one, and fell back on the parent's standard. "We'll see."

Sleepy, Freddie smiled. She knew from his tone that her father was already weakening. "Mrs. Patterson's real nice. She's going to let us have Show and Tell every Friday."

"So you said." And he'd been worried, Spence thought. "I get the feeling you like school."

"It's neat." She yawned hugely. "Did you fill out all the forms?"

"They'll be ready for you to take in tomorrow." All five hundred of them, he thought with a sigh. "Time to unplug the batteries, funny face."

"One more story. The made-up kind." She yawned again, comforted by the soft cotton of his shirt beneath her cheek and the familiar scent of his after-shave.

He gave in, knowing she would sleep long before he got to the happy ever after. He wove a story around a beautiful, dark-haired princess from a foreign land, and the knight who tried to rescue her from her ivory tower.

Foolishness, Spence thought even as he added a sor-
cerer and a two-headed dragon. He knew his thoughts were
drifting toward Natasha again. She was certainly beautiful, but he didn't think he'd ever met a woman less in need
of rescuing.

It was just his bad luck that he had to pass her shop every
day to and from campus.

He'd ignore her. If anything, he should be grateful to
her. She'd made him want, made him feel things he hadn't
thought he could anymore. Maybe now that he and Freddie were settled, he'd start socializing again. There were
plenty of attractive, single women at the college. But the
idea of dating didn't fill him with delight.

Socializing, Spence corrected. Dating was for teenagers and conjured up visions of drive-in movies, pizza and
sweaty palms. He was a grown man, and it was certainly
time he started enjoying female companionship again. Over
the age of five, he thought, looking at Freddie's small hand
balled in his palm.

Just what would you think, he asked silently, if I brought
a woman home to dinner? It made him remember how big
and hurt her eyes had been when he and Angela had swept
out of the condo for evenings at the theater or the opera.

It won't ever be like that again, he promised as he shifted
her from his chest to the pillow. He settled the grinning
Raggedy Ann beside her, then tucked the covers under her
chin. Resting a hand on the bedpost, he glanced around
the room.

It already had Freddie's stamp on it. The dolls lining
the shelves with books jumbled beneath them, the fuzzy,
pink elephant slippers beside her oldest and most favored
sneakers. The room had that little-girl scent of shampoo

and crayons. A night-light in the shape of a unicorn assured that she wouldn't wake up in the dark and be afraid.

He stayed a moment longer, finding himself as soothed
by the light as she. Quietly he stepped out, leaving her door
open a few inches.

Downstairs he found Vera carrying a tray of coffee. The
Mexican housekeeper was wide from shoulders to hips, and
gave the impression of a small, compact freight train when
she moved from room to room. Since Freddie's birth, she
had proven not only efficient but indispensable. Spence
knew it was often possible to insure an employee's loyalty
with a paycheck, but not her love. From the moment Freddie had come home in her silk-trimmed blanket, Vera had
been in love.

She cast an eye up the stairs now, and her lined face
folded into a smile. "She had one big day, huh?"

"Yes, and one she fought ending to the last gasp. Vera,
you didn't have to bother."

She shrugged her shoulders while she carried the coffee into his office. "You said you have to work tonight."

"Yes, for a little while."

"So I make you coffee before I go in and put my feet up
to watch TV." She arranged the tray on his desk, fussing a
bit while she talked. "My baby, she's happy with school and
her new friends." She didn't add that she had wept into her
apron when Freddie had stepped onto the bus. "With the
house empty all day, I have plenty of time to get my work
done. You don't stay up too late, Dr. Kimball."

"No." It was a polite lie. He knew he was too restless for
sleep. "Thank you, Vera."

"*¡De nada!*" She patted her iron-gray hair. "I wanted

to tell you that I like this place very much. I was afraid to leave New York, but now I'm happy."

"We couldn't manage without you."

"Sí." She took this as her due. For seven years she had worked for the *señor*, and basked in the prestige of being housekeeper for an important man—a respected musician, a doctor of music and a college professor. Since the birth of his daughter she had been so in love with *her baby* that she would have worked for Spence, whatever his station.

She had grumbled about moving from the beautiful high-rise in New York, to the rambling house in the small town, but Vera was shrewd enough to know that the *señor* had been thinking of Freddie. Freddie had come home from school only hours before, laughing, excited, with the names of new best friends tumbling from her lips. So Vera was content.

"You are a good father, Dr. Kimball."

Spence glanced over before he sat down behind his desk. He was well aware that there had been a time Vera had considered him a very poor one.

"I'm learning."

"Sí." Casually she adjusted a book on the shelf. "In this big house you won't have to worry about disturbing Freddie's sleep if you play your piano at night."

He looked over again, knowing she was encouraging him in her way to concentrate on his music. "No, it shouldn't disturb her. Good night, Vera."

After a quick glance around to be certain there was nothing more for her to tidy, she left him.

Alone, Spence poured the coffee, then studied the papers on his desk. Freddie's school forms were stacked next to his own work. He had a great deal of preparation ahead of him, before his classes began the following week.

He looked forward to it, even as he tried not to regret that the music that had once played so effortlessly inside his head was still silent.

Chapter 3

Natasha scooped the barrette through the hair above her ear and hoped it would stay fixed for more than five minutes. She studied her reflection in the narrow mirror over the sink in the back of the shop before she decided to add a touch of lipstick. It didn't matter that it had been a long and hectic day or that her feet were all but crying with fatigue. Tonight was her treat to herself, her reward for a job well done.

Every semester she signed up for one course at the college. She chose whatever seemed most fun, most intriguing or most unusual. Renaissance Poetry one year, Automotive Maintenance another. This term, two evenings a week, she would be taking Music History. Tonight she would begin an exploration of a new topic. Everything she learned she would store for her own pleasure, as other women stored diamonds and emeralds. It didn't have to be useful. In Natasha's opinion a glittery necklace wasn't particularly useful, either. It was simply exciting to own.

She had her notebook, her pens and pencils and a flood of enthusiasm. To prepare herself, she had raided the library and pored over related books for the last two weeks. Pride wouldn't allow her to go into class ignorant. Curiosity made her wonder if her instructor could take the dry, distant facts and add excitement.

There was little doubt that this particular instructor was adding dashes of excitement in other quarters. Annie had teased her just that morning about the new professor everyone was talking about. Dr. Spencer B. Kimball.

The name sounded very distinguished to Natasha, quite unlike the description of a hunk that Annie had passed along. Annie's information came from her cousin's daughter, who was majoring in Elementary Education with a minor in Music. A sun-god, Annie had relayed and made Natasha laugh.

A very gifted sun-god, Natasha mused while she turned off lights in the shop. She knew Kimball's work well, or the work he had composed before he had suddenly and inexplicably stopped writing music. Why, she had even danced to his Prelude in D Minor when she had been with the corps de ballet in New York.

A million years ago, she thought as she stepped onto the street. Now she would be able to meet the genius, listen to his views and perhaps find new meanings in many of the classics she already loved.

He was probably the temperamental artiste type, she decided, pleased with the way the evening breeze lifted her hair and cooled her neck. Or a pale eccentric with one earring. It didn't matter. She intended to work hard. Each course she took was a matter of pride to her. It still stung to remember how little she had known when she'd been eighteen. How little she had cared to know, Natasha admitted, other than dance. She had of her own choice closed herself off from so many worlds in order to focus everything on one. When that had been taken away, she had been as lost as a child set adrift on the Atlantic.

She had found her way to shore, just as her family had once found its way across the wilds of the Ukraine to the jungles of Manhattan. She liked herself better—the independent, ambitious American woman she had become. As she was now, she could walk into the big, beautiful old building on campus with as much pride as any freshman student.

There were footsteps echoing in the corridors, distant, dislocated. There was a hushed reverence that Natasha always associated with churches and universities. In a way there was religion here—the belief in learning.

She felt somewhat reverent herself as she made her way to her class. As a child of five in her small farming village, she had never even imagined such a building, or the books and beauty it contained.

Several students were already waiting. A mixed bag, she noted, ranging from college to middle age. All of them seemed to buzz with that excitement of beginning. She saw by the clock that it was two minutes shy of eight. She'd expected Kimball to be there, busily shuffling his papers, peering at them behind glasses, his hair a little wild and streaming to his shoulders.

Absently she smiled at a young man in horn-rims, who was staring at her as if he'd just woken from a dream. Ready to begin, she sat down, then looked up when the same man clumsily maneuvered himself into the desk beside her.

"Hello."

He looked as though she'd struck him with a bat rather than offered a casual greeting. He pushed his glasses nervously up his nose. "Hello. I'm—I'm…Terry Maynard," he finished on a burst as his name apparently came to him at last.

"Natasha." She smiled again. He was on the sunny side of twenty-five and harmless as a puppy.

"I haven't, ah, seen you on campus before."

"No." Though at twenty-seven it amused her to be taken for a coed, she kept her voice sober. "I'm only taking this one class. For fun."

"For fun?" Terry appeared to take music very seriously. "Do you know who Dr. Kimball is?" His obvious awe made him almost whisper the name.

"I've heard of him. You're a Music major?"

"Yes. I hope to, well one day, I hope to play with the New York Symphony." His blunt fingers reached nervously to adjust his glasses. "I'm a violinist."

She smiled again and made his Adam's apple bob. "That's wonderful. I'm sure you're very good."

"What do you play?"

"Five card draw." Then she laughed and settled back in her chair. "I'm sorry. I don't play an instrument. But I love to listen to music and thought I'd enjoy the class." She glanced at the clock on the wall. "If it ever starts, that is. Apparently our esteemed professor is late."

At that moment the esteemed professor was rushing down the corridors, cursing himself for ever agreeing to take on this night class. By the time he had helped Freddie with her homework—how many animals can you find in this picture?—convinced her that brussels sprouts were cute instead of yucky, and changed his shirt because her affectionate hug had transferred some mysterious, sticky substance to his sleeve, he had wanted nothing more than a good book and a warm brandy.

Instead he was going to have to face a roomful of eager faces, all waiting to learn what Beethoven had worn when he'd composed his Ninth Symphony.

In the foulest of moods, he walked into class. "Good evening. I'm Dr. Kimball." The murmurs and rattles quieted. "I must apologize for being late. If you'll all take a seat, we'll dive right in."

As he spoke he scanned the room. And found himself staring into Natasha's astonished face.

"No." She wasn't aware she'd spoken the word aloud, and wouldn't have cared. It was some sort of joke, she thought, and a particularly bad one. This—this *man* in the casually elegant jacket was Spencer Kimball, a musician whose songs she had admired and danced to. The man who, while barely into his twenties had been performing at Carnegie Hall being hailed as a genius. This man who had tried to pick her up in a toy store was the illustrious Dr. Kimball?

It was ludicrous, it was infuriating, it was—

Wonderful, Spence thought as he stared at her. Absolutely wonderful. In fact, it was perfect, as long as he could control the laugh that was bubbling in his throat. So the czarina was one of his students. It was better, much better than a warm brandy and an evening of quiet.

"I'm sure," he said after a long pause, "we'll all find the next few months fascinating."

She should have signed up for Astronomy, Natasha told herself. She could have learned all kinds of interesting things about the planets and stars. Asteroids. She'd have been much better off learning about—what was it?—gravitational pull and inertia. Whatever that was. Surely it was much more important for her to find out how many moons revolved around Jupiter than to study Burgundian composers of the fifteenth century.

She would transfer, Natasha decided. First thing in the morning she would make the arrangements. In fact, she would get up and walk out right now if she wasn't certain Dr. Spencer Kimball would smirk.

Running her pencil between her fingers, she crossed her legs and determined not to listen.

It was a pity his voice was so attractive.

Impatient, Natasha looked at the clock. Nearly an hour to go. She would do what she did when she waited at the dentist's office. Pretend she was someplace else. Struggling to block Spence's voice from her mind she began to swing her foot and doodle on her pad.

She didn't notice when her doodles became notes, or when she began to hang on every word. He made fifteenth-century musicians seem alive and vital—and their music as real as flesh and blood. Rondeaux, vieralais, ballades. She could almost hear the three-part chansons of the dawning Renaissance, the reverent, soaring Kyries and Glorias of the masses.

She was caught up, involved in that ancient rivalry between church and state and music's part in the politics. She could see huge banqueting halls filled with elegantly dressed aristocrats, feasting on music as well as food.

"Next time we'll be discussing the Franco-Flemish school and rhythmic developments." Spence gave his class an easy smile. "And I'll try to be on time."

Was it over? Natasha glanced at the clock again and was shocked to see it was indeed after nine.

"Incredible, isn't he?"

She looked at Terry. His eyes were gleaming behind his lenses. "Yes." It cost her to admit it, but truth was truth.

"You should hear him in theory class." He noticed with envy that several students were grouped around his idol. As yet, Terry hadn't worked up the nerve to approach him. "I'll—see you Thursday."

"What? Oh. Good night, Terry."

"I could, ah, give you a ride home if you want." The fact that he was nearly out of gas and his muffler was currently held on by a coat hanger didn't enter his mind.

She favored him with an absent smile that had his heart doing a cha-cha. "That's nice of you, but I don't live far."

She hoped to breeze out of the classroom while Spence was still occupied. She should have known better.

He simply put a hand on her arm and stopped her. "I'd like to speak with you a moment, Natasha."

"I'm in a hurry."

"It won't take long." He nodded to the last of his departing students, then eased back against his desk and grinned at her. "I should have paid more attention to my roster, but then again, it's nice to know there are still surprises in the world."

"That depends on your point of view, Dr. Kimball."

"Spence." He continued to grin. "Class is over."

"So it is." Her regal nod made him think again of Russian royalty. "Excuse me."

"Natasha." He waited, almost seeing impatience shimmer around her as she turned. "I can't imagine that someone with your heritage doesn't believe in destiny."

"Destiny?"

"Of all the classrooms in all the universities in all the world, she walks into mine."

She wouldn't laugh. She'd be damned if she would. But her mouth quirked up at the corners before she controlled it. "And here I was thinking it was just bad luck."

"Why Music History?"

She balanced her notebook on her hip. "It was a toss-up between that and Astronomy."

"That sounds like a fascinating story. Why don't we go down the street for a cup of coffee? You can tell me about it." Now he saw it—molten fury that turned her eyes from rich velvet to sharp jet. "Now why does that infuriate you?" he inquired, almost to himself. "Is an offer of a cup of coffee in this town similiar to an illicit proposition?"

"You should know, Dr. Kimball." She turned, but he reached the door before her, slamming it with enough force to make her step back. He was every bit as angry as herself, she noted. Not that it mattered. It was only that he had seemed a mild sort of man. Detestable, but mild. There was nothing mild about him now. Those fascinating bones and angles in his face might have been carved of stone.

"Clarify."

"Open the door."

"Gladly. After you answer my question." He *was* angry. Spence realized he hadn't felt this kind of hot, blood-pumping rage in years. It felt wonderful. "I realize that just because I'm attracted to you doesn't mean you have to return the favor."

She threw up her chin, hating herself for finding the storm-cloud-gray eyes so hypnotic. "I don't."

"Fine." He couldn't strangle her for that, however much he'd like to. "But, damn it, I want to know why you aim and fire every time I'm around you."

"Because men like you deserve to be shot."

"Men like me," he repeated, measuring out the words. "What exactly does that mean?"

He was standing close, all but looming over her. As in the shop when he had brushed up against her, she felt those bubble bursts of excitement, attraction, confusion. It was more than enough to push her over the edge.

"Do you think because you have a nice face and a pretty smile you can do whatever you like? *Yes,*" she answered before he could speak and slapped her notebook against his chest. "You think you have only to snap your fingers." She demonstrated dramatically. "And a woman will fall into your arms. Not this woman."

Her accent thickened when she was on a roll, he noted, somewhat baffled by her claim. "I don't recall snapping my fingers."

She let loose one short, explicit Ukrainian oath and grabbed the knob. "You want to have a cup of coffee with me? Good. We'll have your coffee—and we'll call your wife and ask her to join us."

"My what?" He closed his hand over hers so that the door was jerked open, then slammed shut again. "I don't have a wife."

"Really?" The single word dripped with scorn; her eyes flashed at him. "And I suppose the woman who came with you to the shop is your sister."

It should have been funny. But he couldn't quite get the joke. "Nina? As a matter of fact, she is."

Natasha yanked open the door with a sound of disgust. "That is pathetic."

Filled with righteous indignation, she stormed down the corridor and out the main door. In a staccato rhythm that matched her mood, her heels beat on the concrete as she started down the steps. When she was abruptly whirled around, she nearly took the last two in a tumble.

"You've got a hell of a nerve."

"I?" she managed. "I have a nerve?"

"You think you've got it all figured out, don't you?" Having the advantage of height, Spence could stare down at her. Natasha saw shadows move over his face as temper colored his voice. He didn't appear awkward now, but every bit in control. "Or I should say you think you've got me figured."

"It takes very little." The fingers on her arm were very firm. She hated knowing that mixed with her own anger was basic sexual attraction. Fighting it off, she tossed back her hair. "You're really very typical."

"I wonder, can your opinion of me get any lower?" Now fury ground edge to edge with desire.

"Doubtful."

"In that case, I might as well satisfy myself."

The notebook flew out of her hand when he dragged her close. She managed a single, startled sound in her throat before his mouth covered hers. Covered, crushed, then conquered.

Natasha would have fought him. Over and over she told herself she *would* fight him. But it was shock—at least, she prayed it was shock—that had her arms falling limply to her sides.

It was wrong. It was unforgivable. And, oh God, it was wonderful. Instinctively he'd found the key to unlock the passion that had lain dormant in her for so long. Her blood swam hot with it. Her mind hazed. Dimly she heard someone laugh as they strolled down the sidewalk below. A beep of a car horn, a shout of greeting, then silence once more.

She murmured, a pitiful protest that shamed her and was easily ignored as his tongue glided over her own. His taste was a banquet after a long fast. Though she kept her hands balled at her sides, she leaned into the kiss.

Kissing her was like walking through a mine field. Any moment he expected the bomb to go off and blow him to pieces. He should have stopped after the first shock, but danger had a thrill of its own.

And she was dangerous. As his fingers dived into her hair, he could feel the ground quiver and quake. It was her—the promise, the threat of titanic passion. He could taste it on her lips, even as she fought to hold it back. He could feel it in her taut, terrified stance. If she released it, she could make him a slave.

Needs such as he'd never known battered his system with heavy fists. Images, all fire and smoke, danced in his brain. Something struggled to break free, like a bird beating at the bars of a cage. He could feel it straining. Then Natasha was pulling away from him, standing apart and staring at him with wide, eloquent eyes.

She couldn't breathe. For an instant she was genuinely afraid she would die on the spot with this unwanted, shameful desire on her conscience. In defiance she took a huge gulp of air.

"I could never hate anyone as much as I hate you."

He shook his head to clear it. She had left him dizzy, dazed and utterly defenseless. For his own sake he waited until he was sure he could speak. "That's a lofty position you put me in, Natasha." He stepped down until they were at eye level. There were tears on her lashes, but they were offset by the condemnation in her eyes. "Let's just be sure you've put me there for the right reasons. Is it because I kissed you, or because you liked it?"

She swung her hand out. He could have avoided the blow easily enough, but thought she deserved a hit. As the crack of the slap echoed, he decided they were even.

"Don't come near me again," she said, breathing hard. "I warn you, if you do, I won't care what I say or who hears me. If it wasn't for your little girl—" She broke off and bent to gather her things. Her pride was shattered, along with her self-esteem. "You don't deserve such a beautiful child."

He caught her arm again, but this time the expression on his face made her blood go cold. "You're right. I never have and probably never will deserve Freddie, but I'm all she has. Her mother—my wife—died three years ago."

He strode off, was caught in the beam of a street lamp, then disappeared into the dark beyond. Her notebook pressed against her chest, Natasha sank weakly onto the bottom step.

What in hell was she going to do now?

There was no choice. No matter how much she hated it, there was really only one course to take. Natasha rubbed the palms of her hands on the thighs of her khakis, then started up the freshly painted wooden steps.

It was a nice house, she thought, stalling. Of course she'd seen it so often that she rarely noticed it anymore. It was one of those sturdy old brick places tucked back from the street and shielded by trees and box hedges.

The summer flowers had yet to fade, but the fall blooms were already staking their claim. Showy delphiniums vied with spicy scented mums, vivid dahlias with starry asters. Someone was caring for them. She could see fresh mulch on the flower beds, damp with watering.

Wanting a little more time, she studied the house. There were curtains at the windows, thin ivory sheers that would let in the light. Higher up she caught a glimpse of a fanciful pattern of unicorns that identified a little girl's room.

She gathered her courage and crossed the porch to the front door. It would be quick, she promised herself. Not painless, but quick. She rapped, released her breath and waited.

The woman who answered was short and wide with a face as brown and wrinkled as a raisin. Natasha found herself fixed by a pair of small, dark eyes while the housekeeper dried her hands on the skirt of a stained apron.

"May I help you?"

"I'd like to see Dr. Kimball if he's in." She smiled, pretending she didn't feel as though she were stepping into the pillory. "I'm Natasha Stanislaski." She saw the housekeeper's little eyes narrow, so that they nearly disappeared into the folds of her face.

Vera had at first taken Natasha for one of the *señor*'s students, and had been prepared to nudge her on her way. "You own the toy store in town."

"That's right."

"Ah." With a nod, she opened the door wider to let Natasha in. "Freddie says you are a very nice lady, who gave her a blue ribbon for her doll. I promised to take her back, but just to look." She gestured for Natasha to follow.

As they made their way down the hall, Natasha caught the hesitant notes of a piano. When she saw her reflection in an old oval mirror, it surprised her that she was smiling.

He was sitting at the piano with the child on his lap, looking over her head while she slowly tapped out "Mary Had a Little Lamb." The sun streamed in through the windows behind them. At that moment she wished she could paint. How else could it be captured?

It was perfect. The light, the shadows, the pale pastels of the room all combined to make the perfect backdrop. The alignment of their heads, their bodies, was too natural and eloquent ever to be posed. The girl was in pink and white, the laces of one sneaker untied. He had taken off his jacket and tie, then rolled up the sleeves of the pale dress shirt to the elbows like a workman.

There was the fragile shine of the child's hair, the deeper glow of his. The child leaned back against her father, her head resting just under his collarbone; the faintest smile of pleasure lighted her face. Over it all was the simple nursery rhyme music she was playing.

He had his hands on the knees of her jeans, his long, beautiful fingers tapping the time in tandem with the tick of the antique metronome. She could see it all, the love, the patience, the pride.

"No, please," Natasha whispered, holding out a hand to Vera. "Don't disturb them."

"You play now, Daddy." Freddie tilted her head toward his. Her hair wisped around her face where it had escaped from its clips. "Play something pretty."

"Für Elise." Natasha recognized it instantly, that soft, romantic, somehow lonely music. It went straight to her heart as she watched his fingers stroke, caress, seduce the keys.

What was he thinking? She could see that his thoughts had turned inward—to the music, to himself. There was an effortlessness in the way his fingers flowed over the keys, and yet she knew that kind of beauty was never achieved without the greatest effort.

The song swelled, note after note, unbearably sad, impossibly beautiful, like the vase of waxy calla lilies that rested on the glossy surface of the piano.

Too much emotion, Natasha thought. Too much pain, though the sun was still shining through the gauzy curtains and the child on his lap continued to smile. The urge to go to him, to put a comforting hand onto his shoulder, to hold both against her heart, was so strong that she had to curl her fingers into her palms.

Then the music drifted away, the last note lingering like a sigh.

"I like that one," Freddie told him. "Did you make it up?"

"No." He looked at his fingers, spreading them, flexing them, then letting them rest on hers. "Beethoven did." Then he was smiling again, pressing his lips to the soft curve of his daughter's neck. "Had enough for today, funny face?"

"Can I play outside until dinner?"

"Well… What'll you give me?"

It was an old game and a favorite one. Giggling, she swiveled on his lap and gave him a hard, smacking kiss. Still squealing from the bear hug, she spotted Natasha. "Hi!"

"Miss Stanislaski would like to see you, Dr. Kimball." At his nod, Vera walked back to the kitchen.

"Hello." Natasha managed to smile, even when Spence lifted his daughter and turned. She wasn't over the music yet. It was still pouring through her like tears. "I hope I haven't come at a bad time."

"No." After a last squeeze, he set Freddie down, and she immediately bounded to Natasha.

"We're all finished with my lesson. Did you come to play?"

"No, not this time." Unable to resist, Natasha bent to stroke Freddie's cheek. "Actually I came to talk to your father." But she was a coward, Natasha thought in disgust. Rather than look at him, she continued to address Freddie. "How do you like school? You have Mrs. Patterson, don't you?"

"She's nice. She didn't even yell when Mikey Towers's icky bug collection got loose in the classroom. And I can read all of *Go, Dog, Go*."

Natasha crouched so that they were eye to eye. "Do you like my hat?"

Freddie laughed, recognizing the line from the Dr. Seuss classic. "I like the dog party part the best."

"So do I." Automatically she tied Freddie's loose laces. "Will you come to the store and visit me soon?"

"Okay." Delighted with herself, Freddie raced for the door. "Bye Miss Stanof—Stanif—"

"Tash." She sent Freddie a wink. "All the kids call me Tash."

"Tash." Freddie grinned at the sound of the name, then streaked away.

She listened to Freddie's sneakers squeak down the hall, then took a long breath. "I'm sorry to disturb you at home, but I felt it would be more…" What was the word? Appropriate, comfortable? "It would be better."

"All right." His eyes were very cool, not like those of the man who had played such sad and passionate music. "Would you like to sit down?"

"No." She said it too quickly, then reminded herself that it was better if they were both stiffly polite. "It won't take long. I only want to apologize."

"Oh? For something specific?"

Fire blazed in her eyes. He enjoyed seeing it, particularly since he'd spent most of the night cursing her. "When I make a mistake, I make a point of admitting it. But since you behaved so—" Oh, why did she always lose her English when she was angry?

"Unconscionably?" he suggested.

Her brow shot up into her fall of hair. "So you admit it."

"I thought you were the one who was here to admit something." Enjoying himself, he sat on the arm of a wing chair in pale blue damask. "Don't let me interrupt."

She was tempted, very tempted, to turn on her heel and stalk out. Pride was equally as strong as temper. She would do what she had come to do, then forget it.

"What I said about you—about you and your daughter was unfair and untrue. Even when I was...mistaken about other things, I knew it was untrue. And I'm very sorry I said it."

"I can see that." Out of the corner of his eye he caught a movement. He turned his head in time to see Freddie make her sprinter's rush for the swings. "We'll forget it."

Natasha followed his gaze and softened. "She really is a beautiful child. I hope you let her come into the shop from time to time."

The tone of her voice had him studying Natasha more carefully. Was it longing, sorrow? "I doubt I could keep her away. You're very fond of children."

Natasha brought her emotions under control with a quick jerk. "Yes, of course. In my business it's a requirement. I won't keep you, Dr. Kimball."

He rose to accept the hand she had formally held out. "Spence," he corrected, gently tightening his fingers on hers. "What else was it you were mistaken about?"

So it wasn't going to be easy. Then again, Natasha thought she deserved a dose of humiliation. "I thought you were married, and was very angry and insulted when you asked me out."

"You're taking my word now that I'm not married."

"No. I looked it up in the library in *Who's Who*."

He stared at her for a moment longer, then threw back his head and laughed. "God, what a trusting soul. Find anything else that interested you?"

"Only things that would fill your ego. You still have my hand."

"I know. Tell me, Natasha, did you dislike me on general principles, or only because you thought I was a married man and had no business flirting with you?"

"Flirting?" She nearly choked on the word. "There was nothing so innocent in the way you looked at me. As if..."

"As if—?" he prompted.

As if we were already lovers, she thought, and felt her skin heat. "I didn't like it," she said shortly.

"Because you thought I was married?"

"Yes. No," she said, correcting herself when she realized where that could lead. "I just didn't like it." He brought her hand to his lips. "Don't," she managed.

"How would you like me to look at you?"

"It isn't necessary for you to look at all."

"But it is." He could feel it again, that high-strung passion, just waiting to burst free from whatever cell she had locked it in. "You'll be sitting right in front of me tomorrow night in class."

"I'm going to transfer."

"No, you won't." He brushed a finger over the small gold hoop in her ear. "You enjoyed it too much. I could see the wheels turning in that fabulous head of yours. And if you did," he continued before she could sputter out a response, "I'd just make a nuisance of myself in your shop."

"Why?"

"Because you're the first woman I've wanted in longer than I can remember."

Excitement rippled up her spine like chain lightning. Before she could prevent it, the memory of that stormy kiss curved back to weaken her. Yes, that had been a man who had wanted. And had, no matter how she had resisted, made her want, too.

But that had only been one kiss, fueled by lust despite

the moonlight and soft air. She knew heartbreakingly well where such desires could lead.

"That's nonsense."

"Simple honesty," he murmured, fascinated by the emotions that came and went in her dark eyes. "I thought it best, since we'd gotten off to such a shaky beginning. Since you've determined for yourself that I'm not married, knowing I'm attracted to you shouldn't insult you."

"I'm not insulted," she said carefully. "I'm just not interested."

"Do you always kiss men you're not interested in?"

"I didn't kiss you." She jerked her hand free. "You kissed me."

"We can fix that." He gathered her close. "This time kiss me back."

She could have pulled away. His arms weren't banding her as they had before, but were wrapped loosely, coaxingly around her. His lips were soft this time, soft, persuasive, patient. She could feel the warmth seep into her bloodstream like a drug. With a little moan, she slipped her hands up his back and held on.

It was like holding a candle and feeling the wax slowly melt as the fire burned at its center. He could feel her yield degree by degree until her lips parted for his own, accepting, inviting. But even as she gave, he could sense some strong, hard core that resisted, held back. She didn't want to feel whatever he was making her feel.

Impatient, he dragged her closer. Though her body molded itself to his and her head fell back in erotic surrender, there was still a part of her standing just out of his reach. What she gave him only stirred his appetite for more.

She was breathless when he released her. It took an effort, too much of an effort, Natasha thought, to level herself. But once she had, her voice was steady.

"I don't want to be involved."

"With me, or with anyone?"

"With anyone."

"Good." He brushed a hand over her hair. "It'll be simpler to change your mind."

"I'm very stubborn," she muttered.

"Yes, I've noticed. Why don't you stay for dinner?"

"No."

"All right. I'll take you to dinner Saturday night."

"No."

"Seven-thirty. I'll pick you up."

"No."

"You wouldn't want me to come by the shop Saturday afternoon and embarrass you."

Out of patience, she stalked to the door. "I can't understand how a man that could play music with such sensitivity could be such a clod."

Just lucky, I guess, he thought when the door slammed. Alone again, he caught himself whistling.

Chapter 4

Saturdays in a toy store were noisy, crowded and chaotic. They were supposed to be. To a child even the word Saturday was magic—it meant a magic twenty-four hours when school was too faraway to be a problem. There were bikes to be ridden, games to be played, races to be won. For as long as Natasha had been running The Fun House, she had enjoyed Saturdays as much as her pint-size clientele.

It was one more black mark against Spence that he was the reason she couldn't enjoy this one.

She'd told him no, she reminded herself as she rang up sales on a set of jacks, three plastic dinosaurs and a pint of blowing bubbles. And she'd meant no.

The man didn't seem to understand plain English.

Why else would he have sent her the single red rose? And to the shop, of all places? she thought now, trying to scowl at it. Annie's romantic enthusiasm had been impossible to hold off. Even when Natasha had ignored the flower, Annie had rescued it, running across the street to buy a plastic bud vase so that it could have a place of honor on the checkout counter.

Natasha did her best not to look at it, not to stroke the tightly closed petals, but it wasn't as easy to ignore the fragile scent that wafted toward her every time she rang up a sale.

Why did men think they could soften up a woman with a flower?

Because they could, Natasha admitted, biting off a sigh as she glanced toward it.

That didn't mean she was going out to dinner with him. Tossing back her hair, Natasha counted out the pile of sweaty pennies and nickels the young Hampston boy passed her for his monthly comic-book purchase. Life should be so simple, she thought as the boy rushed out with the latest adventures of Commander Zark. Damn it, it was that simple. On a deep breath she steeled her determination. Her life was exactly that simple, no matter how Spence tried to complicate it. To prove it, she intended to go home, soak in a hot tub, then spend the rest of her evening stretched out on the sofa, watching an old movie and eating popcorn.

He'd been clever. She left the counter to go into the next aisle to referee a huffy disagreement between the Freedmont brothers about how they should spend their pooled resources. She wondered if the esteemed professor looked at their relationship—their nonrelationship, she corrected—as a chess match. She'd always been too reckless to succeed at that particular game, but she had a feeling Spence would play it patiently and well. All the same, if he thought she would be easily checkmated, he had a surprise coming.

Spence had led her second class brilliantly, never looking at her any longer than he had looked at any of his other students, answering her questions in the same tone he used with others. Yes, a very patient player.

Then, just when she'd relaxed, he'd passed her that first red rose as she walked out of class. A very smart move to endanger her queen.

If she'd had any spine at all, Natasha thought now, she would have dropped it onto the floor and ground it under her heel. But she hadn't, and now had to scramble to keep one play ahead of him. Because it had caught her off guard, Natasha told herself. Just like the one that had been delivered to the shop this morning.

If he kept it up, people were going to begin to talk. In a town this size, news items like red roses bounced from shop to pub, from pub to front stoop and from front stoop to backyard gossip sessions. She needed to find a way to stop it. At the moment, she couldn't come up with anything better than ignoring it. Ignoring Spence, she added. How she wished she could.

Bringing herself back to the problem at hand, Natasha hooked an arm around each of the squabbling Freedmont boys in a mock headlock.

"Enough. If you keep calling each other names like nerd and…what was the other?"

"Dork," the taller of the boys told her with relish.

"Yes, dork." She couldn't resist committing it to memory. "That's a good one. If you keep it up, I'll tell your mother not to let you come in for two weeks."

"Aw, Tash."

"That means everyone else will see all the creepy things I get in for Halloween before either of you." She let that threat hang, giving the two little necks a quick squeeze. "So, I'll make a suggestion. Flip a coin and decide whether to buy the football or the magic set. Whatever you don't get now, you ask for for Christmas. Good idea?"

The boys grimaced at each other from either side of her. "Pretty good."

"No, you have to say it's very good, or I'll knock your heads together."

She left them arguing over which coin to use for the fatal flip.

"You missed your calling," Annie commented when the brothers raced off with the football.

"How's that?"

"You should be working for the UN." She nodded out the front window; the boys were practicing passing on their way down the street. "There aren't many tougher nuts than the Freedmont brothers."

"I make them afraid of me first, then offer them a dignified way out."

"See? Definitely UN material."

With a laugh, Natasha shook her head. "Other people's problems are the easiest to solve." Weakening, she glanced toward the rose again. If she had one wish at the moment, it would be for someone to come along and solve her own.

An hour later she felt a tug on the hem of her skirt.

"Hi."

"Freddie, hello." She flicked her finger over a bow that was trying to hold back Freddie's flyaway hair. It was tied from the blue ribbon Natasha had given her on her first visit. "Don't you look pretty today."

Freddie beamed, female to female. "Do you like my outfit?"

Natasha surveyed the obviously new blue denim overalls, parade stiff with sizing. "I like it very much. I have a pair just like them."

"You do?" Nothing, since Freddie had decided to make Natasha her newest heroine, could have pleased her more. "My daddy got them for me."

"That's nice." Despite her better judgment, Natasha scanned the shop for him. "Did he, ah, bring you in today?"

"No, Vera did. You said it was all right just to look."

"Sure it is. I'm glad you came in." And she was, Natasha realized. Just as she was stupidly disappointed that Freddie hadn't brought her daddy.

"I'm not supposed to touch anything." Freddie tucked her itchy fingers into her pockets. "Vera said I should look with my eyes and not with my hands."

"That's very good advice." And some Natasha wouldn't have minded others passing along to nimble-fingered children. "But some things are okay to touch. You just ask me."

"Okay. I'm going to join the Brownies and get a uniform and everything."

"That's wonderful. You'll come in and show it to me?"

Delight nearly split Freddie's face in two. "Okay. It has a hat, and I'm going to learn how to make pillows and candle holders and all kinds of things. I'll make you something."

"I'd like that." She tidied Freddie's lopsided bow.

"Daddy said you were going to eat dinner with him in a restaurant tonight."

"Well, I—"

"I don't like restaurants very much, except for pizza, so I'm going to stay home, and Vera's going to fix tortillas for me and JoBeth. We get to eat in the kitchen."

"That sounds nice."

"If you don't like the restaurant, you can come back and have some. Vera always makes a lot."

Uttering a helpless little sigh, Natasha bent to tie Freddie's left shoelace. "Thank you."

"Your hair smells pretty."

Half in love, Natasha leaned closer to sniff Freddie's. "So does yours."

Fascinated by Natasha's tangle of curls, Freddie reached out to touch. "I wish my hair was like yours," she said. "It's straight as a pin," she added, quoting her Aunt Nina.

Smiling, Natasha brushed at the fragile wisps over Freddie's brow. "When I was a little girl, we put an angel on top of the Christmas tree every year. She was very beautiful, and she had hair just like yours."

Pleasure came flushing into Freddie's cheeks.

"Ah, there you are." Vera shuffled down the crowded aisle, straw carryall on one arm, a canvas bag on the other. "Come, come, we must get back home before your father thinks we are lost." She held out a hand for Freddie and nodded to Natasha. "Good afternoon, miss."

"Good afternoon." Curious, Natasha raised a brow. She was being summed up again by the little dark eyes, and definitely being found wanting, Natasha thought. "I hope you'll bring Freddie back to visit soon."

"We will see. It is as hard for a child to resist a toy store as it is for a man to resist a beautiful woman."

Vera led Freddie down the aisle, not looking back when the girl waved and grinned over her shoulder.

"Well," Annie murmured as she stuck her head around the corner. "What brought that on?"

With a humorless smile, Natasha shoved a pin back into her hair. "At a guess, I would say the woman believes I have designs on her employer."

Annie gave an unladylike snort. "If anything, the employer has designs on you. I should be so lucky." Her sigh was only a little envious. "Now that we know the new hunk on the block isn't married, all's right with the world. Why didn't you tell me you were going out with him?"

"Because I wasn't."

"But I heard Freddie say—"

"He asked me out," Natasha clarified. "I said no."

"I see." After a brief pause, Annie tilted her head. "When did you have the accident?"

"Accident?"

"Yes, the one where you suffered brain damage."

Natasha's face cleared with a laugh, and she started toward the front of the shop.

"I'm serious," Annie said as soon as they had five free minutes. "Dr. Spencer Kimball is gorgeous, unattached and…" She leaned over the counter to sniff at the rose. "Charming. Why aren't you taking off early to work on real problems, like what to wear tonight?"

"I know what I'm wearing tonight. My bathrobe."

Annie couldn't resist the grin. "Aren't you rushing things just a tad? I don't think you should wear your robe until at least your third date."

"There's not going to be a first one." Natasha smiled at her next customer and rang up a sale.

It took Annie forty minutes to work back to the subject at hand. "Just what are you afraid of?"

"The IRS."

"Tash, I'm serious."

"So am I." When her pins worked loose again, she gave up and yanked them out. "Every American businessperson is afraid of the IRS."

"We're talking about Spence Kimball."

"No," Natasha corrected. "You're talking about Spence Kimball."

"I thought we were friends."

Surprised by Annie's tone, Natasha stopped tidying the racetrack display her Saturday visitors had wrecked. "We are. You know we are."

"Friends talk to each other, Tash, confide in each other, ask advice." Puffing out a breath, Annie stuffed her hands into the pockets of her baggy jeans. "Look, I know that things happened to you before you came here, things you're still carrying around but never talk about. I figured I was being a better friend by not asking you about it."

Had she been so obvious? Natasha wondered. All this time she'd been certain she had buried the past and all that went with it—deeply. Feeling a little helpless, she reached out to touch Annie's hand. "Thank you."

With a dismissive shrug, Annie turned to flick the lock on the front door. The shop was empty now, the bustle of the afternoon only an echo. "Remember when you let me cry on your shoulder after Don Newman dumped me?"

Natasha pressed her lips into a thin line. "He wasn't worth crying over."

"I enjoyed crying over him," Annie returned with a quick, amused smile. "I needed to cry and yell and moan and get a little drunk. You were right there for me, saying all those great, nasty things about him."

"That was the easy part," Natasha remembered. "He was a dork." It pleased her tremendously to use the young Freedmont boy's insult.

"Yeah, but he was a terrific-looking dork." Annie allowed herself a brief reminiscence. "Anyway, you helped me over that rough spot until I convinced myself I was better off without him. You've never needed my shoulder, Tash, because you've never let a guy get past this." She lifted a hand, pressing her palm against empty air.

Amused, Natasha leaned back against the counter. "And what is that?"

"The Great Stanislaski Force Field," Annie told her. "Guaranteed to repel all males from the age of twenty-five to fifty."

Natasha lifted a brow, not quite sure if she was amused any longer. "I'm not certain if you're trying to flatter or insult me."

"Neither. Just listen to me a minute, okay?" Annie took a deep breath to keep herself from rushing through something she thought should be taken step-by-step. "Tash, I've seen you brush off guys with less effort than you'd swat away a gnat. And just as automatically," she added when Natasha remained silent. "You're very pleasant about it, and also very definite. I've never seen you give any man a second's thought once you've politely shown him the door. I've even admired you for it, for being so sure of yourself, so comfortable with yourself that you didn't need a date on Saturday night to keep your ego out of the dirt."

"Not sure of myself," Natasha murmured. "Just apathetic about relationships."

"All right." Annie nodded slowly. "I'll accept that. But this time it's different."

"What is?" Natasha skirted the counter and began to tally the day's sales.

"You see? You know I'm going to mention his name, and you're nervous."

"I'm not nervous," Natasha lied.

"You've been nervous, moody and distracted since Kimball walked into the shop a couple of weeks ago. In over three years, I've never seen you give a man more than five minutes' thought. Until now."

"That's only because this one is more annoying than

most." At Annie's shrewd look, Natasha gave up. "All right, there is…something," she admitted. "But I'm not interested."

"You're afraid to be interested."

Natasha didn't like the sound of that, but forced herself to shrug it off. "It's the same thing."

"No, it's not." Annie put a hand over Natasha's and squeezed. "Look, I'm not pushing you toward this guy. For all I know, he could have murdered his wife and buried her in the rose garden. All I'm saying is, you're not going to be comfortable with yourself until you stop being afraid."

Annie was right, Natasha thought later as she sat on her bed with her chin on her hand. She was moody, she was distracted. And she was afraid. Not of Spence, Natasha assured herself. No man would ever frighten her again. But she was afraid of the feelings he stirred up. Forgotten, unwanted feelings.

Did that mean she was no longer in charge of her emotions? No. Did that mean she would act irrationally, impulsively, just because needs and desires had pried their way back into her life? No. Did that mean she would hide in her room, afraid to face a man? A most definite no.

She was only afraid because she had yet to test herself, Natasha thought, moving toward her closet. So tonight she would have dinner with the persistent Dr. Kimball, prove to herself that she was strong and perfectly capable of resisting a fleeting attraction, then get back to normal.

Natasha frowned at her wardrobe. With a restless move of her shoulders she pulled out a deep blue cocktail dress with a jeweled belt. Not that she was dressing for him. He was really irrelevant. It was one of her favorite dresses, Natasha thought as she stripped off her robe, and she rarely had the opportunity to wear anything but work clothes.

He knocked at precisely seven twenty-eight. Natasha detested herself for anxiously watching the clock. She had reapplied her lipstick twice, checked and rechecked the contents of her purse and fervently wished that she had delayed taking her stand.

She was acting like a teenager, Natasha told herself as she walked to the door. It was only dinner, the first and last dinner she intended to share with him. And he was only a man, she added, pulling the door open.

An outrageously attractive man.

He looked wonderful, was all she could think, with his hair swept back from his face, and that half smile in his eyes. It had never occurred to her that a man could be gut-wrenchingly sexy in a suit and a tie.

"Hi." He held out another red rose.

Natasha nearly sighed. It was a pity the smoke-gray suit didn't make him seem more professorial. Giving in a little, she tapped the blossom against her cheek. "It wasn't the roses that changed my mind."

"About what?"

"About having dinner with you." She stepped back, deciding that she had no choice but to let him in while she put the flower into water.

He smiled then, fully, and exasperated her by looking charming and cocky at the same time. "What did?"

"I'm hungry." She set her short velvet jacket on the arm of the sofa. "I'll put this in water. You can sit if you like."

She wasn't going to give him an inch, Spence thought as he watched her walk away. Oddly enough, that only made her more interesting. He took a deep breath, shaking his head. Incredible. Just when he was convinced that nothing smelled sexier than soap, she put something on that made him think of midnight and weeping violins.

Deciding that he was safer thinking of something else, he studied the room. She preferred vivid colors, he mused, noting the emerald and teal slashes of the pillows on a sapphire-blue couch. There was a huge brass urn beside it, stuffed with silky peacock feathers. Candles of varying sizes and shades were set around the room so that it smelled, romantically, of vanilla and jasmine and gardenia. A shelf in the corner was crammed with books that ran the gamut from popular fiction to classic literature by way of home improvements for the novice.

The table surfaces were crowded with mementos, framed pictures, dried bouquets, fanciful statuettes inspired by fairy tales. There was a gingerbread house no bigger than his palm, a girl dressed as Red Riding Hood, a pig peeking out of the window of a tiny straw house, a beautiful woman holding a single glass slipper.

Practical tips on plumbing, passionate colors and fairy tales, he mused, touching a fingertip to the tiny crystal slipper. It was as curious and as intriguing a combination as the woman herself.

Hearing her come back into the room, Spence turned. "These are beautiful," he said, gesturing to one of the figures. "Freddie's eyes would pop out."

"Thank you. My brother makes them."

"Makes them?" Fascinated, Spence picked up the gingerbread house to study it more closely. It was carved from polished wood, then intricately painted so that each licorice whip and lollipop looked good enough to eat. "It's incredible. You rarely see workmanship like this."

Whatever her reservations, she warmed toward him and crossed the room to join him. "He's been carving and sculpting since he was a child. One day his art will be in galleries and museums."

"It should be already."

The sincerity in his voice hit her most vulnerable spot, her love of family. "It's not so easy. He's young and hardheaded and proud, so he keeps his job, hammering wood, instead of carving it to bring in money for the family. But one day..." She smiled at the collection. "He makes these for me, because I struggled so hard to learn to read English from this book of fairy tales I found in the boxes of things the church gave us when we came to New York. The pictures were so pretty, and I wanted so badly to know the stories that went with them."

She caught herself, embarrassed to have said anything. "We should go."

He only nodded, having already decided to pry gently until she told him more. "You should wear your jacket." He lifted it from the sofa. "It's getting chilly."

The restaurant he'd chosen was only a short drive away and sat on one of the wooded hills that overlooked the Potomac. If Natasha had been given a guess, she would have been on target with his preference for a quiet, elegant backdrop and discreetly speedy service. Over her first glass of wine, she told herself to relax and enjoy.

"Freddie was in the shop today."

"So I heard." Amused, Spence lifted his own glass. "She wants her hair curled."

Natasha's puzzled look became a smile; she lifted a hand to her own. "Oh. That's sweet."

"Easy for you to say. I've just gotten the hang of pigtails."

To her surprise, Natasha could easily picture him patiently braiding the soft, flaxen tresses. "She's beautiful."

The image of him holding the girl on his lap at the piano slipped back into her mind. "She has your eyes."

"Don't look now," Spence murmured, "but I believe you've given me a compliment."

Feeling awkward, Natasha lifted the menu. "To soften the blow," she told him. "I'm about to make up for skipping lunch this afternoon."

True to her word, she ordered generously. As long as she was eating, Natasha figured, the interlude would go smoothly. Over appetizers she was careful to steer the conversation toward subjects they had touched on in class. Comfortably they discussed late fifteenth-century music with its four-part harmonies and traveling musicians. Spence appreciated her genuine curiosity and interest, but was equally determined to explore more personal areas.

"Tell me about your family."

Natasha slipped a hot, butter-drenched morsel of lobster into her mouth, enjoying the delicate, almost decadent flavor. "I'm the oldest of four," she began, then became abruptly aware that his fingertips were playing casually with hers on the tablecloth. She slid her hand out of reach.

Her maneuver had him lifting his glass to hide a smile. "Are you all spies?"

A flicker of temper joined the lights that the candle brought to her eyes. "Certainly not."

"I wondered, since you seem so reluctant to talk about them." His face sober, he leaned toward her. "Say 'Get moose and squirrel.'"

Her mouth quivered before she gave up and laughed. "No." She dipped her lobster in melted butter again, coating it slowly, enjoying the scent, then the taste and texture. "I have two brothers and a sister. My parents still live in Brooklyn."

"Why did you move here, to West Virginia?"

"I wanted a change." She lifted a shoulder. "Didn't you?"

"Yes." A faint line appeared between his brows as he studied her. "You said you were about Freddie's age when you came to the States. Do you remember much about your life before that?"

"Of course." For some reason she sensed he was thinking more of his daughter than of her own memories of the Ukraine. "I've always believed impressions made on us in those first few years stay the longest. Good or bad, they help form what we are." Concerned, she leaned closer, smiling. "Tell me, when you think about being five, what do you remember?"

"Sitting at the piano, doing scales." It came so clearly that he nearly laughed. "Smelling hothouse roses and watching the snow outside the window. Being torn between finishing my practice and getting to the park to throw snowballs at my nanny."

"Your nanny," Natasha repeated, but with a chuckle rather than a sneer he noted. She cupped her chin in her hands, leaning closer, alluring him with the play of light and shadow over her face. "And what did you do?"

"Both."

"A responsible child."

He ran a fingertip down her wrist and surprised a shiver out of her. Before she moved her hand away, he felt her pulse scramble. "What do you remember about being five?"

Because her reaction annoyed her, she was determined to show him nothing. She only shrugged. "My father bringing in wood for the fire, his hair and coat all covered with snow. The baby crying—my youngest brother. The smell of the bread my mother had baked. Pretending to be asleep while I listened to Papa talk to her about escape."

"Were you afraid?"

"Yes." Her eyes blurred with the memory. She didn't often look back, didn't often need to. But when she did, it came not with the watery look of old dreams, but clear as glass. "Oh, yes. Very afraid. More than I will ever be again."

"Will you tell me?"

"Why?"

His eyes were dark, and fixed on her face. "Because I'd like to understand."

She started to pass it off, even had the words in her mind. But the memory remained too vivid. "We waited until spring and took only what we could carry. We told no one, no one at all, and set off in the wagon. Papa said we were going to visit my mother's sister who lived in the west. But I think there were some who knew, who watched us go with tired faces and big eyes. Papa had papers, badly forged, but he had a map and hoped we would avoid the border guards."

"And you were only five?"

"Nearly six by then." Thinking, she ran a fingertip around and around the rim of her glass. "Mikhail was between four and five, Alex just two. At night, if we could risk a fire, we would sit around it and Papa would tell stories. Those were good nights. We would fall asleep listening to his voice and smelling the smoke from the fire. We went over the mountains and into Hungary. It took us ninety-three days."

He couldn't imagine it, not even when he could see it reflected so clearly in her eyes. Her voice was low, but the emotions were all there, bringing it richness. Thinking of the little girl, he took her hand and waited for her to go on.

"My father had planned for years. Perhaps he had

dreamed it all of his life. He had names, people who would help defectors. There was war, the cold one, but I was too young to understand. I understood the fear, in my parents, in the others who helped us. We were smuggled out of Hungary into Austria. The church sponsored us, brought us to America. It was a long time before I stopped waiting for the police to come and take my father away."

She brought herself back, embarrassed to have spoken of it, surprised to find her hand caught firmly in his.

"That's a lot for a child to deal with."

"I also remember eating my first hot dog." She smiled and picked up her wine again. She never spoke of that time, never. Not even with family. Now that she had, with him, she felt a desperate need to change the subject. "And the day my father brought home our first television. No childhood, even one with nannies, is ever completely secure. But we grow up. I'm a businesswoman, and you're a respected composer. Why don't you write?" She felt his fingers tense on hers. "I'm sorry," she said quickly. "I had no business asking that."

"It's all right." His fingers relaxed again. "I don't write because I can't."

She hesitated, then went on impulse. "I know your music. Something that intense doesn't fade."

"It hasn't mattered a great deal in the past couple of years. Just lately it's begun to matter again."

"Don't be patient."

When he smiled, she shook her head, at once impatient and regal. Her hand was gripping his now, hard and strong.

"No, I mean it. People always say when the time is right, when the mood is right, when the place is right. Years are wasted that way. If my father had waited until we were older, until the trip was safer, we might still be in the

Ukraine. There are some things that should be grabbed with both hands and taken. Life can be very, very short."

He could feel the urgency in the way her hands gripped his. And he could see the shadow of regret in her eyes. The reason for both intrigued him as much as her words.

"You may be right," he said slowly, then brought the palm of her hand to his lips. "Waiting isn't always the best answer."

"It's getting late." Natasha pulled her hand free, then balled it into a fist on her lap. But that didn't stop the heat from spearing her arm. "We should go."

She was relaxed again when he walked her to her door. During the short drive home he had made her laugh with stories of Freddie's ploys to interest him in a kitten.

"I think cutting pictures of cats from a magazine to make you a poster was very clever." She turned to lean back against her front door. "You are going to let her have one?"

"I'm trying not to be a pushover."

Natasha only smiled. "Big old houses like yours tend to get mice in the winter. In fact, in a house of that size, you'd be wise to take two of JoBeth's kittens."

"If Freddie pulls that one on me, I'll know exactly where she got it." He twirled one of Natasha's curls around his fingers. "And you have a quiz coming up next week."

Natasha lifted both brows. "Blackmail, Dr. Kimball?"

"You bet."

"I intend to ace your quiz, and I have a strong feeling that Freddie could talk you into taking the entire litter all by herself, if she put her mind to it."

"Just the little gray one."

"You've already been to see them."

"A couple of times. You're not going to ask me in?"

"No."

"All right." He slipped his arms around her waist.

"Spence—"

"I'm just taking your advice," he murmured as he skimmed his lips over her jaw. "Not being patient." He brought her closer; his mouth brushed her earlobe. "Taking what I want." His teeth scraped over her bottom lip. "Not wasting time."

Then he was crushing his mouth against hers. He could taste the faintest tang of wine on her lips and knew he could get drunk on that alone. Her flavors were rich, exotic, intoxicating. Like the hint of autumn in the air, she made him think of smoking fires, drifting fog. And her body was already pressed eagerly against his in an instantaneous acknowledgment.

Passion didn't bloom, it didn't whisper. It exploded so that even the air around them seemed to shudder with it.

She made him feel reckless. Unaware of what he murmured to her, he raced his lips over her face, coming back, always coming back to her heated, hungry mouth. In one rough stroke he took his hands over her.

Her head was spinning. If only she could believe it was the wine. But she knew it was he, only he who made her dizzy and dazed and desperate. She wanted to be touched. By him. On a breathless moan, she let her head fall back, and the urgent trail of his lips streaked down her throat.

Feeling this way had to be wrong. Old fears and doubts swirled inside her, leaving empty holes that begged to be filled. And when they were filled, with liquid, shimmering pleasure, the fear only grew.

"Spence." Her fingers dug into his shoulders; she fought a war between the need to stop him and the impossible desire to go on. "Please."

He was as shaken as she and took a moment, burying

his face in her hair. "Something happens to me every time I'm with you. I can't explain it."

She wanted badly to hold him against herself, but forced her arms to drop to her sides. "It can't continue to happen."

He drew away, just far enough to be able to take her face into both hands. The chill of the evening and the heat of passion had brought color to her cheeks. "If I wanted to stop it, which I don't, I couldn't."

She kept her eyes level with his and tried not to be moved by the gentle way he cradled her face. "You want to go to bed with me."

"Yes." He wasn't certain if he wanted to laugh or curse her for being so matter-of-fact. "But it's not quite that simple."

"Sex is never simple."

His eyes narrowed. "I'm not interested in having sex with you."

"You just said—"

"I want to make love with you. There's a difference."

"I don't choose to romanticize it."

The annoyance in his eyes vanished as quickly as it had appeared. "Then I'm sorry I'll have to disappoint you. When we make love, whenever, wherever, it's going to be very romantic." Before she could evade, he closed his mouth over hers. "That's a promise I intend to keep."

Chapter 5

"Natasha! Hey, ah, Natasha!"

Broken out of thoughts that weren't particularly productive, Natasha glanced over and spied Terry. He was wearing a long yellow-and white-striped scarf in defense against a sudden plunge in temperature that had sprinkled frost on the ground. As he raced after her, it flapped awkwardly behind him. By the time he reached her, his glasses had slipped crookedly down to the tip of his reddening nose.

"Hi, Terry."

The hundred-yard dash had winded him. He dearly hoped it wouldn't aggravate his asthma. "Hi. I was—I saw you heading in." He'd been waiting hopefully for her for twenty minutes.

Feeling a bit like a mother with a clumsy child, she straightened his glasses, then wrapped the scarf more securely around his skinny neck. His rapid breathing fogged his lenses. "You should be wearing gloves," she told him, then patting his chilled hand, led him up the steps.

Overwhelmed, he tried to speak and only made a strangled sound in his throat.

"Are you catching a cold?" Searching through her purse, she found a tissue and offered it.

He cleared his throat loudly. "No." But he took the tissue and vowed to keep it until the day he died. "I was just wondering if tonight—after class—you know, if you don't have anything to do… You've probably got plans, but if you don't, then maybe…we could have a cup of coffee. Two cups," he amended desperately. "I mean you could have your own cup, and I'd have one." So saying, he turned a thin shade of green.

The poor boy was lonely, Natasha thought, giving him an absent smile. "Sure." It wouldn't hurt to keep him company for an hour or so, she decided as she walked into class. And it would help her keep her mind off…

Off the man standing in front of the class, Natasha reflected with a scowl; the man who had kissed the breath out of her two weeks before and who was currently laughing with a sassy little blonde who couldn't have been a day over twenty.

Her mood grim, she plopped down at her desk and poked her nose into a textbook.

Spence knew the moment she walked into the room. He was more than a little gratified to have seen the huffy jealousy on her face before she stuck a book in front of it. Apparently fate hadn't been dealing him such a bad hand when it kept him up to his ears in professional and personal problems for the last couple of weeks. Between leaky plumbing, PTA and Brownie meetings and a faculty conference, he hadn't had an hour free. But now things were running smoothly again. He studied the top of Natasha's head. He intended to make up for lost time.

Sitting on the edge of his desk, he opened a discussion of the distinctions between sacred and secular music during the baroque period.

She didn't want to be interested. Natasha was sure he knew it. Why else would he deliberately call on her for an opinion—twice?

Oh, he was clever, she thought. Not by a flicker, not by the slightest intonation did he reveal a more personal relationship with her. No one in class would possibly suspect that this smooth, even brilliant lecturer had kissed her senseless, not once, not twice, but three times. Now he calmly talked of early seventeenth-century operatic developments.

In his black turtleneck and gray tweed jacket he looked casually elegant and totally in charge. And of course, as always, he had the class in the palms of those beautiful hands he eloquently used to make a point. When he smiled over a student's comment, Natasha heard the little blonde two seats behind her sigh. Because she'd nearly done so herself, Natasha stiffened her spine.

He probably had a whole string of eager women. A man who looked like him, talked like him, kissed like him was bound to. He was the type that made promises to one woman at midnight and snuggled up to another over breakfast in bed.

Wasn't it fortunate she no longer believed in promises?

Something was going on inside that fabulous head of hers, Spence mused. One moment she was listening to him as if he had the answers to the mysteries of the universe on the tip of his tongue. The next, she was sitting rigidly and staring off into space, as though she wished herself somewhere else. He would swear that she was angry, and that the anger was directed squarely at him. Why was an entirely different matter.

Whenever he'd tried to have a word with her after class over the last couple of weeks, she'd been out of the building like a bullet. Tonight he would have to outmaneuver her.

She stood the moment class was over. Spence watched her smile at the man sitting across from her. Then she bent down to pick up the books and pencils the man scattered as he rose.

What was his name? Spence wondered. Maynard. That was it. Mr. Maynard was in several of his classes, and managed to fade into the background in each one. Yet at the moment the unobtrusive Mr. Maynard was crouched knee to knee with Natasha.

"I think we've got them all." Natasha gave Terry's glasses a friendly shove back up his nose.

"Thanks."

"Don't forget your scarf—" she began, then looked up. A hand closed over her arm and helped her to her feet. "Thank you, Dr. Kimball."

"I'd like to talk to you, Natasha."

"Would you?" She gave the hand on her arm a brief look, then snatched up her coat and books. Feeling as though she were on a chessboard again, she decided to aggressively counter his move. "I'm sorry, it'll have to wait. I have a date."

"A date?" he managed, getting an immediate picture of someone dark, dashing and muscle-bound.

"Yes. Excuse me." She shook off his hand and stuck an arm into the sleeve of her coat. Since the men on either side of her seemed equally paralyzed, she shifted the books to her other arm and struggled to find the second sleeve. "Are you ready, Terry?"

"Well, yeah, sure. Yeah." He was staring at Spence with a mixture of awe and trepidation. "But I can wait if you want to talk to Dr. Kimball first."

"There's no need." She scooped up his arm and pulled him to the door.

Women, Spence thought as he sat down at a desk. He'd already accepted the fact that he had never understood them. Apparently he never would.

"Jeez, Tash, don't you think you should have seen what Dr. Kimball wanted?"

"I know what he wanted," she said between her teeth as she pushed open the main doors. The rush of autumn air cooled her cheeks. "I wasn't in the mood to discuss it tonight." When Terry tripped over the uneven sidewalk, she realized she was still dragging him and slowed her pace. "Besides, I thought we were going to have some coffee."

"Right." When she smiled at him, he tugged on his scarf as if to keep from strangling.

They walked into a small lounge where half the little square tables were empty. At the antique bar two men were muttering over their beers. A couple in the corner were all but sitting on each other's laps and ignoring their drinks.

She'd always liked this room with its dim lighting and old black-and-white posters of James Dean and Marilyn Monroe. It smelled of cigarettes and jug wine. There was a big portable stereo on a shelf above the bar that played an old Chuck Berry number loudly enough to make up for the lack of patrons. Natasha felt the bass vibrate through her chair as she sat down.

"Just coffee, Joe," she called to the man behind the bar

before she leaned her elbows on the table. "So," she said to Terry, "how's everything going?"

"Okay." He couldn't believe it. He was here, sitting with her. On a date. She'd called it a date herself.

It would take a little prodding. Patient, she shrugged out of her coat. The overheated room had her pushing the sleeves of her sweater past her elbows. "It must be different for you here. Did you ever tell me where you were going to college before?"

"I graduated from Michigan State." Because his lenses were fogged again, Natasha seemed to be shrouded by a thin, mysterious mist. "When I, ah, heard that Dr. Kimball would be teaching here, I decided to take a couple years of graduate study."

"You came here because of Spence—Dr. Kimball?"

"I didn't want to miss the opportunity. I went to New York last year to hear him lecture." Terry lifted a hand and nearly knocked over a bowl of sugar. "He's incredible."

"I suppose," she murmured as their coffee was served.

"Where you been hiding?" the bartender asked, giving her shoulder a casual squeeze. "I haven't seen you in here all month."

"Business is good. How's Darla?"

"History." Joe gave her a quick, friendly wink. "I'm all yours, Tash."

"I'll keep it in mind." With a laugh, she turned back to Terry. "Is something wrong?" she asked when she saw him dragging at his collar.

"Yes. No. That is… Is he your boyfriend?"

"My…" To keep herself from laughing in Terry's face, she took a sip of coffee. "You mean Joe? No." She cleared her throat and sipped again. "No, he's not. We're just…" She searched for a word. "Pals."

"Oh." Relief and insecurity warred. "I just thought, since he... Well."

"He was only joking." Wanting to put Terry at ease again, she squeezed his hand. "What about you? Do you have a girl back in Michigan?"

"No. There's nobody. Nobody at all." He turned his hand over, gripping hers.

Oh, my God. As realization hit, Natasha felt her mouth drop open. Only a fool would have missed it, she thought as she stared into Terry's adoring, myopic eyes. A fool, she added, who was so tied up with her own problems that she missed what was happening under her nose. She was going to have to be careful, Natasha decided. Very careful.

"Terry," she began. "You're very sweet—"

That was all it took to make his hand shake. Coffee spilled down his shirt. Moving quickly, Natasha shifted chairs so that she was beside him. Snatching paper napkins from the dispenser, she began to blot the stain.

"It's a good thing they never serve it hot in this place. If you soak this in cold water right away, you should be all right."

Overcome, Terry grabbed both of her hands. Her head was bent close, and the scent of her hair was making him dizzy. "I love you," he blurted, and took aim with his mouth; his glasses slid down his nose.

Natasha felt his lips hit her cheekbone, cold and trembly. Because her heart went out to him, she decided that being careful wasn't the right approach. Firmness was called for, quickly.

"No, you don't." Her voice was brisk, she pulled back far enough to dab at the spill on the table.

"I don't?" Her response threw him off. It was nothing like any of the fantasies he'd woven. There was the one where he'd saved her from a runaway truck. And another where he'd played the song he was writing for her and she had collapsed in a passionate, weeping puddle into his arms. His imagination hadn't stretched far enough to see her wiping up coffee and calmly telling him he wasn't in love at all.

"Yes, I do." He snatched at her hand again.

"That's ridiculous," she said, and smiled to take the sting out of the words. "You like me, and I like you, too."

"No, it's more than that. I—"

"All right. Why do you love me?"

"Because you're beautiful," he managed, losing his grip as he stared into her face again. "You're the most beautiful woman I've ever seen."

"And that's enough?" Disengaging her hand from his, she linked her fingers to rest her chin on them. "What if I told you I was a thief—or that I liked to run down small, furry animals with my car? Maybe I've been married three times and have murdered all my husbands in their sleep."

"Tash—"

She laughed, but resisted the temptation to pet his cheek. "I mean, you don't know me enough to love me. If you did, what I looked like wouldn't matter."

"But—but I think about you all the time."

"Because you've told yourself it would be nice to be in love with me." He looked so forlorn that she took a chance and laid one hand upon his. "I'm very flattered."

"Does this mean you won't go out with me?"

"I'm out with you now." She pushed her cup of coffee in front of him. "As friends," she said before the light could dawn again in his eyes. "I'm too old to be anything but your friend."

"No, you're not."

"Oh, yes." Suddenly she felt a hundred. "Yes, I am."

"You think I'm stupid," he muttered. In place of confused excitement came a crushing wave of humiliation. He could feel his cheeks sting with it.

"No, I don't." Her voice softened, and she reached once more for his hands. "Terry, listen—"

Before she could stop him, he pushed back his chair. "I've got to go."

Cursing herself, Natasha picked up his striped scarf. There was no use in following him now. He needed time, she decided. And she needed air.

The leaves were beginning to turn, and a few that had fallen early scraped along the sidewalk ahead of the wind. It was the kind of evening Natasha liked best, but now she barely noticed it. She'd left her coffee untouched to take a long, circular walk through town.

Heading home, she thought of a dozen ways she could have handled Terry's infatuation better. Through her clumsiness she had wounded a sensitive, vulnerable boy. It could have been avoided, all of it, if she had been paying attention to what was happening in front of her face.

Instead she'd been blinded by her own unwelcome feelings for someone else.

She knew too well what it was to believe yourself in love, desperately, hopelessly in love. And she knew how it hurt to discover that the one you loved didn't return those feelings. Cruel or kind, the rejection of love left the heart bruised.

Uttering a sigh, she ran a hand over the scarf in her pocket. Had she ever been so trusting and defenseless? Yes, she answered herself. That and much, much more.

It was about damn time, Spence thought as he watched her start up the walk. Obviously her mind was a million miles away. On her date, he decided and tried not to grind his teeth. Well, he was going to see to it that she had a lot more to think about in very short order.

"Didn't he walk you home?"

Natasha stopped dead with an involuntary gasp. In the beam of her porch light she saw Spence sitting on her stoop. That was all she needed, she thought while she dragged a hand through her hair. With Terry she'd felt as though she'd kicked a puppy. Now she was going to have to face down a large, hungry wolf.

"What are you doing here?"

"Freezing."

She nearly laughed. His breath was puffing out in white steam. With the windchill, she imagined that the effective temperature was hovering around twenty-five degrees Fahrenheit. After a moment, Natasha decided she must be a very poor sport to be amused at the thought of Spence sitting on cold concrete for the past hour.

He rose as she continued down the walk. How could she have forgotten how tall he was? "Didn't you invite your friend back for a drink?"

"No." She reached out and twisted the knob. Like most of the doors in town, it was unlocked. "If I had, you'd be very embarrassed."

"That's not the word for it."

"I suppose I'm lucky I didn't find you waiting up for me inside."

"You would have," he muttered, "if it had occurred to me to try the door."

"Good night."

"Wait a damn minute." He slapped his palm on the door before she could close it in his face. "I didn't sit out here in the cold for my health. I want to talk to you."

There was something satisfying in the brief, fruitless push-push they played with the door. "It's late."

"And getting later by the second. If you close the door, I'm just going to beat on it until all your neighbors poke their heads out their windows."

"Five minutes," she said graciously, because she had planned to grant him that in any case. "I'll give you a brandy, then you'll go."

"You're all heart, Natasha."

"No." She laid her coat over the back of the couch. "I'm not."

She disappeared into the kitchen without another word. When she returned with two snifters of brandy, he was standing in the center of the room, running Terry's scarf through his fingers.

"What kind of game are you playing?"

She set down his brandy, then sipped calmly at her own. "I don't know what you mean."

"What are you doing, going out on dates with some college kid who's still wet behind the ears?"

Both her back and her voice stiffened. "It's none of your business whom I go out with."

"It is now," Spence replied, realizing it now mattered to him.

"No, it's not. And Terry's a very nice young man."

"Young's the operative word." Spence tossed the scarf aside. "He's certainly too young for you."

"Is that so?" It was one thing for her to say it, and quite another to have Spence throw it at her like an accusation. "I believe that's for me to decide."

"Hit a nerve that time," Spence muttered to himself. There had been a time—hadn't there?—when he had been considered fairly smooth with women. "Maybe I should have said you're too old for him."

"Oh, yes." Despite herself, she began to see the humor of it. "That's a great deal better. Would you like to drink this brandy or wear it?"

"I'll drink it, thanks." He lifted the glass, but instead of bringing it to his lips, took another turn around the room. He was jealous, Spence realized. It was rather pathetic, but he was jealous of an awkward, tongue-tied grad student. And while he was about it, he was making a very big fool of himself. "Listen, maybe I should start over."

"I don't know why you would want to start something over you should never have begun."

But like a dog with a bone, he couldn't stop gnawing. "It's just that he's obviously not your type."

Fire blazed again. "Oh, and you'd know about my type?"

Spence held up his free hand. "All right, one straight question before my foot is permanently lodged in my mouth. Are you interested in him?"

"Of course I am." Then she cursed herself; it was impossible to use Terry and his feelings as a barricade against Spence. "He's a very nice boy."

Spence almost relaxed, then spotted the scarf again, still spread over the back of her couch. "What are you doing with that?"

"I picked it up for him." The sight of it, bright and a little foolish on the jewel colors of her couch, made her feel like the most vicious kind of femme fatale. "He left it behind after I broke his heart. He thinks he's in love with me." Miserable, she dropped into a chair. "Oh, go away. I don't know why I'm talking to you."

The look on her face made him want to smile and stroke

her hair. He thought better of it and kept his tone brisk. "Because you're upset, and I'm the only one here."

"I guess that'll do." She didn't object when Spence sat down across from her. "He was very sweet and nervous, and I had no idea what he was feeling—or what he thought he was feeling. I should have realized, but I didn't until he spilled his coffee all over his shirt, and... Don't laugh at him."

Spence continued to smile as he shook his head. "I'm not. Believe me, I know exactly how he must have felt. There are some women who make you clumsy."

Their eyes met and held. "Don't flirt with me."

"I'm past flirting with you, Natasha."

Restless, she rose to pace the room. "You're changing the subject."

"Am I?"

She waved an impatient hand as she paced. "I hurt his feelings. If I had known what was happening, I might have stopped it. There is nothing," she said passionately, "nothing worse than loving someone and being turned away."

"No." He understood that. And he could see by the shadows haunting her eyes that she did, too. "But you don't really believe he's in love with you."

"He believes it. I ask him why he thinks it, and do you know what he says?" She whirled back, her hair swirling around her shoulders with the movement. "He says because he thinks I'm beautiful. That's it." She threw up her hands and started to pace again. Spence only watched, caught up in her movements and by the musical cadence that agitation brought to her voice. "When he says it, I want to slap him and say—what's wrong with you? A face is nothing but a face. You don't know my mind or my heart. But he has big, sad eyes, so I can't yell at him."

"You never had a problem yelling at me."

"You don't have big, sad eyes, and you're not a boy who thinks he's in love."

"I'm not a boy," he agreed, catching her by the shoulders from behind. Even as she stiffened, he turned her around. "And I like more than your face, Natasha. Though I like that very much."

"You don't know anything about me, either."

"Yes, I do. I know you lived through experiences I can hardly imagine. I know you love and miss your family, that you understand children and have a natural affection for them. You're organized, stubborn and passionate." He ran his hands down her arms, then back to her shoulders. "I know you've been in love before." He tightened his grip before she could pull away. "And you're not ready to talk about it. You have a sharp, curious mind and caring heart, and you wish you weren't attracted to me. But you are."

She lowered her lashes briefly to veil her eyes. "Then it would seem you know more of me than I of you."

"That's easy to fix."

"I don't know if I want to. Or why I should."

His lips brushed hers, then retreated before she could respond or reject. "There's something there," he murmured. "That's reason enough."

"Maybe there is," she began. "No." She drew back when he would have kissed her again. "Don't. I'm not very strong tonight."

"A good way to make me feel guilty if I press my advantage."

She felt twin rushes of disappointment and relief when he released her. "I'll make you dinner," she said on impulse.

"Now?"

"Tomorrow. Just dinner," she added, wondering if she

should already be regretting the invitation. "If you bring Freddie."

"She'd like that. So would I."

"Good. Seven o'clock." Natasha picked up his coat and held it out. "Now you have to go."

"You should learn to say what's on your mind." With a half laugh, Spence took the coat from her. "One more thing."

"Only one?"

"Yeah." He swung her back into his arms for one long, hard, mind-numbing kiss. He had the satisfaction of seeing her sink weakly onto the arm of the sofa when he released her.

"Good night," he said, then stepping outside, gulped in a deep breath of cold air.

It was the first time Freddie had been asked out to a grown-up dinner, and she waited impatiently while her father shaved. Usually she enjoyed watching him slide the razor through the white foam on his face. There were even times when she secretly wished she were a boy, so that she could look forward to the ritual. But tonight she thought her father was awfully slow.

"Can we go now?"

Standing in his bathrobe, Spence rinsed off the traces of lather. "It might be a better idea if I put some pants on."

Freddie only rolled her eyes. "When are you going to?"

Spence scooped her up to bite gently at her neck. "As soon as you beat it."

Taking him at his word, she raced downstairs to prowl the foyer and count to sixty. Around the fifth round, she sat on the bottom step to play with the buckle of her left shoe.

Freddie had it all figured out. Her father was going to

marry either Tash or Mrs. Patterson, because they were both pretty and had nice smiles. Afterward, the one he married would come and live in their new house. Soon she would have a new baby sister. A baby brother would do in a pinch, but it was definitely a second choice. Everybody would be happy, because everybody would like each other a lot. And her daddy would play his music late at night again.

When she heard Spence start down, Freddie jumped up and whirled around to face him. "Daddy, I counted to sixty a jillion times."

"I bet you left out the thirties again." He took her coat from the hall closet and helped bundle her into it.

"No, I didn't." At least she didn't think she had. "You took forever." With a sigh, she pulled him to the door.

"We're still going to be early."

"She won't mind."

At that moment, Natasha was pulling a sweater over her head and wondering why she had invited anyone to dinner, particularly a man every instinct told her to avoid. She'd been distracted all day, worrying if the food would be right, if she'd chosen the most complementary wine. And now she was changing for the third time.

Totally out of character, she told herself as she frowned at her reflection in the mirror. The casual blue sweater and leggings calmed her. If she looked at ease, Natasha decided she would be at ease. She fastened long silver columns at her ears, gave her hair a quick toss, then hurried back to the kitchen. She had hardly checked her sauce when she heard the knock.

They were early, she thought, allowing herself one mild oath before going to the door.

They looked wonderful. Agitation vanished in a smile. The sight of the little girl with her hand caught firmly in her father's went straight to her heart. Because it came naturally, she bent to kiss Freddie on both cheeks. "Hello."

"Thank you for asking me to dinner." Freddie recited the sentence, then looked at her father for approval.

"You're welcome."

"Aren't you going to kiss Daddy, too?"

Natasha hesitated, then caught Spence's quick, challenging grin. "Of course." She brushed her lips formally against his cheeks. "That is a traditional Ukrainian greeting."

"I'm very grateful for *glasnost*." Still smiling, he took her hand and brought it to his lips.

"Are we going to have borscht?" Freddie wanted to know.

"Borscht?" Natasha lifted a brow as she helped Freddie out of her coat.

"When I told Mrs. Patterson that me and Daddy were going to have dinner at your house, she said that borscht was Russian for beet soup." Freddie managed not to say she thought it sounded gross, but Natasha got the idea.

"I'm sorry I didn't make any," she said, straight faced. "I made another traditional dish instead. Spaghetti and meatballs."

It was easy, surprisingly so. They ate at the old gateleg table by the window, and their talk ranged from Freddie's struggles with arithmetic to Neapolitan opera. It took only a little prodding for Natasha to talk of her family. Freddie wanted to know everything there was about being a big sister.

"We didn't fight very much," Natasha reflected as she drank after-dinner coffee and balanced Freddie on her knee. "But when we did, I won, because I was the oldest. And the meanest."

"You're not mean."

"Sometimes when I'm angry I am." She looked at Spence, remembering—and regretting—telling him he didn't deserve Freddie. "Then I'm sorry."

"When people fight, it doesn't always mean they don't like each other," Spence murmured. He was doing his best not to think how perfect, how perfectly right his daughter looked cuddled on Natasha's lap. Too far, too fast, he warned himself. For everyone involved.

Freddie wasn't sure she understood, but she was only five. Then she remembered happily that she would soon be six. "I'm going to have a birthday."

"Are you?" Natasha looked appropriately impressed. "When?"

"In two weeks. Will you come to my party?"

"I'd love to." Natasha looked at Spence as Freddie recited all the wonderful treats that were in store.

It wasn't wise to get so involved with the little girl, she warned herself. Not when the little girl was attached so securely to a man who made Natasha long for things she had put behind her. Spence smiled at her. No, it wasn't wise, she thought again. But it was irresistible.

Chapter 6

"Chicken pox." Spence said the two words again. He stood in the doorway and watched his little girl sleep. "It's a hell of a birthday present, sweetie."

In two days his daughter would be six, and by then, according to the doctor, she'd be covered with the itchy rash that was now confined to her belly and chest.

It was going around, the pediatrician had said. It would run its course. Easy for him to say, Spence thought. It wasn't his daughter whose eyes were teary. It wasn't his baby with a hundred-and-one-degree temperature.

She'd never been sick before, Spence realized as he rubbed his tired eyes. Oh, the sniffles now and again, but nothing a little TLC and baby aspirin hadn't put right. He dragged a hand through his hair; Freddie moaned in her sleep and tried to find a cool spot on her pillow.

The call from Nina hadn't helped. He'd had to come down hard to prevent her from catching the shuttle and arriving on his doorstep. That hadn't stopped her telling him that Freddie had undoubtedly caught chicken pox because she was attending public school. That was nonsense, of course, but when he looked at his little girl, tossing in her bed, her face flushed with fever, the guilt was almost unbearable.

Logic told him that chicken pox was a normal part of childhood. His heart told him that he should be able to find a way to make it go away.

For the first time he realized how much he wanted someone beside him. Not to take things over, not to smooth over the downside of parenting. Just to be there. To understand what it felt like when your child was sick or hurt or unhappy. Someone to talk to in the middle of the night, when worries or pleasures kept you awake.

When he thought of that someone, he thought only of Natasha.

A big leap, he reminded himself and walked back to the bedside. One he wasn't sure he could make again and land on both feet.

He cooled Freddie's forehead with the damp cloth Vera had brought in. Her eyes opened.

"Daddy."

"Yes, funny face. I'm right here."

Her lower lip trembled. "I'm thirsty."

"I'll go get you a cold drink."

Sick or not, she knew how to maneuver. "Can I have Kool Aid?"

He pressed a kiss on her cheek. "Sure. What kind?"

"The blue kind."

"The blue kind." He kissed her again. "I'll be right back." He was halfway down the stairs when the phone rang simultaneously with a knock on the door. "Damn it. Vera, get the phone, will you?" Out of patience, he yanked open the front door.

The smile Natasha had practiced all evening faded. "I'm sorry. I've come at a bad time."

"Yeah." But he reached out to pull her inside. "Hang on a minute. Vera—oh good," he added when he saw the housekeeper hovering. "Freddie wants some Kool Aid, the blue kind."

"I will make it." Vera folded her hands in front of her apron. "Mrs. Barklay is on the phone."

"Tell her—" Spence broke off, swearing as Vera's mouth pruned. She didn't like to tell Nina anything. "All right, I'll get it."

"I should go," Natasha put in, feeling foolish. "I only came by because you weren't at class tonight, and I wondered if you were well."

"It's Freddie." Spence glanced at the phone and wondered if he could strangle his sister over it. "She has the chicken pox."

"Oh. Poor thing." She had to smother the automatic urge to go up and look in on the child herself. Not your child, Natasha reminded herself. Not your place. "I'll get out of your way."

"I'm sorry. Things are a little confused."

"Don't be. I hope she's well soon. Let me know if I can do anything."

At that moment Freddie called for her father in a voice that was half sniffle and half croak.

It was Spence's quick helpless glance up the stairs that had Natasha ignoring what she thought was her better judgment. "Would you like me to go up for a minute? I could sit with her until you have things under control again."

"No. Yes." Spence blew out a long breath. If he didn't

deal with Nina now, she'd only call back. "I'd appreciate it." Reaching the end of his rope, he yanked up the phone receiver. "Nina."

Natasha followed the glow of the night-light into Freddie's room. She found her sitting up in bed, surrounded by dolls. Two big tears were sliding down her cheeks. "I want my daddy," she said obviously miserable.

"He'll be right here." Her heart lost, Natasha sat down on the bed and drew Freddie into her arms.

"I don't feel good."

"I know. Here, blow your nose."

Freddie complied, then settled her head on Natasha's breast. She sighed, finding it pleasantly different from her father's hard chest or Vera's cushy one. "I went to the doctor and got medicine, so I can't go to my Brownie meeting tomorrow."

"There'll be other meetings, as soon as the medicine makes you well."

"I have chicken pox," Freddie announced, torn between discomfort and pride. "And I'm hot and itchy."

"It's a silly thing, the chicken pox," Natasha said soothingly. She tucked Freddie's tousled hair behind one ear. "I don't think chickens get it at all."

Freddie's lips turned up, just a little. "JoBeth had it last week, and so did Mikey. Now I can't have a birthday party."

"You'll have a party later, when everyone's well again."

"That's what Daddy said." A fresh tear trailed down her cheek. "It's not the same."

"No, but sometimes not the same is even better."

Curious, Freddie watched the light glint off the gold hoop in Natasha's ear. "How?"

"It gives you more time to think about how much fun you'll have. Would you like to rock?"

"I'm too big to rock."

"I'm not." Wrapping Freddie in a blanket, Natasha carried her to the white wicker rocker. She cleared it of stuffed animals, then tucked one particularly worn rabbit in Freddie's arms. "When I was a little girl and I was sick, my mother would always rock me in this big, squeaky chair we had by the window. She would sing me songs. No matter how bad I felt, when she rocked me I felt better."

"My mother didn't rock me." Freddie's head was aching, and she wanted badly to pop a comforting thumb into her mouth. She knew she was too old for that. "She didn't like me."

"That's not true." Natasha instinctively tightened her arms around the child. "I'm sure she loved you very much."

"She wanted my daddy to send me away."

At a loss, Natasha lowered her cheek to the top of Freddie's head. What could she say now? Freddie's words had been too matter-of-fact to dismiss as a fantasy. "People sometimes say things they don't mean, and that they regret very much. Did your daddy send you away?"

"No."

"There, you see?"

"Do you like me?"

"Of course I do." She rocked gently, to and fro. "I like you very much."

The movement, the soft female scent and voice lulled Freddie. "Why don't you have a little girl?"

The pain was there, deep and dull. Natasha closed her eyes against it. "Perhaps one day I will."

Freddie tangled her fingers in Natasha's hair, comforted. "Will you sing, like your mother did?"

"Yes. And you try to sleep."

"Don't go."

"No, I'll stay awhile."

Spence watched them from the doorway. In the shadowed light they looked achingly beautiful, the tiny, flaxen-haired child in the arms of the dark, golden-skinned woman. The rocker whispered as it moved back and forth while Natasha sang some old Ukrainian folk song from her own childhood.

It moved him as completely, as uniquely as holding the woman in his own arms had moved him. And yet so differently, so quietly that he wanted to stand just as he was, watching through the night.

Natasha looked up and saw him. He looked so frazzled that she had to smile.

"She's sleeping now."

If his legs were weak, he hoped it was because he'd climbed up and down the stairs countless times in the last twenty-four hours. Giving in to them, he sat down on the edge of the bed.

He studied his daughter's flushed face, nestled peacefully in the crook of Natasha's arm. "It's supposed to get worse before it gets better."

"Yes, it does." She stroked a hand down Freddie's hair. "We all had it when we were children. Amazingly, we all survived."

He blew out a long breath. "I guess I'm being an idiot."

"No, you're very sweet." She watched him as she continued to rock, wondering how difficult it had been for him to raise a baby without a mother's love. Difficult enough, she decided, that he deserved credit for seeing that his daughter was happy, secure and unafraid to love. She smiled again.

"Whenever one of us was sick as children, and still today, my father would badger the doctor, then he would go to church to light candles. After that he would say this old gypsy chant he'd learned from his grandmother. It's covering all the bases."

"So far I've badgered the doctor." Spence managed a smile of his own. "You wouldn't happen to remember that chant?"

"I'll say it for you." Carefully she rose, lifting Freddie in her arms. "Should I lay her down?"

"Thanks." Together they tucked in the blankets. "I mean it."

"You're welcome." She looked over the sleeping child, and though her smile was easy, she was beginning to feel awkward. "I should go. Parents of sick children need their rest."

"At least I can offer you a drink." He held up the glass. "How about some Kool Aid? It's the blue kind."

"I think I'll pass." She moved around the bed toward the door. "When the fever breaks, she'll be bored. Then you'll really have your work cut out for you."

"How about some pointers?" He took Natasha's hand as they started down the steps.

"Crayons. New ones. The best is usually the simplest."

"How is it someone like you doesn't have a horde of children of her own?" He didn't have to feel her stiffen to know he'd said the wrong thing. He could see the sorrow come and go in her eyes. "I'm sorry."

"No need." Recovered, she picked up her coat from where she'd laid it on the newel post. "I'd like to come and see Freddie again, if it's all right."

He took her coat and set it down again. "If you won't take the blue stuff, how about some tea? I could use the company."

"All right."

"I'll just—" He turned and nearly collided with Vera.

"I will fix the tea," she said after a last look at Natasha.

"Your housekeeper thinks I have designs on you."

"I hope you won't disappoint her," Spence said as he led Natasha into the music room.

"I'm afraid I must disappoint both of you." Then she laughed and wandered to the piano. "But you should be very busy. All the young women in college talk about Dr. Kimball." She tucked her tongue into her cheek. "You're a hunk, Spence. Popular opinion is equally divided between you and the captain of the football team."

"Very funny."

"I'm not joking. But it's fun to embarrass you." She sat and ran her fingers over the keys. "Do you compose here?"

"I did once."

"It's wrong of you not to write." She played a series of chords. "Art's more than a privilege. It's a responsibility." She searched for the melody, then with a sound of impatience shook her head. "I can't play. I was too old when I tried to learn."

He liked the way she looked sitting there, her hair falling over her shoulders, half curtaining her face, her fingers resting lightly on the keys of the piano he had played since childhood.

"If you want to learn, I'll teach you."

"I'd rather you write a song." It was more than impulse, she thought. Tonight he looked as though he needed a friend. She smiled and held out a hand. "Here, with me."

He glanced up as Vera carried in a tray. "Just set it there, Vera. Thank you."

"You will want something else?"

He looked back at Natasha. Yes, he would want something else. He wanted it very much. "No. Good night." He listened to the housekeeper's shuffling steps. "Why are you doing this?"

"Because you need to laugh. Come, write a song for me. It doesn't have to be good."

He did laugh. "You want me to write a bad song for you?"

"It can be a terrible song. When you play it for Freddie, she'll hold her ears and giggle."

"A bad song's about all I can do these days." But he was amused enough to sit down beside her. "If I do this, I have to have your solemn oath that it won't be repeated for any of my students."

"Cross my heart."

He began to noodle with the keys, Natasha breaking in now and then to add her inspiration. It wasn't as bad as it might have been, Spence considered as he ran through some chords. No one would call it brilliant, but it had a certain primitive charm.

"Let me try." Tossing back her hair, Natasha struggled to repeat the notes.

"Here." As he sometimes did with his daughter, he put his hands over Natasha's to guide them. The feeling, he realized, was entirely different. "Relax." His murmur whispered beside her ear.

She only wished she could. "I hate to do poorly at anything," she managed. With his palms firmly over her hands, she struggled to concentrate on the music.

"You're doing fine." Her hair, soft and fragrant, brushed his cheek.

As they bent over the keys, it didn't occur to him that he hadn't played with the piano in years. Oh, he had played— Beethoven, Gershwin, Mozart and Bernstein, but hardly for fun.... It had been much too long since he had sat before the keys for entertainment.

"No, no, an A minor maybe."

Natasha stubbornly hit a B major again. "I like this better."

"It throws it off."

"That's the point."

He grinned at her. "Want to collaborate?"

"You do better without me."

"I don't think so." His grin faded; he cupped her face in one hand. "I really don't think so."

This wasn't what she had intended. She had wanted to lighten his mood, to be his friend. She hadn't wanted to stir these feelings in both of them, feelings they would be wiser to ignore. But they were there, pulsing. No matter how strong her will, she couldn't deny them. Even the light touch of his fingers on her face made her ache, made her yearn, made her remember.

"The tea's getting cold." But she didn't pull away, didn't try to stand. When he leaned over to touch his mouth to hers, she only shut her eyes. "This can't go anywhere," she murmured.

"It already has." His hand moved up her back, strong, possessive, in contrast with the light play of his lips. "I think about you all the time, about being with you, touching you. I've never wanted anyone the way I want you." Slowly he ran a hand down her throat, over her shoulder, along her arm until their fingers linked over the piano keys. "It's like a thirst, Natasha, a constant thirst. And when I'm with you like this, I know it's the same for you."

She wanted to deny it, but his mouth was roaming hungrily over her face, taunting hers to tremble with need. And she did need, to be held like this, wanted like this. It had been easy in the past to pretend that being desired wasn't necessary. No, she hadn't had to pretend. Until now, until him, it had been true.

Now, suddenly, like a door opening, like a light being switched on, everything had changed. She yearned for him, and her blood swam faster, just knowing he wanted her. Even for a moment, she told herself as her hands clutched at his hair to pull his mouth to hers. Even for this moment.

It was there again, that whirlwind of sensation that erupted the instant they came together. Too fast, too hot, too real to be borne. Too stunning to be resisted.

It was as though he were the first, though he was not. It was as though he were the only one, though that could never be. As she poured herself into the kiss, she wished desperately that her life could begin again in that moment, with him.

There was more than passion here. The emotions that swirled inside her nearly swallowed him. There was desperation, fear and a bottomless generosity that left him dazed. Nothing would ever be simple again. Knowing it, a part of him tried to pull back, to think, to reason. But the taste of her, hot, potent, only drew him closer to the flame.

"Wait." For the first time she admitted her own weakness and let her head rest against his shoulder. "This is too fast."

"No." He combed his fingers through her hair. "It's taken years already."

"Spence." Struggling for balance, she straightened. "I don't know what to do," she said slowly, watching him. "It's important for me to know what to do."

"I think we can figure it out." But when he reached for her again, she rose quickly and stepped away.

"This isn't simple for me." Unnerved, she pushed back her hair with both hands. "I know it might seem so, because of the way I respond to you. I know that it's easier for men, less personal somehow."

He rose very carefully, very deliberately. "Why don't you explain that?"

"I only mean that I know that men find things like this less difficult to justify."

"Justify," he repeated, rocking back on his heels. How could he be angry so quickly, after being so bewitched? "You make this sound like some kind of crime."

"I don't always find the right words," she snapped. "I'm not a college professor. I didn't speak English until I was eight, couldn't read it for longer than that."

He checked his temper as he studied her. Her eyes were dark with something more than anger. She was standing stiffly, head up, but he couldn't tell if her stand was one of pride or self-defense. "What does that have to do with anything?"

"Nothing. And everything." Frustrated, she whirled back into the hallway to snatch up her coat. "I hate feeling stupid—hate being stupid. I don't belong here. I shouldn't have come."

"But you did." He grabbed her by her shoulders, so that her coat flew out to fall onto the bottom step. "Why did you?"

"I don't know. It doesn't matter why."

He gave her an impatient squeeze. "Why do I feel as if I'm having two conversations at the same time? What's going on in that head of yours, Natasha?"

"I want you," she said passionately. "And I don't want to."

"You want me." Before she could jerk away, he pulled her against himself. There was no patience in this kiss, no persuasion. It took and took, until she was certain she could have nothing left to give. "Why does that bother you?" he murmured against her lips.

Unable to resist, she ran her hands over his face, memorizing the shape. "There are reasons."

"Tell me about them."

She shook her head, and this time when she pulled back, he released her. "I don't want my life to change. If something happened between us, yours would not, but mine might. I want to be sure it doesn't."

"Does this lead back to that business about men and women thinking differently?"

"Yes."

That made him wonder who had broken her heart, and he didn't smile. "You look more intelligent than that. What I feel for you has already changed my life."

That frightened her, because it made her want to believe it. "Feelings come and go."

"Yes, they do. Some of them. What if I told you I was falling in love with you?"

"I wouldn't believe you." Her voice shook, and she bent to pick up her coat. "And I would be angry with you for saying it."

Maybe it was best to wait until he could make her believe. "And if I told you that until I met you, I didn't know I was lonely?"

She lowered her eyes, much more moved by this than she would have been by any words of love. "I would have to think."

He touched her again, just a hand to her hair. "Do you think everything through?"

Her eyes were eloquent when she looked at him. "Yes."

"Then think about this. It wasn't my intention to seduce you—not that I haven't given that a great deal of thought on my own, but I didn't see it happening with my daughter sick upstairs."

"You didn't seduce me."

"Now she's taking potshots at my ego."

That made her smile. "There was no seduction. That implies planned persuasion. I don't want to be seduced."

"I'll keep that in mind. All the same, I don't think I want to dissect all this like a Music major with a Beethoven concerto. It ruins the romance in much the same way."

She smiled again. "I don't want romance."

"That's a pity." And a lie, he thought, remembering the way she'd looked when he'd given her a rose. "Since chicken pox is going to be keeping me busy for the next week or two, you'll have some time. Will you come back?"

"To see Freddie." She shrugged into her coat, then relented. "And to see you."

She did. What began as just a quick call to bring Freddie a get-well present turned into the better part of an evening, soothing a miserable, rash-ridden child and an exhausted, frantic father. Surprisingly she enjoyed it, and made a habit over the next ten days of dropping in over her lunch break to spell a still-suspicious Vera, or after work to give Spence a much-needed hour of peace and quiet.

As far as romance went, bathing an itchy girl in corn starch left a lot to be desired. Despite it, Natasha found herself only more attracted to Spence and more in love with his daughter.

She watched him do his best to cheer the miserably uncomfortable patient on her birthday, then helped him deal with the pair of kittens that were Freddie's favored birthday gift. As the rash faded and boredom set in, Natasha pumped up Spence's rapidly fading imagination with stories of her own.

"Just one more story."

Natasha smoothed Freddie's covers under her chin. "That's what you said three stories ago."

"You tell good ones."

"Flattery will get you nowhere. It's past my bedtime." Natasha lifted a brow at the big red alarm clock. "And yours."

"The doctor said I could go back to school on Monday. I'm not 'fectious."

"Infectious," Natasha corrected. "You'll be glad to see your friends again."

"Mostly." Stalling, Freddie played with the edge of her blanket. "Will you come and see me when I'm not sick?"

"I think I might." She leaned over to make a grab and came up with a mewing kitten. "And to see Lucy and Desi."

"And Daddy."

Cautious, Natasha scratched the kitten's ears. "Yes, I suppose."

"You like him, don't you?"

"Yes. He's a very good teacher."

"He likes you, too." Freddie didn't add that she had seen her father kiss Natasha at the foot of her bed just the night before, when they'd thought she was asleep. Watching them had given her a funny feeling in her stomach. But after a minute it had been a good funny feeling. "Will you marry him and come and live with us?"

"Well, is that a proposal?" Natasha managed to smile. "I think it's nice that you'd want me to, but I'm only friends with your daddy. Like I'm friends with you."

"If you came to live with us, we'd still be friends."

The child, Natasha reflected, was as clever as her father. "Won't we be friends if I live in my own house?"

"I guess." The pouty lower lip poked out. "But I'd like it better if you lived here, like JoBeth's mom does. She makes cookies."

Natasha leaned toward her, nose to nose. "So, you want me for my cookies."

"I love you." Freddie threw her arms around Natasha's neck and clung. "I'd be a good girl if you came."

Stunned, Natasha hugged the girl tight and rocked. "Oh, baby, I love you, too."

"So you'll marry us."

Put like that, Natasha wasn't sure whether to laugh or cry. "I don't think getting married right now is the answer for any of us. But I'll still be your friend, and come visit and tell you stories."

Freddie gave a long sigh. She knew when an adult was evading, and realized that it would be smart to retreat a step. Particularly when she had already made up her mind. Natasha was exactly what she wanted for a mother. And there was the added bonus that Natasha made her daddy laugh. Freddie decided then and there that her most secret and solemn Christmas wish would be for Natasha to marry her father and bring home a baby sister.

"Promise?" Freddie demanded.

"Cross my heart." Natasha gave her a kiss on each cheek. "Now you go to sleep. I'll find your daddy so he can come up and kiss you good-night."

Freddie closed her eyes, her lips curved with her own secret smile.

Carrying the kitten, Natasha made her way downstairs. She'd put off her monthly books and an inventory to visit tonight. More than a little midnight oil would be burned, she decided, rubbing the kitten against her cheek.

She would have to be careful with Freddie now, and with herself. It was one thing for her to have fallen in love with the youngster, but quite another for the girl to love her enough to want her for a mother. How could she expect a child of six to understand that adults often had problems and fears that made it impossible for them to take the simple route?

The house was quiet, but a light was shining from the music room. She set down the kitten, knowing he would unerringly race to the kitchen.

She found Spence in the music room, spread on the two-cushion sofa so that his legs hung over one end. In sloppy sweats and bare feet he looked very little like the brilliant composer and full professor of music. Nor had he shaved. Natasha was forced to admit that the shadow of stubble only made him more attractive, especially when combined with tousled hair a week or two late for the barber.

He was sleeping deeply, a throw pillow crunched under his head. Natasha knew, because Vera had unbent long enough to tell her that Spence had stayed up throughout two nights during the worst of his daughter's fever and discomfort.

She was aware, too, that he had juggled his schedule at the college with trips home during the day. More than once during her visits she'd found him up to his ears in paperwork.

Once she had thought him pampered, a man who'd come by his talents and his position almost by birth. Perhaps he had been born with his talent, she thought now, but he worked hard, for himself and for his child. There was nothing she could admire more in a man.

I'm falling in love with him, she admitted. With his smile and his temper, his devotion and his drive. Perhaps, just perhaps they could give something to each other. Cautiously, carefully, with no promises between them.

She wanted to be his lover. She had never wanted such a thing before. With Anthony it had just happened, overwhelming her, sweeping her up and away, then leaving her shattered. It wouldn't be that way with Spence. Nothing would ever hurt her that deeply again. And with him there was a chance, just a chance of happiness.

Shouldn't she take it? Moving quietly, she unfolded the throw of soft blue wool that was draped along the back of the couch to spread it over him. It had been a long time since she'd taken a risk. Perhaps the time was here. She bent to brush her lips over his brow. And the man.

Chapter 7

The black cat screeched a warning. A rushing gust of wind blew open the door with an echoing slam and maniacal laughter rolled in. What sounded like ooze dripped down the walls, plunking dully onto the bare concrete floor as the prisoners rattled their chains. There was a piercing scream followed by a long, desperate moan.

"Great tunes," Annie commented and popped a gum ball into her mouth.

"I should have ordered more of those records." Natasha took an orange fright wig and turned a harmless stuffed bear into a Halloween ghoul. "That's the last one."

"After tonight you'll have to start thinking Christmas, anyway." Annie pushed back her pointed black hat, then grinned, showing blackened teeth. "Here come the Freedmont boys." She rubbed her hands together and tried out a cackle. "If this costume's worth anything, I should be able to turn them into frogs."

She didn't quite manage that, but sold them fake blood and latex scars.

"I wonder what those little dears have in store for the neighborhood tonight," Natasha mused.

"Nothing good." Annie ducked under a hanging bat. "Shouldn't you get going?"

"Yes, in a minute." Stalling, Natasha fiddled with her dwindling supply of masks and fake noses. "The pig snouts sold better than I'd imagined. I didn't realize so many people would want to dress up as livestock." She picked one up to hold it over her nose. "Maybe we should keep them out year round."

Recognizing her friend's tactics, Annie ran her tongue over her teeth to keep from grinning. "It was awfully nice of you to volunteer to help decorate for Freddie's party tonight."

"It's a little thing," Natasha said and hated herself for being nervous. She replaced the snout, then ran her finger over a wrinkled elephant trunk attached to oversize glasses. "Since I suggested the idea of her having a Halloween party to make up for her missed birthday, I thought I should help."

"Uh-huh. I wonder if her daddy's going to come as Prince Charming."

"He is not Prince Charming."

"The Big Bad Wolf?" On a laugh, Annie held up her hands in a gesture of peace. "Sorry. It's just such a kick to see you unnerved."

"I'm not unnerved." That was a big lie, Natasha admitted while she packed up some of her contributions to the party. "You know, you're welcome to come."

"And I appreciate it. I'd rather stay home and guard my house from preadolescent felons. And don't worry," she added before Natasha could speak again. "I'll lock up."

"All right. Maybe I'll just—" Natasha broke off as the door jingled open. Another customer, she thought, would give her a little more time. When she spotted Terry, there was no way of saying who was more surprised. "Hello."

He swallowed over the huge lump in his throat and tried to look beyond her costume. "Tash?"

"Yes." Hoping he'd forgiven her by now, she smiled and held out a hand. He'd changed his seat in class, and every time she had tried to approach him, he'd darted off. Now he stood trapped, embarrassed and uncertain. He touched her outstretched hand, then stuck his own into his pocket.

"I didn't expect to see you here."

"No?" She tilted her head. "This is my shop." She wondered if it would strike him that she had been right when she'd said how little he knew her, and her voice softened. "I own it."

"You own it?" He looked around, unable to hide the impression it made on him. "Wow. That's something."

"Thank you. Did you come to buy something or just to look?"

Instantly he colored. It was one thing to go into a store, and another to go into one where the owner was a woman he'd professed to love. "I just…ah…"

"Something for Halloween?" she prompted. "They have parties at the college."

"Yeah, well, I kind of thought I might slip into a couple. I guess it's silly really, but…"

"Halloween is very serious business here at The Fun House," Natasha told him solemnly. As she spoke, another scream ripped from the speakers. "You see?"

Embarrassed that he'd jumped, Terry managed a weak smile. "Yeah. Well, I was thinking, maybe a mask or something. You know." His big, bony hands waved in space, then retreated to his pockets.

"Would you like to be scary or funny?"

"I don't, ah, I haven't thought about it."

Understanding, Natasha resisted the urge to pat his cheek. "You might get some ideas when you look at what we have left. Annie, this is my friend, Terry Maynard. He's a violinist."

"Hi." Annie watched his glasses slide down his nose after his nervous nod of greeting and thought him adorable. "We're running low, but we've still got some pretty good stuff. Why don't you come over and take a look? I'll help you pick one out."

"I have to run." Natasha began gathering up her two shopping bags, hoping that the visit had put them back on more solid ground. "Have a good time at your party, Terry."

"Thanks."

"Annie, I'll see you in the morning."

"Right. Don't bob for too many apples." Pushing her pointed hat out of her eyes again, Annie grinned at Terry. "So, you're a violinist."

"Yeah." He gave Natasha's retreating back one last look. When the door closed behind her he felt a pang, but only a small one. "I'm taking some graduate classes at the college."

"Great. Hey, can you play 'Turkey in the Straw'?"

Outside Natasha debated running home to get her car. The cool, clear air changed her mind. The trees had turned. The patchwork glory of a week before, with its scarlets and vivid oranges and yellows, had blended into a dull russet. Dry, curling leaves spun from the branches to crowd against the curbs and scatter on the sidewalks. They crackled under her feet as she began the short walk.

The hardiest flowers remained, adding a spicy scent so different from the heavy fragrances of summer. Cooler, cleaner, crisper, Natasha thought as she drew it in.

She turned off the main street to where hedges and big trees shielded the houses. Jack-o'-lanterns sat on stoops and porches, grinning as they waited to be lighted at dusk. Here and there effigies in flannel shirts and torn jeans hung from denuded branches. Witches and ghosts stuffed with straw sat on steps, waiting to scare and delight the wandering trick-or-treaters.

If anyone had asked her why she had chosen a small town in which to settle, this would have been one of her answers. People here took the time—the time to carve a pumpkin, the time to take a bundle of old clothes and fashion it into a headless horseman. Tonight, before the moon rose, children could race along the streets, dressed as fairies or goblins. Their goody bags would swell with store-bought candy and homemade cookies, while adults pretended not to recognize the miniature hoboes, clowns and demons. The only thing the children would have to fear was make-believe.

Her child would have been seven.

Natasha paused for a moment, pressing a hand to her stomach until the grief and the memory could be blocked. How many times had she told herself the past was past? And how many times would that past sneak up and slice at her?

True, it came less often now, but still so sharply and always unexpectedly. Days could go by, even months, then it surfaced, crashing over her, leaving her a little dazed, a little tender, like a woman who had walked into a wall.

A car engine was gunned. A horn blasted. "Hey, Tash."

She blinked and managed to lift a hand in passing salute, though she couldn't identify the driver, who continued on his way.

This was now, she told herself, blinking to focus again on the swirl of leaves. This was here. There was never any going back. Years before she had convinced herself that the only direction was forward. Deliberately she took a long, deep breath, relieved when she felt her system level. Tonight wasn't the time for sorrows. She had promised another child a party, and she intended to deliver.

She had to smile when she started up the steps of Spence's home. He had already been working, she noted. Two enormous jack-o'-lanterns flanked the porch. Like Comedy and Tragedy, one grinned and the other scowled. Across the railing a white sheet had been shaped and spread so that the ghost it became seemed to be in full flight. Cardboard bats with red eyes swooped down from the eaves. In an old rocker beside the door sat a hideous monster who held his laughing head in his hand. On the door was a full-size cutout of a witch stirring a steaming cauldron.

Natasha knocked under the hag's warty nose. She was laughing when Spence opened the door. "Trick or treat," she said.

He couldn't speak at all. For a moment he thought he was imagining things, had to be. The music-box gypsy was standing before him, gold dripping from her ears and her wrists. Her wild mane of hair was banded by a sapphire scarf that flowed almost to her waist with the corkscrew curls. More gold hung around her neck, thick, ornate chains that only accented her slenderness. The red dress was snug, scooped at the bodice and full in the skirt, with richly colored scarfs tied at the waist.

Her eyes were huge and dark, made mysterious by some womanly art. Her lips were full and red, turned up now as she spun in a saucy circle. It took him only seconds to see it all, down to the hints of black lace at the hem. He felt as though he'd been standing in the doorway for hours.

"I have a crystal ball," she told him, reaching into her pocket to pull out a small, clear orb. "If you cross my palm with silver, I'll gaze into it for you."

"My God," he managed. "You're beautiful."

She only laughed and stepped inside. "Illusions. Tonight is meant for them." With a quick glance around, she slipped the crystal back into her pocket. But the image of the gypsy and the mystery remained. "Where's Freddie?"

His hand had gone damp on the knob. "She's…" It took a moment for his brain to kick back into gear. "She's at JoBeth's. I wanted to put things together when she wasn't around."

"A good idea." She studied his gray sweats and dusty sneakers. "Is this your costume?"

"No. I've been hanging cobwebs."

"I'll give you a hand." Smiling, she held up her bags. "I have some tricks and I have some treats. Which would you like first?"

"You have to ask?" he said quietly, then hooking an arm around her waist, brought her up hard against himself. She threw her head back, words of anger and defiance in her eyes and on the tip of her tongue. Then his mouth found hers. The bags slipped out of her hands. Freed, her fingers dived into his hair.

This wasn't what she wanted. But it was what she needed. Without hesitation her lips parted, inviting intimacy. She heard his quiet moan of pleasure merge with her own. It seemed right, somehow it seemed perfectly right to be holding him like this, just inside his front door, with the scents of fall flowers and fresh polish in the air, and the sharp-edged breeze of autumn rushing over them.

It was right. He could taste and feel the rightness with her body pressed against his own, her lips warm and agile. No illusion this. No fantasy was she, despite the colorful scarfs and glittering gold. She was real, she was here, and she was his. Before the night was over, he would prove it to both of them.

"I hear violins," he murmured as he trailed his lips down her throat.

"Spence." She could only hear her heartbeat, like thunder in her head. Struggling for sanity, she pushed away. "You make me do things I tell myself I won't." After a deep breath she gave him a steady look. "I came to help you with Freddie's party."

"And I appreciate it." Quietly he closed the door. "Just like I appreciate the way you look, the way you taste, the way you feel."

She shouldn't have been so aroused by only a look. Couldn't be, not when the look told her that whatever the crystal in her pocket promised, he already knew their destiny. "This is a very inappropriate time."

He loved the way her voice could take on that regal tone, czarina to peasant. "Then we'll find a better one."

Exasperated, she hefted the bags again. "I'll help you hang your cobwebs, if you promise to be Freddie's father—and only Freddie's father while we do."

"Okay." He didn't see any other way he'd survive an evening with twenty costumed first-graders. And the party, he thought, wouldn't last forever. "We'll be pals for the duration."

She liked the sound of it. Choosing a bag, she reached inside. She held up a rubber mask of a bruised, bloodied and scarred face. Competently she slipped it over Spence's head. "There. You look wonderful."

He adjusted it until he could see her through both eye-holes, and had a foolish and irresistible urge to look at himself in the hall mirror. Behind the mask he grinned. "I'll suffocate."

"Not for a couple of hours yet." She handed him the second bag. "Come on. It takes time to build a haunted house."

It took them two hours to transform Spence's elegantly decorated living room into a spooky dungeon, fit for rats and screams of torture. Black and orange crepe paper hung on the walls and ceiling. Angel-hair cobwebs draped the corners. A mummy, arms folded across its chest leaned in a corner. A black-caped witch hung in the air, suspended on her broom. Thirsty and waiting for dusk, an evil-eyed Dracula lurked in the shadows, ready to pounce.

"You don't think it's too scary?" Spence asked as he hung up a Pin-the-Nose-on-the-Pumpkin game. "They're first-graders."

Natasha flicked a finger over a rubber spider that hung by a thread and sent him spinning. "Very mild. My brothers made a haunted house once. They blindfolded Rachel and me to take us through. Mikhail put my hand in a bowl of grapes and told me it was eyes."

"Now that's disgusting," Spence decided.

"Yes." It delighted her to remember it. "Then there was this spaghetti—"

"Never mind," he interrupted. "I get the idea."

She laughed, adjusting her earring. "In any case, I had a wonderful time and have always wished I'd thought of it first. The children tonight would be very disappointed if we didn't have some monsters waiting for them. After they've been spooked, which they desperately want to be, you turn on the lights, so they see it's all pretend."

"Too bad we're out of grapes."

"It's all right. When Freddie's older, I'll show you how to make a bloodied severed hand out of a rubber glove."

"I can't wait."

"What about food?"

"Vera's been a Trojan." With his mask on top of his head, Spence stood back to study the whole room. It felt good, really good to look at the results, and to know that he and Natasha had produced them together. "She's made everything from deviled eggs to witch's brew punch. You know what would have been great? A fog machine."

"That's the spirit." His grin made her laugh and long to kiss him. "Next year."

He liked the sound of that, he realized. Next year, and the year after. A little dazed at the speed with which his thoughts were racing, he only studied her.

"Is something wrong?"

"No." He smiled. "Everything's just fine."

"I have the prizes here." Wanting to rest her legs, Natasha sat on the arm of a chair beside a lounging ghoul. "For the games and costumes."

"You didn't have to do that."

"I told you I wanted to. This is my favorite." She pulled out a skull, then flicking a switch, set it on the floor where it skimmed along, disemboded, its empty eyes blinking.

"Your favorite." Tongue in cheek, Spence picked it up where it vibrated in his hand.

"Yes. Very gruesome." She tilted her head. "Say 'Alas, poor Yorick!'"

He only laughed and switched it off. Then he pulled down his mask. "'O, that this too, too solid flesh would melt.'" She was chuckling when he came over and lifted her to her feet. "Give us a kiss."

"No," she decided after a moment. "You're ugly."

"Okay." Obligingly he pushed the mask up again. "How about it?"

"Much worse." Solemnly she slid the mask down again. "Very funny."

"No, but it seemed necessary." Linking her arm with his, she studied the room. "I think you'll have a hit."

"We'll have a hit," he corrected. "You know Freddie's crazy about you."

"Yes." Natasha gave him an easy smile. "It's mutual."

They heard the front door slam and a shout. "Speaking of Freddie."

Children arrived first in trickles, then in a flood. When the clock struck six, the room was full of ballerinas and pirates, monsters and superheroes. The haunted house brought gasps and shrieks and shudders. No one was brave enough to make the tour alone, though many made it twice, then a third time. Occasionally a stalwart soul was coura- geous enough to poke a finger into the mummy or touch the vampire's cape.

When the lights were switched on there were moans of disappointment and a few relieved sighs. Freddie, a life- size Raggedy Ann, tore open her belated birthday presents with abandon.

"You're a very good father," Natasha murmured.

"Thanks." He linked his fingers with hers, no longer questioning why it should be so right for them to stand to- gether and watch over his daughter's party. "Why?"

"Because you haven't once retreated for aspirin, and you hardly winced when Mikey spilled punch on your rug."

"That's because I have to save my strength for when Vera sees it." Spence dodged, in time to avoid a collision with a fairy princess being chased by a goblin. There were squeals from every corner of the room, punctuated by the crashing and moaning of the novelty record on the stereo. "As for the aspirin… How long can they keep this up?"

"Oh, a lot longer than we can."

"You're such a comfort."

"We'll have them play games now. You'll be surprised how quickly two hours can pass."

She was right. By the time the numbered noses had all been stuck in the vicinity of the pumpkin head, when musical chairs was only a fond memory, after the costume parade and judging, when the last apple bobbed alone and the final clothespin had clunked into a mason jar, parents began to trail in to gather up their reluctant Frankensteins and ghoulies. But the fun wasn't over.

In groups and clutches, trick-or-treaters canvassed the neighborhood for candy bars and caramel apples. The wind-rushed night and crackling leaves were things they would remember long after the last chocolate drop had been consumed.

It was nearly ten before Spence managed to tuck an exhausted and thrilled Freddie into bed. "It was the best birthday I ever had," she told him. "I'm glad I got the chicken pox."

Spence rubbed a finger over a smeared orange freckle the cold cream had missed. "I don't know if I'd go that far, but I'm glad you had fun."

"Can I have—?"

"No." He kissed her nose. "If you eat one more piece of candy you'll blow up."

She giggled, and because she was too tired to try any

strategy, snuggled into her pillow. Memories were already swirling in her head. "Next year I want to be a gypsy like Tash. Okay?"

"Sure. Go to sleep now. I'm going to take Natasha home, but Vera's here."

"Are you going to marry Tash soon, so she can stay with us?"

Spence opened his mouth, then closed it again as Freddie yawned hugely. "Where do you get these ideas?" he muttered.

"How long does it take to get a baby sister?" she asked as she drifted off.

Spence rubbed a hand over his face, grateful that she had fallen asleep and saved him from answering.

Downstairs he found Natasha cleaning up the worst of the mess. She flicked back her hair as he came in. "When it looks as bad as this, you know you've had a successful party." Something in his expression had her narrowing her eyes. "Is something wrong?"

"No. No, it's Freddie."

"She has a tummy ache," Natasha said, instantly sympathetic.

"Not yet." He shrugged it off with a half laugh. "She always manages to surprise me. Don't," he said and took the trash bag from her. "You've done enough."

"I don't mind."

"I know."

Before he could take her hand, she linked her own. "I should be going. Tomorrow's Saturday—our busiest day."

He wondered what it would be like if they could simply walk upstairs together, into his bedroom. Into his bed. "I'll take you home."

"That's all right. You don't have to."

"I'd like to." The tension was back. Their eyes met, and he understood that she felt it as well. "Are you tired?"

"No." It was time for some truths, she knew. He had done what she'd asked and been only Freddie's father during the party. Now the party was over. But not the night.

"Would you like to walk?"

The corners of her lips turned up, then she put her hand into his. "Yes. I would."

It was colder now, with a bite in the air warning of winter. Above, the moon was full and chillingly white. Clouds danced over it, sending shadows shifting. Over the rustle of leaves they heard the echoing shouts and laughter of lingering trick-or-treaters. Inevitably the big oak on the corner had been wrapped in bathroom tissue by teenagers.

"I love this time," Natasha murmured. "Especially at night when there's a little wind. You can smell smoke from the chimneys."

On the main street, older children and college students still stalked in fright masks and painted faces. A poor imitation of a wolf howl bounced along the storefronts, followed by a feminine squeal and laughter. A car full of ghouls paused long enough for them to lean out the windows and screech.

Spence watched the car turn a corner, its passengers still howling. "I can't remember being anywhere that Halloween was taken so seriously."

"Wait until you see what happens at Christmas."

Natasha's own pumpkin was glowing on her stoop beside a bowl half-filled with candy bars. There was a sign on her door. Take Only One. Or Else.

Spence shook his head at it. "That really does it?"

Natasha merely glanced at the sign. "They know me."

Leaning over, Spence plucked one. "Can I have a brandy to go with it?"

She hesitated. If she let him come in, it was inevitable that they would pick up where the earlier kiss had left off. It had been two months, she thought, two months of wondering, of stalling, of pretending. They both knew it had to stop sooner or later.

"Of course." She opened the door and let him in.

Wound tight, she went into the kitchen to pour drinks. It was yes or it was no, she told herself. She had known the answer long before this night, even prepared for it. But what would it be like with him? What would she be like? And how, when she had shared herself with him in that most private way, would she be able to pretend she didn't need more?

Couldn't need more, Natasha reminded herself. Whatever her feelings for him, and they were deeper, much deeper than she dared admit, life had to continue as it was. No promises, no vows. No broken hearts.

He turned when she came back into the room, but didn't speak. His own thoughts were mixed and confused. What did he want? Her, certainly. But how much, how little could he accept? He'd been sure he'd never feel this way again. More than sure that he would never want to. Yet it seemed so easy to feel, every time he looked at her.

"Thanks." He took the brandy, watching her as he sipped. "You know, the first time I lectured, I stood at the podium and my mind went completely blank. For one terrible moment I couldn't think of anything I'd planned to say. I'm having exactly the same problem now."

"You don't have to say anything."

"It's not as easy as I thought it would be." He took her hand, surprised to find it cold and unsteady. Instinctively he lifted it to press his lips to the palm. It helped, knowing she was as nervous as he. "I don't want to frighten you."

"This frightens me." She could feel sensation spear her. "Sometimes people say I think too much. Maybe it's true. If it is, it's because I feel too much. There was a time…." She took her hand from his, wanting to be strong on her own. "There was a time," she repeated, "when I let what I felt decide for me. There are some mistakes that you pay for until you die."

"This isn't a mistake." He set down the brandy to take her face between his hands.

Her fingers curled around his wrists. "I don't want it to be. There can't be any promises, Spence, because I'd rather not have them than have them broken. I don't need or want pretty words. They're too easily said." Her grip tightened. "I want to be your lover, but I need respect, not poetry."

"Are you finished?"

"I need for you to understand," she insisted.

"I'm beginning to. You must have loved him a great deal."

She dropped her hands, but steadied herself before she answered. "Yes."

It hurt, surprising him. He could hardly be threatened by someone from her past. He had a past, as well. But he *was* threatened, and he *was* hurt. "I don't care who he was, and I don't give a damn what happened." That was a lie, he realized, and one he'd have to deal with sooner or later. "But I don't want you thinking of him when you're with me."

"I don't, not the way you mean."

"Not in any way."

She raised a brow. "You can't control my thoughts or anything else about me."

"You're wrong." Fueled by impotent jealousy, he pulled

her into his arms. The kiss was angry, demanding, possessive. And tempting. Tempting her so close to submission
that she struggled away.

"I won't be taken." Her voice was only more defiant because she was afraid she was wrong.

"Your rules, Natasha?"

"Yes. If they're fair."

"To whom?"

"Both of us." She pressed her fingers against her temples for a moment. "We shouldn't be angry," she said more
quietly. "I'm sorry." She offered a shrug and a quick smile.
"I'm afraid. It's been a long time since I've been with anyone—since I've wanted to be."

He picked up his brandy, staring into it as it swirled.
"You make it hard for me to stay mad."

"I'd like to think we were friends. I've never been friends
with a lover."

And he'd never been in love with a friend. It was a
huge and frightening admission, and one he was certain
he couldn't make out loud. Perhaps, if he stopped being
clumsy, he could show her.

"We are friends." He held out a hand, then curled his
fingers around hers. "Friends trust each other, Natasha."

"Yes."

He looked at their joined hands. "Why don't we—?" A
noise at the window had him breaking off and glancing
over. Before he could move, Natasha tightened her hold. It
took only a moment to see that she wasn't frightened, but
amused. She brought a finger from her free hand to her lips.

"I think it's a good idea to be friends with my professor," she said, lifting her voice and making a go-ahead
gesture to Spence.

"I, ah, I'm glad Freddie and I have found so many nice

people since we've moved." Puzzled, he watched Natasha root through a drawer.

"It's a nice town. Of course, sometimes there are problems. You haven't heard about the woman who escaped from the asylum."

"What asylum?" At her impatient glance, he covered himself. "No, I guess not."

"The police are keeping very quiet about it. They know she's in the area and don't want people to panic." Natasha flicked on the flashlight she'd uncovered and nodded in approval as the batteries proved strong. "She's quite insane, you know, and likes to kidnap small children. Especially young boys. Then she tortures them, hideously. On a night with a full moon she creeps up on them, so silently, so evilly. Then before they can scream, she grabs them around the throat."

So saying, she whipped up the shade on the window. With the flashlight held under her chin, she pressed her face against the glass and grinned.

Twin screams echoed. There was a crash, a shout, then the scramble of feet.

Weak from laughter, Natasha leaned against the windowsill. "The Freedmont boys," she explained when she'd caught her breath. "Last year they hung a dead rat outside Annie's door." She pressed a hand to her heart as Spence came over to peer out the window. All he could see were two shadows racing across the lawn.

"I think the tables are well-turned."

"Oh, you should have seen their faces." She dabbed a tear from her lashes. "I don't think their hearts will start beating again until they pull the covers over their heads."

"This should be a Halloween they don't forget."

"Every child should have one good scare they remember

always." Still smiling, she stuck the light under her chin again. "What do you think?"

"It's too late to scare me away." He took the flashlight and set it aside. Closing his hand over hers, he drew her to her feet. "It's time to find out how much is illusion, how much is reality." Slowly he pulled the shade down.

Chapter 8

It was very real. Painfully real. The feel of his mouth against hers left no doubt that she was alive and needy. The time, the place, meant nothing. Those could have been illusions. But he was not. Desire was not. She felt it spring crazily inside her at only a meeting of lips.

No, it wasn't simple. She had known since she had first tasted him, since she had first allowed herself to touch him that whatever happened between them would never be simple. Yet that was what she had been so certain she'd wanted. Simplicity, a smooth road, an easy path.

Not with him. And not ever again.

Accepting, she twined her arms around him. Tonight there would be no past, no future. Only one moment taken in both hands, gripped hard and enjoyed.

Answer for answer, need for need, they clung together. The low light near the door cast their silhouettes onto the wall, one shadow. It shifted when they did, then stilled.

When he swept her into his arms, she murmured a protest. She had said she wouldn't be taken and had meant it. Yet cradled there she didn't feel weak. She felt loved. In gratitude and in acceptance she pressed her lips to his throat. As he carried her toward the bedroom, she allowed herself to yield.

Then there was only moonlight. It crept through the thin curtain, softly, quietly, as a lover might creep through the window to find his woman. Her lover said nothing as he set her on her feet by the bed. His silence told her everything.

He'd imagined her like this. It seemed impossible, yet he had. The image had been clear and vivid. He had seen her with her hair in wild tangles around her face, with her eyes dark and steady, her skin gleaming like the gold she wore. And in his imaginings, he'd seen much, much more.

Slowly he reached up to slip the scarf from her hair, to let it float soundlessly to the floor. She waited. With his eyes on hers he loosened another and another of the slashes of color—sapphire, emerald, amber—until they lay like jewels at her feet. She smiled. With his fingertips he drew the dress off her shoulders, then pressed his lips to the skin he'd bared.

A sigh and a shudder. Then she reached for him, struggling to breathe while she pulled his shirt over his head. His skin was taut and smooth under her palms. She could feel the quiver of muscle at the passage of her hands. As her eyes stayed on his, she could see the flash and fury of passion that darkened them.

He had to fight every instinct to prevent himself from tearing the dress from her, ripping aside the barriers and taking what she was offering. She wouldn't stop him. He could see it in her eyes, part challenge, part acknowledgment and all desire.

But he had promised her something. Though she claimed she wanted no promises, he intended to keep it. She would have romance, as much as he was capable of giving her.

Fighting for patience, he undid the range of buttons down her back. Her lips were curved when she pressed them to his chest. Her hands were smooth when she slipped his pants over his hips. As the dress slid to the floor, he brought her close for a long, luxurious kiss.

She swayed. It seemed foolish to her, but she was dizzy. Colors seemed to dance in her head to some frantic symphony she couldn't place. Her bracelets jingled when he lifted her hand to press a small circle of kisses upon her wrist. Material rustled, more notes to the song, when he slipped petticoat after colorful petticoat over her hips.

He hadn't believed she could be so beautiful. But now, standing before him in only a thin red chemise and the glitter of gold, she was almost more than a man could bear. Her eyes were nearly closed, but her head was up—a habit of pride that suited her well. Moonlight swam around her.

Slowly she lifted her arms, crossing them in front of her to push the slender straps from her shoulders. The material trembled over her breasts, then clung for a fleeting instant before it slithered to the floor at their feet. Now there was only the glitter of gold against her skin. Exciting, erotic, exotic. She waited, then lifted her arms again—to him.

"I want you," she said.

Flesh met flesh, drawing twin moans from each of them. Mouth met mouth, sending shock waves of pleasure and pain through both. Desire met desire, driving out reason.

Inevitable. It was the only thought that filtered through the chaos in her mind as her hands raced over him. No force this strong, no need this deep could be anything but inevitable. So she met that force, met that need, with all of her heart.

Patience was forgotten. She was a hunger in him already too long denied. He wanted all, everything she was, everything she had. Before he could demand, she was giving. When they tumbled onto the bed, his hands were already greedily searching to give and to take pleasure.

Could he have known it would be so huge, so consuming? Everything about her was vivid and honed sharp. Her taste an intoxicating mix of honey and whiskey, both heated. Her skin as lush as a rose petal drenched in evening dew. Her scent as dark as his own passion. Her need as sharp as a freshly whetted blade.

She arched against him, offering, challenging, crying out when he sought and found each secret. Pleasure arrowed into him as her small, agile body pressed against his. Strong, willful, she rolled over him to exploit and explore until his breath was a fire in his lungs and his body a mass of sensation. Half-mad, he tumbled with her over the bed and spread a tangle of sheets around them. When he lifted himself over her, he could see the wild curtain of her hair like a dark cloud, the deep, rich glow of her eyes as they clung to his. Her breathing was as hurried as his own, her body as willing.

Never before, he realized, and never again would he find anyone who matched him so perfectly. Whatever he needed, she needed, whatever he wanted, she wanted. Before he could ask, she was answering. For the first time in his life, he knew what it was to make love with mind and heart and soul as well as body.

She thought of no one and of nothing but him. When he touched her, it was as though she'd never been touched before. When he said her name, it was the first time she'd heard it. When his mouth sought hers, it was a first kiss, the one she'd been waiting for, wishing for all of her life.

Palm to palm their hands met, fingers gripping hard like

one soul grasping another. They watched each other as he filled her. And there was a promise, felt by both. In a moment of panic she shook her head. Then he was moving in her, and she with him.

"Again," was all he said as he pulled her against him.

"Spence."

"Again." His mouth covered hers, waking her out of a half dream and into fresh passion.

He wanted her just as much, now that he knew what they could make between them, but with a fire that held steady on slow burn. This time, though desire was still keen, the madness was less intense. He could appreciate the subtle curves, the soft angles, the lazy sighs he could draw out of her with only a touch. It was like making love to some primitive goddess, naked but for the gold draped over her skin. After so long a thirst he quenched himself slowly, leisurely after that first, greedy gulp.

How had she ever imagined she had known what it was to love a man, or to be loved by one? There were pleasures here that as a woman she knew she had never tasted before. This was what it was to be steeped, to be drowned, to be sated. She ran her hands over him, absorbing the erotic sensations of the flick of his tongue, the scrape of his teeth, the play of those clever fingertips. No, these were new pleasures, very new. And their taste was freedom.

As the moon soared high into the night, so did she.

"I thought I had imagined what it would be like to be with you." Her head resting on his shoulder, Spence trailed his fingers up and down her arm. "I didn't even come close."

"I thought I would never be here with you." She smiled into the dark. "I was very wrong."

"Thank God. Natasha—"

With a quick shake of her head, she put a finger to his lips. "Don't say too much. It's easy to say too much in the moonlight." And easy to believe it, she added silently.

Though impatient, he bit back the words he wanted to say. He had made a mistake once before by wanting too much, too quickly. He was determined not to make mistakes with Natasha. "Can I tell you that I'll never look at gold chains in quite the same way again?"

With a little chuckle she pressed a kiss to his shoulder. "Yes, you can tell me that."

He toyed with her bracelets. "Can I tell you I'm happy?"

"Yes."

"Are you?"

She tilted her head to look at him. "Yes. Happier than I thought I could be. You make me feel…" She smiled, making a quick movement with her shoulders. "Like magic."

"Tonight was magic."

"I was afraid," she murmured. "Of you, of this. Of myself," she admitted. "It's been a very long time for me."

"It's been a long time for me, too." At her restless movement, he caught her chin in his hand. "I haven't been with anyone since before my wife died."

"Did you love her very much? I'm sorry," she said quickly and closed her eyes tight. "I have no business asking that."

"Yes, you do." He kept his fingers firm. "I loved her once, or I loved the idea of her. That idea was gone long before she died."

"Please. Tonight isn't the time to talk about things that were."

When she sat up, he went with her, cupping her forearms in his hands. "Maybe not. But there are things I need to tell you, things we will talk about."

"Is what happened before so important?"

He heard the trace of desperation in her voice and wished he could find the reason. "I think it could be."

"This is now." She closed her hands over his. It was as close to a promise as she dared make. "Now I want to be your friend and your lover."

"Then be both."

She calmed herself with a deliberate effort.

"Perhaps I don't want to talk about other women while I'm in bed with you."

He could feel that she was braced and ready to argue. In a move that threw her off, he leaned closer to touch his lips to her brow. "We'll let you use that one for now."

"Thank you." She brushed a hand through his hair. "I'd like to spend this night with you, all night." With a half smile, she shook her head. "You can't stay."

"I know." He caught her hand to bring it to his lips. "Freddie would have some very awkward questions for me if I wasn't around for breakfast in the morning."

"She's a very lucky girl."

"I don't like leaving this way."

She smiled and kissed him. "I understand, as long as the other woman is only six."

"I'll see you tomorrow." Bending closer, he deepened the kiss.

"Yes." On a sigh she wrapped her arms around him. "Once more," she murmured, drawing him down to the bed. "Just once more."

In her cramped office at the back of the shop, Natasha sat at her desk. She had come in early to catch up on the practical side of business. Her ledger was up-to-date, her invoices had been filled. With Christmas less than two months away, she had completed her orders. Early merchandise was already stacked wherever room could be found. It made her feel good to be surrounded by the wishes of children, and to know that on Christmas morning what was now stored in boxes would cause cries of delight and wonder.

But there were practicalities as well. She had only begun to think of displays, decorations and discounts. She would have to decide soon whether she wanted to hire part-time help for the seasonal rush.

Now, at midmorning, with Annie in charge of the shop, she had textbooks and notes spread out. Before business there were studies, and she took both very seriously.

There was to be a test on the baroque era, and she intended to show her teacher—her lover—that she could hold her own.

Perhaps it shouldn't have been so important to prove she could learn and retain. But there had been times in her life, times she was certain Spence could never understand, when she had been made to feel inadequate, even stupid. The little girl with broken English, the thin teenager who'd thought more about dance than schoolbooks, the dancer who'd fought so hard to make her body bear the insults of training, the young woman who had listened to her heart, not her head.

She was none of those people any longer, and yet she was all of them. She needed Spence to respect her intelligence, to see her as an equal, not just as the woman he desired.

She was being foolish. On a sigh, Natasha leaned back in her chair to toy with the petals of the red rose that stood at her elbow. Even more than foolish, she was wrong. Spence was nothing like Anthony. Except for the vaguest of physical similarities, those two men were almost opposites. True, one was a brilliant dancer, the other a brilliant musician, but Anthony had been selfish, dishonest, and in the end cowardly.

She had never known a man more generous, a man kinder than Spence. He was compassionate and honest. Or was that her heart talking? To be sure. But the heart, she thought, didn't come with a guarantee like a mechanical toy. Every day she was with him, she fell deeper and deeper in love. So much in love, she thought, that there were moments, terrifying moments, when she wanted to toss aside everything and tell him.

She had offered her heart to a man before, a heart pure and fragile. When it had been given back to her, it had been scarred.

No, there were no guarantees.

How could she dare risk that again? Even knowing that what was happening to her now was different, very different from what had happened to the young girl of seventeen, how could she possibly take the chance of leaving herself open again to that kind of pain and humiliation?

Things were better as they were, she assured herself. They were two adults, enjoying each other. And they were friends.

Taking the rose out of its vase, she stroked it along her cheek. It was a pity that she and her friend could only find a few scattered hours to be alone. There was a child to consider, then there were schedules and responsibilities. But in those hours when her friend became her lover, she knew the true meaning of bliss.

Bringing herself back, she slipped the flower into the vase and shifted her concentration to her studies. Within five minutes the phone rang.

"Good morning, Fun House."

"Good morning, businessperson."

"Mama!"

"So, you are busy or you have a moment to talk to your mother?"

Natasha cradled the phone in both hands, loving the sound of her mother's voice. "Of course I have a moment. All the moments you like."

"I wondered, since you have not called me in two weeks."

"I'm sorry." For two weeks a man had been the center of her life. But she could hardly tell that to her mother. "How are you and Papa and everyone?"

"Papa and me and everyone are good. Papa gets a raise."

"Wonderful."

"Mikhail doesn't see the Italian girl anymore." Nadia gave thanks in Ukrainian and made Natasha laugh. "Alex, he sees all the girls. Smart boy, my Alex. And Rachel has time for nothing but her studies. What of Natasha?"

"Natasha is fine. I'm eating well and getting plenty of sleep," she added before Nadia could ask.

"Good. And your store?"

"We're about to get ready for Christmas, and I expect a better year than last."

"I want you to stop sending your money."

"I want you to stop worrying about your children."

Nadia's sigh made Natasha smile. It was an old argument. "You are a very stubborn woman."

"Like my mama."

That was true enough, and Nadia clearly didn't intend to concede. "We will talk about this when you come for Thanksgiving."

Thanksgiving, Natasha thought. How could she have forgotten? Clamping the receiver between ear and shoulder, she flipped through her calendar. It was less than two weeks away. "I can't argue with my mother on Thanksgiving." Natasha made a note for herself to call the train station. "I'll be up late Wednesday evening. I'll bring the wine."

"You bring yourself."

"Myself and the wine." Natasha scribbled another note to herself. It was a difficult time to take off, but she had never missed—and would never miss—a holiday at home. "I'll be so glad to see all of you again."

"Maybe you bring a friend."

It was another old routine, but this time, for the first time, Natasha hesitated. No, she told herself with a shake of her head. Why would Spence want to spend Thanksgiving in Brooklyn?

"Natasha?" Nadia's well-honed instincts had obviously picked up her daughter's mental debate. "You have friend?"

"Of course. I have a lot of friends."

"Don't be smart with your mama. Who is he?"

"He's no one." Then she rolled her eyes as Nadia began tossing out questions. "All right, all right. He's a professor at the college, a widower," she added. "With a little girl. I was just thinking they might like company for the holiday, that's all."

"Ah."

"Don't give me that significant ah, Mama. He's a friend, and I'm very fond of the little girl."

"How long you know him?"

"They just moved here late this summer. I'm taking one of his courses, and the little girl comes in the shop sometimes." It was all true, she thought. Not all the truth, but all true. She hoped her tone was careless. "If I get around to it, I might ask him if he'd like to come up."

"The little girl, she can sleep with you and Rachel."

"Yes, if—"

"The professor, he can take Alex's room. Alex can sleep on the couch."

"He may already have plans."

"You ask."

"All right. If it comes up."

"You ask," Nadia repeated. "Now go back to work."

"Yes, Mama. I love you."

Now she'd done it, Natasha thought as she hung up. She could almost see her mother standing beside the rickety telephone table and rubbing her hands together.

What would he think of her family, and they of him? Would he enjoy a big, rowdy meal? She thought of the first dinner they had shared, the elegant table, the quiet, discreet service. He probably has plans anyway, Natasha decided. It just wasn't something she was going to worry about.

Twenty minutes later the phone rang again. It was probably her mother, Natasha thought, calling with a dozen questions about this "friend." Braced, Natasha picked up the receiver. "Good morning, Fun House."

"Natasha."

"Spence?" Automatically she checked her watch. "Why aren't you at the university? Are you sick?"

"No. No. I came home between classes. I've got about an hour. I need you to come."

"To your house?" There was an urgency in his voice, but it had nothing to do with disaster and everything to do with excitement. "Why? What is it?"

"Just come, will you? It's nothing I can explain. I have to show you. Please."

"Yes, all right. Are you sure you're not sick?"

"No." She heard his laugh and relaxed. "No, I'm not sick. I've never felt better. Hurry up, will you?"

"Ten minutes." Natasha snatched up her coat. He'd sounded different. Happy? No, elated, ecstatic. What did a man have to be ecstatic about in the middle of the morning? Perhaps he was sick. Pulling on her gloves, she dashed into the shop.

"Annie, I have to—" She stopped, blinked, then stared at the image of Annie being kissed, soundly, by Terry Maynard. "I...excuse me."

"Oh, Tash, Terry just... Well, he..." Annie blew the hair out of her eyes and grinned foolishly. "Are you going out?"

"Yes, I have to see someone." She bit her lip to keep from grinning back. "I won't be more than an hour. Can you manage?"

"Sure." Annie smoothed down her hair, while Terry stood beside her, turning various shades of red. "It has been a quiet morning. Take your time."

Perhaps the world had decided to go crazy today, Natasha thought as she rushed down the street. First her mother calling, already preparing to kick Alex out of his bed for a stranger. Spence demanding she come to his house and see...something in the middle of the day. And now Annie and Terry, kissing each other beside the cash register. Well, she could only deal with one at a time. It looked as though Spence was first on the list.

She took his steps two at a time, convinced he was suffering from some sort of fever. When he pulled open the door before she reached it, she was certain of it. His eyes were bright, his color up. His sweater was rumpled and his tie unknotted.

"Spence, are you—?"

Before she could get the words out, he was snatching her up, crushing his mouth to hers as he swung her around and around. "I thought you'd never get here."

"I came as quickly as I could." Instinctively she put a hand to his cheek. Then the look in his eyes had her narrowing her own. No, it wasn't a fever, she decided. At least it wasn't the kind that required medical attention. "If you had me run all the way over here for that, I'm going to hit you very hard."

"For—no," he answered on a laugh. "Though it's a wonderful idea. A really wonderful idea." He kissed her again until she thoroughly agreed with him. "I feel like I could make love with you for hours, days, weeks."

"They might miss you in class," she murmured. Steadying herself, she stepped back. "You sounded excited. Did you win the lottery?"

"Better. Come here." Remembering the door, he slammed it shut, then pulled her into the music room. "Don't say anything. Just sit."

She obliged, but when he went to the piano, she started to stand again. "Spence, I'd enjoy a concert, but—"

"Don't talk," he said impatiently. "Just listen."

And he began to play.

It took only moments for her to realize it was nothing she'd heard before. Nothing that had been written before. A tremor ran through her body. She clasped her hands tightly in her lap.

Passion. Each note swelled with it, soared with it, wept with it. She could only stare, seeing the intensity in his eyes and the fluid grace of his fingers on the keys. The beauty of it ripped at her, digging deep into heart and into soul. How could it be that her feelings, her most intimate feelings could be put to music?

As the tempo built, her pulse beat thickly. She couldn't have spoken, could hardly breathe. Then the music flowed into something sad and strong. And alive. She closed her eyes as it crashed over her, unaware that tears had begun to spill onto her cheeks.

When it ended, she sat very still.

"I don't have to ask you what you think," Spence murmured. "I can see it."

She only shook her head. She didn't have the words to tell him. There were no words. "When?"

"Over the last few days." The emotion the song had wrenched from him came flooding back. Rising, he went to her to take her hands and pulled her to her feet. As their fingers met, she could feel the intensity he'd poured into his music. "It came back." He pressed her hands to his lips. "At first it was terrifying. I could hear it in my head, the way I used to. It's like being plugged into heaven, Natasha. I can't explain it."

"No. You don't have to. I heard it."

She understood, he thought. Somehow he'd been sure she would. "I thought it was just wishful thinking, or that when I sat down there..." He looked back at the piano. "That it would vanish. But it didn't. It flowed. God, it's like being given back your hands or your eyes."

"It was always there." She lifted her hands to his face. "It was just resting."

"No, *you* brought it back. I told you once, my life had changed when I met you. I didn't know how much. It's for you, Natasha."

"No, it's for you. Very much for you." Wrapping her arms around him, she pressed her mouth to his. "It's just the beginning."

"Yes." He dragged his hands through her hair so that her face was tilted to his. "It is." His grip only tightened when she would have pulled away. "If you heard that, if you understood that, you know what I mean. And you know what I feel."

"Spence, it would be wrong for you to say anything now. Your emotions are all on the surface. What you feel about your music is easily confused with other things."

"That's nonsense. You don't want to hear me tell you that I love you."

"No." Panic skidded up her spine. "No, I don't. If you care for me at all, you won't."

"It's a hell of a position you put me in."

"I'm sorry. I want you to be happy. As long as things go on as they are—"

"And how long can things go on as they are?"

"I don't know. I can't give you back the words you want to give to me. Even feeling them, I can't." Her eyes lifted again to meet his. "I wish I could."

"Am I still competing against someone else?"

"No." Quickly she reached out to take his hands. "No. What I felt for—before," she corrected, "was a fantasy. A girl's make-believe. This is real. I'm just not strong enough to hold on to it."

Or too strong to give in to it, he thought. And it was hurting her. Perhaps because he wanted her so badly, his impatience was adding pressure that would break them apart instead of bring them together.

"Then I won't tell you that I love you." He kissed her brow. "And that I need you in my life." He kissed her lips, lightly. "Not yet." His fingers curled tightly over hers. "But there'll come a time, Natasha, when I will tell you. When you'll listen. When you'll answer me."

"You make it sound like a threat."

"No, it's one of those promises you don't want to hear."

He kissed her on both cheeks, casually enough to confuse her. "I have to get back."

"Yes, so do I." She picked up her gloves, only to run them restlessly through her hands. "Spence, it meant a very great deal that you wanted to share this with me. I know what it's like to lose part of yourself. I'm very proud of you and for you. And I'm glad that you celebrated this with me."

"Come back, have dinner with me. I haven't begun to celebrate."

She smiled again. "I'd like that."

She didn't often buy champagne, but it seemed appropriate. Even necessary. A bottle of wine was little enough to offer for what he had given her that morning. The music itself was a gift she would always treasure. With it, he'd given her time and a glimpse of hope.

Perhaps he did love her. If she believed it, she could allow herself time to let it strengthen. If she believed it, she would have to tell him everything. It was that, even more than her own fears that still held her back.

She needed time for that, as he did.

But tonight was for celebrating.

She knocked and tried a sober smile for Vera. "Good evening."

"Miss." With this noncommittal greeting, Vera opened the door wider. She kept her thoughts on Natasha very much to herself. True, the woman made the *señor* happy and seemed very fond of Freddie. But after more than three years of having them to herself, Vera was very cautious of sharing. "Dr. Kimball is in the music room with Freddie."

"Thank you. I brought some wine."

"I will take it."

With only a little sigh, Natasha watched Vera walk away.

The more the housekeeper held firm, the more determined Natasha was to win her over.

She heard Freddie's giggles as she approached the music room. And others, she realized. When she reached the door, she spotted Freddie and JoBeth clinging to each other and squealing. And why not? Natasha thought with a grin. Spence was wearing a ridiculous helmet and aiming a cardboard spool like a weapon.

"Stowaways aboard my ship are fed to the Beta Monster," he warned them. "He has six-foot teeth and bad breath."

"No!" Eyes wide, heart pounding with delight and dread, Freddie scrambled for cover. "Not the Beta Monster."

"He likes little girls best." With an evil laugh, he scooped the squealing JoBeth under one arm. "He swallows little boys whole, but he chews and chews and chews when I feed him girls."

"That's gross." JoBeth covered her mouth with both hands.

"You bet." So saying, Spence made a dive and came up with a squirming Freddie. "Say your prayers, you're about to be the main course." Then with a muffled "Oomph," he tumbled onto the couch with both of them.

"We vanquished you!" Freddie announced, climbing over him. "The Wonder Sisters vanquished you."

"This time, but next time it's the Beta Monster." As he blew the hair out of his eyes, he spotted Natasha in the doorway. "Hi." She thought his smile was adorably sheepish. "I'm a space pirate."

"Oh. Well, that explains it." Before she could step into the room, both girls deserted the space pirate to launch themselves at her.

"We always beat him," Freddie told her. "Always, always."

"I'm glad to hear it. I wouldn't want anyone I know to be eaten by the Beta Monster."

"He just made it up," JoBeth said wisely. "Dr. Kimball makes things up real good."

"Yes, I know."

"JoBeth's going to stay for dinner, too. You're going to be Daddy's guest and she's going to be mine. You get to have seconds first."

"That's very polite." She bent to kiss Freddie's cheeks, then JoBeth's. "How is your mama?"

"She's going to have a baby." JoBeth screwed up her face and shrugged her shoulders.

"I heard." Natasha smoothed JoBeth's hair. "Are you taking care of her?"

"She doesn't get sick in the mornings anymore, but Daddy says she'll be fat soon."

Miserably envious, Freddie shifted from one foot to the other. "Let's go up to my room," she told JoBeth. "We can play with the kittens."

"You will wash your hands and faces," Vera told them as she came in with the ice bucket and glasses. "Then you will come down to dinner, walking like ladies, not running like elephants." She nodded to Spence. "Miss Stanislaski brought champagne."

"Thank you, Vera." Belatedly he remembered to remove his helmet.

"Dinner in fifteen minutes," she stated, then went out.

"Now she knows I have designs on you," Natasha muttered. "And is certain I'm after your great wealth."

With a laugh, he pried the cork free. "That's all right, I

know you're only after my body." Wine frothed to the lip of the glasses, then receded.

"I like it very much. Your body." With a smile she accepted the flute of champagne.

"Then maybe you'd like to enjoy it later." He touched the rim of his glass to hers. "Freddie twisted my arm and got me to agree to a sleep-over at the Rileys'. So I don't feel left out, maybe I can stay with you tonight. All night."

Natasha took her first sip of wine, letting the taste explode on her tongue. "Yes," she said, and smiled at him.

Chapter 9

Natasha watched the shadows dancing from the lights the candles tossed around the room. Soothing, they played over the curtains, the top rung of the old ladder-back chair in the corner, over the coxcomb she had impulsively slipped into an empty milk bottle and set on her dresser. Her room, she thought. It had always been very much hers. Until…

With a half sigh she let her hand rest on Spence's heart.

It was no longer quiet; the wind had risen to toss a late, cold rain against the panes. Outside it was a chilled, gusty night that promised a chilled, frosty morning. Winter often came early to the little town snuggled in the foothills of the Blue Ridge. But she was warm, beautifully warm, in Spence's arms.

The silence between them was easy, as the loving had been. Curled close, they lay still, content to let the hours pass, one lazy second at a time. Each of them quietly celebrated the knowledge that in the morning they wouldn't wake alone. His hand skimmed over her thigh, her hip, until it linked with hers.

There was music playing inside her head—the song he had given her that morning. She knew she would remember each note, each chord, for the rest of her life. And it was only the beginning for him, or a new beginning. The idea of that delighted her. In the years to come she would hear his music and remember the time they had had together. On hearing it she would celebrate again, even if his music took him away.

Still, she had to ask.

"Will you go back to New York?"

He brushed his lips through her hair. "Why?"

"You're composing again." She could imagine him there, in evening dress, attending the opening of his own symphony.

"I don't need to be in New York to compose. And if I did, there are more reasons to stay here."

"Freddie."

"Yes, there's Freddie. And there's you."

Her restless movement rustled the sheets. She could see him after the symphony at some small intimate party, the Rainbow Room perhaps, or a private club. He would be dancing with a beautiful woman.

"The New York you lived in is different from mine."

"I imagine." He wondered why that should matter to her. "Do you ever think of going back?"

"To live, no. But to visit." It was silly, she thought, to be nervous about asking such a simple thing. "My mother called me today."

"Is everything all right?"

"Yes. She only called to remind me about Thanksgiving.

I'd almost forgotten. Every year we have a big dinner and eat too much. Do you go home for the holiday?"

"I am home."

"I mean to your family." She shifted to watch his face.

"I only have Freddie. And Nina," he added. "She always goes out to the Waldorf."

"Your parents. I've never asked you if you still have them, or where they live."

"They're in Cannes." Or was it Monte Carlo? It occurred to him suddenly that he didn't know for certain. The ties there were loose, comfortably so for everyone involved.

"Won't they come back for the holidays?"

"They never come to New York in the winter."

"Oh." Try as she might, she couldn't picture the holidays without family.

"We never ate at home on Thanksgiving. We always went out, were usually traveling." His memories of his childhood were more of places than people, more of music than words. "When I was married to Angela, we usually met friends at a restaurant and went to the theater."

"But—" She caught herself and fell silent.

"But what?"

"Once you had Freddie..."

"Nothing changed." He shifted onto his back to stare at the ceiling. He'd wanted to tell her about his marriage, about himself—the man he had been—but had put it off. For too long, he reflected. How could he expect to build, when he had yet to clear away the emotional rubble of his past? "I've never explained to you about Angela."

"It's not necessary." She took his hand again. She'd wanted to invite him to a meal, not dredge up old ghosts.

"It is for me." Sitting up, he reached for the bottle of

champagne they had brought back with them. Filling both glasses, he handed her one.

"I don't need explanations, Spence."

"But you'll listen?"

"Yes, if it's important to you."

He took a moment to gather his thoughts. "I was twenty-five when I met her. On top of the world as far as my music went, and to be honest, at twenty-five, very little else mattered to me. I had spent my life traveling, doing exactly what I pleased and being successful in what was most important to me. I don't believe anyone had ever told me, 'No, you can't have that. No, you can't do that.' When I saw her, I wanted her."

He paused to sip, to look back. Beside him Natasha stared into her glass, watching bubbles rise. "And she wanted you."

"In her way. The pity was that her attraction for me was as shallow as mine for her. And in the end just as destructive. I loved beautiful things." With a half laugh he tilted his glass again. "And I was used to having them. She was exquisite, like a delicate porcelain doll. We moved in the same circles, attended the same parties, preferred the same literature and music."

Natasha shifted her glass from one hand to the other, wishing his words didn't make her feel so miserable. "It's important to have things in common."

"Oh, we had plenty in common. She was as spoiled and as pampered as I, as self-absorbed and as ambitious. I don't think we shared any particularly admirable qualities."

"You're too hard on yourself."

"You didn't know me then." He found himself profoundly grateful for that. "I was a very rich young man who took everything I had for granted, because I had always had it. Things change," he murmured.

"Only people who are born with money can consider it a disadvantage."

He glanced over to see her sitting cross-legged, the glass cupped in both hands. Her eyes were solemn and direct, and made him smile at himself. "Yes, you're right. I wonder what might have happened if I had met you when I was twenty-five." He touched her hair, but didn't dwell on the point. "In any case, Angela and I were married within a year and bored with each other only months after the ink had dried on the marriage certificate."

"Why?"

"Because at that time we were so much alike. When it started to fall apart, I wanted badly to fix it. I'd never failed at anything. The worst of it was, I wanted the marriage to work more for my own ego than because of my feelings for her. I was in love with the image of her and the image we made together."

"Yes." She thought of herself and her feelings for Anthony. "I understand."

"Do you?" The question was only a murmur. "It took me years to understand it. In any case, once I did, there were other considerations."

"Freddie," Natasha said again.

"Yes, Freddie. Though we still lived together and went through the motions of marriage, Angela and I had drifted apart. But in public and in private we were...civilized. I can't tell you how demeaning and destructive a civilized marriage can be. It's a cheat, Natasha, to both parties. And we were equally to blame. Then one day she came home furious, livid. I remember how she stalked over to the bar, tossing her mink aside so that it fell on the floor. She poured a drink, drank it down, then threw the glass against the wall. And told me she was pregnant."

Her throat dry, Natasha drank. "How did you feel?"

"Stunned. Rocked. We'd never planned on having children. We were much too much children, spoiled children ourselves. Angela had had a little more time to think it all through and had her answer. She wanted to go to Europe to a private clinic and have an abortion."

Something tightened inside Natasha. "Is that what you wanted?"

He wished, how he wished he could have answered unequivocally no. "At first I didn't know. My marriage was falling apart, I'd never given a thought to having children. It seemed sensible. And then, I'm not sure why, but I was furious. I guess it was because it was the easy way again, the easy way out for both of us. She wanted me to snap my fingers and get rid of this...inconvenience."

Natasha stared down at her own balled fist. His words were hitting much too close to home. "What did you do?"

"I made a bargain with her. She would have the baby, and we would give the marriage another shot. She would have the abortion and I would divorce her, and make certain that she didn't get what she considered her share of the Kimball money."

"Because you wanted the child."

"No." It was a painful admission, one that still cost him. "Because I wanted my life to run the way I'd imagined it would. I knew if she had an abortion, we would never put the pieces back. I thought perhaps if we shared this, we'd pull it all together again."

Natasha remained silent for a moment, absorbing his words and seeing them reflected in her own memories. "People sometimes think a baby will fix what's broken."

"And it doesn't," he finished. "Nor should it have to. By the time Freddie was born, I was already losing my grip on my music. I couldn't write. Angela had delivered Freddie, then passed her over to Vera, as though she were no more than a litter of kittens. I was little better."

"No." She reached out to take his wrist. "I've seen you with her. I know how you love her."

"Now. What you said to me that night on the steps of the college, about not deserving her. It hurt because it was true." He saw Natasha shake her head but went on. "I'd made a bargain with Angela, and for more than a year I kept it. I barely saw the child, because I was so busy escorting Angela to the ballet or the theater. I'd stopped working completely. I did nothing. I never fed her or bathed her or cuddled her at night. Sometimes I'd hear her crying in the other room and wonder—what is that noise? Then I'd remember."

He picked up the bottle to top off his glass. "Sometime before Freddie was two I stepped back and looked at what I'd done with my life. And what I hadn't done. It made me sick. I had a child. It took more than a year for it to sink in. I had no marriage, no wife, no music, but I had a child. I decided I had an obligation, a responsibility, and it was time to pull myself up and deal with it. That's how I thought of Freddie at first, when I finally began to think of her. An obligation." He drank again, then shook his head. "That was little better than ignoring her. Finally I looked, really looked at that beautiful little girl and fell in love. I picked her up out of her crib, scared to death, and just held her. She screamed for Vera."

He laughed at that, then stared once more into his wine. "It took months before she was comfortable around me. By that time I'd asked Angela for a divorce. She'd snapped up my offer without a blink. When I told her I was keeping the child, she wished me luck and walked out. She never came back to see Freddie, not once in all the months the lawyers were battling over a settlement. Then I heard that she'd been killed. A boating accident in the Mediterranean. Sometimes I'm afraid Freddie remembers what her mother was like. More, I'm afraid she'll remember what I was like."

Natasha remembered how Freddie had spoken of her mother when they had rocked. Setting aside her glass, she took Spence's face in her hand. "Children forgive," she told him. "Forgiveness is easy when you're loved. It's harder, so much harder to forgive yourself. But you must."

"I think I've begun to."

Natasha took his glass and set it aside. "Let me love you," she said simply, and enfolded him.

It was different now that passion had mellowed. Slower, smoother, richer. As they knelt on the bed, their mouths met dreamily—a long, lazy exploration of tastes that had become hauntingly familiar. She wanted to show him what he meant to her, and that what they had together, tonight, was worlds apart from what had been. She wanted to comfort, excite and cleanse.

A sigh, then a murmur, then a low, liquid moan. The sounds were followed by a light, breezy touch. Fingertips trailing on flesh. She knew his body now as well as her own, every angle, every plane, every vulnerability. When his breath caught on a tremble, her laughter came quietly. Watching him in the shifting candlelight, she brushed kisses at his temple, his cheek, the corner of his mouth, his throat. There a pulse beat for her, heavy and fast.

She was as erotic as any fantasy, her body swaying first to, then away from his. Her eyes stayed on him, glowing, aware, and her hair fell in a torrent of dark silk over her naked shoulders.

When he touched her, skimming his hands up and over, her head fell back. But there was nothing of submission in the gesture. It was a demand. Pleasure me.

On a groan he lowered his mouth to her throat and felt the need punch like a fist through his gut. His open mouth growing greedy, he trailed down her, pausing to linger at the firm swell of her breast. He could feel her heart, almost taste it, as its beat grew fast and hard against his lips. Her hands came to his hair, gripping tight while she arched like a bow.

Before he could think he reached for her and sent her spiraling over the first crest.

Breathless, shuddering, she clung, managing only a confused murmur as he laid her back on the bed. She struggled for inner balance, but he was already destroying will and mind and control.

This was seduction. She hadn't asked for it, hadn't wanted it. Now she welcomed it. She couldn't move, couldn't object. Helpless, drowning in her own pleasure, she let him take her where he willed. His mouth roamed freely over her damp skin. His hands played her as skillfully as they might a fine-tuned instrument. Her muscles went lax.

Her breath began to rush through her lips. She heard music. Symphonies, cantatas, preludes. Weakness became strength and she reached for him, wanting only to feel his body fit against her own.

Slowly, tormentingly, he slid up her, leaving trails of heat and ice, of pleasure and pain. His own body throbbed as she moved under him. He found her mouth, diving deep, holding back even when her fingers dug into his hips.

Again and again he brought them both shivering to the edge, only to retreat, prolonging dozens of smaller pleasures. Her throat was a long white column he could feast on as she rose to him. Her arms wrapped themselves fast around him like taut silk. Her breath rushed along his cheek, then into his mouth, where it formed his own name like a prayer against his lips.

When he slipped into her, even pleasure was shattered.

Natasha awoke to the scent of coffee and soap, and the enjoyable sensation of having her neck nuzzled.

"If you don't wake up," Spence murmured into her ear, "I'm going to have to crawl back into bed with you."

"All right," she said on a sigh and snuggled closer.

Spence took a long, reluctant look at her shoulders, which the shifting sheets had bared. "It's tempting, but I should be home in an hour."

"Why?" Her eyes still closed, she reached out. "It's early."

"It's nearly nine."

"Nine? In the morning?" Her eyes flew open. She shot up in bed, and he wisely moved the cup of coffee out of harm's way. "How can it be nine?"

"It comes after eight."

"But I never sleep so late." She pushed back her hair with both hands, then managed to focus. "You're dressed."

"Unfortunately," he agreed, even more reluctantly when the sheets pooled around her waist. "Freddie's due home at ten. I had a shower." Reaching out, he began to toy with her hair. "I was going to wake you, see if you wanted to join me, but you looked so terrific sleeping I didn't have the heart." He leaned over to nip at her bottom lip. "I've never watched you sleep before."

The very idea of it had the blood rushing warm under her skin. "You should have gotten me up."

"Yes." With a half smile he offered her the coffee. "I can see I made a mistake. Easy with the coffee," he warned. "It's really terrible. I've never made it before."

Eyeing him, she took a sip, then grimaced. "You really should have wakened me." But she valiantly took another sip, thinking how sweet it was of him to bring it to her. "Do you have time for breakfast? I'll make you some."

"I'd like that. I was going to grab a doughnut from the bakery down the street."

"I can't make pastries like Ye Old Sweet Shoppe, but I can fix you eggs." Laughing, she set the cup aside. "And coffee."

In ten minutes she was wrapped in a short red robe, frying thin slices of ham. He liked watching her like this, her hair tousled, eyes still heavy with sleep. She moved competently from stove to counter, like a woman who had grown up doing such chores as a matter of course.

Outside a thin November rain was falling from a pewter sky. He heard the muffled sound of footsteps from the apartment above, then the faint sound of music. Jazz from the neighbor's radio. And there was the sizzle of meat grilling, the hum of the baseboard heater under the window. Morning music, Spence thought.

"I could get used to this," he said, thinking aloud.

"To what?" Natasha popped two slices of bread into the toaster.

"To waking up with you, having breakfast with you."

Her hands fluttered once, as if her thoughts had suddenly taken a sharp turn. Then, very deliberately they began to work again. And she said nothing at all.

"That's the wrong thing to say again, isn't it?"

"It isn't right or wrong." Her movements brisk, she brought him a cup of coffee. She would have turned away once more, but he caught her wrist. When she forced herself to look at him, she saw that the expression in his eyes was very intense. "You don't want me to fall in love with you, Natasha, but neither one of us have a choice about it."

"There's always a choice," she said carefully. "It's sometimes hard to make the right one, or to know the right one."

"Then it's already been made. I am in love with you."

He saw the change in her face, a softening, a yielding, and something in her eyes, something deep and shadowed and incredibly beautiful. Then it was gone. "The eggs are going to burn."

His hand balled into a fist as she walked back to the stove. Slowly, carefully he flexed his fingers. "I said I love you, and you're worried about eggs burning."

"I'm a practical woman, Spence. I've had to be." But it was hard to think, very hard, when her mind and heart were dragging her in opposing directions. She fixed the plates with the care she might have given to a state dinner. Going over and over the words in her head, she set the plates on the table, then sat down across from him.

"We've only known each other a short time."

"Long enough."

She moistened her lips. What she heard in his voice was more hurt than anger. She wanted nothing less than to hurt him. "There are things about me you don't know. Things I'm not ready to tell you."

"They don't matter."

"They do." She took a deep breath. "We have something. It would be ridiculous to try to deny it. But love—there is no bigger word in the world. If we share that word, things will change."

"Yes."

"I can't let them. From the beginning I told you there could be no promises, no plans. I don't want to move my life beyond what I have now."

"Is it because I have a child?"

"Yes, and no." For the first time since he'd met her, nerves showed in the way she linked and unlinked her fingers. "I would love Freddie even if I hated you. For herself. Because I care for you, I only love her more. But for you and me to take what we have and make something more from this would change even that. I'm not ready to take on the responsibilities of a child." Under the table she pressed her hand hard against her stomach. "But with or without Freddie, I don't want to take the next step with you. I'm sorry, and I understand if you don't want to see me again."

Torn between frustration and fury, he rose to pace to the window. The rain was still falling thinly, coldly upon the dying flowers outside. She was leaving something out, something big and vital. She didn't trust him yet, Spence realized. After everything they'd shared, she didn't yet trust him. Not enough.

"You know I can't stop seeing you, any more than I can stop loving you."

You could stop being in love, she thought, but found herself afraid to tell him. It was selfish, hideously so, but she wanted him to love her. "Spence, three months ago I didn't even know you."

"So I'm rushing things."

She moved her shoulder and began to poke at her eggs.

He studied her from behind, the way she held herself, how her fingers moved restlessly from her fork to her cup, then back again. He wasn't rushing a damn thing, and they both knew it. She was afraid. He leaned against the window, thinking it through. Some jerk had broken her heart, and she was afraid to have it broken again.

All right, he thought. He could get around that. A little time and the most subtle kind of pressure. He would get around it, he promised himself. For the first part of his life, he'd thought nothing would ever be as important to him as his music. In the last few years he'd learned differently. A child was infinitely more important, more precious and more beautiful. Now he'd been taught in a matter of weeks that a woman could be as important, in a different way, but just as important.

Freddie had waited for him, bless her. He would wait for Natasha.

"Want to go to a matinee?"

She'd been braced for anger, so only looked blankly over her shoulder. "What?"

"I said would you like to go to a matinee? The movies." Casually he walked back to the table to join her. "I promised Freddie I'd take her to the movies this afternoon."

"I—yes." A cautious smile bloomed. "I'd like to go with you. You're not angry with me?"

"Yes, I am." But he returned her smile as he began to eat. "I figured if you came along, you'd buy the popcorn."

"Okay."

"The jumbo size."

"Ah, now I begin to see the strategy. You make me feel guilty, so I spend all my money."

"That's right, and when you're broke, you'll have to marry me. Great eggs," he added when her mouth dropped open. "You should eat yours before they get cold."

"Yes." She cleared her throat. "Since you've offered me an invitation, I have one for you. I was going to mention it last night, but you kept distracting me."

"I remember." He rubbed his foot over hers. "You're easily distracted, Natasha."

"Perhaps. It was about my mother's phone call and Thanksgiving. She asked me if I wanted to bring someone along." She frowned at her eggs. "I imagine you have plans."

His smile was slow and satisfied. Perhaps the wait wouldn't be as long as he'd thought. "Are you asking me to Thanksgiving dinner at your mother's?"

"My mother asked," Natasha said precisely. "She always makes too much food, and she and Papa enjoy company. When it came up, I thought about you and Freddie."

"I'm glad to know that you think about us."

"It's nothing," she said, annoyed with herself for stringing out what should have been a simple invitation. "I always take the train up on Wednesday after work and come back Friday evening. Since there is no school, it occurred to me that you both might enjoy the trip."

"Do we get borscht?"

The corners of her lips curved. "I could ask." She pushed her plate aside when she saw the gleam in his eyes. He wasn't laughing, she thought, as much as planning. "I don't want you to get the wrong idea. It's simply an invitation from friend to friend."

"Right."

She frowned at him. "I think Freddie would enjoy a big family meal."

"Right again."

His easy agreement had her blowing out a frustrated breath. "Just because it's at my parents' home doesn't mean I'm taking you there for…" She waved her hand as she searched for an appropriate phrase. "For approval, or to show you off."

"You mean your father won't take me into the den and ask me my intentions?"

"We don't have a den," she muttered. "And no. I'm a grown woman." Because Spence was grinning, she lifted a brow. "He will, perhaps, study you discreetly."

"I'll be on my best behavior."

"Then you'll come?"

He sat back, sipping his coffee and smiling to himself. "I wouldn't miss it."

Chapter 10

Freddie sat in the backseat with a blanket tucked up to her chin and clutched her Raggedy Ann. Because she wanted to drift with her own daydreams she pretended to sleep, and pretended so well that she actually dozed from time to time. It was a long drive from West Virginia to New York, but she was much too excited to be bored.

There was soft music on the car radio. She was enough of her father's daughter to recognize Mozart, and child enough to wish there were words to sing along to. Vera had already been dropped off at her sister's in Manhattan, where the housekeeper would holiday until Sunday. Now Spence was directing the big, quiet car through the traffic toward Brooklyn.

Freddie was only a little disappointed that they hadn't taken the train, but liked snuggling up and listening to her father and Natasha talk. She didn't pay much attention to what they said. Their voices were enough.

She was almost sick with excitement at the idea of meeting Natasha's family and sharing a big turkey dinner. Though she didn't like turkey very much, Natasha had told her that there would be plenty of cranberry sauce and succotash. Freddie had never eaten succotash, but the name was so funny, she knew it would be good. Even if it wasn't, even if it was disgusting, she was determined to be polite and clean her plate. JoBeth had told her that her grandmother got upset if JoBeth didn't eat all her vegetables, so Freddie wasn't taking any chances.

Lights flickered over her closed lids. Her lips curved a little as she heard Natasha's laugh merging with her father's. In her imaginings they were already a family. Instead of Raggedy Ann, Freddie was carefully tending to her baby sister as they all drove through the night to her grandparents' house. It was just like the song, she thought, but she didn't know if they were going over any rivers. And she didn't think they would pass through the woods.

Her baby sister's name was Katie, and she had black, curly hair like Natasha. Whenever Katie cried, Freddie was the only one who could make her happy again. Katie slept in a white crib in Freddie's room, and Freddie always made sure she was covered with a pink blanket. Babies caught colds, Freddie knew. When they did, you had to give them medicine out of a little dropper. They couldn't blow their noses themselves. Everyone said that Katie took her medicine best from Freddie.

Delighted with herself, Freddie snuggled the doll closer. "We're going to Grandmother's," she whispered, and began to build a whole new fantasy around the visit.

The trouble was, Freddie wasn't sure that the people she was pretending were her grandparents would like her. Not everyone liked kids, she thought. Maybe they wished she wasn't coming to visit. When she got there, they would want her to sit in a chair with her hands folded on her lap. That was the way Aunt Nina told her young ladies sat. Freddie hated being a young lady. But she would have to sit for just hours, not interrupting, not talking too loud, and never, never running in the house.

They would get mad and frown at her if she spilled something on the floor. Maybe they would yell. She'd heard JoBeth's father yell, especially when JoBeth's big brother, who was in third grade already and was supposed to know better, had taken one of his father's golf clubs to hit at rocks in the backyard. One of the rocks had crashed right through the kitchen window.

Maybe she would break a window. Then Natasha wouldn't marry her daddy and come to stay with them. She wouldn't have a mother or a baby sister, and Daddy would stop playing his music at night again.

Almost paralyzed by her thoughts, Freddie shrank against the seat as the car slowed.

"Yes, turn right here." At the sight of her old neighborhood, Natasha's spirits rose even higher. "It's about halfway down, on the left. You might be able to find a space… yes, there." She spotted a parking space behind her father's ancient pickup. Obviously the Stanislaskis had put out the word that their daughter and friends were coming, and the neighbors had cooperated.

It was like that here, she thought. The Poffenbergers had lived on one side, the Andersons on the other for as long as Natasha could remember. One family would bring food when there was illness, another would mind a child after school. Joys and sorrows were shared. And gossip abounded.

Mikhail had dated the pretty Anderson girl, then had

ended up as best man at her wedding, when she'd married one of his friends. Natasha's parents had stood as godparents for one of the Poffenberger babies. Perhaps that was why, when Natasha had found she'd needed a new place and a new start, she had picked a town that had reminded her of home. Not in looks, but in ties.

"What are you thinking?" Spence asked her.

"Just remembering." She turned her head to smile at him. "It's good to be back." She stepped onto the curb, shivered once in the frosty air, then opened the back door for Freddie while Spence popped the trunk. "Freddie, are you asleep?"

Freddie kept herself balled tight, but squeezed her eyes open. "No."

"We're here. It's time to get out."

Freddie swallowed, clutching the doll to her chest. "What if they don't like me?"

"What's this?" Crouching, Natasha brushed the hair from Freddie's cheeks. "Have you been dreaming?"

"They might not like me and wish I wasn't here. They might think I'm a pest. Lots of people think kids're pests."

"Lots of people are stupid then," Natasha said briskly, buttoning up Freddie's coat.

"Maybe. But they might not like me, anyway."

"What if you don't like them?"

That was something that hadn't occurred to her. Mulling it over, Freddie wiped her nose with the back of her hand before Natasha could come up with a tissue. "Are they nice?"

"I think so. After you meet them, you can decide. Okay?"

"Okay."

"Ladies, maybe you could pick another time to have a conference." Spence stood a few feet away, loaded down with luggage. "What was that all about?" he asked when they joined him on the sidewalk.

"Girl talk," Natasha answered with a wink that made Freddie giggle.

"Great." He started up the worn concrete steps behind Natasha. "Nothing I like better than to stand in the brisk wind holding three hundred pounds of luggage. What did you pack in here? Bricks?"

"Only a few, along with some essentials." Delighted with him, she turned and kissed his cheek—just as Nadia opened the door.

"Well." Pleased, Nadia folded her arms across her chest. "I told Papa you would come before Johnny Carson was over."

"Mama." Natasha rushed up the final steps to be enfolded in Nadia's arms. There was the scent she always remembered. Talc and nutmeg. And, as always, there was the strong, sturdy feel of her mother's body. Nadia's dark and sultry looks were just as strong, more so, perhaps, with the lines etched by worry, laughter and time.

Nadia murmured an endearment, then drew Natasha back to kiss her cheeks. She could see herself as she had been twenty years before. "Come on, you leave our guests standing in the cold."

Natasha's father bounded into the hall to pluck her off the floor and toss her into the air. He wasn't a tall man, but the arms beneath his work shirt were thick as cinder blocks from his years in the construction trade. He gave a robust laugh as he kissed her.

"No manners," Nadia declared as she shut the door. "Yuri, Natasha brings guests."

"Hello." Yuri thrust out a calloused hand and pumped Spence's. "Welcome."

"This is Spence and Freddie Kimball." As she made

introductions, Natasha noticed Freddie slip her hand into her father's.

"We are happy to meet you." Because warmth was her way, Nadia greeted them both with kisses. "I will take your coats, and you please come in and sit. You will be tired."

"We appreciate you having us," Spence began. Then, sensing that Freddie was nervous, he picked her up and carried her into the living room.

It was small, the wallpaper old and the furniture worn. But there were lace doilies on the arms of the chairs, the woodwork gleamed in the yellow lamplight from vigorous polishing, and here and there were exquisitely worked pillows. Framed family pictures fought for space among the potted plants and knicknacks.

A husky wheeze had Spence glancing down. There was an old gray dog in the corner. His tail began to thump when he saw Natasha. With obvious effort he rose and waddled to her.

"Sasha." She crouched to bury her face in the dog's fur. She laughed as he sat down again and leaned against her. "Sasha is a very old man," she explained to Freddie. "He likes best now to sleep and eat."

"And drink vodka," Yuri put in. "We will all have some. Except you," he added and flicked a finger down Freddie's nose. "You would have some champagne, huh?"

Freddie giggled, then bit her lip. Natasha's father didn't look exactly like she'd imagined a grandfather. He didn't have snow-white hair and a big belly. Instead his hair was black and white at the same time, and he had no belly at all. He talked funny, with a deep, rumbly kind of voice. But he smelled good, like cherries. And his smile was nice.

"What's vodka?"

"Russian tradition," Yuri answered her. "A drink we make from grain."

Freddie wrinkled her nose. "That sounds yucky," she said, then immediately bit her lip again. But at Yuri's burst of laughter she managed a shy smile.

"Natasha will tell you that her papa always teases little girls." Nadia poked an elbow into Yuri's ribs. "It's because he is really just little boy at heart. You would like hot chocolate?"

Freddie was torn between the comfort of her father's hand and one of her favorite treats. And Nadia was smiling at her, not with that goofy look grown-ups sometimes put on when they had to talk to kids. It was a warm smile, just like Natasha's.

"Yes, ma'am."

Nadia gave a nod of approval at the child's manners. "Maybe you would like to come with me. I show you how to make it with big, fat marshmallows."

Forgetting shyness, Freddie took her hand from Spence's and put it into Nadia's. "I have two cats," she told Nadia proudly as they walked into the kitchen. "And I had chicken pox on my birthday."

"Sit, sit," Yuri ordered, gesturing toward the couch. "We have a drink."

"Where are Alex and Rachel?" With a contented sigh, Natasha sank into the worn cushions.

"Alex takes his new girlfriend to the movies. Very pretty," Yuri said, rolling his bright, brown eyes. "Rachel is at lecture. Big-time lawyer from Washington, D.C. comes to college."

"And how is Mikhail?"

"Very busy. They remodel apartment in Soho." He passed out glasses, tapping each before he drank. "So," he said to Spence as he settled in his favorite chair, "you teach music."

"Yes. Natasha's one of my best students in Music History."

"Smart girl, my Natasha." He settled back in his chair and studied Spence. But not, as Natasha had hoped, discreetly. "You are good friends."

"Yes," Natasha put in, uneasy about the gleam in her father's eyes. "We are. Spence just moved into town this summer. He and Freddie used to live in New York."

"So. This is interesting. Like fate."

"I like to think so," Spence agreed, enjoying himself. "It was especially fortunate that I have a little girl and Natasha owns a very tempting toy store. Added to that, she signed up for one of my classes. It made it difficult for her to avoid me when she was being stubborn."

"She is stubborn," Yuri agreed sadly. "Her mother is stubborn. Me, I am very agreeable."

Natasha gave a quick snort.

"Stubborn and disrespectful women run in my family." Yuri took another healthy drink. "It is my curse."

"Perhaps one day I'll be fortunate enough to say the same." Spence smiled over the rim of his glass. "When I convince Natasha to marry me."

Natasha sprang up, ignoring her father's grin. "Since the vodka's gone to your head so quickly, I'll see if Mama has any extra hot chocolate."

Yuri pushed himself out of his chair to reach for the bottle as Natasha disappeared. "We'll leave the chocolate to the women."

Natasha awoke at first light with Freddie curled in her arms. She was in the bed of her childhood, in a room where she and her sister had spent countless hours talking, laughing, arguing. The wallpaper was the same. Faded roses. Whenever her mother had threatened to paint it, both she and Rachel had objected. There was something comforting about waking up to the same walls from childhood through adolescence to adulthood.

Turning her head, she could see her sister's dark hair against the pillow of the next bed. The sheets and blankets were in tangles. Typical, Natasha thought with a smile. Rachel had more energy asleep than most people had fully awake. She had come in the night before after midnight, bursting with enthusiasm over the lecture she had attended, full of hugs and kisses and questions.

Natasha brushed a kiss over Freddie's hair, then carefully shifted her. The child snuggled into the pillow without making a sound. Quietly Natasha rose. She took a moment to steady herself when the floor tilted. Four hours' sleep, she decided, was bound to make anyone light-headed. Gathering her clothes, she went off to shower and dress.

Arriving downstairs, she caught the scent of coffee brewing. It didn't seem to appeal to her, but she followed it into the kitchen.

"Mama." Nadia was already at the counter, busily rolling out piecrusts. "It's too early to cook."

"On Thanksgiving it's never too early." She lifted her cheek for a kiss. "You want coffee?"

Natasha pressed a hand to her uneasy stomach. "No. I don't think so. I assume that bundle of blankets on the couch is Alex."

"He gets in very late." Nadia pursed her lips briefly in disapproval, then shrugged. "He's not a boy anymore."

"No. You'll just have to face it, Mama, you have grown children—and you raised them very well."

"Not so well that Alex learns to pick up his socks." But she smiled, hoping her youngest son wouldn't deprive her of that last vestige of motherhood too soon.

"Did Papa and Spence stay up very late?"

"Papa likes talking to your friend. He's a nice man." Nadia laid a circle of dough on a pie plate, then took up another chunk to roll out. "Very handsome."

"Yes," Natasha agreed, but cautiously.

"He has good job, is responsible, loves his daughter."

"Yes," Natasha said again.

"Why don't you marry him when he wants you to?"

She'd figured on this. Biting back a sigh, Natasha leaned on the kitchen table. "There are a lot of nice, responsible and handsome men, Mama. Should I marry them all?"

"Not so many as you think." Smiling to herself, Nadia started on a third crust. "You don't love him?" When Natasha didn't answer, Nadia's smile widened. "Ah."

"Don't start. Spence and I have only known each other for a few months. There's a lot he doesn't know about me."

"So tell him."

"I don't seem to be able to."

Nadia put down her rolling pin to cup her daughter's face in two floury hands. "He is not like the other one."

"No, he's not. But—"

Impatient, Nadia shook her head. "Holding on to something that's gone only makes a sickness inside. You have a good heart, Tash. Trust it."

"I want to." She wrapped her arms around her mother and held tight. "I do love him, Mama, but it still scares me. And it still hurts." On a long breath she drew back. "I want to borrow Papa's truck."

Nadia didn't ask where she was going. Didn't need to. "Yes. I can go with you."

Natasha only kissed her mother's cheek and shook her head.

She'd been gone an hour before Spence made his bleary-eyed way downstairs. He and the gray dog exchanged glances of sympathy. Yuri had been generous with the vodka the night before, to guests and pets. At the moment, Spence felt as though a chain gang were chipping rock in his head. Operating on automatic, he found the kitchen, following the scents of baking, and blissfully, coffee.

Nadia took one look, laughed broadly and gestured to the table. "Sit." She poured a cup of coffee, strong and black. "Drink. I fix you breakfast."

Like a dying man, Spence clutched the cup in both hands. "Thanks. I don't want to put you out."

Nadia merely waved a hand as she reached for a cast-iron skillet. "I know a man with a hangover. Yuri poured you too much vodka."

"No. I took care of that all on my own." He opened the aspirin bottle she set on the table. "Bless you, Mrs. Stanislaski."

"Nadia. You call me Nadia when you get drunk in my house."

"I don't remember feeling like this since college." So saying he downed three aspirins. "I can't imagine why I thought it was fun at the time." He managed a weak smile. "Something smells wonderful."

"You will like my pies." She pushed fat sausages around in the skillet. "You met Alex last night."

"Yes." Spence didn't object when she filled his cup a

second time. "That was cause enough for one more drink. You have a beautiful family, Nadia."

"They make me proud." She laughed as the sausage sizzled. "They make me worry. You know, you have daughter."

"Yes." He smiled at her, picturing what Natasha would look like in a quarter of a century.

"Natasha is the only one who moves far away. I worry most for her."

"She's very strong."

Nadia only nodded as she added eggs to the pan. "Are you patient, Spence?"

"I think so."

Nadia glanced over her shoulder. "Don't be too patient."

"Funny. Natasha once told me the same thing."

Pleased, Nadia popped bread into the toaster. "Smart girl."

The kitchen door swung open. Alex, dark, rumpled and heavy-eyed, grinned. "I smelled breakfast."

The first snow was falling, small, thin flakes that swirled in the wind and vanished before they hit the ground. There were some things, Natasha knew, that were beautiful and very precious, and here for only such a short time.

She stood alone, bundled against the cold she didn't feel. Except inside. The light was pale gray, but not dreary, not with the tiny, dancing snowflakes. She hadn't brought flowers. She never did. They would look much too sad on such a tiny grave.

Lily. Closing her eyes, she let herself remember how it had felt to hold that small, delicate life in her arms. Her baby. *Milaya.* Her little girl. Those beautiful blue eyes, Natasha remembered, those exquisite miniature hands.

Like the flower she had been named for, Lily had been

so lovely, and had lived such a brief, brief time. She could see Lily, small and red and wrinkled, her little hands fisted when the nurse had first laid her in Natasha's arms. She could feel even now that sweet ache that tugged when Lily had nursed at her breast. She remembered the feel of that soft, soft skin and the smell of powder and lotion, the comfort of rocking late at night with her own baby girl on her shoulder.

So quickly gone, Natasha thought. A few precious weeks. No amount of time, no amount of prayer would ever make her understand it. Accept, perhaps, but never understand.

"I love you, Lily. Always." She bent to press her palm against the cold grass. Rising again, she turned and walked away through the lightly dancing snow.

Where had she gone? There could be a dozen places, Spence assured himself. It was foolish to be worried. But he couldn't help it. Some instinct was at work here, heightened by the certainty that Natasha's family knew exactly where she was, but refused to say.

The house was already filled with noise, laughter, and the smells of the celebrational meal to come. He tried to shake off the feeling that wherever Natasha was, she needed him.

There was so much she hadn't told him. That had become crystal clear when he saw the pictures in the living room. Natasha in tights and dance shoes, in ballet skirts and toe shoes. Natasha with her hair streaming behind her, caught at the apex of a grand jeté.

She'd been a dancer, quite obviously a professional, but had never mentioned it.

Why had she given it up? Why had she kept something

that had been an important part of her life a secret from him?

Coming out of the kitchen, Rachel saw him with one of the photographs in his hand. She kept silent for a moment, studying him. Like her mother, she approved of what she saw. There was a strength here and a gentleness. Her sister needed and deserved both.

"It's a beautiful picture."

He turned. Rachel was taller than Natasha, more willowy. Her dark hair was cut short in a sleek cap around her face. Her eyes, more gold than brown, dominated. "How old was she?"

Rachel dipped her hands into the pockets of her trousers as she crossed the room. "Sixteen, I think. She was in the corps de ballet then. Very dedicated. I always envied Tash her grace. I was a klutz." She smiled and gently changed the subject. "Always taller and skinnier than the boys, knocking things over with my elbows. Where's Freddie?"

Spence set down the picture. Without saying it, Rachel had told him that if he had questions, they were for Natasha. "She's upstairs, watching the Macy's parade with Yuri."

"He never misses it. Nothing disappointed him more than when we grew too old to want to sit in his lap and watch the floats."

A laughing squeal from the second floor had them both turning toward the stairs. Feet clomped. A pink whirlwind in her jumpsuit, Freddie came dashing down to launch herself at Spence. "Daddy, Papa makes bear noises. *Big* bear noises."

"Did he rub his beard on your cheek?" Rachel wanted to know.

"It's scratchy." She giggled, then wriggled down to run upstairs once more, hoping he'd do it again.

"She's having the time of her life," Spence decided.

"So's Papa. How's your head?"

"Better, thanks." He heard the sound of the truck pulling up outside, and glanced toward the window.

"Mama needs my help." Rachel slipped back into the kitchen.

He was at the door waiting for her. Natasha looked very pale, very tired, but she smiled when she saw him. "Good morning." Because she needed him, she slipped her arms around his waist and held tight.

"Are you all right?"

"Yes." She was now, she realized, when he was holding her like this. Stronger, she pulled back. "I thought you might sleep late."

"No, I've been up awhile. Where have you been?"

She unwound her scarf. "There was something I needed to do." After peeling off her coat, she hung it in the narrow closet. "Where is everyone?"

"Your mother and Rachel are in the kitchen. The last time I looked, Alex was on the phone."

This time the smile came easily. "Sweet-talking a girl."

"Apparently. Freddie's up with your father, watching the parade."

"And putting him in heaven." She touched her fingertips to Spence's cheek. "Will you kiss me?"

There was some need here, he thought as he bent toward her. Some deep, private need she still refused to share. Her lips were cold when his met them, but they softened, then warmed. At last they curved.

"You're very good for me, Spence."

"I was hoping you'd catch on to that." He gave her bottom lip a playful nip. "Better?"

"Much. I'm glad you're here." She squeezed his hand. "How do you feel about some of Mama's hot chocolate?"

Before he could answer, Freddie came sprinting down the steps again, one shoelace trailing, to throw her arms around Natasha's waist. "You're back!"

"So I am." Natasha bent to kiss the top of Freddie's head. "What have you been up to?"

"I'm watching the parade with Papa. He can talk just like Donald Duck, and he lets me sit on his lap."

"I see." Leaning closer, Natasha took a sniff. There was the telltale fragrance of gumdrops lingering on Freddie's breath. "Does he still hog all the yellow ones?"

Freddie giggled, casting a quick, cautious look at her father. Spence had a much different view of gumdrops than Yuri. "It's okay. I like the red ones best."

"How many red ones?" Spence asked her.

Freddie lifted her shoulders and let them fall. It was, Spence noted with some amusement, almost a mirror image of Natasha's habitual gesture. "Not too many. Will you come up and watch with us?" She tugged at Natasha's hand. "It's almost time for Santa Claus."

"In a little while." Out of habit, Natasha crouched to tie Freddie's shoelace. "Tell Papa that I won't mention the gumdrops to Mama. If he saves me some."

"Okay." She dashed up the stairs.

"He's made quite an impression on her," Spence observed.

"Papa makes impressions on everyone." She started to rise, and felt the room spin. Before she could sink to the floor again, Spence had her arms.

"What is it?"

"Nothing." She pressed a hand to her head, waiting for the dizziness to pass. "I stood up too fast, that's all."

"You're pale. Come sit down." He had an arm hooked around her waist, but she shook her head.

"No, I'm fine, really. Just a little tired." Relieved that the room had steadied, she smiled at him. "Blame it on Rachel. She would have talked through the night if I hadn't fallen asleep on her in self-defense."

"Have you eaten anything?"

"I thought you were a doctor of music." She smiled again and patted his cheek. "Don't worry, the minute I go into the kitchen, Mama will start feeding me."

Just then the front door opened. Spence watched Natasha's face light up. "Mikhail!" With a laugh, she threw herself into the arms of her brother.

He had the dark, blinding good looks that ran in the family. The tallest of the brood, he had to bend to gather Natasha close. His hair curled over his ears and collar. His coat was worn, his boots were scarred. His hands, as they stroked Natasha's hair, were wide-palmed and beautiful.

It took Spence only seconds to see that while Natasha loved all of her family deeply, there was a separate and special bond here.

"I've missed you." She drew back just far enough to kiss his cheeks, then hugged him close again. "I've really missed you."

"Then why don't you come more often?" He pushed her away, wanting a good long look. He didn't care for the pallor in her cheeks, but since her hands were still cold, he realized she'd been out. And he knew where she'd spent that morning. He murmured something in Ukrainian, but she only shook her head and squeezed his hands tight. With a shrug very like her own, he put the subject aside.

"Mikhail, I want you to meet Spence."

As he took off his coat, Mikhail turned to study Spence.

Unlike Alex's friendly acceptance or Rachel's subtle measuring, this was an intense and prolonged stare that left Spence in no doubt that if Mikhail didn't approve, he wouldn't hesitate to say so.

"I know your work," he said at length. "It's excellent."

"Thank you." Spence met look for look. "I can say the same about yours." When Mikhail lifted one dark brow, Spence continued. "I've seen the figures you carved for Natasha."

"Ah." A glimmer of a smile curved Mikhail's mouth. "My sister always was fond of fairy tales." There was a squeal from upstairs, followed by rumbling laughter.

"That's Freddie," Natasha explained. "Spence's daughter. She's making Papa's day."

Mikhail slipped a thumb through one belt loop. "You are a widower."

"That's right."

"And now you teach at college."

"Yes."

"Mikhail," Natasha interrupted. "Don't play big brother. I'm older than you."

"But I'm bigger." Then with a quick, flashing grin, he tossed an arm around her shoulder. "So what's to eat?"

Too much, Spence decided as the family gathered around the table late that afternoon. The huge turkey in the center of the hand-crocheted tablecloth was only the beginning. Faithful to her adopted country's holiday, Nadia had prepared a meal that was an American tradition from the chestnut dressing to the pumpkin pies.

Wide-eyed, Freddie gawked, staring at platter after platter. The room was full of noise as everyone talked over and around everyone else. The china was mismatched. Old

Sasha lay sprawled under the table near her feet, hoping for a few unobtrusive handouts. She was sitting on a wobbly chair and the New York Yellow Pages. As far as she was concerned, it was the best day of her life.

Alex and Rachel began to argue over some childhood infraction. Mikhail joined in to tell them they were both wrong. When her opinion was sought, Natasha just laughed and shook her head, then turned to Spence and murmured something into his ear that made him chuckle.

Nadia, her cheeks rosy with the pleasure of having her family together, slipped a hand into Yuri's as he lifted his glass.

"Enough," he said, and effectively silenced the table. "You can argue later about who let white mice loose in science lab. Now we toast. We are thankful for this food that Nadia and my girls have fixed for us. And more thankful for the friends and family who are here together to enjoy it. We give thanks, as we did on our first Thanksgiving in our country, that we are free."

"To freedom," Mikhail said as he lifted his glass.

"To freedom," Yuri agreed. His eyes misted and he looked around the table. "And to family."

Chapter 11

That evening, with Freddie dozing in his lap, Spence listened to Yuri tell stories of the old country. While the meal had been a noisy competition for conversation, this hour was one of quiet and content. Across the room Rachel and Alex played a trivia game. They argued often, but without heat.

In the corner, Natasha and Mikhail sat close, dark heads together. Spence could hear their murmurs and noted that one often reached to touch the other's hand, to touch a cheek. Nadia sat smiling, interrupting Yuri occasionally to correct or comment as she worked another pillow cover.

"Woman." Yuri pointed at his wife with the stem of his after-dinner pipe. "I remember like yesterday."

"You remember as you like to remember."

"Tak." He stuck the pipe back into his mouth. "And what I remember makes better story."

When Freddie stirred, Spence shifted her. "I'd better put her to bed."

"I will do it." Nadia set her needlework aside and rose. "I would like to." Making soothing noises, she lifted Freddie. Sleepy and agreeable, Freddie snuggled into her neck.

"Will you rock me?"

"Yes." Touched, Nadia kissed her hair as she started toward the steps. "I will rock you in the chair where I rocked all my babies."

"And sing?"

"I will sing you a song my mother sang to me. You would like that?"

Freddie gave a yawn and a drowsy nod.

"You have a beautiful daughter." Like Spence, Yuri watched them turn up the steps. "You must bring her back often."

"I think I'll have a hard time keeping her away."

"She is always welcome, as you are." Yuri took a puff on his pipe. "Even if you don't marry my daughter."

That statement brought on ten seconds of humming silence until Alex and Rachel bent back over their game, smothering grins. Spence didn't bother to smother his own as Natasha rose.

"There isn't enough milk for the morning," she decided on the spot. "Spence, why don't you walk with me to get some?"

"Sure."

A few moments later they stepped outside, wrapped in coats and scarves. The air had a bite that Natasha welcomed. Overhead the sky was clear as black glass and icy with stars.

"He didn't mean to embarrass you," Spence began.

"Yes, he did."

Spence didn't bother to hold back the chuckle, and draped an arm over her shoulders. "I suppose he did. I like your family."

"So do I. Most of the time."

"You're lucky to have them. Watching Freddie here has made me realize how important family is. I don't suppose I've really tried to get closer to Nina or my parents."

"They're still family. Perhaps we're as close as we are, because when we came here we only had each other."

"It's true my family never crossed the mountains into Hungary in a wagon."

That made her laugh. "Rachel was always jealous that she hadn't been born yet. When she was little, she would get back by saying she was more American, because she'd been born in New York. Then not long ago, someone said to her that if she wanted to be a lawyer, she should think of changing or shortening her name." With a new laugh, Natasha looked up at him. "She became very insulted and very Ukrainian."

"It's a good name. You could always keep it profession-ally after you marry me."

"Don't start."

"Must be your father's influence." He glanced at the dark shop, where a Closed sign hung on the door. "The store's closed."

"I know." She turned into his arms. "I just wanted to walk. Now that we're standing here in a dark doorway, alone, I can kiss you."

"Good point." Spence lowered his mouth to hers.

Natasha was annoyed with herself for dozing off and on during the drive home. She felt as though she'd spent a week mountain climbing, rather than less than forty-eight hours in her family home. By the time she shook herself awake for the last time, they were crossing the Maryland border into West Virginia.

"Already." She straightened in her seat and cast an apologetic glance at Spence. "I didn't help you drive."

"It's all right. You looked like you needed the rest."

"Too much food, too little sleep." She looked back at Freddie, who was sleeping soundly. "We've been poor company for you."

"You can make up for it. Come home with me for a while."

"All right." It was the least she could do, Natasha thought. With Vera away until Sunday, she could help him tuck Freddie into bed and fix him a light meal.

When they pulled up in front of the house, they managed the suitcases and the sleeping child between them. "I'll take her up," he murmured. "It won't take long."

Natasha waited in the kitchen, brewing tea and making sandwiches. It was ridiculous, she thought. She not only was exhausted but starving. By the time Spence came down again, she had Vera's worktable set.

"She's sleeping like a rock." He scanned the table. "You read my mind."

"With two unconscious passengers you couldn't stop and eat."

"What have we got?"

"Old Ukrainian tradition." She pulled back her chair. "Tuna fish."

"Wonderful," Spence decided after the first bite.

It was more than the sandwich. He liked having her there, sitting across from him in the glare of the kitchen light with the house quiet around them. "I guess you'll open the shop tomorrow."

"Absolutely. It'll be a madhouse from now until Christmas. I've hired a college student part-time, and he starts tomorrow." She lifted her cup and grinned at him over the rim. "Guess who it is."

"Melony Trainor," he said, naming one of his most attractive students and earning a punch on the shoulder.

"No. She's too busy flirting with men to work. Terry Maynard."

"Maynard? Really?"

"Yes. He can use the money to buy a new muffler for his car. And…" She paused dramatically. "He and Annie are an item."

"No kidding?" He was grinning as he sat back. "Well, he certainly got over having his life shattered quickly."

Natasha lifted a brow. "It wasn't shattered, only shaken. They've been seeing each other almost every night for three weeks."

"Sounds serious."

"I think it is. But Annie's worried she's too old for him."

"How much older is she?"

Natasha leaned forward and lowered her voice. "Oh, very much older. Nearly an entire year."

"Cradle robber."

With a laugh she leaned back again. "It's nice to see them together. I only hope they don't forget to wait on customers because they're mooning at each other." She shrugged, and went back to her tea. "I think I'll go in early and start on the decorations."

"You'll be tired at the end of the day. Why don't you come here for dinner?"

Curious, she tilted her head. "You cook?"

"No." He grinned and polished off his sandwich. "But I do great takeout. You can get a whole box of chicken or pizza with the works. I've even been known to come up with oriental seafood."

"I'll leave the menu to you." She rose to clear the table, but he took her hand.

"Natasha." He stood, using his free hand to stroke her hair. "I want to thank you for sharing the last couple of days with me. It meant a lot."

"To me too."

"Still, I've missed being alone with you." He bent to brush his lips over hers. "Come upstairs with me. I want very much to make love with you in my bed."

She didn't answer. Nor did she hesitate. Slipping an arm around his waist, she went with him.

He left the bedside light on low. She could just see the dark, masculine colors he'd chosen for his room. Midnight blue, forest green. An oil painting in a heavy, ornate frame dominated one wall. She could see the silhouettes of exquisite antiques. The bed was big, a generous private space covered by a thick, soft quilt. A special space, Natasha realized, knowing he had never brought another woman to this bed, to this room.

In the mirror over the bureau she caught their reflections as they stood side by side and saw herself smile when he touched a hand to her cheek.

There was time, time to savor. The fatigue she had felt earlier had vanished. Now she felt only the glow that came from loving and being loved. Words were too difficult, but when she kissed him, her heart spoke for her.

Slowly they undressed each other.

She slipped his sweater over his head. He undid the buttons of her cardigan, then pushed it from her shoulders. Keeping her eyes on his, she unfastened his shirt. He slid up the cotton sweater, letting his fingers trail until she was free of it. She unhooked his trousers. He flipped the three snaps that held her slacks at the waist. Keeping his hands light, he drew the teddy down her body as she tugged away the last barrier between them.

Quietly they moved together, her palms pressing against his back, his skimming up her sides. Heads tilting first this way, then that, they experimented with long, lingering kisses. Enjoyment. Their bodies warming, their mouths seeking, it seemed so easy here.

They drew back in unspoken agreement. Spence pulled down the quilt. They slipped under it together.

Intimacy had no rival, Natasha thought. There was nothing to compare with this. Their bodies rubbed against each other, so that the sheets whispered with each movement. Her sigh answered his murmurs. The flavor and fragrance of his skin was familiar, personal. His touch, gentle, then persuasive, then demanding, was everything she wanted.

She was simply beautiful. Not just her body, not just that exquisite face, but her spirit. When she moved with him, there was a harmony more intense than any he could create with music. She was his music—her laugh, her voice, her gestures. He knew of no way to tell her. Only to show her.

He made love with her as though it were the first and the only time. Never had she felt so elegant, so graceful. Never had she felt so strong or so sure.

When he rose over her, when she rose to meet him, it was perfect.

"I'd like you to stay."

Natasha turned her face into his throat. "I can't. Freddie would ask questions in the morning I don't know how to answer."

"I have a very simple answer. I'll tell her the truth. I'm in love with you."

"That's not simple."

"It is the truth." He shifted so that he could look at her. Her eyes were shadowed in the dim light. "I do love you, Natasha."

"Spence—"

"No. No logic or excuses. We're past that. Tell me if you believe me."

She looked into his eyes and saw what she already knew. "Yes, I believe you."

"Then tell me what you feel. I need to know."

He had a right to know, she thought, though she could all but taste the panic on her tongue. "I love you. And I'm afraid."

He brought her hand to his lips to press a kiss firmly against her fingers. "Why?"

"Because I was in love before, and nothing, nothing could have ended as badly."

There was that shadow again, he thought impatiently. The shadow from her past that he could neither fight nor conquer because it was nameless.

"Neither of us have come into this without a few bruises, Natasha. But we have a chance to make something new, something important."

She knew he was right, felt he was right, yet still held back. "I wish I were so sure. Spence, there are things you don't know about me."

"That you were a dancer."

She shifted then, to gather the sheets to her breast and sit up. "Yes. Once."

"Why haven't you mentioned it?"

"Because it was over."

He drew the hair away from her face. "Why did you stop?"

"I had a choice to make." The ache came back, but briefly. She turned to him and smiled. "I was not so good. Oh, I was adequate, and perhaps in time I would have been good enough to have been a principal dancer. Perhaps… It was something I wanted very badly once. But wanting something doesn't always make it happen."

"Will you tell me about it?"

It was a beginning, one she knew she had to make. "It's not very exciting." She lifted her hands, then let them fall onto the sheet. "I started late, after we came here. Through the church my parents met Martina Latovia. Many years ago she was an important Soviet dancer who defected. She became friends with my mother and offered to give me classes. It was good for me, the dance. I didn't speak English well, so it was hard to make friends. Everything was so different here, you see."

"Yes, I can imagine."

"I was nearly eight by that time. It becomes difficult to teach the body, the joints, to move as they weren't meant to move. But I worked very hard. *Madame* was kind and encouraging. My parents were so proud." She laughed a little, but warmly. "Papa was sure I would be the next Pavlova. The first time I danced *en pointe*, Mama cried. Dance is obsession and pain and joy. It's a different world, Spence. I can't explain. You have to know it, be a part of it."

"You don't have to explain."

She looked over at him. "No, not to you," she murmured. "Because of the music. I joined the corps de ballet when I was almost sixteen. It was wonderful. Perhaps I didn't know there were other worlds, but I was happy."

"What happened?"

"There was another dancer." She shut her eyes. It was important to take this slowly, carefully. "You've heard of him, I imagine. Anthony Marshall."

"Yes." Spence had an immediate picture of a tall, blond man with a slender build and incredible grace. "I've seen him dance many times."

"He was magnificent. Is," she corrected. "Though it's been years since I've seen him dance. We became involved. I was young. Too young. And it was a very big mistake."

Now the shadow had a name. "You loved him."

"Oh yes. In a naive and idealistic kind of way. The only way a girl can love at seventeen. More, I thought he loved me. He told me he did, in words, in actions. He was very charming, romantic…and I wanted to believe him. He promised me marriage, a future, a partnership in dance, all the things I wanted to hear. He broke all those promises, and my heart."

"So now you don't want to hear promises from me."

"You're not Anthony," she murmured, then lifted a hand to his cheek. Her eyes were dark and beautiful, her voice only more exotic as emotions crowded. "Believe me, I know that. And I don't compare, not now. I'm not the same woman who built dreams on a few careless words."

"What I've said to you hasn't been careless."

"No." She leaned closer to rest her cheek against his. "Over the past months I've come to see that, and to understand that what I feel for you is different from anything I've felt before." There was more she wanted to tell him, but the words clogged her throat. "Please, let that be enough for now."

"For now. It won't be enough forever."

She turned her mouth to his. "Just for now."

* * *

How could it be? Natasha asked herself. How could it be that when she was just beginning to trust herself, to trust her heart, that this should happen? How could she face it again?

It was like a play run backward and started again, when her life had changed so drastically and completely. She sat back on her bed, no longer concerned about dressing for work, about starting a normal day. How could things be normal now? How could she expect them to be normal ever again?

She held the little vial in her hand. She had followed the instructions exactly. Just a precaution, she had told herself. But she'd known in her heart. Since the visit to her parents two weeks before she'd known. And had avoided facing the reality.

It was not the flu that made her queasy in the mornings. It was not overwork or stress that caused her to be so tired, or that brought on the occasional dizzy spells. The simple test that she'd bought over the counter in the drugstore had told her what she'd already known and feared.

She was carrying a child. Once again she was carrying a child. The rush of joy and wonder was totally eclipsed by the bone-deep fear that froze her.

How could it be? She was no longer a foolish girl and had taken precautions. Romance aside, she had been practical enough, responsible enough to visit her doctor and begin taking those tiny little pills, when she had realized where her relationship with Spence was bound to go. Yet she was pregnant. There was no denying it.

How could she tell him? Covering her face with her hands, Natasha rocked back and forth to give herself some small comfort. How could she go through all of it again, when that time years before was still so painfully etched on her memory?

She had known Anthony no longer loved her, if he had ever. But when she'd learned she was carrying his child, she had been thrilled. And so certain that he would share her delight. When she'd gone to him, almost bubbling over, glowing with the joy of it, his cruelty had all but cut her in two.

How grudgingly he'd let her into his apartment, Natasha remembered. How difficult it had been for her to continue to smile when she'd seen his table set for two, the candles lighted, the wine chilling—as he'd so often prepared the stage when he'd loved her. Now he'd set that stage for someone else. But she'd persuaded herself that it didn't matter. Once she'd told him, everything would change.

Everything had.

"What the hell are you talking about?" She remembered the fury in his eyes as he'd stared at her.

"I went to the doctor this afternoon. I'm pregnant, almost two months." She reached out for him. "Anthony—"

"That's an old game, Tash." He'd said it casually, but perhaps he'd been shaken. He'd stalked to the table to pour a glass of wine.

"It's not a game."

"No? Then how could you be so stupid?" He'd grabbed her arm and given her a quick shake, his magnificent mane of hair flying. "If you've gotten yourself in trouble, don't expect to come running to me to fix it."

Dazed, she'd lifted a hand to rub her arm where his fingers had bit in. It was only that he didn't understand, she'd told herself. "I'm having a child. Your child. The doctor says the baby will come in July."

"Maybe you're pregnant." He'd shrugged as he'd downed the wine. "It doesn't concern me."

"It must."

He'd looked at her then, his glass held aloft, his eyes cool. "How do I know it's mine?"

At that she'd paled. As she'd stood there, she'd remembered how it had felt when she'd almost stepped in front of a bus on her first trip to New York City. "You know. You have to know."

"I don't have to know anything. Now, if you'll excuse me, I'm expecting someone."

In desperation she'd reached out for him. "Anthony, don't you understand? I'm carrying our baby."

"Your baby," he corrected. "Your problem. If you want some advice, get rid of it."

"Get—" She hadn't been so young or so naive that she hadn't understood his meaning. "You can't mean it."

"You want to dance, Tash? Try picking classes back up after taking off nine months to give birth to some brat you're going to end up giving away in any case. Grow up."

"I have grown up." She'd laid a hand on her stomach, in protection and defense. "And I will have this child."

"Your choice." He'd gestured with his wineglass. "Don't expect to pull me into it. I've got a career to think of. You're probably better off," he decided. "Talk some loser into marrying you and set up housekeeping. You'd never be any better than mediocre at dance anyway."

So she had had the child and loved it—for a brief, brief time. Now there was another. She couldn't bear to love it, couldn't bear to want it. Not when she knew what it was like to lose.

Frantic, she threw the vial across the room and began pulling clothes out of her closet. She had to get away. She had to think. She would get away, Natasha promised herself, then pressed her fingers against her eyes until she calmed. But she had to tell him.

This time she drove to his house, struggling for calm as the car brought her closer. Because it was Saturday, children were playing in yards and on the sidewalk. Some called out to her as she passed, and she managed to lift a hand in a wave. She spotted Freddie wrestling with her kittens on the grass.

"Tash! Tash!" Lucy and Desi darted for cover, but Freddie raced to the car. "Did you come to play?"

"Not today." Summoning a smile, Natasha kissed her cheeks. "Is your daddy home?"

"He's playing music. He plays music a lot since we came here. I drew a picture. I'm going to send it to Papa and Nana."

Natasha struggled to keep the smile in place at Freddie's names for her parents. "They will like that very much."

"Come on, I'll show you."

"In a little while. I need to speak to your father first. By myself."

Freddie's bottom lip threatened. "Are you mad at him?"

"No." She pressed a finger to Freddie's nose. "Go find your kittens. I'll talk to you before I go."

"Okay." Reassured, Freddie raced off, sending out whoops that would have the kittens cowering in the bushes, Natasha reflected.

It was better to keep her mind a blank, she decided as she

knocked on the front door. Then she would take it slowly, logically, like an adult.

"Miss." Vera opened the door, her expression less remote than usual. Freddie's description of the Thanksgiving holiday in Brooklyn had done a great deal to win her over.

"I'd like to see Dr. Kimball if he's not busy."

"Come in." She found herself frowning a bit as she studied Natasha. "Are you all right, miss? You're very pale."

"Yes, I'm fine. Thank you."

"Would you like tea?"

"No—no, I can't stay long."

Though Vera privately thought Natasha looked like a cornered rabbit, she nodded. "You'll find him in the music room. He's been up half the night working."

"Thank you." Clutching her bag, Natasha started down the hall. She could hear the music he was playing, something weepy. Or perhaps it was her own mood, she thought; she blinked back tears.

When she saw him, she remembered the first time she had walked into that room. Perhaps she had started to fall in love with him that day, when he had sat there with a child on his lap, surrounded by sunlight.

She pulled off her gloves, running them through her nervous hands as she watched him. He was lost in it, both captor and captive of the music. Now she would change his life. He hadn't asked for this, and they both knew that loving wasn't always enough.

"Spence." She murmured his name when the music stopped, but he didn't hear. She could see the intensity was still on him as he scribbled on staff paper. He hadn't shaved. It made her want to smile, but instead her eyes filled. His shirt was rumpled and open at the collar. His hair was tousled. As she watched, he ran a hand through it. "Spence," she repeated.

He looked up—annoyed at first. Then he focused and smiled at her. "Hi. I didn't expect to see you today."

"Annie's watching the shop." She knit her hands. "I needed to see you."

"I'm glad you did." He rose, though the music was still filling his head. "What time is it anyway?" Absently he glanced at his watch. "Too early to ask you for lunch. How about some coffee?"

"No." Even the thought of coffee made her stomach roll. "I don't want anything. I needed to tell you...." Her fingers knotted. "I don't know how. I want you to know I never intended—this isn't intended to put you under obligation...."

The words trailed off again, he shook his head and started toward her. "If something's wrong, why don't you tell me?"

"I'm trying to."

He took her hand to lead her to the couch. "The best way's often straight out."

"Yes." She put her hand to her spinning head. "You see, I..." She saw the concern in his eyes, then everything went black....

She was lying on the sofa, and Spence was kneeling beside her, chafing her wrists. "Take it easy," he murmured. "Just lie still. I'll call a doctor."

"No. There's no need." Carefully she pushed herself up. "I'm all right."

"The hell you are." Her skin was clammy under his hand. "You're like ice, and pale as a ghost. Damn it, Natasha, why didn't you tell me you weren't well? I'll take you to the hospital."

"I don't need the hospital or the doctor." Hysteria was bubbling under her heart. She fought it back and forced herself to speak. "I'm not sick, Spence. I'm pregnant."

Chapter 12

"What?" It was the best he could do; he sank back onto his heels and stared at her. "What did you say?"

She wanted to be strong, had to be. He looked as though she'd hit him with a blunt instrument. "I'm pregnant," she repeated, then made a helpless gesture. "I'm sorry."

He only shook his head, waiting for it to sink in. "Are you sure?"

"Yes." It was best to be matter-of-fact, Natasha told herself. He was a civilized man. There would be no accusations, no cruelty. "This morning I took a test. I suspected before, for a couple of weeks, but..."

"Suspected." His hand curled into a fist on the cushion. She didn't look furious, as Angela had. She looked destroyed. "And you didn't mention it."

"I saw no need until I knew. There was no point in upsetting you."

"I see. Is that what you are, Natasha? Upset?"

"What I am is pregnant," she said briskly. "And I felt it was only right to tell you. I'm going away for a few days." Though she still felt shaky, she managed to stand.

"Away?" Confused, afraid she would faint again, furious, he caught her. "Now just a damn minute. You drop in, tell me you're pregnant, and now you calmly tell me you're going away?" He felt something sharp punch into his gut. Its name was fear. "Where?"

"Just away." She heard her own voice, snappish and rude, and pressed a hand to her head. "I'm sorry, I'm not handling this well. I need some time. I need to go away."

"What you need to do is sit down until we talk this out."

"I can't talk about it." She felt the pressure inside her build like floodwaters against a dam. "Not yet—not until I...I only wanted to tell you before I left."

"You're not going anywhere." He grabbed her arm to pull her back. "And you damn well will talk about it. What do you want from me? Am I supposed to say, 'Well, that's interesting news, Natasha. See you when you get back'?"

"I don't want anything." When her voice rose this time, she couldn't control it. Passions, grief, fears, poured out even as the tears began. "I never wanted anything from you. I didn't want to fall in love with you, I didn't want to need you in my life. I didn't want your child inside me."

"That's clear enough." His grip tightened, and he let his own temper free. "That's crystal clear. But you do have my child inside you, and now we're going to sit down and talk about what we're going to do about it."

"I tell you I need time."

"I've already given you more than enough time, Natasha. Apparently fate's taken a hand again, and you're going to have to face it."

"I can't go through this again. I won't."

"Again? What are you talking about?"

"I had a child." She jerked away to cover her face with her hands. Her whole body began to quake. "I had a child. Oh, God."

Stunned, he put a gentle hand upon her shoulder. "You have a child?"

"Had." The tears seemed to be shooting up, hot and painful, from the center of her body. "She's gone."

"Come sit down, Natasha. Talk to me."

"I can't. You don't understand. I lost her. My baby. I can't bear the thought of going through it all again." She tore herself away. "You don't know, you can't know, how much it hurts."

"No, but I can see it." He reached for her again. "I want you to tell me about this, so I can understand."

"What would that change?"

"We'll have to see. It isn't good for you to get so upset now."

"No." She swiped a hand over her cheek. "It doesn't do any good to be upset. I'm sorry I'm behaving like this."

"Don't apologize. Sit down. I'll get you some tea. We'll talk." He led her to a chair and she went unresistingly. "I'll only be a minute."

He was away for less than that, he was sure, but when he came back, she was gone.

Mikhail carved from a block of cherrywood and listened to the blast of rock and roll through his earphones. It suited the mood he could feel from the wood. Whatever was inside—and he wasn't sure just what that was yet— was young and full of energy. Whenever he carved, he listened, whether it was to blues or Bach or simply the rush and whoosh of traffic four floors below his window. It left his mind free to explore whatever medium his hands were working in.

Tonight his mind was too cluttered, and he knew he was stalling. He glanced over his worktable and across his cramped and cluttered two-room apartment. Natasha was curled in the overstuffed, badly sprung chair he'd salvaged off the street the previous summer. She had a book in her hands, but Mikhail didn't think she'd turned a page in more than twenty minutes. She, too, was stalling.

As annoyed with himself as with her, he pulled off the headphones. He only had to turn to be in the kitchen. Saying nothing, he put a pot onto one of the two temperamental gas burners and brewed tea. Natasha made no comment. When he brought over two cups, setting hers on the scarred surface of a nearby table, she glanced up blankly.

"Oh. *Dyakuyu.*"

"It's time to tell me what's going on."

"Mikhail—"

"I mean it." He dropped onto the mismatched hassock at her feet. "You've been here nearly a week, Tash."

She managed a small smile. "Ready to kick me out?"

"Maybe." But he put a hand over hers, rubbing lightly. "I haven't asked any questions, because that was what you wanted. I haven't told Mama and Papa that you arrived at my door one evening, looking pale and frightened, because you asked me to say nothing."

"And I appreciate it."

"Well, stop appreciating it." He made one of his characteristically abrupt gestures. "Talk to me."

"I told you I needed to get away for a little while, and I didn't want Mama and Papa to fuss over me." She moved her shoulders, then reached for her tea. "You don't fuss."

"I'm about to. Tell me what's wrong." He leaned over and cupped her chin in one hand. "Tash, tell me."

"I'm pregnant," she blurted out, then shakily set the tea down again.

He opened his mouth, but when the words didn't come, he simply wrapped his arms around her. Taking a long, labored breath, she held on.

"You're all right? You're well?"

"Yes. I went to the doctor a couple days ago. He says I'm fine. We're fine."

He drew back to study her face. "The college professor?"

"Yes. There hasn't been anyone but Spence."

Mikhail's dark eyes kindled. "If the bastard's treated you badly—"

"No." She found it odd that she was able to smile and caught Mikhail's fisted hands in hers. "No, he's never treated me badly."

"So he doesn't want the child." When Natasha merely looked down at their joined hands, Mikhail narrowed his eyes. "Natasha?"

"I don't know." She pulled away to stand and pace through Mikhail's collection of beat-up furniture and blocks of wood and stone.

"You haven't told him?"

"Of course I told him." As she moved, her hands clasped and unclasped. To calm herself, she stopped by Mikhail's Christmas tree—a one-foot evergreen in a pot that she'd decorated with bits of colored paper. "I just didn't give him much of a chance to say anything when I did. I was too upset."

"You don't want the child."

She turned at that, her eyes wide. "How can you say that? How could you think that?"

"Because you're here, instead of working things out with the college professor."

"I needed time to think."

"You think too much."

It wasn't anything he hadn't said before. Natasha's jaw set. "This isn't a matter of deciding between a blue dress and a red one. I'm having a child."

"*Tak*. Why don't you sit down and relax before you give it wrinkles."

"I don't want to sit down." She began to prowl again, shoving a box out of her way with one foot. "I didn't want to get involved with him in the first place. Even when I did, when he made it impossible for me to do otherwise, I knew it was important to keep some distance. I wanted to make sure I didn't make the same mistakes again. And now..." She made a helpless gesture.

"He isn't Anthony. This baby isn't Lily." When she turned around, her eyes were so drenched with emotion that he rose to go to her. "I loved her, too."

"I know."

"You can't judge by what's gone, Tash." Gently he kissed her cheeks. "It isn't fair to you, your professor or the child."

"I don't know what to do."

"Do you love him?"

"Yes, I love him."

"Does he love you?"

"He says—"

He caught her restless hands in his own. "Don't tell me what he says, tell me what you know."

"Yes, he loves me."

"Then stop hiding and go home. You should be having this conversation with him, not with your brother."

* * *

He was slowly going out of his mind. Every day Spence went by Natasha's apartment, certain that this time she would answer the door. When she didn't, he stalked over to harass Annie in the shop. He barely noticed the Christmas decorations in shop windows, the fat, cheerful Santas, the glittery angels, the colored lights strung around the houses. When he did, it was to scowl at them.

It had taken all of his efforts to make a show of holiday spirit for Freddie. He'd taken her to pick out a tree, spent hours decorating it with her and complimenting her crumbling popcorn strings. Dutifully he'd listened to her ever-growing Christmas list, and had taken her to the mall to sit in Santa's lap. But his heart wasn't in it.

It had to stop, he told himself and he stared out the window at the first snowfall. Whatever crisis he was facing, whatever chaos his life was in, he wouldn't see Freddie's Christmas spoiled.

She asked about Natasha every day. It only made it more difficult because he had no answers. He'd watched Freddie play an angel in her school's Christmas pageant and wished Natasha had been with him.

And what of their child? He could hardly think of anything else. Even now Natasha might be carrying the baby sister Freddie so coveted. The baby, Spence had already realized, that he desperately wanted. Unless... He didn't want to think of where she had gone, what she had done. How could he think of anything else?

There had to be a way to find her. When he did, he would beg, plead, browbeat and threaten until she came back to him.

She'd had a child. The fact left him dazed. A child she had lost, Spence remembered. But how, and when? Questions that needed answering crowded his mind. She had said she loved him, and he knew that saying it had been difficult for her. Even so, she had yet to trust him.

"Daddy." Freddie bounced into the room, her mind full of the Christmas that was only six days away. "We're making cookies."

He glanced over his shoulder to see Freddie grinning, her mouth smeared with red and green sugar. Spence swooped her up to hold her close. "I love you, Freddie."

She giggled, then kissed him. "I love you, too. Can you come make cookies with us?"

"In a little while. I have to go out first." He was going to go to the shop, corner Annie and find out where Natasha had gone. No matter what the redhead said, Spence didn't believe that Natasha would have left her assistant without a number where she could be reached.

Freddie's lip poked out while she fiddled with Spence's top button. "When will you come back?"

"Soon." He kissed her again before he set her down. "When I come back, I'll help you bake cookies. I promise."

Content, Freddie rushed back to Vera. She knew her father always kept his promises.

Natasha stood outside the front door as the snow fell. There were lights strung along the roof and around the posts. She wondered how they would look when they were lighted. There was a full-size Santa on the door, his load of presents making him bend from the waist. She remembered the witch that had stood there on Halloween. On that first night she and Spence had made love. On that night, she was certain, their child had been conceived.

For a moment she almost turned back, telling herself she should go to her apartment, unpack, catch her breath. But that would only be hiding again. She'd hidden long enough. Gathering her courage, she knocked.

The moment Freddie opened the door, the little girl's eyes shone. She let out a squeal and all but jumped into Natasha's arms. "You're back, you're back! I've been waiting for you forever."

Natasha held her close, swaying back and forth. This was what she wanted, needed, she realized as she buried her face in Freddie's hair. How could she have been such a fool? "It's only been a little while."

"It's been days and days. We got a tree and lights, and I already wrapped your present. I bought it myself at the mall. Don't go away again."

"No," Natasha murmured. "I won't." She set Freddie down to step inside and close out the cold and snow.

"You missed my play. I was an angel."

"I'm sorry."

"We made the halos in school and got to keep them, so I can show you how I looked."

"I'd like that."

Certain everything was back to normal, Freddie took her hand. "I tripped once, but I remembered all my lines. Mikey forgot his. I said 'A child is born in Bethlehem,' and 'Peace on Earth,' and sang 'Gloria in selfish Deo.'"

Natasha laughed for the first time in days. "I wish I had heard that. You will sing it for me later?"

"Okay. We're baking cookies." Still holding Natasha's hand, she began to drag her toward the kitchen.

"Is your daddy helping you?"

"No, he had to go out. He said he'd come back soon and bake some. He promised."

Torn between relief and disappointment, Natasha followed Freddie into the kitchen.

"Vera, Tash is back."

"I see." Vera pursed her lips. Just when she'd thought Natasha *might* be good enough for the *señor* and her baby, the woman had gone off without a word. Still, she knew her duty. "Would you like some coffee or tea, miss?"

"No, thank you. I don't want to be in your way."

"You have to stay." Freddie tugged at Natasha's hand again. "Look, I've made snowmen and reindeers and Santas." She plucked what she considered one of her best creations from the counter. "You can have one."

"It's beautiful." Natasha looked down at the snowman with red sugar clumped on his face and the brim of his hat broken off.

"Are you going to cry?" Freddie asked.

"No." She managed to blink back the mist of tears. "I'm just glad to be home."

As she spoke, the kitchen door opened. Natasha held her breath when Spence stepped into the room. He didn't speak. His hand still on the door, he stopped to stare. It was as if he'd conjured her up out of his own chaotic thoughts. There was snow melting in her hair and on the shoulders of her coat. Her eyes were bright, teary.

"Daddy, Tash is home," Freddie announced, running to him. "She's going to bake cookies with us."

Vera briskly untied her apron. Whatever doubts she'd had about Natasha were eclipsed by the look on her face. Vera knew a woman in love when she saw her. "We need more flour. Come, Freddie, we will go buy some."

"But I want to—"

"You want to bake, we need flour to bake. Come, we'll get your coat." Businesslike, Vera bustled Freddie out of the room.

Alone, Spence and Natasha stood where they were; the

moment stretched out. The heat in the kitchen was making her dizzy. Natasha stripped off her coat and laid it over the back of a chair. She wanted to talk to him, reasonably. That couldn't be done if she fainted at his feet.

"Spence." The word seemed to echo off the walls, and she took a deep breath. "I was hoping we could talk."

"I see. Now you've decided talking's a good idea."

She started to speak, then changed her mind. When the oven timer went off behind her, she turned automatically to take up the hot mitt and remove the latest batch of cookies from the oven. She took her time setting them on the cooling rack.

"You're right to be angry with me. I behaved very badly toward you. Now I have to ask you to listen to me, and hope you can forgive me."

He studied her for one long, silent moment. "You certainly know how to defuse an argument."

"I didn't come to argue with you. I've had time to think, and I realize that I chose a very poor way to tell you about the baby, then to leave as I did." She looked down at her hands, her tightly laced fingers. "To just run away was inexcusable. I can only tell you that I was afraid and confused and too emotional to think clearly."

"One question," he interjected, then waited until she lifted her head. He needed to see her face. "Is there still a baby?"

"Yes." The blank puzzlement in her eyes became awareness. Awareness became regret. "Oh, Spence, I'm sorry, so sorry to have caused you to think that I might have…" She blinked away tears, knowing her emotions were still too close to the surface. "I'm sorry. I went to Mikhail's to stay with him a few days." She let out a shaky breath. "May I sit?"

He only nodded, then moved to the window as she slid behind the table. Laying his palms upon the counter, he looked out at the snow. "I've been going out of my mind, wondering where you were, how you were. The state you were in when you left, I was terrified you'd do something rash before we could talk it through."

"I could never do what you thought, Spence. This is our baby."

"You said you didn't want it." He turned again. "You said you wouldn't go through it again."

"I was afraid," Natasha admitted. "And it's true I hadn't wanted to get pregnant, not now. Not ever. I'd like to tell you everything."

He wanted badly, much too badly, just to reach out to her, to hold her and tell her that nothing mattered. Because he knew it did matter, he busied himself at the stove. "Do you want some coffee?"

"No. It makes me sick now." She smiled a little when he fumbled with the pot. "Please, would you sit down?"

"All right." He sat down across from her, then spread his hands. "Go ahead."

"I told you that I had been in love with Anthony while I was with the corps de ballet. I was just seventeen when we became lovers. He was the first for me. There's been no one for me until you."

"Why?"

The answer was much easier than she'd believed. "I'd never loved again until you. The love I feel for you is much different from the fantasies I had for Anthony. With you it isn't dreams and knights and princes. With you it's real and solid. Day-to-day. Ordinary—ordinary in the most beautiful way. Can you understand?"

He looked at her. The room was quiet, insulated by the snow. It smelled of warm cookies and cinnamon. "Yes."

"I was afraid to feel this strongly for you, for anyone, because what happened between Anthony and me..." She waited a moment, surprised that there was no pain now, only sadness. "I had believed him, everything he said, everything he promised me. When I discovered he made many of the same promises to other women, I was crushed. We argued, and he sent me away like a child who had displeased him. A few weeks later I discovered I was pregnant. I was thrilled. I could only think that I was carrying Anthony's child and that when I told him, he would see that we belonged together. Then I told him."

Spence reached for her hand without a word.

"It was not as I had imagined. He was angry. The things he said.... It doesn't matter," she went on. "He didn't want me, he didn't want the child. In those few moments I grew up years. He wasn't the man I had wanted him to be, but I had the child. I wanted that baby." Her fingers tightened on his. "I so desperately wanted that baby."

"What did you do?"

"The only thing I could. There could be no dancing now. I left the company and went home. I know it was a burden for my parents, but they stood by me. I got a job in a department store. Selling toys." She smiled at that.

"It must have been difficult for you." He tried to imagine her, a teenager, pregnant, deserted by the father of her child, struggling to hold it all together.

"Yes, it was. It was also a wonderful time. My body changed. After the first month or two when I felt so fragile, I began to feel strong. So strong. I would sit in bed at night and read books on babies and birthing. I would ask Mama dozens of questions. I knit—badly," she said with a quiet laugh. "Papa built a bassinet, and Mama sewed a white skirt with pink and blue ribbons. It was beautiful." She felt the tears well up and shook her head. "Could I have some water?"

He rose, and filling a glass from the tap, set it beside her. "Take your time, Natasha." Because he knew they both needed it, he stroked her hair. "You don't have to tell me everything at once."

"I need to." She sipped slowly, waiting for him to sit down again. "I called her Lily," she murmured. "She was so lovely, so tiny and soft. I had no idea it was possible to love anything, anyone, the way you love a child. I would watch her sleep for hours, so thrilled, so awed that she had come from me."

The tears were falling now, soundlessly. One fell onto the back of her hand. "It was hot that summer, and I would take her out in this little carriage to get air and sunshine. People would stop to look at her. She hardly cried, and when I nursed her, she would put a hand on my breast and watch me with those big eyes. You know what it is. You have Freddie."

"I know. There's nothing like having a child."

"Or losing one," Natasha said softly. "It was so quick. She was only five weeks old. I woke up in the morning, surprised that she had slept through the night. My breasts were full of milk. The bassinet was by my bed. I reached down for her, picked her up. At first I didn't understand, didn't believe...." She broke off to press her hands to her eyes. "I remember screaming and screaming—Rachel rushing up out of the next bed, the rest of the family running in—Mama taking her from me." The silent tears turned to weeping. Her face now covered by her hands, she let go in a way she usually only allowed herself in private.

There was nothing he could say, nothing to be said. Instead of searching for meaningless words, he rose to crouch beside her and gather her into his arms. The passion of her grief held sway. Then on a half sob, she turned and clung to him, accepting comfort.

Her hands were fisted against his back. Gradually they relaxed as he kept her close. The hot tears slowed, and the pain, now shared, eased.

"I'm all right," she managed at length. Pulling away, she began to fumble in her bag for a tissue. Spence took it from her to dry her cheeks himself. "The doctor called it crib death. No reason," she said as she closed her eyes once more. "That was somehow worse. Not knowing why, not being sure if I could have stopped it."

"No." He took both her hands and she opened her eyes. "Don't do that. Listen to me. I can only imagine what it would be like to go through what you went through, but I know that when truly horrible things happen, it's usually out of our control."

"It took me a long time to accept what I can never understand." She turned over her hands in his. "A long time to start living again, going back to work, finally moving here, starting my business. I think I would have died without my family." She gave herself a moment, sipping the water to cool her dry throat. "I didn't want to love anyone again. Then there was you. And Freddie."

"We need you, Natasha. And you need us."

"Yes." She took his hand to press it to her lips. "I want you to understand. Spence, when I learned I was pregnant, it all came flying back at me. I tell you, I don't think I could survive going through that again. I'm so afraid to love this child. And I already do."

"Come here." He lifted her to her feet, keeping her hands

locked tight in his. "I know that you loved Lily, and that you'll always love her and grieve for her. So will I now. What happened before can't be changed, but this is a different place, a different time. A different child. I want you to understand that we're going to go through this pregnancy, the birth and the rearing together. Whether you want me or not."

"I'm afraid."

"Then we'll be afraid together. And when this baby is eight and rides a two-wheeler for the first time, we'll be afraid together."

Her lips trembled into a smile. "When you say it, I can almost believe it."

"Believe it." He bent to kiss her. "Because it's a promise."

"Yes, it's time for promises." Her smile grew. "I love you." It was so easy to say it now. So easy to feel it. "Will you hold me?"

"On one condition." He rubbed away a drying tear with his thumb. "I want to tell Freddie she's expecting a baby brother or sister. I think it would make a great Christmas present for her."

"Yes." She felt stronger, surer. "I want us to tell her."

"All right, you've got five days."

"Five days for what?"

"To make whatever plans you want to make, to arrange to have your family come down, buy a dress, whatever you need to do to get ready for the wedding."

"But—"

"No buts." He framed her face with his hands and silenced her. "I love you, I want you. You're the best thing to come into my life since Freddie, and I don't intend to lose you. We've made a child, Natasha." Watching her, he laid a hand on her stomach, gently possessive. "A child I want. A child I already love."

In a gesture of trust, she placed her hand on his. "I won't be afraid if you're with me."

"We have a date here Christmas Eve. I'm going to wake up Christmas morning with my wife."

She steadied herself by putting her hands on his forearms. "Just like that?"

"Just like that."

With a laugh, she threw her arms around his neck and said one word. "Yes."

Epilogue

Christmas Eve was the most beautiful day in the year as far as Natasha was concerned. It was a time to celebrate life and love and family.

The house was quiet when she came in. She was drawn to the tree and the light. She sent an angel spinning on one branch, then turned to study the room.

On the table there was a papier-mâché reindeer with only one ear. Compliments of Freddie's second-grade art class. Beside it stood a pudgy snowman holding a lantern. An exquisite porcelain crèche was displayed on the mantel. Beneath it hung four stockings. A fire crackled in the grate.

A year before she had stood before the fire and promised to love, honor and cherish. They had been the easiest promises she had ever had to keep. Now this was her home.

Home. She took a deep breath to draw in the scents of pine and candles. It was so good to be home. Last-minute shoppers had crowded The Fun House until late in the afternoon. Now there was only family.

"Mama." Freddie raced in, trailing a bright red ribbon. "You're home."

"I'm home." Laughing, Natasha scooped her up to spin her around.

"We took Vera to the airport so she can spend Christmas with her sister, then we watched the planes. Daddy said when you got home we'd have dinner, then sing Christmas carols."

"Daddy's absolutely right." Natasha draped the ribbon over Freddie's shoulder. "What's this?"

"I'm wrapping a present, all by myself. It's for you."

"For me? What is it?"

"I can't tell you."

"Yes, you can. Watch." She dropped onto the couch to run her fingers along Freddie's ribs. "It'll be easy," she said as Freddie squealed and squirmed.

"Torturing the child again," Spence commented from the doorway.

"Daddy!" Springing up, Freddie raced to him. "I didn't tell."

"I knew I could count on you, funny face. Look who woke up." He bounced a baby on his hip.

"Here, Brandon." Madly in love, Freddie passed up the ribbon so that he could play with it. "It's pretty, just like you."

At six months, young Brandon Kimball was chubby, rosy-cheeked and delighted with the world in general. He clutched the ribbon in one hand and reached for Freddie's hair with the other.

Walking over, Natasha held out her arms. "Such a big

boy," she murmured as her son reached for her. Gathering him close, she pressed a kiss to his throat. "So beautiful."

"He looks just like his mother." Spence stroked a hand over Brandon's thick, black curls. As if he approved of the statement, Brandon let out a gurgling laugh. When he wriggled, Natasha set him down to crawl on the rug.

"It's his first Christmas." Natasha watched him scoot over to torment one of the cats and saw Lucy dart under the sofa. She's no fool, Natasha thought happily.

"And our second." He turned Natasha into his arms. "Happy anniversary."

Natasha kissed him once, then twice. "Have I told you today that I love you?"

"Not since I called you this afternoon."

"Much too long ago." She slipped her arms around his waist. "I love you. Thank you for the most wonderful year of my life."

"You're very welcome." He glanced over her head only long enough to see that Freddie had prevented Brandon from pulling an ornament from a low branch. "But it's only going to get better."

"Do you promise?"

He smiled and lowered his mouth to hers again. "Absolutely."

Freddie stopped crawling with Brandon to watch them. A baby brother had turned out to be nice, after all, but she was still holding out for that baby sister. She smiled as she saw her parents embrace.

Maybe next Christmas.

* * * * *

LURING A LADY

Chapter 1

She wasn't a patient woman. Delays and excuses were barely tolerated, and never tolerated well. Waiting—and she was waiting now—had her temper dropping degree by degree toward ice. With Sydney Hayward icy anger was a great deal more dangerous than boiling rage. One frigid glance, one frosty phrase could make the recipient quake. And she knew it.

Now she paced her new office, ten stories up in midtown Manhattan. She swept from corner to corner over the deep oatmeal-colored carpet. Everything was perfectly in place, papers, files, coordinated appointment and address books. Even her brass-and-ebony desk set was perfectly aligned, the pens and pencils marching in a straight row across the polished mahogany, the notepads carefully placed beside the phone.

Her appearance mirrored the meticulous precision and tasteful elegance of the office. Her crisp beige suit was all straight lines and starch, but didn't disguise the fact that there was a great pair of legs striding across the carpet. With it she wore a single strand of pearls, earrings to match and a slim gold watch, all very discreet and exclusive. As a Hayward, she'd been raised to be both.

Her dark auburn hair was swept off her neck and secured with a gold clip. The pale freckles that went with the hair were nearly invisible after a light dusting of powder. Sydney felt they made her look too young and too vulnerable. At twenty-eight she had a face that reflected her breeding. High, slashing cheekbones, the strong, slightly pointed chin, the small straight nose. An aristocratic face, it was pale as porcelain, with a softly shaped mouth she knew could sulk too easily, and large smoky-blue eyes that people often mistook for guileless.

Sydney glanced at her watch again, let out a little hiss of breath, then marched over to her desk. Before she could pick up the phone, her intercom buzzed.

"Yes."

"Ms. Hayward. There's a man here who insists on seeing the person in charge of the Soho project. And your four-o'clock appointment—"

"It's now four-fifteen," Sydney cut in, her voice low and smooth and final. "Send him in."

"Yes, ma'am, but he's not Mr. Howington."

So Howington had sent an underling. Annoyance hiked Sydney's chin up another fraction. "Send him in," she repeated, and flicked off the intercom with one frosted pink nail. So, they thought she'd be pacified with a junior executive. Sydney took a deep breath and prepared to kill the messenger.

It was years of training that prevented her mouth from dropping open when the man walked in. No, not walked, she corrected. Swaggered. Like a black-patched pirate over the rolling deck of a boarded ship.

She wished she'd had the foresight to have fired a warning shot over his bow.

Her initial shock had nothing to do with the fact that he was wildly handsome, though the adjective suited perfectly. A mane of thick, curling black hair flowed just beyond the nape of his neck, to be caught by a leather thong in a short ponytail that did nothing to detract from rampant masculinity. His face was rawboned and lean, with skin the color of an old gold coin. Hooded eyes were nearly as black as his hair. His full lips were shadowed by a day or two's growth of beard that gave him a rough and dangerous look.

Though he skimmed under six foot and was leanly built, he made her delicately furnished office resemble a doll's house.

What was worse was the fact that he wore work clothes. Dusty jeans and a sweaty T-shirt with a pair of scarred boots that left a trail of dirt across her pale carpet. They hadn't even bothered with the junior executive, she thought as her lips firmed, but had sent along a common laborer who hadn't had the sense to clean up before the interview.

"You're Hayward?" The insolence in the tone and the slight hint of a Slavic accent had her imagining him striding up to a camp fire with a whip tucked in his belt.

The misty romance of the image made her tone unnecessarily sharp. "Yes, and you're late."

His eyes narrowed fractionally as they studied each other across the desk. "Am I?"

"Yes. You might find it helpful to wear a watch. My time is valuable if yours is not. Mr...."

"Stanislaski." He hooked his thumbs in the belt loops

of his jeans, shifting his weight easily, arrogantly onto one hip. "Sydney's a man's name."

She arched a brow. "Obviously you're mistaken."

He skimmed his gaze over her slowly, with as much interest as annoyance. She was pretty as a frosted cake, but he hadn't come straight and sweaty from a job to waste time with a female. "Obviously. I thought Hayward was an old man with a bald head and a white mustache."

"You're thinking of my grandfather."

"Ah, then it's your grandfather I want to see."

"That won't be possible, Mr. Stanislaski, as my grandfather's been dead for nearly two months."

The arrogance in his eyes turned quickly to compassion. "I'm sorry. It hurts to lose family."

She couldn't say why, of all the condolences she had received, these few words from a stranger touched her. "Yes, it does. Now, if you'll take a seat, we can get down to business."

Cold, hard and distant as the moon. Just as well, he thought. It would keep him from thinking of her in more personal ways—at least until he got what he wanted.

"I have sent your grandfather letters," he began as he settled into one of the trim Queen Anne chairs in front of the desk. "Perhaps the last were misplaced during the confusion of death."

An odd way to put it, Sydney thought, but apt. Her life had certainly been turned upside down in the past few months. "Correspondence should be addressed to me." She sat, folding her hands on the desk. "As you know Hayward Industries is considering several firms—"

"For what?"

She struggled to shrug off the irritation of being interrupted. "I beg your pardon?"

"For what are you considering several firms?"

If she had been alone, she would have sighed and shut her eyes. Instead, she drummed her fingers on the desk. "What position do you hold, Mr. Stanislaski?"

"Position?"

"Yes, yes, what is it you do?"

The impatience in her voice made him grin. His teeth were very white, and not quite straight. "You mean, what is it I do? I work with wood."

"You're a carpenter?"

"Sometimes."

"Sometimes," she repeated, and sat back. Behind her, buildings punched into a hard blue sky. "Perhaps you can tell me why Howington Construction sent a sometimes carpenter to represent them in this interview."

The room smelled of lemon and rosemary and only reminded him that he was hot, thirsty and as impatient as she. "I could—if they had sent me."

It took her a moment to realize he wasn't being deliberately obtuse. "You're not from Howington?"

"No. I'm Mikhail Stanislaski, and I live in one of your buildings." He propped a dirty boot on a dusty knee. "If you're thinking of hiring Howington, I would think again. I once worked for them, but they cut too many corners."

"Excuse me." Sydney gave the intercom a sharp jab. "Janine, did Mr. Stanislaski tell you he represented Howington?"

"Oh, no, ma'am. He just asked to see you. Howington called about ten minutes ago to reschedule. If you—"

"Never mind." Sitting back again, she studied the man

who was grinning at her. "Apparently I've been laboring under a misconception."

"If you mean you made a mistake, yes. I'm here to talk to you about your apartment building in Soho."

She wanted, badly, to drag her hands through her hair. "You're here with a tenant complaint?"

"I'm here with many tenants' complaints," he corrected.

"You should be aware that there's a certain procedure one follows in this kind of matter."

He lifted one black brow. "You own the building, yes?"

"Yes, but—"

"Then it's your responsibility."

She stiffened. "I'm perfectly aware of my responsibilities, Mr. Stanislaski. And now…"

He rose as she did, and didn't budge an inch. "Your grandfather made promises. To honor him, you must keep them."

"What I must do," she said in a frigid voice, "is run my business." And she was trying desperately to learn how. "You may tell the other tenants that Hayward is at the point of hiring a contractor as we're quite aware that many of our properties are in need of repair or renovation. The apartments in Soho will be dealt with in turn."

His expression didn't change at the dismissal, nor did the tone of his voice or the spread-legged, feet-planted stance. "We're tired of waiting for our turn. We want what was promised to us, now."

"If you'll send me a list of your demands—"

"We have."

She set her teeth. "Then I'll look over the files this evening."

"Files aren't people. You take the rent money every month, but you don't think of the people." He placed his hands on the desk and leaned forward. Sydney caught a wisp of sawdust and sweat that was uncomfortably appealing. "Have you seen the building, or the people who live in it?"

"I have reports," she began.

"Reports." He swore—it wasn't in a language she understood, but she was certain it was an oath. "You have your accountants and your lawyers, and you sit up here in your pretty office and look through papers." With one quick slash of the hand, he dismissed her office and herself. "But you know nothing. It's not you who's cold when the heat doesn't work, or who must climb five flights of stairs when the elevator is broken. You don't worry that the water won't get hot or that the wiring is too old to be safe."

No one spoke to her that way. No one. Her own temper was making her heart beat too fast. It made her forget that she was facing a very dangerous man. "You're wrong. I'm very concerned about all of those things. And I intend to correct them as soon as possible."

His eyes flashed and narrowed, like a sword raised and turned on its edge. "This is a promise we've heard before."

"Now, it's my promise, and you haven't had that before."

"And we're supposed to trust you. You, who are too lazy or too afraid to even go see what she owns."

Her face went dead white, the only outward sign of fury. "I've had enough of your insults for one afternoon, Mr. Stanislaski. Now, you can either find your way out, or I'll call security to help you find it."

"I know my way," he said evenly. "I'll tell you this, Miss Sydney Hayward, you will begin to keep those promises within two days, or we'll go to the building commissioner, and the press."

Sydney waited until he had stalked out before she sat

again. Slowly she took a sheet of stationery from the drawer then methodically tore it into shreds. She stared at the smudges his big wide-palmed hands had left on her glossy desk and chose and shredded another sheet. Calmer, she punched the intercom. "Janine, bring me everything you've got on the Soho project."

An hour later, Sydney pushed the files aside and made two calls. The first was to cancel her dinner plans for the evening. The second was to Lloyd Bingham, her grandfather's—now her—executive assistant.

"You just caught me," Lloyd told her as he walked into Sydney's office. "I was on my way out. What can I do for you?"

Sydney shot him a brief glance. He was a handsome, ambitious man who preferred Italian tailors and French food. Not yet forty, he was on his second divorce and liked to escort society women who were attracted to his smooth blond looks and polished manners. Sydney knew that he had worked hard and long to gain his position with Hayward and that he had taken over the reins during her grandfather's illness the past year.

She also knew that he resented her because she was sitting behind a desk he considered rightfully his.

"For starters, you can explain why nothing has been done about the Soho apartments."

"The unit in Soho?" Lloyd took a cigarette from a slim gold case. "It's on the agenda."

"It's been on the agenda for nearly eighteen months. The first letter in the file, signed by the tenants, was dated almost two years ago and lists twenty-seven specific complaints."

"And I believe you'll also see in the file that a number of

them were addressed." He blew out a thin stream of smoke as he made himself comfortable on one of the chairs.

"A number of them," Sydney repeated. "Such as the furnace repairs. The tenants seemed to think a new furnace was required."

Lloyd made a vague gesture. "You're new to the game, Sydney. You'll find that tenants always want new, better and more."

"That may be. However, it hardly seems cost-effective to me to repair a thirty-year-old furnace and have it break down again two months later." She held up a finger before he could speak. "Broken railings in stairwells, peeling paint, an insufficient water heater, a defective elevator, cracked porcelain…" She glanced up. "I could go on, but it doesn't seem necessary. There's a memo here, from my grandfather to you, requesting that you take over the repairs and maintenance of this building."

"Which I did," Lloyd said stiffly. "You know very well that your grandfather's health turned this company upside down over the last year. That apartment complex is only one of several buildings he owned."

"You're absolutely right." Her voice was quiet but without warmth. "I also know that we have a responsibility, a legal and a moral responsibility to our tenants, whether the building is in Soho or on Central Park West." She closed the folder, linked her hands over it and, in that gesture, stated ownership. "I don't want to antagonize you, Lloyd, but I want you to understand that I've decided to handle this particular property myself."

"Why?"

She granted him a small smile. "I'm not entirely sure. Let's just say I want to get my feet wet, and I've decided to make this property my pet project. In the meantime, I'd like you to look over the reports on the construction firms, and give me your recommendations." She offered him another file. "I've included a list of the properties, in order of priority. We'll have a meeting Friday, ten o'clock, to finalize."

"All right." He tapped out his cigarette before he rose. "Sydney, I hope you won't take offense, but a woman who's spent most of her life traveling and buying clothes doesn't know much about business, or making a profit."

She did take offense, but she'd be damned if she'd show it. "Then I'd better learn, hadn't I? Good night, Lloyd."

Not until the door closed did she look down at her hands. They were shaking. He was right, absolutely right to point out her inadequacies. But he couldn't know how badly she needed to prove herself here, to make something out of what her grandfather had left her. Nor could he know how terrified she was that she would let down the family name. Again.

Before she could change her mind, she tucked the file into her briefcase and left the office. She walked down the wide pastel corridor with its tasteful watercolors and thriving ficus trees, through the thick glass doors that closed in her suite of offices. She took her private elevator down to the lobby, where she nodded to the guard before she walked outside.

The heat punched like a fist. Though it was only mid-June, New York was in the clutches of a vicious heat wave with temperatures and humidity spiraling gleefully. She had only to cross the sidewalk to be cocooned in the waiting car, sheltered from the dripping air and noise. After giving her driver the address, she settled back for the ride to Soho.

Traffic was miserable, snarling and edgy. But that would only give her more time to think. She wasn't certain what she was going to do when she got there. Nor was she sure what she would do if she ran into Mikhail Stanislaski again.

He'd made quite an impression on her, Sydney mused. Exotic looks, hot eyes, a complete lack of courtesy. The worst part was the file had shown that he'd had a perfect right to be rude and impatient. He'd written letter after letter during the past year, only to be put off with half-baked promises.

Perhaps if her grandfather hadn't been so stubborn about keeping his illness out of the press. Sydney rubbed a finger over her temple and wished she'd taken a couple of aspirin before she'd left the office.

Whatever had happened before, she was in charge now. She intended to respect her inheritance and all the responsibilities that went with it. She closed her eyes and fell into a half doze as her driver fought his way downtown.

Inside his apartment, Mikhail carved a piece of cherry-wood. He wasn't sure why he continued. His heart wasn't in it, but he felt it more productive to do something with his hands.

He kept thinking about the woman. Sydney. All ice and pride, he thought. One of the aristocrats it was in his blood to rebel against. Though he and his family had escaped to America when he had still been a child, there was no denying his heritage. His ancestors had been Gypsies in the Ukraine, hot-blooded, hot tempered and with little respect for structured authority.

Mikhail considered himself to be American—except when it suited him to be Russian.

Curls of wood fell on the table or the floor. Most of his cramped living space was taken up with his work—blocks and slabs of wood, even an oak burl, knives, chisels, hammers, drills, calipers. There was a small lathe in the corner and jars that held brushes. The room smelled of linseed oil, sweat and sawdust.

Mikhail took a pull from the beer at his elbow and sat back to study the cherry. It wasn't ready, as yet, to let him see what was inside. He let his fingers roam over it, over the grain, into the grooves, while the sound of traffic and music and shouts rose up and through the open window at his back.

He had had enough success in the past two years that he could have moved into bigger and more modern dwellings. He liked it here, in this noisy neighborhood, with the bakery on the corner, the bazaarlike atmosphere on Canal, only a short walk away, the women who gossiped from their stoops in the morning, the men who sat there at night.

He didn't need wall-to-wall carpet or a sunken tub or a big stylish kitchen. All he wanted was a roof that didn't leak, a shower that offered hot water and a refrigerator that would keep the beer and cold cuts cold. At the moment, he didn't have any of those things. And Miss Sydney Hayward hadn't seen the last of him.

He glanced up at the three brisk knocks on his door, then grinned as his down-the-hall neighbor burst in. "What's the story?"

Keely O'Brian slammed the door, leaned dramatically against it, then did a quick jig. "I got the part." Letting out a whoop, she raced to the table to throw her arms around Mikhail's neck. "I got it." She gave him a loud, smacking kiss on one cheek. "I got it." Then the other.

"I told you you would." He reached back to ruffle her short cap of dusty blond hair. "Get a beer. We'll celebrate."

"Oh, Mik." She crossed to the tiny refrigerator on long, slim legs left stunningly revealed by a pair of neon green shorts. "I was so nervous before the audition I got the hiccups, then I drank a gallon of water and sloshed my way through the reading." She tossed the cap into the trash before toasting herself. "And I still got it. A movie of the week. I'll probably only get like sixth or seventh billing, but I don't get murdered till the third act." She took a sip, then let out a long, bloodcurdling scream. "That's what I have to do when the serial killer corners me in the alley. I really think my scream turned the tide."

"No doubt." As always, her quick, nervous speech amused him. She was twenty-three, with an appealing coltish body, lively green eyes and a heart as wide as the Grand Canyon. If Mikhail hadn't felt so much like her brother right from the beginning of their relationship, he would have long since attempted to talk her into bed.

Keely took a sip of beer. "Hey, do you want to order some Chinese or pizza or something? I've got a frozen pizza, but my oven is on the blink again."

The simple statement made his eyes flash and his lips purse. "I went today to see Hayward."

The bottle paused on the way to her lips. "In person? You mean like, face-to-face?"

"Yes." Mikhail set aside his carving tools, afraid he would gouge the wood.

Impressed, Keely walked over to sit on the windowsill. "Wow. So, what's he like?"

"He's dead."

She choked on the beer, watching him wide-eyed as she pounded on her chest. "Dead? You didn't…"

"Kill him?" This time Mikhail smiled. Another thing he enjoyed about Keely was her innate flare for the dramatic. "No, but I considered killing the new Hayward—his granddaughter."

"The new landlord's a woman? What's she like?"

"Very beautiful, very cold." He was frowning as he skimmed his fingertips over the wood grain. "She has red hair and white skin. Blue eyes like frost on a lake. When she speaks, icicles form."

Keely grimaced and sipped. "Rich people," she said, "can afford to be cold."

"I told her she has two days before I go to the building commissioner."

This time Keely smiled. As much as she admired Mikhail, she felt he was naive in a lot of ways. "Good luck. Maybe we should take Mrs. Bayford's idea about a rent strike. Of course, then we risk eviction, but…hey." She leaned out the open window. "You should see this car. It's like a Lincoln or something—with a driver. There's a woman getting out of the back." More fascinated than envious, she let out a long, appreciative breath. "*Harper's Bazaar*'s version of the executive woman." Grinning, she shot a glance over her shoulder. "I think your ice princess has come slumming."

Outside, Sydney studied the building. It was really quite lovely, she thought. Like an old woman who had maintained her dignity and a shadow of her youthful beauty. The red brick had faded to a soft pink, smudged here and there by soot and exhaust. The trimming paint was peeling and cracked, but that could be easily remedied. Taking out a legal pad, she began to take notes.

She was aware that the men sitting out on the stoop were watching her, but she ignored them. It was a noisy place, she noted. Most of the windows were open and there was a variety of sounds—televisions, radios, babies crying, someone singing "The Desert Song" in a warbling soprano. There were useless little balconies crowded with potted flowers, bicycles, clothes drying in the still, hot air.

Shading her eyes, she let her gaze travel up. Most of the railings were badly rusted and many had spokes missing. She frowned, then spotted Mikhail, leaning out of a window on the top floor, nearly cheek to cheek with a stunning blonde. Since he was bare chested and the blonde was wearing the tiniest excuse for a tank top, Sydney imagined she'd interrupted them. She acknowledged him with a frigid nod, then went back to her notes.

When she started toward the entrance, the men shifted to make a path for her. The small lobby was dim and oppressively hot. On this level the windows were apparently painted shut. The old parquet floor was scarred and scraped, and there was a smell, a very definite smell, of mold. She studied the elevator dubiously. Someone had hand-lettered a sign above the button that read Abandon Hope Ye Who Enter Here.

Curious, Sydney punched the up button and listened to the grinding rattles and wheezes. On an impatient breath, she made more notes. It was deplorable, she thought. The unit should have been inspected, and Hayward should have been slapped with a citation. Well, she was Hayward now.

The doors squeaked open, and Mikhail stepped out.

"Did you come to look over your empire?" he asked her.

Very deliberately she finished her notes before she met his gaze. At least he had pulled on a shirt—if you could call it that. The thin white T-shirt was ripped at the sleeves and mangled at the hem.

"I believe I told you I'd look over the file. Once I did, I thought it best to inspect the building myself." She glanced at the elevator, then back at him. "You're either very brave or very stupid, Mr. Stanislaski."

"A realist," he corrected with a slow shrug. "What happens, happens."

"Perhaps. But I'd prefer that no one use this elevator until it's repaired or replaced."

He slipped his hands into his pockets. "And will it be?"

"Yes, as quickly as possible. I believe you mentioned in your letter that some of the stair railings were broken."

"I've replaced the worst of them."

Her brow lifted. "You?"

"There are children and old people in this building."

The simplicity of his answer made her ashamed. "I see. Since you've taken it on yourself to represent the tenants, perhaps you'd take me through and show me the worst of the problems."

As they started up the stairs, she noted that the railing was obviously new, an unstained line of wood that was sturdy under her hand. She made a note that it had been replaced by a tenant.

He knocked on apartment doors. People greeted him enthusiastically, her warily. There were smells of cooking—meals just finished, meals yet to be eaten. She was offered strudel, brownies, goulash, chicken wings. Some of the complaints were bitter, some were nervous. But Sydney saw for herself that Mikhail's letters hadn't exaggerated.

By the time they reached the third floor, the heat was making her dizzy. On the fourth, she refused the offer of spaghetti and meatballs—wondering how anyone could bear to cook in all this heat—and accepted a glass of water. Dutifully she noted down how the pipes rattled and thumped. When they reached the fifth floor, she was wishing desperately for a cool shower, a chilled glass of chardonnay and the blissful comfort of her air-conditioned apartment.

Mikhail noted that her face was glowing from the heat. On the last flight of stairs, she'd been puffing a bit, which pleased him. It wouldn't hurt the queen to see how her subjects lived. He wondered why she didn't at least peel off her suit jacket or loosen a couple of those prim buttons on her blouse.

He wasn't pleased with the thought that he would enjoy doing both of those things for her.

"I would think that some of these tenants would have window units." Sweat slithered nastily down her back. "Air-conditioning."

"The wiring won't handle it," he told her. "When people turn them on, it blows the fuses and we lose power. The hallways are the worst," he went on conversationally. "Airless. And up here is worst of all. Heat rises."

"So I've heard."

She was white as a sheet, he noted, and swore. "Take off your jacket."

"I beg your pardon?"

"You're stupid." He tugged the linen off her shoulders and began to pull her arms free.

The combination of heat and his rough, purposeful fingers had spots dancing in front of her eyes. "Stop it."

"Very stupid. This is not a boardroom."

His touch wasn't the least bit loverlike, but it was very disturbing. She batted at his hands the moment one of her arms was free. Ignoring her, Mikhail pushed her into his apartment.

"Mr. Stanislaski," she said, out of breath but not out of dignity. "I will not be pawed."

"I have doubts you've ever been pawed in your life, Your Highness. What man wants frostbite? Sit."

"I have no desire to—"

He simply shoved her into a chair, then glanced over where Keely stood in the kitchen, gaping. "Get her some water," he ordered.

Sydney caught her breath. A fan whirled beside the chair and cooled her skin. "You are the rudest, most ill-mannered, most insufferable man I've ever been forced to deal with."

He took the glass from Keely and was tempted to toss the contents into Sydney's beautiful face. Instead he shoved the glass into her hand. "Drink."

"Jeez, Mik, have a heart," Keely murmured. "She looks beat. You want a cold cloth?" Even as she offered, she couldn't help but admire the ivory silk blouse with its tiny pearl buttons.

"No, thank you. I'm fine."

"I'm Keely O'Brian, 502."

"Her oven doesn't work," Mikhail said. "And she gets no hot water. The roof leaks."

"Only when it rains." Keely tried to smile but got no response. "I guess I'll run along. Nice to meet you."

When they were alone, Sydney took slow sips of the tepid water. Mikhail hadn't complained about his own apartment, but she could see from where she sat that the linoleum on the kitchen floor was ripped, and the refrigerator was hopelessly small and out-of-date. She simply didn't have the energy to look at the rest.

His approach had been anything but tactful, still the bottom line was he was right and her company was wrong.

He sat on the edge of the kitchen counter and watched as color seeped slowly back into her cheeks. It relieved him. For a moment in the hall he'd been afraid she would faint. He already felt like a clod.

"Do you want food?" His voice was clipped and un-friendly. "You can have a sandwich."

She remembered that she was supposed to be dining at Le Cirque with the latest eligible bachelor her mother had chosen. "No, thank you. You don't think much of me, do you?"

He moved his shoulders in the way she now recognized as habit. "I think of you quite a bit."

She frowned and set the glass aside. The way he said it left a little too much to the imagination. "You said you were a carpenter?"

"I am sometimes a carpenter."

"You have a license?"

His eyes narrowed. "A contractor's license, yes. For remodeling, renovations."

"Then you'd have a list of other contractors you've worked with—electricians, plumbers, that sort of thing."

"Yes."

"Fine. Work up a bid on repairs, including the finish work, painting, tile, replacing fixtures, appliances. Have it on my desk in a week." She rose, picking up her crumpled jacket.

He stayed where he was as she folded the jacket over her arm, lifted her briefcase. "And then?"

She shot him a cool look. "And then, Mr. Stanislaski, I'm going to put my money where your mouth is. You're hired."

Chapter 2

"Mother, I really don't have time for this."

"Sydney, dear, one always has time for tea." So saying, Margerite Rothchild Hayward Kinsdale LaRue poured ginseng into a china cup. "I'm afraid you're taking this real estate business too seriously."

"Maybe because I'm in charge," Sydney muttered without looking up from the papers on her desk.

"I can't imagine what your grandfather was thinking of. But then, he always was an unusual man." She sighed a moment, remembering how fond she'd been of the old goat. "Come, darling, have some tea and one of these delightful little sandwiches. Even Madam Executive needs a spot of lunch."

Sydney gave in, hoping to move her mother along more quickly by being agreeable. "This is really very sweet of you. It's just that I'm pressed for time today."

"All this corporate nonsense," Margerite began as Sydney sat beside her. "I don't know why you bother. It would have been so simple to hire a manager or whatever." Margerite added a squirt of lemon to her cup before she sat back. "I realize it might be diverting for a while, but the thought of you with a career. Well, it seems so pointless."

"Does it?" Sydney murmured, struggling to keep the bitterness out of her voice. "I may surprise everyone and be good at it."

"Oh, I'm sure you'd be wonderful at whatever you do, darling." Her hand fluttered absently over Sydney's. The girl had been so little trouble as a child, she thought. Margerite really hadn't a clue how to deal with this sudden and—she was sure—temporary spot of rebellion. She tried placating. "And I was delighted when Grandfather Hayward left you all those nice buildings." She nibbled on a sandwich, a striking woman who looked ten years younger than her fifty years, groomed and polished in a Chanel suit. "But to actually become involved in running things." Baffled, she patted her carefully tinted chestnut hair. "Well, one might think it's just a bit unfeminine. A man is easily put off by what he considers a high-powered woman."

Sydney gave her mother's newly bare ring finger a pointed look. "Not every woman's sole ambition centers around a man."

"Oh, don't be silly." With a gay little laugh, Margerite patted her daughter's hand. "A husband isn't something a woman wants to be without for long. You mustn't be discouraged because you and Peter didn't work things out. First marriages are often just a testing ground."

Reining in her feelings, Sydney set her cup down carefully. "Is that what you consider your marriage to Father? A testing ground?"

"We both learned some valuable lessons from it, I'm

sure." Confident and content, she beamed at her daughter. "Now, dear, tell me about your evening with Channing. How was it?"

"Stifling."

Margerite's mild blue eyes flickered with annoyance. "Sydney, really."

"You asked." To fortify herself, Sydney picked up her tea again. Why was it, she asked herself, that she perpetually felt inadequate around the woman who had given birth to her. "I'm sorry, Mother, but we simply don't suit."

"Nonsense. You're perfectly suited. Channing Warfield is an intelligent, successful man from a very fine family."

"So was Peter."

China clinked against china as Margerite set her cup in its saucer. "Sydney, you must not compare every man you meet with Peter."

"I don't." Taking a chance, she laid a hand on her mother's. There was a bond there, there had to be. Why did she always feel as though her fingers were just sliding away from it? "Honestly, I don't compare Channing with anyone. The simple fact is, I find him stilted, boring and pretentious. It could be that I'd find any man the same just now. I'm not interested in men at this point of my life, Mother. I want to make something of myself."

"Make something of yourself," Margerite repeated, more stunned than angry. "You're a Hayward. You don't need to make yourself anything else." She plucked up a napkin to dab at her lips. "For heaven's sake, Sydney, you've been divorced from Peter for four years. It's time you found a suitable husband. It's women who write the invitations," she reminded her daughter. "And they have a policy of excluding beautiful, unattached females. You have a place in society, Sydney. And a responsibility to your name."

The familiar clutching in her stomach had Sydney setting the tea aside. "So you've always told me."

Satisfied that Sydney would be reasonable, she smiled. "If Channing won't do, there are others. But I really think you shouldn't be so quick to dismiss him. If I were twenty years younger...well." She glanced at her watch and gave a little squeak. "Dear me, I'm going to be late for the hairdresser. I'll just run and powder my nose first."

When Margerite slipped into the adjoining bath, Sydney leaned her head back and closed her eyes. Where was she to put all these feelings of guilt and inadequacy? How could she explain herself to her mother when she couldn't explain herself to herself?

Rising, she went back to her desk. She couldn't convince Margerite that her unwillingness to become involved again had nothing to do with Peter when, in fact, it did. They had been friends, damn it. She and Peter had grown up with each other, had cared for each other. They simply hadn't been in love with each other. Family pressure had pushed them down the aisle while they'd been too young to realize the mistake. Then they had spent the best part of two years trying miserably to make the marriage work.

The pity of it wasn't the divorce, but the fact that when they had finally parted, they were no longer friends. If she couldn't make a go of it with someone she'd cared for, someone she'd had so much in common with, someone she'd liked so much, surely the lack was in her.

All she wanted to do now was to feel deserving of her grandfather's faith in her. She'd been offered a different kind of responsibility, a different kind of challenge. This time, she couldn't afford to fail.

Wearily she answered her intercom. "Yes, Janine."

"Mr. Stanislaski's here, Miss Hayward. He doesn't have

an appointment, but he says he has some papers you wanted to see."

A full day early, she mused, and straightened her shoulders. "Send him in."

At least he'd shaved, she thought, though this time there were holes in his jeans. Closing the door, he took as long and as thorough a look at her. As if they were two boxers sizing up the competition from neutral corners.

She looked just as starched and prim as before, in one of her tidy business suits, this time in pale gray, with all those little silver buttons on her blouse done up to her smooth white throat. He glanced down at the tea tray with its delicate cups and tiny sandwiches. His lips curled.

"Interrupting your lunch, Hayward?"

"Not at all." She didn't bother to stand or smile but gestured him across the room. "Do you have the bid, Mr. Stanislaski?"

"Yes."

"You work fast."

He grinned. "Yes." He caught a scent—rather a clash of scents. Something very subtle and cool and another, florid and overly feminine. "You have company?"

Her brow arched. "Why do you ask?"

"There is perfume here that isn't yours." Then with a shrug, he handed her the papers he carried. "The first is what must be done, the second is what should be done."

"I see." She could feel the heat radiating off him. For some reason it felt comforting, life affirming. As if she'd stepped out of a dark cave into the sunlight. Sydney made certain her fingers didn't brush his as she took the papers. "You have estimates from the subcontractors?"

"They are there." While she glanced through his work,

he lifted one of the neat triangles of bread, sniffed at it like a wolf. "What is this stuff in here?"

She barely looked up. "Watercress."

With a grunt, he dropped it back onto the plate. "Why would you eat it?"

She looked up again, and this time, she smiled. "Good question."

She shouldn't have done that, he thought as he shifted his hands to his pockets. When she smiled, she changed. Her eyes warmed, her lips softened, and beauty became approachable rather than aloof.

It made him forget he wasn't the least bit interested in her type of woman.

"Then I'll ask you another question."

Her lips pursed as she scanned the list. She liked what she saw. "You seem to be full of them today."

"Why do you wear colors like that? Dull ones, when you should be wearing vivid. Sapphire or emerald."

It was surprise that had her staring at him. As far as she could remember, no one had ever questioned her taste. In some circles, she was thought to be quite elegant. "Are you a carpenter or a fashion consultant, Mr. Stanislaski?"

His shoulders moved. "I'm a man. Is this tea?" He lifted the pot and sniffed at the contents while she continued to gape at him. "It's too hot for tea. You have something cold?"

Shaking her head, she pressed her intercom. "Janine, bring in something cold for Mr. Stanislaski, please." Because she had a nagging urge to get up and inspect herself in a mirror, she cleared her throat. "There's quite a line of demarcation between your must and your should list, Mr.—"

"Mikhail," he said easily. "It's because there are more things you should do than things you must. Like life."

"Now a philosopher," she muttered. "We'll start with the must, and perhaps incorporate some of the should. If we work quickly, we could have a contract by the end of the week."

His nod was slow, considering. "You, too, work fast."

"When necessary. Now first, I'd like you to explain to me why I should replace all the windows."

"Because they're single glazed and not efficient."

"Yes, but—"

"Sydney, dear, the lighting in there is just ghastly. Oh." Margerite stopped at the doorway. "I beg your pardon, I see you're in a meeting." She would have looked down her nose at Mikhail's worn jeans, but she had a difficult time getting past his face. "How do you do?" she said, pleased that he had risen at her entrance.

"You are Sydney's mother?" Mikhail asked before Sydney could shoo Margerite along.

"Why, yes." Margerite's smile was reserved. She didn't approve of her daughter being on a first-name basis in her relationships with the help. Particularly when that help wore stubby ponytails and dirty boots. "How did you know?"

"Real beauty matures well."

"Oh." Charmed, Margerite allowed her smile to warm fractionally. Her lashes fluttered in reflex. "How kind."

"Mother, I'm sorry, but Mr. Stanislaski and I have business to discuss."

"Of course, of course." Margerite walked over to kiss the air an inch from her daughter's cheek. "I'll just be running along. Now, dear, you won't forget we're to have lunch next week? And I wanted to remind you that… Stanislaski," she repeated, turning back to Mikhail. "I thought you looked familiar. Oh, my." Suddenly breathless, she laid a hand on her heart. "You're Mikhail Stanislaski?"

"Yes. Have we met?"

"No. Oh, no, we haven't, but I saw your photo in *Art/ World*. I consider myself a patron." Face beaming, she skirted the desk and, under her daughter's astonished gaze, took his hands in hers. To Margerite, the ponytail was now artistic, the tattered jeans eccentric. "Your work, Mr. Stanislaski—magnificent. Truly magnificent. I bought two of your pieces from your last showing. I can't tell you what a pleasure this is."

"You flatter me."

"Not at all," Margerite insisted. "You're already being called one of the top artists of the nineties. And you've commissioned him." She turned to beam at her speechless daughter. "A brilliant move, darling."

"I—actually, I—"

"I'm delighted," Mikhail interrupted, "to be working with your daughter."

"It's wonderful." She gave his hands a final squeeze. "You must come to a little dinner party I'm having on Friday on Long Island. Please, don't tell me you're already engaged for the evening." She slanted a look from under her lashes. "I'll be devastated."

He was careful not to grin over her head at Sydney. "I could never be responsible for devastating a beautiful woman."

"Fabulous. Sydney will bring you. Eight o'clock. Now I must run." She patted her hair, shot an absent wave at Sydney and hurried out just as Janine brought in a soft drink.

Mikhail took the glass with thanks, then sat again. "So," he began, "you were asking about windows."

Sydney very carefully relaxed the hands that were balled into fists under her desk. "You said you were a carpenter."

"Sometimes I am." He took a long, cooling drink. "Sometimes I carve wood instead of hammering it."

If he had set out to make a fool of her—which she wasn't sure he hadn't—he could have succeeded no better. "I've spent the last two years in Europe," she told him, "so I'm a bit out of touch with the American art world."

"You don't have to apologize," he said, enjoying himself.

"I'm not apologizing." She had to force herself to speak calmly, to not stand up and rip his bid into tiny little pieces. "I'd like to know what kind of game you're playing, Stanislaski."

"You offered me work, on a job that has some value for me. I am accepting it."

"You lied to me."

"How?" He lifted one hand, palm up. "I have a contractor's license. I've made my living in construction since I was sixteen. What difference does it make to you if people now buy my sculpture?"

"None." She snatched up the bids again. He probably produced primitive, ugly pieces in any case, she thought. The man was too rough and unmannered to be an artist. All that mattered was that he could do the job she was hiring him to do.

But she hated being duped. To make him pay for it, she forced him to go over every detail of the bid, wasting over an hour of his time and hers.

"All right then." She pushed aside her own meticulous notes. "Your contract will be ready for signing on Friday."

"Good." He rose. "You can bring it when you pick me up. We should make it seven."

"Excuse me?"

"For dinner." He leaned forward. For a shocking moment, she thought he was actually going to kiss her. She went rigid as a spear, but he only rubbed the lapel of her suit between his thumb and forefinger. "You must wear something with color."

She pushed the chair back and stood. "I have no intention of taking you to my mother's home for dinner."

"You're afraid to be with me." He said so with no little amount of pride.

Her chin jutted out. "Certainly not."

"What else could it be?" With his eyes on hers, he strolled around the desk until they were face-to-face. "A woman like you could not be so ill-mannered without a reason."

The breath was backing up in her lungs. Sydney forced it out in one huff. "It's reason enough that I dislike you."

He only smiled and toyed with the pearls at her throat. "No. Aristocrats are predictable, Hayward. You would be taught to tolerate people you don't like. For them, you would be the most polite."

"Stop touching me."

"I'm putting color in your cheeks." He laughed and let the pearls slide out of his fingers. Her skin, he was sure, would be just as smooth, just as cool. "Come now, Sydney, what will you tell your charming mother when you go to her party without me? How will you explain that you refused to bring me?" He could see the war in her eyes, the one fought between pride and manners and temper, and laughed again. "Trapped by your breeding," he murmured. "This is not something I have to worry about myself."

"No doubt," she said between her teeth.

"Friday," he said, and infuriated her by flicking a finger down her cheek. "Seven o'clock."

"Mr. Stanislaski," she murmured when he reached the

door. As he turned back, she offered her coolest smile. "Try to find something in your closet without holes in it."

She could hear him laughing at her as he walked down the hallway. If only, she thought as she dropped back into her chair. If only she hadn't been so well-bred, she could have released some of this venom by throwing breakables at the door.

She wore black quite deliberately. Under no circumstances did she want him to believe that she would fuss through her wardrobe, looking for something colorful because he'd suggested it. And she thought the simple tube of a dress was both businesslike, fashionable and appropriate.

On impulse, she had taken her hair down so that it fluffed out to skim her shoulders—only because she'd tired of wearing it pulled back. As always, she had debated her look for the evening carefully and was satisfied that she had achieved an aloof elegance.

She could hear the music blasting through his door before she knocked. It surprised her to hear the passionate strains of *Carmen*. She rapped harder, nearly gave in to the urge to shout over the aria, when the door swung open. Behind it was the blond knockout in a skimpy T-shirt and skimpier shorts.

"Hi." Keely crunched a piece of ice between her teeth and swallowed. "I was just borrowing an ice tray from Mik—my freezer's set on melt these days." She managed to smile and forced herself not to tug on her clothes. She felt like a peasant caught poaching by the royal princess. "I was just leaving." Before Sydney could speak, she dashed back inside to scoop up a tray of ice. "Mik, your date's here."

Sydney winced at the term *date* as the blond bullet streaked past her. "There's no need for you to rush off—"

"Three's a crowd," Keely told her on the run and, with a quick fleeting grin, kept going.

"Did you call me?" Mikhail came to the bedroom doorway. There was one, very small white towel anchored at his waist. He used another to rub at his wet, unruly hair. He stopped when he spotted Sydney. Something flickered in his eyes as he let his gaze roam down the long, cool lines of the dress. Then he smiled. "I'm late," he said simply.

She was grateful she'd managed not to let her mouth fall open. His body was all lean muscle, long bones and bronzed skin—skin that was gleaming with tiny drops of water that made her feel unbearably thirsty. The towel hung dangerously low on his hips. Dazed, she watched a drop of water slide down his chest, over his stomach and disappear beneath the terry cloth.

The temperature in the room, already steamy, rose several degrees.

"You're…" She knew she could speak coherently—in a minute. "We said seven."

"I was busy." He shrugged. The towel shifted. Sydney swallowed. "I won't be long. Fix a drink." A smile, wicked around the edges, tugged at his mouth. A man would have to be dead not to see her reaction—not to be pleased by it. "You look…hot, Sydney." He took a step forward, watching her eyes widen, watching her mouth tremble open. With his gaze on hers, he turned on a small portable fan. Steamy air stirred. "That will help," he said mildly.

She nodded. It was cooling, but it also brought the scent of his shower, of his skin into the room. Because she could see the knowledge and the amusement in his eyes, she got a grip on herself. "Your contracts." She set the folder down on a table. Mikhail barely glanced at them.

"I'll look and sign later."

"Fine. It would be best if you got dressed." She had to swallow another obstruction in her throat when he smiled at her. Her voice was edgy and annoyed. "We'll be late."

"A little. There's cold drink in the refrigerator," he added as he turned back to the bedroom. "Be at home."

Alone, she managed to take three normal breaths. Degree by degree she felt her system level. Any man who looked like that in a towel should be arrested, she thought, and turned to study the room.

She'd been too annoyed to take stock of it on her other visit. And too preoccupied, she admitted with a slight frown. A man like that had a way of keeping a woman preoccupied. Now she noted the hunks of wood, small and large, the tools, the jars stuffed with brushes. There was a long worktable beneath the living room window. She wandered toward it, seeing that a few of those hunks of wood were works in progress.

Shrugging, she ran a finger over a piece of cherry that was scarred with grooves and gouges. Rude and primitive, just as she'd thought. It soothed her ruffled ego to be assured she'd been right about his lack of talent. Obviously a ruffian who'd made a momentary impression on the capricious art world.

Then she turned and saw the shelves.

They were crowded with his work. Long smooth columns of wood, beautifully shaped. A profile of a woman with long, flowing hair, a young child caught in gleeful laughter, lovers trapped endlessly in a first tentative kiss. She couldn't stop herself from touching, nor from feeling. His work ranged from the passionate to the charming, from the bold to the delicate.

Fascinated, she crouched down to get a closer look at the pieces on the lower shelves. Was it possible, she wondered, that a man with such rough manners, with such cocky arrogance possessed the wit, the sensitivity, the compassion to create such lovely things out of blocks of wood?

With a half laugh Sydney reached for a carving of a tiny kangaroo with a baby peeking out of her pouch. It felt as smooth and as delicate as glass. Even as she replaced it with a little sigh, she spotted the miniature figurine. Cinderella, she thought, charmed as she held it in her fingertips. The pretty fairy-tale heroine was still dressed for the ball, but one foot was bare as Mikhail had captured her in her dash before the clock struck twelve. For a moment, Sydney thought she could almost see tears in the painted eyes.

"You like?"

She jolted, then stood up quickly, still nestling the figurine in her hand. "Yes—I'm sorry."

"You don't have to be sorry for liking." Mikhail rested a hip, now more conservatively covered in wheat-colored slacks, on the worktable. His hair had been brushed back and now curled damply nearly to his shoulders.

Still flustered, she set the miniature back on the shelf. "I meant I should apologize for touching your work."

A smile tugged at his lips. It fascinated him that she could go from wide-eyed delight to frosty politeness in the blink of an eye. "Better to be touched than to sit apart, only to be admired. Don't you think?"

It was impossible to miss the implication in the tone of his voice, in the look in his eyes. "That would depend."

As she started by, he shifted, rose. His timing was perfect. She all but collided with him. "On what?"

She didn't flush or stiffen or retreat. She'd become accustomed to taking a stand. "On whether one chooses to be touched."

He grinned. "I thought we were talking about sculpture."

So, she thought on a careful breath, she'd walked into that one. "Yes, we were. Now, we really will be late. If you're ready, Mr. Stanislaski—"

"Mikhail." He lifted a hand casually to flick a finger at the sapphire drop at her ear. "It's easier." Before she could reply, his gaze came back and locked on hers. Trapped in that one long stare, she wasn't certain she could remember her own name. "You smell like an English garden at teatime," he murmured. "Very cool, very appealing. And just a little too formal."

It was too hot, she told herself. Much too hot and close. That was why she had difficulty breathing. It had nothing to do with him. Rather, she wouldn't allow it to have anything to do with him. "You're in my way."

"I know." And for reasons he wasn't entirely sure of, he intended to stay there. "You're used to brushing people aside."

"I don't see what that has to do with—"

"An observation," he interrupted, amusing himself by toying with the ends of her hair. The texture was as rich as the color, he decided, pleased she had left it free for the evening. "Artists observe. You'll find that some people don't brush aside as quickly as others." He heard her breath catch, ignored her defensive jerk as he cupped her chin in his hand. He'd been right about her skin—smooth as polished pearls. Patiently he turned her face from side to side. "Nearly perfect," he decided. "Nearly perfect is better than perfect."

"I beg your pardon?"

"Your eyes are too big, and your mouth is just a bit wider than it should be."

Insulted, she slapped his hand away. It embarrassed and

infuriated her that she'd actually expected a compliment. "My eyes and mouth are none of your business."

"Very much mine," he corrected. "I'm doing your face."

When she frowned, a faint line etched between her brows. He liked it. "You're doing what?"

"Your face. In rosewood, I think. And with your hair down like this."

Again she pushed his hand away. "If you're asking me to model for you, I'm afraid I'm not interested."

"It doesn't matter whether you are. I am." He took her arm to lead her to the door.

"If you think I'm flattered—"

"Why should you be?" He opened the door, then stood just inside, studying her with apparent curiosity. "You were born with your face. You didn't earn it. If I said you sang well, or danced well, or kissed well, you could be flattered."

He eased her out, then closed the door. "Do you?" he asked, almost in afterthought.

Ruffled and irritated, she snapped back. "Do I what?"

"Kiss well?"

Her brows lifted. Haughty arches over frosty eyes. "The day you find out, you can be flattered." Rather pleased with the line, she started down the hall ahead of him.

His fingers barely touched her—she would have sworn it. But in the space of a heartbeat her back was to the wall and she was caged between his arms, with his hands planted on either side of her head. Both shock and a trembling river of fear came before she could even think to be insulted.

Knowing he was being obnoxious, enjoying it, he kept his lips a few scant inches from hers. He recognized the curling in his gut as desire. And by God, he could deal with that. And her. Their breath met and tangled, and he smiled. Hers had come out in a quick, surprised puff.

"I think," he said slowly, consideringly, "you have yet to learn how to kiss well. You have the mouth for it." His gaze lowered, lingered there. "But a man would have to be patient enough to warm that blood up first. A pity I'm not patient."

He was close enough to see her quick wince before her eyes went icy. "I think," she said, borrowing his tone, "that you probably kiss very well. But a woman would have to be tolerant enough to hack through your ego first. Fortunately, I'm not tolerant."

For a moment he stood where he was, close enough to swoop down and test both their theories. Then the smile worked over his face, curving his lips, brightening his eyes. Yes, he could deal with her. When he was ready.

"A man can learn patience, *milaya*, and seduce a woman to tolerance."

She pressed against the wall, but like a cat backed into a corner, she was ready to swipe and spit. He only stepped back and cupped a hand over her elbow.

"We should go now, yes?"

"Yes." Not at all sure if she was relieved or disappointed, she walked with him toward the stairs.

Chapter 3

Margerite had pulled out all the stops. She knew it was a coup to have a rising and mysterious artist such as Stanislaski at her dinner party. Like a general girding for battle, she had inspected the floral arrangements, the kitchens, the dining room and the terraces. Before she was done, the caterers were cursing her, but Margerite was satisfied.

She wasn't pleased when her daughter, along with her most important guest, was late.

Laughing and lilting, she swirled among her guests in a frothy gown of robin's-egg blue. There was a sprinkling of politicians, theater people and the idle rich. But the Ukrainian artist was her coup de grace, and she was fretting to show him off.

And, remembering that wild sexuality, she was fretting to flirt.

The moment she spotted him, Margerite swooped.

"Mr. Stanislaski, how marvelous!" After shooting her daughter a veiled censorious look, she beamed.

"Mikhail, please." Because he knew the game and played it at his will, Mikhail brought her hand to his lips and lingered over it. "You must forgive me for being late. I kept your daughter waiting."

"Oh." She fluttered, her hand resting lightly, possessively on his arm. "A smart woman will always wait for the right man."

"Then I'm forgiven."

"Absolutely." Her fingers gave his an intimate squeeze. "This time. Now, you must let me introduce you around, Mikhail." Linked with him, she glanced absently at her daughter. "Sydney, do mingle, darling."

Mikhail shot a quick, wicked grin over his shoulder as he let Margerite haul him away.

He made small talk easily, sliding into the upper crust of New York society as seamlessly as he slid into the working class in Soho or his parents' close-knit neighborhood in Brooklyn. They had no idea he might have preferred a beer with friends or coffee at his mother's kitchen table.

He sipped champagne, admired the house with its cool white walls and towering windows, and complimented Margerite on her art collection.

And all the while he chatted, sipped and smiled, he watched Sydney.

Odd, he thought. He would have said that the sprawling elegance of the Long Island enclave was the perfect setting for her. Her looks, her demeanor, reminded him of glistening shaved ice in a rare porcelain bowl. Yet she didn't quite fit. Oh, she smiled and worked the room as skillfully as her mother. Her simple black dress was as exclusive as any of the more colorful choices in the room. Her sapphires winked as brilliantly as any of the diamonds or emeralds.

But…it was her eyes, Mikhail realized. There wasn't laughter in them, but impatience. It was as though she were thinking—let's get this done and over with so I can get on to something important.

It made him smile. Remembering that he'd have the long drive back to Manhattan to tease her made the smile widen. It faded abruptly as he watched a tall blond man with football shoulders tucked into a silk dinner jacket kiss Sydney on the mouth.

Sydney smiled into a pair of light blue eyes under golden brows. "Hello, Channing."

"Hello, yourself." He offered a fresh glass of wine. "Where did Margerite find the wild horses?"

"I'm sorry?"

"To drag you out of that office." His smile dispensed charm like penny candy. Sydney couldn't help but respond.

"It wasn't quite that drastic. I have been busy."

"So you've told me." He approved of her in the sleek black dress in much the same way he would have approved of a tasteful accessory for his home. "You missed a wonderful play the other night. It looks like Sondheim's got another hit on his hands." Never doubting her acquiescence, he took her arm to lead her into dinner. "Tell me, darling, when are you going to stop playing the career woman and take a break? I'm going up to the Hamptons for the weekend, and I'd love your company."

Dutifully she forced her clamped teeth apart. There was no use resenting the fact he thought she was playing. Everyone did. "I'm afraid I can't get away just now." She took her seat beside him at the long glass table in the airy dining room. The drapes were thrown wide so that the garden seemed to spill inside with the pastel hues of early roses, late tulips and nodding columbine.

She wished the dinner had been alfresco so she could have sat among the blossoms and scented the sea air.

"I hope you don't mind a little advice."

Sydney nearly dropped her head into her hand. The chatter around them was convivial, glasses were clinking, and the first course of stuffed mushrooms was being served. She felt she'd just been clamped into a cell. "Of course not, Channing."

"You can run a business or let the business run you."

"Hmm." He had a habit of stating his advice in clichés. Sydney reminded herself she should be used to it.

"Take it from someone with more experience in these matters."

She fixed a smile on her face and let her mind wander.

"I hate to see you crushed under the heel of responsibility," he went on. "And after all, we know you're a novice in the dog-eat-dog world of real estate." Gold cuff links, monogrammed, winked as he laid a hand on hers. His eyes were sincere, his mouth quirked in that I'm-only-looking-out-for-you smile. "Naturally, your initial enthusiasm will push you to take on more than is good for you. I'm sure you agree."

Her mind flicked back. "Actually, Channing, I enjoy the work."

"For the moment," he said, his voice so patronizing she nearly stabbed him with her salad fork. "But when reality rushes in you may find yourself trampled under it. Delegate, Sydney. Hand the responsibilities over to those who understand them."

If her spine had been any straighter, it would have

snapped her neck. "My grandfather entrusted Hayward to me."

"The elderly become sentimental. But I can't believe he expected you to take it all so seriously." His smooth, lightly tanned brow wrinkled briefly in what she understood was genuine if misguided concern. "Why, you've hardly attended a party in weeks. Everyone's talking about it."

"Are they?" She forced her lips to curve over her clenched teeth. If he offered one more shred of advice, she would have to upend the water goblet in his lap. "Channing, why don't you tell me about the play?"

At the other end of the table, tucked between Margerite and Mrs. Anthony Lowell of the Boston Lowells, Mikhail kept a weather eye on Sydney. He didn't like the way she had her head together with pretty boy. No, by God, he didn't. The man was always touching her. Her hand, her shoulder. Her soft, white, bare shoulder. And she was just smiling and nodding, as though his words were a fascination in themselves.

Apparently the ice queen didn't mind being pawed if the hands doing the pawing were as lily-white as her own.

Mikhail swore under his breath.

"I beg your pardon, Mikhail?"

With an effort, he turned his attention and a smile toward Margerite. "Nothing. The pheasant is excellent."

"Thank you. I wonder if I might ask what Sydney's commissioned you to sculpt."

He flicked a black look down the length of the table. "I'll be working on the project in Soho."

"Ah." Margerite hadn't a clue what Hayward might own in Soho. "Will it be an indoor or outdoor piece?"

"Both. Who is the man beside Sydney? I don't think I met him."

"Oh, that's Channing, Channing Warfield. The Warfields are old friends."

"Friends," he repeated, slightly mollified.

Conspiratorially Margerite leaned closer. "If I can confide, Wilhelmina Warfield and I are hoping they'll make an announcement this summer. They're such a lovely couple, so suitable. And since Sydney's first marriage is well behind her—"

"First marriage?" He swooped down on that tidbit of information like a hawk on a dove. "Sydney was married before?"

"Yes, but I'm afraid she and Peter were too young and impetuous," she told him, conveniently overlooking the family pressure that had brought the marriage about. "Now, Sydney and Channing are mature, responsible people. We're looking forward to a spring wedding."

Mikhail picked up his wine. There was an odd and annoying scratching in his throat. "What does this Channing Warfield do?"

"Do?" The question baffled her. "Why, the Warfields are in banking, so I suppose Channing does whatever one does in banking. He's a devil on the polo field."

"Polo," Mikhail repeated with a scowl so dark Helena Lowell choked on her pheasant. Helpfully Mikhail gave her a sharp slap between the shoulder blades, then offered her her water goblet.

"You're, ah, Russian, aren't you, Mr. Stanislaski?" Helena asked. Images of Cossacks danced in her head.

"I was born in the Ukraine."

"The Ukraine, yes. I believe I read something about your family escaping over the border when you were just a child."

"We escaped in a wagon, over the mountains into Hungary, then into Austria and finally settled in New York."

"A wagon." Margerite sighed into her wine. "How romantic."

Mikhail remembered the cold, the fear, the hunger. But he only shrugged. He doubted romance was always pretty, or comfortable.

Relieved that he looked approachable again, Helena Lowell began to ask him questions about art.

After an hour, he was glad to escape from the pretensions of the society matron's art school jargon. Guests were treated to violin music, breezy terraces and moon-kissed gardens. His hostess fluttered around him like a butterfly, lashes batting, laughter trilling.

Margerite's flirtations were patently obvious and didn't bother him. She was a pretty, vivacious woman currently between men. Though he had privately deduced she shared little with her daughter other than looks, he considered her harmless, even entertaining. So when she offered to show him the rooftop patio, he went along.

The wind off the sound was playful and fragrant. And it was blessedly quiet following the ceaseless after-dinner chatter. From the rail, Mikhail could see the water, the curve of beach, the serene elegance of other homes tucked behind walls and circling gardens.

And he could see Sydney as she strolled to the shadowy corner of the terrace below with her arm tucked through Channing's.

"My third husband built this house," Margerite was saying. "He's an architect. When we divorced, I had my choice between this house and the little villa in Nice. Naturally, with so many of my friends here, I chose this." With a sigh, she turned to face him, leaning prettily on the rail. "I must say, I love this spot. When I give house parties people are spread out on every level, so it's both cozy and private. Perhaps you'll join us some weekend this summer."

"Perhaps." The answer was absent as he stared down at Sydney. The moonlight made her hair gleam like polished mahogany.

Margerite shifted, just enough so that their thighs brushed. Mikhail wasn't sure if he was more surprised or more amused. But to save her pride, he smiled, easing away slowly. "You have a lovely home. It suits you."

"I'd love to see your studio." Margerite let the invitation melt into her eyes. "Where you create."

"I'm afraid you'd find it cramped, hot and boring."

"Impossible." Smiling, she traced a fingertip over the back of his hand. "I'm sure I'd find nothing about you boring."

Good God, the woman was old enough to be his mother, and she was coming on to him like a misty-eyed virgin primed for her first tumble. Mikhail nearly sighed, then reminded himself it was only a moment out of his life. He took her hand between both of his hands.

"Margerite, you're charming. And I'm—" he kissed her fingers lightly "—unsuitable."

She lifted a finger and brushed it over his cheek. "You underestimate yourself, Mikhail."

No, but he realized how he'd underestimated her.

On the terrace below, Sydney was trying to find a graceful way to discourage Channing. He was attentive, dignified, solicitous, and he was boring her senseless.

It was her lack, she was sure. Any woman with half a soul would be melting under the attraction of a man like Channing. There was moonlight, music, flowers. The breeze in the leafy trees smelled of the sea and murmured of romance. Channing was talking about Paris, and his hand was skimming lightly over her bare back.

She wished she was home, alone, with her eyes crossing over a fat file of quarterly reports.

Taking a deep breath, she turned. She would have to tell him firmly, simply and straight out that he needed to look elsewhere for companionship. It was Sydney's bad luck that she happened to glance up to see Mikhail on the rooftop with her mother just when he took Margerite's hand to his lips.

Why the…she couldn't think of anything vile enough to call him. Slime was too simple. Gigolo too slick. He was nuzzling up to her mother. *Her mother.* When only hours before he'd been…

Nothing, Sydney reminded herself and dismissed the tense scene in the Soho hallway from her mind. He'd been posturing and preening, that was all.

And she could have killed him for it.

As she watched, Mikhail backed away from Margerite, laughing. Then he looked down. The instant their eyes met, Sydney declared war.

She whirled on Channing, her face so fierce he nearly babbled. "Kiss me," she demanded.

"Why, Sydney."

"I said kiss me." She grabbed him by the lapels and hauled him against her.

"Of course, darling." Pleased with her change of heart, he cupped her shoulders in his hands and leaned down to her.

His lips were soft, warm, eager. They slanted over hers with practiced precision while his hands slid down her back. He tasted of after-dinner mints. Her body fit well against his.

And she felt nothing, nothing but an empty inner rage. Then a chill that was both fear and despair.

"You're not trying, darling," he whispered. "You know I won't hurt you."

No, he wouldn't. There was nothing at all to fear from Channing. Miserable, she let him deepen the kiss, ordered herself to feel and respond. She felt his withdrawal even before his lips left hers. The twinges of annoyance and puzzlement.

"Sydney, dear, I'm not sure what the problem is." He smoothed down his crinkled lapels. Marginally frustrated, he lifted his eyes. "That was like kissing my sister."

"I'm tired, Channing," she said to the air between them. "I should go in and get ready to go."

Twenty minutes later, the driver turned the car toward Manhattan. In the back seat Sydney sat ramrod straight well over in her corner, while Mikhail sprawled in his. They didn't bother to speak, not even the polite nonentities of two people who had attended the same function.

He was boiling with rage.

She was frigid with disdain.

She'd done it to annoy him, Mikhail decided. She'd let that silk-suited jerk all but swallow her whole just to make him suffer.

Why was he suffering? he asked himself. She was nothing to him.

No, she was something, he corrected, and brooded into the dark. His only problem was figuring out exactly what that something was.

Obviously, Sydney reflected, the man had no ethics, no morals, no shame. Here he was, just sitting there, all innocence and quiet reflection, after his disgraceful behavior. She frowned at the pale image of her own face in the window glass and tried to listen to the Chopin prelude on the stereo. Flirting so blatantly with a woman twenty years older. Sneering, yes positively sneering down from the rooftop.

And she'd hired him. Sydney let out a quiet, hissing breath from between her teeth. Oh, that was something she regretted. She'd let her concern, her determination to do the right thing, blind her into hiring some oversexed, amoral Russian carpenter.

Well, if he thought he was going to start playing patty-cake with her mother, he was very much mistaken.

She drew a breath, turned and aimed one steady glare. Mikhail would have sworn the temperature in the car dropped fifty degrees in a snap.

"You stay away from my mother."

He slanted her a look from under his lashes and gracefully crossed his legs. "Excuse me?"

"You heard me, Boris. If you think I'm going to stand by and watch you put the moves on my mother, think again. She's lonely and vulnerable. Her last divorce upset her and she isn't over it."

He said something short and sharp in his native tongue and closed his eyes.

Temper had Sydney sliding across the seat until she could poke his arm. "What the hell does that mean?"

"You want translation? The simplest is bullshit. Now shut up. I'm going to sleep."

"You're not going anywhere until we settle this. You keep your big, grimy hands off my mother, or I'll turn that building you're so fond of into a parking lot."

His eyes slitted open. She found the glitter of angry eyes immensely satisfying. "A big threat from a small woman," he said in a deceptively lazy voice. She was entirely too close for his comfort, and her scent was swimming in his senses, tangling his temper with something more basic. "You should concentrate on the suit, and let your mother handle her own."

"Suit? What suit?"

"The banker who spent the evening sniffing your ankles."

Her face flooded with color. "He certainly was not. He's entirely too well mannered to sniff at my ankles or anything else. And Channing is my business."

"So. You have your business, and I have mine. Now, let's see what we have together." One moment he was stretched out, and the next he had her twisted over his lap. Stunned, Sydney pressed her hands against his chest and tried to struggle out of his hold. He tightened it. "As you see, I have no manners."

"Oh, I know it." She tossed her head back, chin jutting. "What do you think you're doing?"

He wished to hell he knew. She was rigid as an ice floe, but there was something incredible, and Lord, inevitable, about the way she fit into his arms. Though he was cursing himself, he held her close, close enough that he felt the uneven rise and fall of her breasts against his chest, tasted the sweet, wine-tipped flavor of her breath on his lips.

There was a lesson here, he thought grimly, and she was going to learn it.

"I've decided to teach you how to kiss. From what I saw from the roof, you did a poor job of it with the polo player."

Shock and fury had her going still. She would not squirm or scream or give him the satisfaction of frightening her. His eyes were close and challenging. She thought she understood exactly how Lucifer would have looked as he walked through the gates of his own dark paradise.

"You conceited jerk." Because she wanted to slug him, badly, she fisted her hands closed and looked haughtily down her small, straight nose. "There's nothing you can teach me."

"No?" He wondered if he'd be better off just strangling her and having done with it. "Let's see then. Your Channing put his hands here. Yes?" He slid them over her shoulders. The quick, involuntary shudder chilled her skin. "You afraid of me, *milaya?*"

"Don't be ridiculous." But she was, suddenly and deeply. She swallowed the fear as his thumbs caressed her bare skin.

"Tremble is good. It makes a man feel strong. I don't think you trembled for this Channing."

She said nothing and wondered if he knew his accent had thickened. It sounded exotic, erotic. He wondered he could speak at all with her watching him and waiting.

"His way isn't mine," he muttered. "I'll show you."

His fingers clamped around the back of her neck, pulled her face toward his. He heard her breath catch then shudder out when he paused only a fraction before their lips touched. Her eyes filled his vision, that wide, wary blue. Ignoring the twist in his gut, he smiled, turned his head just an inch and skimmed his lips over her jawline.

She bit back only part of the moan. Instinctively she tipped her head back, giving him access to the long, sensitive column of her throat.

What was he doing to her? Her mind raced frantically to catch up with her soaring body. Why didn't he just get it over with so she could escape with her pride intact?

She'd kill him for this. Crush him. Destroy him.

And oh, it felt wonderful, delicious. Wicked.

He could only think she tasted of morning—cool, spring mornings when the dew slicked over green, green grass and new flowers. She shivered against him, her body still held stiffly away even as her head fell back in surrender.

Who was she? He nibbled lazily over to her ear and burned for her to show him.

A thousand, a million pinpricks of pleasure danced along her skin. Shaken by them, she started to pull away. But his hands slid down her back and melted her spine. All the while his lips teased and tormented, never, never coming against hers to relieve the aching pressure.

She wanted.

The slow, flickering heat kindling in the pit of her stomach.

She yearned.

Spreading, spreading through her blood and bone.

She needed.

Wave after wave of liquid fire lapping, cruising, flowing over her skin.

She took.

In a fire flash her system exploded. Mouth to mouth she strained against him, pressing ice to heat and letting it steam until the air was so thick with it, it clogged in her throat. Her fingers speared through his hair and fisted as she fed greedily on the stunning flavor of her own passion.

This. At last this. He was rough and restless and smelled of man instead of expensive colognes. The words he muttered were incomprehensible against her mouth. But they didn't sound like endearments, reassurances, promises. They sounded like threats.

His mouth wasn't soft and warm and eager, but hot and

hard and ruthless. She wanted that, how she wanted the heedless and hasty meeting of lips and tongues.

His hands weren't hesitant or practiced, but strong and impatient. It ran giddily through her brain that he would take what he wanted, when and where it suited him. The pleasure and power of it burst through her like sunlight. She choked out his name when he tugged her bodice down and filled his calloused hands with her breasts.

He was drowning in her. The ice had melted and he was over his head, too dazed to know if he should dive deeper or scrabble for the surface. The scent, the taste, oh Lord, the texture. Alabaster and silk and rose petals. Every fine thing a man could want to touch, to steal, to claim as his own. His hands raced over her as he fought for more.

On an oath he shifted, and she was under him on the long plush seat of the car, her hair spread out like melted copper, her body moving, moving under his, her white breasts spilling out above the stark black dress and tormenting him into tasting.

She arched, and her fingers dug into his back as he suckled. A deep and delicious ache tugged at the center of her body. And she wanted him there, there where the heat was most intense. There where she felt so soft, so needy.

"Please." She could hear the whimper in her voice but felt no embarrassment. Only desperation. "Mikhail, please."

The throaty purr of her voice burst in his blood. He came back to her mouth, assaulting it, devouring it. Crazed, he hooked one hand in the top of her dress, on the verge of ripping it from her. And he looked, looked at her face, the huge eyes, the trembling lips. Light and shadow washed over it, leaving her pale as a ghost. She was shaking like a leaf beneath his hands.

And he heard the drum of traffic from outside.

He surfaced abruptly, shaking his head to clear it and gulping in air like a diver down too long. They were driving through the city, their privacy as thin as the panel of smoked glass that separated them from her chauffeur. And he was mauling her, yes, mauling her as if he were a reckless teenager with none of the sense God had given him.

The apology stuck in his throat. An "I beg your pardon" would hardly do the trick. Eyes grim, loins aching, he tugged her dress back into place. She only stared at him and made him feel like a drooling heathen over a virgin sacrifice. And Lord help him, he wanted to plunder.

Swearing, he pushed away and yanked her upright. He leaned back in the shadows and stared out of the dark window. They were only blocks from his apartment. Blocks, and he'd very nearly...it wouldn't do to think about what he'd nearly.

"We're almost there." Strain had his voice coming out clipped and hard. Sydney winced away as though it had been a slap.

What had she done wrong this time? She'd felt, and she'd wanted. Felt and wanted more than she ever had before. Yet she had still failed. For that one timeless moment she'd been willing to toss aside pride and fear. There had been passion in her, real and ready. And, she'd thought, he'd felt passion for her.

But not enough. She closed her eyes. It never seemed to be enough. Now she was cold, freezing, and wrapped her arms tight to try to hold in some remnant of heat.

Damn it, why didn't she say something? Mikhail dragged an unsteady hand through his hair. He deserved to be slapped. Shot was more like it. And she just sat there.

As he brooded out the window, he reminded himself that

it hadn't been all his doing. She'd been as rash, pressing that wonderful body against his, letting that wide, mobile mouth make him crazy. Squirting that damnable perfume all over that soft skin until he'd been drunk with it.

He started to feel better.

Yes, there had been two people grappling in the back seat. She was every bit as guilty as he.

"Look, Sydney." He turned and she jerked back like an overwound spring.

"Don't touch me." He heard only the venom and none of the tears.

"Fine." Guilt hammered away at him as the car cruised to the curb. "I'll keep my big, grimy hands off you, Hayward. Call someone else when you want a little romp in the back seat."

Her fisted hands held on to pride and composure. "I meant what I said about my mother."

He shoved the door open. Light spilled in, splashing over his face, turning it frosty white. "So did I. Thanks for the ride."

When the door slammed, she closed her eyes tight. She would not cry. A single tear slipped past her guard and was dashed away. She would not cry. And she would not forget.

Chapter 4

She'd put in a long day. Actually she'd put in a long week that was edging toward sixty hours between office time, luncheon meetings and evenings at home with files. This particular day had a few hours yet to run, but Sydney recognized the new feeling of relief and satisfaction that came with Friday afternoons when the work force began to anticipate Saturday mornings.

Throughout her adult life one day of the week had been the same as the next; all of them a scattershot of charity functions, shopping and lunch dates. There had been no work schedule, and weekends had simply been a time when the parties had lasted longer.

Things had changed. As she read over a new contract, she was glad they had. She was beginning to understand why her grandfather had always been so lusty and full of life. He'd had a purpose, a place, a goal.

Now they were hers.

True, she still had to ask advice on the more technical wordings of contracts and depended heavily on her board when it came to making deals. But she was starting to appreciate—more, she was starting to relish the grand chess game of buying and selling buildings.

She circled what she considered a badly worded clause then answered her intercom.

"Mr. Bingham to see you, Ms. Hayward."

"Send him in, Janine. Oh, and see if you can reach Frank Marlowe at Marlowe, Radcliffe and Smyth."

"Yes, ma'am."

When Lloyd strode in a moment later, Sydney was still huddled over the contract. She held up one finger to give herself a minute to finish.

"Lloyd. I'm sorry, if I lose my concentration on all these *whereases*, I have to start over." She scrawled a note to herself, set it and the contract aside, then smiled at him. "What can I do for you?"

"This Soho project. It's gotten entirely out of hand."

Her lips tightened. Thinking of Soho made her think of Mikhail. Mikhail reminded her of the turbulent ride from Long Island and her latest failure as a woman. She didn't care for it.

"In what way?"

"In every way." With fury barely leashed, he began to pace her office. "A quarter of a million. You earmarked a quarter of a million to rehab that building."

Sydney stayed where she was and quietly folded her hands on the desk. "I'm aware of that, Lloyd. Considering the condition of the building, Mr. Stanislaski's bid was very reasonable."

"How would you know?" he shot back. "Did you get competing bids?"

"No." Her fingers flexed, then relaxed again. It was difficult, but she reminded herself that he'd earned his way up the ladder while she'd been hoisted to the top rung. "I went with my instincts."

"Instincts?" Eyes narrowed, he spun back to her. The derision in his voice was as thick as the pile of her carpet. "You've been in the business for a matter of months, and you have instincts?"

"That's right. I'm also aware that the estimate for rewiring, the plumbing and the carpentry were well in line with other, similar rehabs."

"Damn it, Sydney, we didn't put much more than that into this building last year."

One slim finger began to tap on the desk. "What we did here in the Hayward Building was little more than decorating. A good many of the repairs in Soho are a matter of safety and bringing the facilities up to code."

"A quarter of a million in repairs." He slapped his palms on the desk and leaned forward. Sydney was reminded of Mikhail making a similar gesture. But of course Lloyd's hands would leave no smudge of dirt. "Do you know what our annual income is from those apartments?"

"As a matter of fact I do." She rattled off a figure, surprising him. It was accurate to the penny. "On one hand, it will certainly take more than a year of full occupancy to recoup the principal on this investment. On the other, when people pay rent in good faith, they deserve decent housing."

"Decent, certainly," Lloyd said stiffly. "You're mixing morals with business."

"Oh, I hope so. I certainly hope so."

He drew back, infuriated that she would sit so smug and righteous behind a desk that should have been his. "You're naive, Sydney."

"That may be. But as long as I run this company, it will be run by my standards."

"You think you run it because you sign a few contracts and make phone calls. You've put a quarter million into what you yourself termed your pet project, and you don't have a clue what this Stanislaski's up to. How do you know he isn't buying inferior grades and pocketing the excess?"

"That's absurd."

"As I said, you're naive. You put some Russian artist in charge of a major project, then don't even bother to check the work."

"I intend to inspect the project myself. I've been tied up. And I have Mr. Stanislaski's weekly report."

He sneered. Before Sydney's temper could fray, she realized Lloyd was right. She'd hired Mikhail on impulse and instinct, then because of personal feelings, had neglected to follow through with her involvement on the project.

That wasn't naive. It was gutless.

"You're absolutely right, Lloyd, and I'll correct it." She leaned back in her chair. "Was there anything else?"

"You've made a mistake," he said. "A costly one in this case. The board won't tolerate another."

With her hands laid lightly on the arms of her chair, she nodded. "And you're hoping to convince them that you belong at this desk."

"They're businessmen, Sydney. And though sentiment might prefer a Hayward at the head of the table, profit and loss will turn the tide."

Her expression remained placid, her voice steady. "I'm sure you're right again. And if the board continues to back me, I want one of two things from you. Your resignation or your loyalty. I won't accept anything in between. Now, if you'll excuse me?"

When the door slammed behind him, she reached for the phone. But her hand was trembling, and she drew it back. She plucked up a paper clip and mangled it. Then another, then a third. Between that and the two sheets of stationery she shredded, she felt the worst of the rage subside.

Clearheaded, she faced the facts.

Lloyd Bingham was an enemy, and he was an enemy with experience and influence. She had acted in haste with Soho. Not that she'd been wrong; she didn't believe she'd been wrong. But if there were mistakes, Lloyd would capitalize on them and drop them right in her lap.

Was it possible that she was risking everything her grandfather had given her with one project? Could she be forced to step down if she couldn't prove the worth and right of what she had done?

She wasn't sure, and that was the worst of it.

One step at a time. That was the only way to go on. And the first step was to get down to Soho and do her job.

The sky was the color of drywall. Over the past few days, the heat had ebbed, but it had flowed back into the city that morning like a river, flooding Manhattan with humidity. The pedestrian traffic surged through it, streaming across the intersections in hot little packs.

Girls in shorts and men in wilted business suits crowded around the sidewalk vendors in hopes that an ice-cream bar or a soft drink would help them beat the heat.

When Sydney stepped out of her car, the sticky oppression of the air punched like a fist. She thought of her driver sitting in the enclosed car and dismissed him for the day. Shielding her eyes, she turned to study her building.

Scaffolding crept up the walls like metal ivy. Windows glittered, their manufacturer stickers slashed across the glass. She thought she saw a pair of arthritic hands scraping away at a label at a third-floor window.

There were signs in the doorway, warning of construction in progress. She could hear the sounds of it, booming hammers, buzzing saws, the clang of metal and the tinny sound of rock and roll through portable speakers.

At the curb she saw the plumber's van, a dented pickup and a scattering of interested onlookers. Since they were all peering up, she followed their direction. And saw Mikhail.

For an instant, her heart stopped dead. He stood outside the top floor, five stories up, moving nimbly on what seemed to Sydney to be a very narrow board.

"Man, get a load of those buns," a woman beside her sighed. "They are class A."

Sydney swallowed. She supposed they were. And his naked back wasn't anything to sneeze at, either. The trouble was, it was hard to enjoy it when she had a hideous flash of him plummeting off the scaffolding and breaking that beautiful back on the concrete below.

Panicked, she rushed inside. The elevator doors were open, and a couple of mechanics were either loading or unloading their tools inside it. She didn't stop to ask but bolted up the steps.

Sweaty men were replastering the stairwell between two and three. They took the time to whistle and wink, but she kept climbing. Someone had the television up too loud, probably to drown out the sound of construction. A baby was crying fitfully. She smelled chicken frying.

Without pausing for breath, she dashed from four to five. There was music playing here. Tough and gritty rock, poorly accompanied by a laborer in an off-key tenor.

Mikhail's door was open, and Sydney streaked through. She nearly tumbled over a graying man with arms like tree trunks. He rose gracefully from his crouched position where he'd been sorting tools and steadied her.

"I'm sorry. I didn't see you."

"Is all right. I like women to fall at my feet."

She registered the Slavic accent even as she glanced desperately around the room for Mikhail. Maybe everybody in the building was Russian, she thought frantically. Maybe he'd imported plumbers from the mother country.

"Can I help you?"

"No. Yes." She pressed a hand to her heart when she realized she was completely out of breath. "Mikhail."

"He is just outside." Intrigued, he watched her as he jerked a thumb toward the window.

She could see him there—at least she could see the flat, tanned torso. "Outside. But, but—"

"We are finishing for the day. You will sit?"

"Get him in," Sydney whispered. "Please, get him in."

Before he could respond, the window was sliding up, and Mikhail was tossing one long, muscled leg inside. He said something in his native tongue, laughter in his voice as the rest of his body followed. When he saw Sydney, the laughter vanished.

"Hayward." He tapped his caulking gun against his palm.

"What were you doing out there?" The question came out in an accusing rush.

"Replacing windows." He set the caulking gun aside. "Is there a problem?"

"No, I…" She couldn't remember ever feeling more of a fool. "I came by to check the progress."

"So. I'll take you around in a minute." He walked into the kitchen, stuck his head into the sink and turned the faucet on full cold.

"He's a hothead," the man behind her said, chuckling at his own humor. When Sydney only managed a weak smile, he called out to Mikhail, speaking rapidly in that exotic foreign tongue.

"Tak" was all he said. Mikhail came up dripping, hair streaming over the bandanna he'd tied around it. He shook it back, splattering water, then shrugged and hooked his thumbs in his belt loops. He was wet, sweaty and half-naked. Sydney had to fold her tongue inside her mouth to keep it from hanging out.

"My son is rude." Yuri Stanislaski shook his head. "I raised him better."

"Your—oh." Sydney looked back at the man with the broad face and beautiful hands. Mikhail's hands. "How do you do, Mr. Stanislaski."

"I do well. I am Yuri. I ask my son if you are the Hayward who owns this business. He only says yes and scowls."

"Yes, well, I am."

"It's a good building. Only a little sick. And we are the doctors." He grinned at his son, then boomed out something else in Ukrainian.

This time an answering smile tugged at Mikhail's mouth. "No, you haven't lost a patient yet, Papa. Go home and have your dinner."

Yuri hauled up his tool chest. "You come and bring the pretty lady. Your mama makes enough."

"Oh, well, thank you, but—"

"I'm busy tonight, Papa." Mikhail cut off Sydney's polite refusal.

Yuri raised a bushy brow. "You're stupid tonight," he said in Ukrainian. "Is this the one who makes you sulk all week?"

Annoyed, Mikhail picked up a kitchen towel and wiped his face. "Women don't make me sulk."

Yuri only smiled. "This one would." Then he turned to Sydney. "Now I am rude, too, talking so you don't understand. He is bad influence." He lifted her hand and kissed it with considerable charm. "I am glad to meet you."

"I'm glad to meet you, too."

"Put on a shirt," Yuri ordered his son, then left, whistling.

"He's very nice," Sydney said.

"Yes." Mikhail picked up the T-shirt he'd peeled off hours before, but only held it. "So, you want to see the work?"

"Yes, I thought—"

"The windows are done," he interrupted. "The wiring is almost done. That and the plumbing will take another week. Come."

He moved out, skirting her by a good two feet, then walked into the apartment next door without knocking.

"Keely's," he told her. "She is out."

The room was a clash of sharp colors and scents. The furniture was old and sagging but covered with vivid pillows and various articles of female attire.

The adjoining kitchen was a mess—not with dishes or pots and pans—but with walls torn down to studs and thick wires snaked through.

"It must be inconvenient for her, for everyone, during the construction."

"Better than plugging in a cake mixer and shorting out the building. The old wire was tube and knob, forty years old or more, and frayed. This is Romex. More efficient, safer."

She bent over his arm, studying the wiring. "Well. Hmm."

He nearly smiled. Perhaps he would have if she hadn't smelled so good. Instead, he moved a deliberate foot away. "After the inspection, we will put up new walls. Come."

It was a trial for both of them, but he took her through every stage of the work, moving from floor to floor, showing her elbows of plastic pipe and yards of copper tubing.

"Most of the flooring can be saved with sanding and refinishing. But some must be replaced." He kicked at a square of plywood he'd nailed to a hole in the second-floor landing.

Sydney merely nodded, asking questions only when they seemed intelligent. Most of the workers were gone, off to cash their week's paychecks. The noise level had lowered so that she could hear muted voices behind closed doors, snatches of music or televised car chases. She lifted a brow at the sound of a tenor sax swinging into "Rhapsody in Blue."

"That's Will Metcalf," Mikhail told her. "He's good. Plays in a band."

"Yes, he's good." The rail felt smooth and sturdy under her hand as they went down. Mikhail had done that, she thought. He'd fixed, repaired, replaced, as needed because he cared about the people who lived in the building. He knew who was playing the sax or eating the fried chicken, whose baby was laughing.

"Are you happy with the progress?" she asked quietly.

The tone of her voice made him look at her, something he'd been trying to avoid. A few tendrils of hair had escaped their pins to curl at her temples. He could see a pale dusting of freckles across her nose. "Happy enough. It's you who should answer. It's your building."

"No, it's not." Her eyes were very serious, very sad. "It's yours. I only write the checks."

"Sydney—"

"I've seen enough to know you've made a good start." She was hurrying down the steps as she spoke. "Be sure to contact my office when it's time for the next draw."

"Damn it. Slow down." He caught up with her at the bottom of the steps and grabbed her arm. "What's wrong with you? First you stand in my room pale and out of breath. Now you run away, and your eyes are miserable."

It had hit her, hard, that she had no community of people who cared. Her circle of friends was so narrow, so self-involved. Her best friend had been Peter, and that had been horribly spoiled. Her life was on the sidelines, and she envied the involvement, the closeness she felt in this place. The building wasn't hers, she thought again. She only owned it.

"I'm not running away, and nothing's wrong with me." She had to get out, get away, but she had to do it with dignity. "I take this job very seriously. It's my first major project since taking over Hayward. I want it done right. And I took a chance by..." She trailed off, glancing toward the door just to her right. She could have sworn she'd heard someone call for help. Television, she thought, but before she could continue, she heard the thin, pitiful call again. "Mikhail, do you hear that?"

"Hear what?" How could he hear anything when he was trying not to kiss her again?

"In here." She turned toward the door, straining her ears. "Yes, in here, I heard—"

That time he'd heard it, too. Lifting a fist, he pounded on the door. "Mrs. Wolburg. Mrs. Wolburg, it's Mik."

The shaky voice barely penetrated the wood. "Hurt. Help me."

"Oh, God, she's—"

Before Sydney could finish, Mikhail rammed his shoulder against the door. With the second thud, it crashed open to lean drunkenly on its hinges.

"In the kitchen," Mrs. Wolburg called weakly. "Mik, thank God."

He bolted through the apartment with its starched doilies and paper flowers to find her on the kitchen floor. She was a tiny woman, mostly bone and thin flesh. Her usually neat cap of white hair was matted with sweat.

"Can't see," she said. "Dropped my glasses."

"Don't worry." He knelt beside her, automatically checking her pulse as he studied her pain-filled eyes. "Call an ambulance," he ordered Sydney, but she was already on the phone. "I'm not going to help you up, because I don't know how you're hurt."

"Hip." She gritted her teeth at the awful, radiating pain. "I think I busted my hip. Fell, caught my foot. Couldn't move. All the noise, nobody could hear me calling. Been here two, three hours. Got so weak."

"It's all right now." He tried to chafe some heat into her hands. "Sydney, get a blanket and pillow."

She had them in her arms and was already crouching beside Mrs. Wolburg before he'd finished the order. "Here now. I'm just going to lift your head a little." Gently she set the woman's limp head on the pillow. Despite the raging heat, Mrs. Wolburg was shivering with cold. As she continued to speak in quiet, soothing tones, Sydney tucked the blanket around her. "Just a few more minutes," Sydney murmured, and stroked the clammy forehead.

A crowd was forming at the door. Though he didn't like leaving Sydney with the injured woman, he rose. "I want to keep the neighbors away. Send someone to keep an eye for the ambulance."

"Fine." While fear pumped hard in her heart, she continued to smile down at Mrs. Wolburg. "You have a lovely apartment. Do you crochet the doilies yourself?"

"Been doing needlework for sixty years, since I was pregnant with my first daughter."

"They're beautiful. Do you have other children?"

"Six, three of each. And twenty grandchildren. Five great…" She shut her eyes on a flood of pain, then opened them again and managed a smile. "Been after me for living alone, but I like my own place and my own way."

"Of course."

"And my daughter, Lizzy? Moved clear out to Phoenix, Arizona. Now what would I want to live out there for?"

Sydney smiled and stroked. "I couldn't say."

"They'll be on me now," she muttered, and let her eyes close again. "Wouldn't have happened if I hadn't dropped my glasses. Terribly nearsighted. Getting old's hell, girl, and don't let anyone tell you different. Couldn't see where I was going and snagged my foot in that torn linoleum. Mik told me to keep it taped down, but I wanted to give it a good scrub." She managed a wavery smile. "Least I've been lying here on a clean floor."

"Paramedics are coming up," Mikhail said from behind her. Sydney only nodded, filled with a terrible guilt and anger she was afraid to voice.

"You call my grandson, Mik? He lives up on Eighty-first. He'll take care of the rest of the family."

"Don't worry about it, Mrs. Wolburg."

Fifteen efficient minutes later, Sydney stood on the sidewalk watching as the stretcher was lifted into the back of the ambulance.

"Did you reach her grandson?" she asked Mikhail.

"I left a message on his machine."

Nodding, she walked to the curb and tried to hail a cab.

"Where's your car?"

"I sent him home. I didn't know how long I'd be and it was too hot to leave him sitting there. Maybe I should go back in and call a cab."

"In a hurry?"

She winced as the siren shrieked. "I want to get to the hospital."

Nonplussed, he jammed his hands into his pockets. "There's no need for you to go."

She turned, and her eyes, in the brief moment they held his, were ripe with emotion. Saying nothing, she faced away until a cab finally swung to the curb. Nor did she speak when Mikhail climbed in behind her.

She hated the smell of hospitals. Layers of illness, antiseptics, fear and heavy cleaners. The memory of the last days her grandfather had lain dying were still too fresh in her mind. The Emergency Room of the downtown hospital added one more layer. Fresh blood.

Sydney steeled herself against it and walked through the crowds of the sick and injured to the admitting window.

"You had a Mrs. Wolburg just come in."

"That's right." The clerk stabbed keys on her computer. "You family?"

"No, I—"

"We're going to need some family to fill out these forms. Patient said she wasn't insured."

Mikhail was already leaning over, eyes dangerous, when Sydney snapped out her answer. "Hayward Industries will be responsible for Mrs. Wolburg's medical expenses." She reached into her bag for identification and slapped it onto the counter. "I'm Sydney Hayward. Where is Mrs. Wolburg?"

"In X ray." The frost in Sydney's eyes had the clerk shifting in her chair. "Dr. Cohen's attending."

So they waited, drinking bad coffee among the moans and tears of inner city ER. Sometimes Sydney would lay her head back against the wall and shut her eyes. She appeared to be dozing, but all the while she was thinking what it would be like to be old, and alone and helpless.

He wanted to think she was only there to cover her butt. Oh yes, he wanted to think that of her. It was so much more comfortable to think of her as the head of some bloodless company than as a woman.

But he remembered how quickly she had acted in the Wolburg apartment, how gentle she had been with the old woman. And most of all, he remembered the look in her eyes out on the street. All that misery and compassion and guilt welling up in those big eyes.

"She tripped on the linoleum," Sydney murmured.

It was the first time she'd spoken in nearly an hour, and Mikhail turned his head to study her. Her eyes were still closed, her face pale and in repose.

"She was only walking in her own kitchen and fell because the floor was old and unsafe."

"You're making it safe."

Sydney continued as if she hadn't heard. "Then she could

only lie there, hurt and alone. Her voice was so weak. I nearly walked right by."

"You didn't walk by." His hand hesitated over hers. Then, with an oath, he pressed his palm to the back of her hand. "You're only one Hayward, Sydney. Your grandfather—"

"He was ill." Her hand clenched under Mikhail's, and her eyes squeezed more tightly closed. "He was sick nearly two years, and I was in Europe. I didn't know. He didn't want to disrupt my life. My father was dead, and there was only me, and he didn't want to worry me. When he finally called me, it was almost over. He was a good man. He wouldn't have let things get so bad, but he couldn't... he just couldn't."

She let out a short, shuddering breath. Mikhail turned her hand over and linked his fingers with hers.

"When I got to New York, he was in the hospital. He looked so small, so tired. He told me I was the only Hayward left. Then he died," she said wearily. "And I was."

"You're doing what needs to be done. No one can ask for more than that."

She opened her eyes again, met his. "I don't know."

They waited again, in silence.

It was nearly two hours before Mrs. Wolburg's frantic grandson rushed in. The entire story had to be told again before he hurried off to call the rest of his family.

Four hours after they'd walked into Emergency, the doctor came out to fill them in.

A fractured hip, a mild concussion. She would be moved to a room right after she'd finished in Recovery. Her age made the break serious, but her health helped balance that. Sydney left both her office and home numbers with the doctor and the grandson, requesting to be kept informed of Mrs. Wolburg's condition.

Unbearably weary in body and mind, Sydney walked out of the hospital.

"You need food," Mikhail said.

"What? No, really, I'm just tired."

Ignoring that, he grabbed her arm and pulled her down the street. "Why do you always say the opposite of what I say?"

"I don't."

"See, you did it again. You need meat."

If she kept trying to drag her heels, he was going to pull her arm right out of the socket. Annoyed, she scrambled to keep pace. "What makes you think you know what I need?"

"Because I do." He pulled up short at a light and she bumped into him. Before he could stop it, his hand had lifted to touch her face. "God, you're so beautiful."

While she blinked in surprise, he swore, scowled then dragged her into the street seconds before the light turned.

"Maybe I'm not happy with you," he went on, muttering to himself. "Maybe I think you're a nuisance, and a snob, and—"

"I am not a snob."

He said something vaguely familiar in his native language. Sydney's chin set when she recalled the translation. "It is not bull. You're the snob if you think I am just because I come from a different background."

He stopped, eyeing her with a mixture of distrust and interest. "Fine then, you won't mind eating in here." He yanked her into a noisy bar and grill. She found herself plopped down in a narrow booth with him, hip to hip.

There were scents of meat cooking, onions frying,

spilled beer, all overlaid with grease. Her mouth watered. "I said I wasn't hungry."

"And I say you're a snob, and a liar."

The color that stung her cheeks pleased him, but it didn't last long enough. She leaned forward. "And would you like to know what I think of you?"

Again he lifted a hand to touch her cheek. It was irresistible. "Yes, I would."

She was saved from finding a description in her suddenly murky brain by the waitress.

"Two steaks, medium rare, and two of what you've got on tap."

"I don't like men to order for me," Sydney said tightly.

"Then you can order for me next time and we'll be even." Making himself comfortable, he tossed his arm over the back of the booth and stretched out his legs. "Why don't you take off your jacket, Hayward? You're hot."

"Stop telling me what I am. And stop that, too."

"What?"

"Playing with my hair."

He grinned. "I was playing with your neck. I like your neck." To prove it, he skimmed a finger down it again.

She clamped her teeth on the delicious shudder that followed it down her spine. "I wish you'd move over."

"Okay." He shifted closer. "Better?"

Calm, she told herself. She would be calm. After a cleansing breath, she turned her head. "If you don't..." And his lips brushed over hers, stopping the words and the thought behind them.

"I want you to kiss me back."

She started to shake her head, but couldn't manage it.

"I want to watch you when you do," he murmured. "I want to know what's there."

"There's nothing there."

But his mouth closed over hers and proved her a liar. She fell into the kiss, one hand lost in his hair, the other clamped on his shoulder.

She felt everything. Everything. And it all moved too fast. Her mind seemed to dim until she could barely hear the clatter and bustle of the bar. But she felt his mouth angle over hers, his teeth nip, his tongue seduce.

Whatever she was doing to him, he was doing to her. He knew it. He saw it in the way her eyes glazed before they closed, felt it in the hot, ready passion of her lips. It was supposed to soothe his ego, prove a point. But it did neither.

It only left him aching.

"Sorry to break this up." The waitress slapped two frosted mugs on the table. "Steak's on its way."

Sydney jerked her head back. His arms were still around her, though his grip had loosened. And she, she was plastered against him. Her body molded to his as they sat in a booth in a public place. Shame and fury battled for supremacy as she yanked herself away.

"That was a despicable thing to do."

He shrugged and picked up his beer. "I didn't do it alone." Over the foam, his eyes sharpened. "Not this time, or last time."

"Last time, you…"

"What?"

Sydney lifted her mug and sipped gingerly. "I don't want to discuss it."

He wanted to argue, even started to, but there was a sheen of hurt in her eyes that baffled him. He didn't mind making her angry. Hell, he enjoyed it. But he didn't know what he'd done to make her hurt. He waited until the waitress had set the steaks in front of them.

"You've had a rough day," he said so kindly Sydney gasped. "I don't mean to make it worse."

"It's…" She struggled with a response. "It's been a rough day all around. Let's just put it behind us."

"Done." Smiling, he handed her a knife and fork. "Eat your dinner. We'll have a truce."

"Good." She discovered she had an appetite after all.

Chapter 5

Sydney didn't know how Mildred Wolburg's accident had leaked to the press, but by Tuesday afternoon her office was flooded with calls from reporters. A few of the more enterprising staked out the lobby of the Hayward Building and cornered her when she left for the day.

By Wednesday rumors were flying around the offices that Hayward was facing a multimillion-dollar suit, and Sydney had several unhappy board members on her hands. The consensus was that by assuming responsibility for Mrs. Wolburg's medical expenses, Sydney had admitted Hayward's neglect and had set the company up for a large public settlement.

It was bad press, and bad business.

Knowing no route but the direct one, Sydney prepared a statement for the press and agreed to an emergency board meeting. By Friday, she thought as she walked into the hospital, she would know if she would remain in charge of

Hayward or whether her position would be whittled down to figurehead.

Carrying a stack of paperbacks in one hand and a potted plant in the other, Sydney paused outside of Mrs. Wolburg's room. Because it was Sydney's third visit since the accident, she knew the widow wasn't likely to be alone. Invariably, friends and family streamed in and out during visiting hours. This time she saw Mikhail, Keely and two of Mrs. Wolburg's children.

Mikhail spotted her as Sydney was debating whether to slip out again and leave the books and plant she'd brought at the nurses' station.

"You have more company, Mrs. Wolburg."

"Sydney." The widow's eyes brightened behind her thick lenses. "More books."

"Your grandson told me you liked to read." Feeling awkward, she set the books on the table beside the bed and took Mrs. Wolburg's outstretched hand.

"My Harry used to say I'd rather read than eat." The thin, bony fingers squeezed Sydney's. "That's a beautiful plant."

"I noticed you have several in your apartment." She smiled, feeling slightly more relaxed as the conversation in the room picked up again to flow around them. "And the last time I was here the room looked like a florist's shop." She glanced around at the banks of cut flowers in vases, pots, baskets, even in a ceramic shoe. "So I settled on an African violet."

"I do have a weakness for flowers and growing things. Set it right there on the dresser, will you, dear? Between the roses and the carnations."

"She's getting spoiled." As Sydney moved to comply, the visiting daughter winked at her brother. "Flowers, presents, pampering. We'll be lucky to ever get home-baked cookies again."

"Oh, I might have a batch or two left in me." Mrs. Wolburg preened in her new crocheted bed jacket. "Mik tells me I'm getting a brand-new oven. Eye level, so I won't have to bend and stoop."

"So I think I should get the first batch," Mikhail said as he sniffed the roses. "The chocolate chip."

"Please." Keely pressed a hand to her stomach. "I'm dieting. I'm getting murdered next week, and I have to look my best." She noted Sydney's stunned expression and grinned. *"Death Stalk,"* she explained. "My first TV movie. I'm the third victim of the maniacal psychopath. I get strangled in this really terrific negligee."

"You shouldn't have left your windows unlocked," Mrs. Wolburg told her, and Keely grinned again.

"Well, that's show biz."

Sydney waited until a break in the conversation, then made her excuses. Mikhail gave her a ten-second lead before he slipped a yellow rose out of a vase. "See you later, beautiful." He kissed Mrs. Wolburg on the cheek and left her chuckling.

In a few long strides, he caught up with Sydney at the elevators. "Hey. You look like you could use this." He offered the flower.

"It couldn't hurt." After sniffing the bloom, she worked up a smile. "Thanks."

"You want to tell me why you're upset?"

"I'm not upset." She jabbed the down button again.

"Never argue with an artist about your feelings." Insistently he tipped back her chin with one finger. "I see fatigue and distress, worry and annoyance."

The ding of the elevator relieved her, though she knew he

would step inside the crowded car with her. She frowned a little when she found herself pressed between Mikhail and a large woman carrying a suitcase-sized purse. Someone on the elevator had used an excess of expensive perfume. Fleetingly Sydney wondered if that shouldn't be as illegal as smoking in a closed car.

"Any Gypsies in your family?" she asked Mikhail on impulse.

"Naturally."

"I'd rather you use a crystal ball to figure out the future than analyze my feelings at the moment."

"We'll see what we can do."

The car stopped on each floor. People shuffled off or squeezed in. By the time they reached the lobby, Sydney was hard up against Mikhail's side, with his arm casually around her waist. He didn't bother to remove it after they'd stepped off. She didn't bother to mention it.

"The work's going well," he told her.

"Good." She didn't care to think how much longer she'd be directly involved with the project.

"The electrical inspection is done. Plumbing will perhaps take another week." He studied her abstracted expression. "And we have decided to make the new roof out of blue cheese."

"Hmm." She stepped outside, stopped and looked back at him. With a quick laugh, she shook her head. "That might look very distinctive—but risky with this heat."

"You were listening."

"Almost." Absently she pressed fingers to her throbbing temple as her driver pulled up to the curb. "I'm sorry. I've got a lot on my mind."

"Tell me."

It surprised her that she wanted to. She hadn't been able

to talk to her mother. Margerite would only be baffled. Channing—that was a joke. Sydney doubted that any of her friends would understand how she had become so attached to Hayward in such a short time.

"There really isn't any point," she decided, and started toward her waiting car and driver.

Did she think he would let her walk away, with that worry line between her brows and the tension knotted tight in her shoulders?

"How about a lift home?"

She glanced back. The ride home from her mother's party was still a raw memory. But he was smiling at her in an easy, friendly fashion. Nonthreatening? No, he would never be that with those dark looks and untamed aura. But they had agreed on a truce, and it was only a few blocks.

"Sure. We'll drop Mr. Stanislaski off in Soho, Donald."

"Yes, ma'am."

She took the precaution of sliding, casually, she hoped, all the way over to the far window. "Mrs. Wolburg looks amazingly well, considering," she began.

"She's strong." It was Mozart this time, he noted, low and sweet through the car speakers.

"The doctor says she'll be able to go home with her son soon."

"And you've arranged for the therapist to visit." Sydney stopped passing the rose from hand to hand and looked at him. "She told me," he explained. "Also that when she is ready to go home again, there will be a nurse to stay with her, until she is well enough to be on her own."

"I'm not playing Samaritan," Sydney mumbled. "I'm just trying to do what's right."

"I realize that. I realize, too, that you're concerned for

her. But there's something more on your mind. Is it the papers and the television news?"

Her eyes went from troubled to frigid. "I didn't assume responsibility for Mrs. Wolburg's medical expenses for publicity, good or bad. And I don't—"

"I know you didn't." He cupped a hand over one of her clenched ones. "Remember, I was there. I saw you with her."

Sydney drew a deep breath. She had to. She'd very nearly had a tirade, and a lost temper was hardly the answer. "The point is," she said more calmly, "an elderly woman was seriously injured. Her pain shouldn't become company politics or journalistic fodder. What I did, I did because I knew it was right. I just want to make sure the right thing continues to be done."

"You are president of Hayward."

"For the moment." She turned to look out the window as they pulled up in front of the apartment building. "I see we're making progress on the roof."

"Among other things." Because he was far from finished, he leaned over her and opened the door on her side. For a moment, they were so close, his body pressed lightly to hers. She had an urge, almost desperate, to rub her fingers over his cheek, to feel the rough stubble he'd neglected to shave away. "I'd like you to come up," he told her. "I have something for you."

Sydney caught her fingers creeping up and snatched them back. "It's nearly six. I really should—"

"Come up for an hour," he finished. "Your driver can come back for you, yes?"

"Yes." She shifted away, not sure whether she wanted to get out or simply create some distance between them. "You can messenger your report over."

"I could."

He moved another inch. In defense, Sydney swung her legs out of the car. "All right then, but I don't think it'll take an hour."

"But it will."

She relented because she preferred spending an hour going over a report than sitting in her empty apartment thinking about the scheduled board meeting. After giving her driver instructions, she walked with Mikhail toward the building.

"You've repaired the stoop."

"Tuesday. It wasn't easy getting the men to stop sitting on it long enough." He exchanged greetings with the three who were ranged across it now as Sydney passed through the aroma of beer and tobacco. "We can take the elevator. The inspection certificate is hardly dry."

She thought of the five long flights up. "I can't tell you how glad I am to hear that." She stepped in with him, waited while he pulled the open iron doors closed.

"It has character now," he said as they began the ascent. "And you don't worry that you'll get in to get downstairs and spend the night inside."

"There's good news."

He pulled the doors open again as the car slid to a smooth, quiet stop. In the hallway, the ceiling was gone, leaving bare joists and new wiring exposed.

"The water damage from leaking was bad," Mikhail said conversationally. "Once the roof is finished, we'll replace."

"I've expected some complaints from the tenants, but we haven't received a single one. Isn't it difficult for everyone, living in a construction zone?"

Mikhail jingled his keys. "Inconvenient. But everyone is excited and watches the progress. Mr. Stuben from the third floor comes up every morning before he leaves for work. Every day he says, 'Mikhail, you have your work cut out for you.'" He grinned as he opened the door. "Some days I'd like to throw my hammer at him." He stepped back and nudged her inside. "Sit."

Lips pursed, Sydney studied the room. The furniture had been pushed together in the center—to make it easier to work, she imagined. Tables were stacked on top of chairs, the rug had been rolled up. Under the sheet he'd tossed over his worktable were a variety of interesting shapes that were his sculptures, his tools, and blocks of wood yet to be carved.

It smelled like sawdust, she thought, and turpentine.

"Where?"

He stopped on his way to the kitchen and looked back. After a quick study, he leaned into the jumble and lifted out an old oak rocker. One-handed, Sydney noted, and felt foolish and impressed.

"Here." After setting it on a clear spot, he headed back into the kitchen.

The surface of the rocker was smooth as satin. When Sydney sat, she found the chair slipped around her like comforting arms. Ten seconds after she'd settled, she was moving it gently to and fro.

"This is beautiful."

He could hear the faint creak as the rocker moved and didn't bother to turn. "I made it for my sister years ago when she had a baby." His voice changed subtly as he turned on the kitchen tap. "She lost the baby, Lily, after only a few weeks, and it was painful for Natasha to keep the chair."

"I'm sorry." The creaking stopped. "I can't think of anything worse for a parent to face."

"Because there is nothing." He came back in, carrying a glass of water and a bottle. "Lily will always leave a little scar on the heart. But Tash has three children now. So pain is balanced with joy. Here." He put the glass in her hand, then shook two aspirin out of the bottle. "You have a headache."

She frowned down at the pills he dropped into her palm. True, her head was splitting, but she hadn't mentioned it. "I might have a little one," she muttered. "How do you know?"

"I can see it in your eyes." He waited until she'd sipped and swallowed, then walked behind the chair to circle her temples with his fingers. "It's not such a little one, either."

There was no doubt she should tell him to stop. And she would. Any minute. Unable to resist, she leaned back, letting her eyes close as his fingers stroked away the worst of the pain.

"Is this what you had for me? Headache remedies?"

Her voice was so quiet, so tired that his heart twisted a little. "No, I have something else for you. But it can wait until you're feeling better. Talk to me, Sydney. Tell me what's wrong. Maybe I can help."

"It's something I have to take care of myself."

"Okay. Will that change if you talk to me?"

No, she thought. It was her problem, her future. But what harm would it do to talk it out, to say it all out loud and hear someone else's viewpoint?

"Office politics." She sighed as he began to massage the base of her neck. His rough, calloused fingers were as gentle as a mother's. "I imagine they can be tricky enough when you have experience. All I have is the family name and my grandfather's last wishes. The publicity on Mrs. Wolburg has left my position in the company very shaky. I assumed responsibility without going through channels or consulting legal. The board isn't pleased with me."

His eyes had darkened, but his hands remained gentle. "Because you have integrity?"

"Because I jumped the gun, so to speak. The resulting publicity only made things worse. The consensus is that someone with more savvy could have handled the Wolburg matter—that's how it's referred to at Hayward. The Wolburg matter in a quiet, tidy fashion. There's a board meeting at noon on Friday, and they could very well request that I step down as president."

"And will you?"

"I don't know." He was working on her shoulders now, competently, thoroughly. "I'd like to fight, draw the whole thing out. Then again, the company's been in upheaval for over a year, and having the president and the board as adversaries won't help Hayward. Added to that, my executive vice president and I are already on poor terms. He feels, perhaps justifiably, that he should be in the number one slot." She laughed softly. "There are times I wish he had it."

"No, you don't." He resisted the urge to bend down and press his lips to the long, slender column of her neck. Barely. "You like being in charge, and I think you're good at it."

She stopped rocking to turn her head and stare at him. "You're the first person who's ever said that to me. Most of the people who know me think I'm playing at this, or that I'm experiencing a kind of temporary insanity."

His hand slid lightly down her arm as he came around to crouch in front of her. "Then they don't know you, do they?"

There were so many emotions popping through her as she kept her eyes on his. But pleasure, the simple pleasure of being understood was paramount. "Maybe they don't," she murmured. "Maybe they don't."

"I won't give you advice." He picked up one of her hands because he enjoyed examining it, the long, ringless fingers, the slender wrist, the smooth, cool skin. "I don't know about office politics or board meetings. But I think you'll do what's right. You have a good brain and a good heart."

Hardly aware that she'd turned her hand over under his and linked them, she smiled. The connection was more complete than joined fingers, and she couldn't understand it. This was support, a belief in her, and an encouragement she'd never expected to find.

"Odd that I'd have to come to a Ukrainian carpenter for a pep talk. Thanks."

"You're welcome." He looked back into her eyes. "Your headache's gone."

Surprised, she touched her fingers to her temple. "Yes, yes it is." In fact, she couldn't remember ever feeling more relaxed. "You could make a fortune with those hands."

He grinned and slid them up her arms, pushing the sleeves of her jacket along so he could feel the bare flesh beneath. "It's only a matter of knowing what to do with them, and when." And he knew exactly how he wanted to use those hands on her. Unfortunately, the timing was wrong.

"Yes, well…" It was happening again, those little licks of fire in the pit of her stomach, the trembling heat along her skin. "I really am grateful, for everything. I should be going."

"You have time yet." His fingers glided back down her arms to link with hers. "I haven't given you your present."

"Present?" He was drawing her slowly to her feet. Now they were thigh to thigh, her eyes level with his mouth. It was curved and close, sending her system into overdrive.

He had only to lean down. Inches, bare inches. Imagining it nearly drove him crazy. Not an altogether unpleasant feeling, he discovered, this anticipation, this wondering. If she offered, and only when she offered, would he take.

"Don't you like presents, *milaya?*"

His voice was like hot cream, pouring richly over her. "I...the report," she said, remembering. "Weren't you going to give me your report?"

His thumbs skimmed over her wrists and felt the erratic beat of her pulse. It was tempting, very tempting. "I can send the report. I had something else in mind."

"Something..." Her own mind quite simply shut down.

He laughed, so delighted with her he wanted to kiss her breathless. Instead he released her hands and walked away. She didn't move, not an inch as he strolled over to the shelves and tossed up the drop cloth. In a moment he was back, pressing the little Cinderella into her hand.

"I'd like you to have this."

"Oh, but..." She tried, really tried to form a proper refusal. The words wouldn't come.

"You don't like?"

"No. I mean, yes, of course I like it, it's exquisite. But why?" Her fingers were already curving possessively around it when she lifted her eyes to his. "Why would you give it to me?"

"Because she reminds me of you. She's lovely, fragile, unsure of herself."

The description had Sydney's pleasure dimming. "Most people would term her romantic."

"I'm not most. Here, as she runs away, she doesn't believe enough." He stroked a finger down the delicate folds of the ball gown. "She follows the rules, without question. It's midnight, and she was in the arms of her prince, but she breaks away and runs. Because that was the rule. And she is afraid, afraid to let him see beneath the illusion to the woman."

"She had to leave. She'd promised. Besides, she'd have been humiliated to have been caught there in rags and bare feet."

Tilting his head, Mikhail studied her. "Do you think he cared about her dress?"

"Well, no, I don't suppose it would have mattered to him." Sydney let out an impatient breath as he grinned at her. It was ridiculous, standing here debating the psychology of a fairy-tale character. "In any case, it ended happily, and though I've nothing in common with Cinderella, the figurine's beautiful. I'll treasure it."

"Good. Now, I'll walk you downstairs. You don't want to be late for dinner with your mother."

"She won't be there until eight-thirty. She's always late." Halfway through the door, Sydney stopped. "How did you know I was meeting my mother?"

"She told me, ah, two days ago. We had a drink uptown."

Sydney turned completely around so that he was standing on one side of the threshold, she on the other. "You had drinks with my mother?" she asked, spacing each word carefully.

"Yes." Lazily he leaned on the jamb. "Before you try to turn me into an iceberg, understand that I have no sexual interest in Margerite."

"That's lovely. Just lovely." If she hadn't already put the figurine into her purse, she might have thrown it in his face. "We agreed you'd leave my mother alone."

"We agreed nothing," he corrected. "And I don't bother your mother." There was little to be gained by telling her that Margerite had called him three times before he'd given in and met her. "It was a friendly drink, and after it was done, I think Margerite understood we are unsuitable for anything but friendship. Particularly," he said, holding up a finger to block her interruption, "since I am very sexually interested in her daughter."

That stopped her words cold. She swallowed, struggled for composure and failed. "You are not, all you're interested in is scoring a few macho points."

Something flickered in his eyes. "Would you like to come back inside so that I can show you exactly what I'm interested in?"

"No." Before she could stop herself, she'd taken a retreating step. "But I would like you to have the decency not to play games with my mother."

He wondered if Margerite would leap so quickly to her daughter's defense, or if Sydney would understand that her mother was only interested in a brief affair with a younger man—something he'd made very clear he wanted no part in.

"Since I would hate for your headache to come back after I went to the trouble to rid you of it, I will make myself as clear as I can. I have no intention of becoming romantically, physically or emotionally involved with your mother. Does that suit you?"

"It would if I could believe you."

He didn't move, not a muscle, but she sensed he had cocked, like the hammer on a gun. His voice was low and deadly. "I don't lie."

She nodded, cool as an ice slick. "Just stick to hammering nails, Mikhail. We'll get along fine. And I can find my own way down." She didn't whirl away, but turned slowly and walked to the elevator. Though she didn't look back as she stepped inside, she was well aware that he watched her go.

* * *

At noon sharp, Sydney sat at the head of the long walnut table of the boardroom. Ten men and two women were ranged down either side with crystal tumblers at their elbows, pads and pens at the ready. Heavy brocade drapes were drawn back to reveal a wall of window, tinted to cut the glare of sunlight—had there been any. Instead there was a thick curtain of rain, gray as soot. She could just make out the silhouette of the Times Building. Occasionally a murmur of thunder sneaked in through the stone and glass.

The gloom suited her. Sydney felt exactly like the reckless child summoned to the principal's office.

She scanned the rows of faces, some of whom had belonged in this office, at this very table, since before she'd been born. Perhaps they would be the toughest to sway, those who thought of her as the little girl who had come to Hayward to bounce on Grandfather's knee.

Then there was Lloyd, halfway down the gleaming surface, his face so smug, so confident, she wanted to snarl. No, she realized as his gaze flicked to hers and held. She wanted to win.

"Ladies, gentlemen." The moment the meeting was called to order she rose. "Before we begin discussion of the matter so much on our minds, I'd like to make a statement."

"You've already made your statement to the press, Sydney," Lloyd pointed out. "I believe everyone here is aware of your position."

There was a rippling murmur, some agreement, some dissent. She let it fade before she spoke again. "Nonetheless, as the president, and the major stockholder of Hayward, I will have my say, then the meeting will open for discussion."

Her throat froze as all eyes fixed on her. Some were patient, some indulgent, some speculative.

"I understand the board's unease with the amount of money allocated to the Soho project. Of Hayward's holdings, this building represents a relatively small annual income. However, this small income has been steady. Over the last ten years, this complex has needed—or I should say received—little or no maintenance. You know, of course, from the quarterly reports just how much this property has increased in value in this space of time. I believe, from a purely practical standpoint, that the money I allocated is insurance to protect our investment."

She wanted to stop, to pick up her glass and drain it, but knew the gesture would make her seem as nervous as she was.

"In addition, I believe Hayward has a moral, an ethical and a legal obligation to insure that our tenants receive safe and decent housing."

"That property could have been made safe and decent for half of the money budgeted," Lloyd put in.

Sydney barely glanced at him. "You're quite right. I believe my grandfather wanted more than the minimum required for Hayward. He wanted it to be the best, the finest. I know I do. I won't stand here and quote you figures. They're in your folders and can be discussed at length in a few moments. Yes, the budget for the Soho project is high, and so are Hayward standards."

"Sydney." Howard Keller, one of her grandfather's oldest associates, spoke gently. "None of us here doubt your motives or your enthusiasm. Your judgment, however, in this, and in the Wolburg matter, is something we must consider. The publicity over the past few days has been extremely detrimental. Hayward stock is down a full three percent. That's in addition to the drop we suffered when you took your position as head of the company. Our stockholders are, understandably, concerned."

"The Wolburg matter," Sydney said with steel in her voice, "is an eighty-year-old woman with a fractured hip. She fell because the floor in her kitchen, a floor we neglected to replace, was unsafe."

"It's precisely that kind of reckless statement that will open Hayward up to a major lawsuit," Lloyd put in. He kept his tone the quiet sound of calm reason. "Isn't it the function of insurance investigators and legal to come to a decision on this, after a careful, thoughtful overview of the situation? We can't run our company on emotion and impulse. Miss Hayward's heart might have been touched by the Wolburg matter, but there are procedures, channels to be used. Now that the press has jumped on this—"

"Yes," she broke in. "It's very interesting how quickly the press learned about the accident. It's hard to believe that only days after an unknown, unimportant old lady falls in her downtown apartment, the press is slapping Hayward in the headlines."

"I would imagine she called them herself," Lloyd said.

Her smile was icy. "Would you?"

"I don't think the issue is how the press got wind of this," Mavis Trelane commented. "The point is they did, and the resulting publicity has been shaded heavily against us, putting Hayward in a very vulnerable position. The stockholders want a solution quickly."

"Does anyone here believe Hayward is not culpable for Mrs. Wolburg's injuries?"

"It's not what we believe," Mavis corrected. "And none of us could make a decision on that until a full investigation into the incident. What is relevant is how such matters are handled."

She frowned when a knock interrupted her.

"I'm sorry," Sydney said, and moved away from the table to walk stiffly to the door. "Janine, I explained we weren't to be interrupted."

"Yes, ma'am." The secretary, who had thrown her loyalty to Sydney five minutes after hearing the story, kept her voice low. "This is important. I just got a call from a friend of mine. He works on Channel 6. Mrs. Wolburg's going to make a statement on the Noon News. Any minute now."

After a moment's hesitation, Sydney nodded. "Thank you, Janine."

"Good luck, Ms. Hayward."

Sydney smiled and shut the door. She was going to need it. Face composed, she turned back to the room. "I've just been told that Mrs. Wolburg is about to make a televised statement. I'm sure we're all interested in what she has to say. So with your permission, I'll turn on the set." Rather than waiting for the debate to settle it, Sydney picked up the remote and aimed it at the console in the corner.

While Lloyd was stating that the board needed to concern themselves with the facts and not a publicity maneuver, Channel 6 cut from commercial to Mrs. Wolburg's hospital bed.

The reporter, a pretty woman in her early twenties with eyes as sharp as nails, began the interview by asking the patient to explain how she came by her injury.

Several members of the board shook their heads and muttered among themselves as she explained about tripping on the ripped linoleum and how the noise of the construction had masked her calls for help.

Lloyd had to stop his lips from curving as he imagined Sydney's ship springing another leak.

"And this floor," the reporter continued. "Had the condition of it been reported to Hayward?"

"Oh, sure. Mik—that's Mikhail Stanislaski, the sweet boy up on the fifth floor, wrote letters about the whole building."

"And nothing was done?"

"Nope, not a thing. Why Mr. and Mrs. Kowalski, the young couple in 101, had a piece of plaster as big as a pie plate fall out of their ceiling. Mik fixed it."

"So the tenants were forced to take on the repairs themselves, due to Hayward's neglect."

"I guess you could say that. Up until the last few weeks."

"Oh, and what happened in the last few weeks?"

"That would be when Sydney—that's Miss Hayward—took over the company. She's the granddaughter of old man Hayward. Heard he'd been real sick the last couple years. Guess things got away from him. Anyway, Mik went to see her, and she came out herself that very day to take a look. Not two weeks later, and the building was crawling with construction workers. We got new windows. Got a new roof going on right this minute. All the plumbing's being fixed, too. Every single thing Mik put on the list is going to be taken care of."

"Really? And did all this happen before or after your injury?"

"Before," Mrs. Wolburg said, a bit impatient with the sarcasm. "I told you all that hammering and sawing was the reason nobody heard me when I fell. And I want you to know that Miss Hayward was there checking the place out again that day. She and Mik found me. She sat right there on the floor and talked to me, brought me a pillow and a blanket and stayed with me until the ambulance came. Came to the hospital, too, and took care of all my medical bills. Been to visit me three times since I've been here."

"Wouldn't you say that Hayward, and therefore Sydney Hayward, is responsible for you being here?"

"Bad eyes and a hole in the floor's responsible," she said evenly. "And I'll tell you just what I told those ambulance chasers who've been calling my family. I've got no reason to sue Hayward. They've been taking care of me since the minute I was hurt. Now maybe if they'd dallied around and tried to make like it wasn't any of their doing, I'd feel differently. But they did what was right, and you can't ask for better than that. Sydney's got ethics, and as long as she's in charge I figure Hayward has ethics, too. I'm pleased to live in a building owned by a company with a conscience."

Sydney stayed where she was after the interview ended. Saying nothing, she switched off the set and waited.

"You can't buy that kind of goodwill," Mavis decided. "Your method may have been unorthodox, Sydney, and I don't doubt there will still be some backwash to deal with, but all in all, I think the stockholders will be pleased."

The discussion labored on another thirty minutes, but the crisis had passed.

The moment Sydney was back in her own office, she picked up the phone. The receiver rang in her ear twelve times, frustrating her, before it was finally picked up on the other end.

"Yeah?"

"Mikhail?"

"Nope, he's down the hall."

"Oh, well then, I—"

"Hang on." The phone rattled, clanged then clattered as

the male voice boomed out Mikhail's name. Feeling like a
fool, Sydney stayed on the line.

"Hello?"

"Mikhail, it's Sydney."

He grinned and grabbed the jug of ice water out of the
refrigerator. "Hello, anyway."

"I just saw the news. I suppose you knew."

"Caught it on my lunch break. So?"

"You asked her to do it?"

"No, I didn't." He paused long enough to gulp down
about a pint of water. "I told her how things were, and she
came up with the idea herself. It was a good one."

"Yes, it was a good one. And I owe you."

"Yeah?" He thought about it. "Okay. Pay up."

Why she'd expected him to politely refuse to take credit
was beyond her. "Excuse me?"

"Pay up, Hayward. You can have dinner with me on
Sunday."

"Really, I don't see how one has to do with the other."

"You owe me," he reminded her, "and that's what I want.
Nothing fancy, okay? I'll pick you up around four."

"Four? Four in the afternoon for dinner?"

"Right." He pulled a carpenter's pencil out of his pocket.
"What's your address?"

He let out a low whistle as she reluctantly rattled it off.
"Nice." He finished writing it on the wall. "Got a phone
number? In case something comes up."

She was scowling, but she gave it to him. "I want to
make it clear that—"

"Make it clear when I pick you up. I'm on the clock,
and you're paying." On impulse he outlined her address
and phone number with a heart. "See you Sunday. Boss."

Chapter 6

Sydney studied her reflection in the cheval glass critically and cautiously. It wasn't as if it were a date. She'd reminded herself of that several hundred times over the weekend. It was more of a payment, and no matter how she felt about Mikhail, she owed him. Haywards paid their debts.

Nothing formal. She'd taken him at his word there. The little dress was simple, its scooped neck and thin straps a concession to the heat. The nipped in waist was flattering, the flared skirt comfortable. The thin, nearly weightless material was teal blue. Not that she'd paid any attention to his suggestion she wear brighter colors.

Maybe the dress was new, purchased after a frantic two hours of searching—but that was only because she'd wanted something new.

The short gold chain with its tiny links and the hoops at her ears were plain but elegant. She'd spent longer than

usual on her makeup, but that was only because she'd been
experimenting with some new shades of eyeshadow.

After much debate, she'd opted to leave her hair down.
Then, of course, she'd had to fool with it until the style
suited her. Fluffed out, skimming just above her shoulders
seemed casual enough to her. And sexy. Not that she cared
about being sexy tonight, but a woman was entitled to a
certain amount of vanity.

She hesitated over the cut-glass decanter of perfume, remembering how Mikhail had described her scent. With a
shrug, she touched it to pulse points. It hardly mattered if
it appealed to him. She was wearing it for herself.

Satisfied, she checked the contents of her purse, then
her watch. She was a full hour early. Blowing out a long
breath, she sat down on the bed. For the first time in her
life, she actively wished for a drink.

An hour and fifteen minutes later, after she had wandered through the apartment, plumping pillows, rearranging
statuary then putting it back where it had been in the first
place, he knocked on the door. She stopped in the foyer,
found she had to fuss with her hair another moment, then
pressed a hand to her nervous stomach. Outwardly composed, she opened the door.

It didn't appear he'd worried overmuch about his attire.
The jeans were clean but faded, the high-tops only slightly
less scuffed than his usual work boots. His shirt was tucked
in—a definite change—and was a plain, working man's
cotton the color of smoke. His hair flowed over the collar,
so black, so untamed no woman alive could help but fan-
tasize about letting her fingers dive in.

He looked earthy, a little wild, and more than a little
dangerous.

And he'd brought her a tulip.

"I'm late." He held out the flower, thinking she looked as cool and delicious as a sherbert parfait in a crystal dish. "I was working on your face."

"You were—what?"

"Your face." He slid a hand under her chin, his eyes narrowing in concentration. "I found the right piece of rosewood and lost track of time." As he studied, his fingers moved over her face as they had the wood, searching for answers. "You will ask me in?"

Her mind, empty as a leaky bucket, struggled to fill again. "Of course. For a minute." She stepped back, breaking contact. "I'll just put this in water."

When she left him, Mikhail let his gaze sweep the room. It pleased him. This was not the formal, professionally decorated home some might have expected of her. She really lived here, among the soft colors and quiet comfort. Style was added by a scattering of Art Nouveau, in the bronzed lamp shaped like a long, slim woman, and the sinuous etched flowers on the glass doors of a curio cabinet displaying a collection of antique beaded bags.

He noted his sculpture stood alone in a glossy old shadow box, and was flattered.

She came back, carrying the tulip in a slim silver vase. "I admire your taste."

She set the vase atop the curio. "Thank you."

"Nouveau is sensuous." He traced a finger down the flowing lines of the lamp. "And rebellious."

She nearly frowned before she caught herself. "I find it attractive. Graceful."

"Graceful, yes. Also powerful."

She didn't care for the way he was smiling at her, as if he knew a secret she didn't. And that the secret was her.

"Yes, well, I'm sure as an artist you'd agree art should have power. Would you like a drink before we go?"

"No, not before I drive."

"Drive?"

"Yes. Do you like Sunday drives, Sydney?"

"I…" She picked up her purse to give her hands something to do. There was no reason, none at all, for her to allow him to make her feel as awkward as a teenager on a first date. "I don't get much opportunity for them in the city." It seemed wise to get started. She moved to the door, wondering what it would be like to be in a car with him. Alone. "I didn't realize you kept a car."

His grin was quick and a tad self-mocking as they moved out into the hall. "A couple of years ago, after my art had some success, I bought one. It was a little fantasy of mine. I think I pay more to keep it parked than I did for the car. But fantasies are rarely free."

In the elevator, he pushed the button for the garage. "I think about it myself," she admitted. "I miss driving, the independence of it, I suppose. In Europe, I could hop in and zoom off whenever I chose. But it seems more practical to keep a driver here than to go to war every time you need a parking space."

"Sometime we'll go up north, along the river, and you can drive."

The image was almost too appealing, whipping along the roads toward the mountains upstate. She thought it was best not to comment. "Your report came in on Friday," she began.

"Not today." He reached down to take her hand as they stepped into the echoing garage. "Talking reports can wait till Monday. Here." He opened the door of a glossy red-and-cream MG. The canvas top was lowered. "You don't mind the top down?" he asked as she settled inside.

Sydney thought of the time and trouble she'd taken with her hair. And she thought of the freedom of having even a hot breeze blow through it. "No, I don't mind."

He climbed into the driver's seat, adjusting long legs, then gunned the engine. After taking a pair of mirrored sunglasses off the dash, he pulled out. The radio was set on rock. Sydney found herself smiling as they cruised around Central Park.

"You didn't mention where we were going."

"I know this little place. The food is good." He noted her foot was tapping along in time with the music. "Tell me where you lived in Europe."

"Oh, I didn't live in any one place. I moved around. Paris, Saint Tropez, Venice, London, Monte Carlo."

"Perhaps you have Gypsies in your blood, too."

"Perhaps." Not Gypsies, she thought. There had been nothing so romantic as wanderlust in her hopscotching travels through Europe. Only dissatisfaction, and a need to hide until wounds had healed. "Have you ever been?"

"When I was very young. But I would like to go back now that I am old enough to appreciate it. The art, you see, and the atmosphere, the architecture. What places did you like best?"

"A little village in the countryside of France where they milked cows by hand and grew fat purple grapes. There was a courtyard at the inn where I stayed, and the flowers were so big and bright. In the late afternoon you could sit and drink the most wonderful white wine and listen to the doves coo." She stopped, faintly embarrassed. "And of course, Paris," she said quickly. "The food, the shopping, the ballet. I knew several people, and enjoyed the parties."

Not so much, he thought, as she enjoyed sitting alone and listening to cooing doves.

"Do you ever think about going back to the Soviet Union?" she asked him.

"Often. To see the place where I was born, the house we lived in. It may not be there now. The hills where I played as a child. They would be."

His glasses only tossed her own reflection back at her. But she thought, behind them, his eyes would be sad. His voice was. "Things have changed so much, so quickly in the last few years. Glasnost, the Berlin Wall. You could go back."

"Sometimes I think I will, then I wonder if it's better to leave it a memory—part bitter, part sweet, but colored through the eyes of a child. I was very young when we left."

"It was difficult."

"Yes. More for my parents who knew the risks better than we. They had the courage to give up everything they had ever known to give their children the one thing they had never had. Freedom."

Moved, she laid a hand over his on the gearshift. Margerite had told her the story of escaping into Hungary in a wagon, making it seem like some sort of romantic adventure. It didn't seem romantic to Sydney. It seemed terrifying. "You must have been frightened."

"More than I ever hope to be again. At night I would lie awake, always cold, always hungry, and listen to my parents talk. One would reassure the other, and they would plan how far we might travel the next day—and the next. When we came to America, my father wept. And I understood it was over. I wasn't afraid anymore."

Her own eyes had filled. She turned away to let the wind

dry them. "But coming here must have been frightening, too. A different place, different language, different culture."

He heard the emotion in her voice. Though touched, he didn't want to make her sad. Not today. "The young adjust quickly. I had only to give the boy in the next house a bloody nose to feel at home."

She turned back, saw the grin and responded with a laugh. "Then, I suppose, you became inseparable friends."

"I was best man at his wedding only two years ago."

With a shake of her head, she settled back. It was then she noticed they were crossing the bridge over to Brooklyn. "You couldn't find a place to have dinner in Manhattan?"

His grin widened. "Not like this one."

A few minutes later, he was cruising through one of the old neighborhoods with its faded brick row houses and big, shady trees. Children scrambled along the sidewalks, riding bikes, jumping rope. At the curb where Mikhail stopped, two boys were having a deep and serious transaction with baseball cards.

"Hey, Mik!" Both of them jumped up before he'd even climbed out of the car. "You missed the game. We finished an hour ago."

"I'll catch the next one." He glanced over to see that Sydney had already gotten out and was standing in the street, studying the neighborhood with baffled and wary eyes. He leaned over and winked. "I got a hot date."

"Oh, man." Twelve-year-old disgust prevented either of them from further comment.

Laughing, Mikhail walked over to grab Sydney's hand and pull her to the sidewalk. "I don't understand," she began as he led her across the concrete heaved up by the roots of a huge old oak. "This is a restaurant?"

"No." He had to tug to make her keep up with him as he climbed the steps. "It's a house."

"But you said—"

"That we were going to dinner." He shoved the door open and took a deep sniff. "Smells like Mama made Chicken Kiev. You'll like."

"Your mother?" She nearly stumbled into the narrow entranceway. Scattered emotions flew inside her stomach like a bevy of birds. "You brought me to your parents' house?"

"Yes, for Sunday dinner."

"Oh, good Lord."

He lifted a brow. "You don't like Chicken Kiev?"

"No. Yes. That isn't the point. I wasn't expecting—"

"You're late," Yuri boomed. "Are you going to bring the woman in or stand in the doorway?"

Mikhail kept his eyes on Sydney's. "She doesn't want to come in," he called back.

"That's not it," she whispered, mortified. "You might have told me about this so I could have…oh, never mind." She brushed past him to take the couple of steps necessary to bring her into the living room. Yuri was just hauling himself out of a chair.

"Mr. Stanislaski, it's so nice of you to have me." She offered a hand and had it swallowed whole by his.

"You are welcome here. You will call me Yuri."

"Thank you."

"We are happy Mikhail shows good taste." Grinning, he used a stage whisper. "His mama, she didn't like the dancer with the blond hair."

"Thanks, Papa." Casually Mikhail draped an arm over Sydney's shoulders—felt her resist the urge to shrug it off. "Where is everyone?"

"Mama and Rachel are in the kitchen. Alex is later than

you. Alex sees all the girls, at the same time," Yuri told Sydney. "It should confuse him, but it does not."

"Yuri, you have not taken the trash out yet." A small woman with an exotic face and graying hair came out of the kitchen, carrying silverware in the skirt of her apron.

Yuri gave his son an affectionate thump on the back that nearly had Sydney pitching forward. "I wait for Mikhail to come and take it."

"And Mikhail will wait for Alex." She set the flatware down on a heavy table at the other end of the room, then came to Sydney. Her dark eyes were shrewd, not unfriendly, but quietly probing. She smelled of spice and melted butter. "I am Nadia, Mikhail's mother." She offered a hand. "We are happy to have you with us."

"Thank you. You have a lovely home."

She had said it automatically, meaningless politeness. But the moment the words were out, Sydney realized they were true. The entire house would probably fit into one wing of her mother's Long Island estate, and the furniture was old rather than antique. Doilies as charming and intricate as those she had seen at Mrs. Wolburg's covered the arms of chairs. The wallpaper was faded, but that only made the tiny rosebuds scattered over it seem more lovely.

The strong sunlight burst through the window and showed every scar, every mend. Just as it showed how lovingly the woodwork and table surfaces had been polished.

Out of the corner of her eye she caught a movement. As she glanced over, she watched a plump ball of gray fur struggling, whimpering from under a chair.

"That is Ivan," Yuri said, clucking to the puppy. "He is only a baby." He sighed a little for his old mutt Sasha who had died peacefully at the age of fifteen six months before. "Alex brings him home from pound."

"Saved you from walking the last mile, right, Ivan?" Mikhail bent down to ruffle his fur. Ivan thumped his tail while giving Sydney nervous looks. "He is named for Ivan the Terrible, but he's a coward."

"He's just shy," Sydney corrected, then gave in to need and crouched down. She'd always wanted a pet, but boarding schools didn't permit them. "There, aren't you sweet?" The dog trembled visibly for a moment when she stroked him, then began to lick the toes that peeked out through her sandals.

Mikhail began to think the pup had potential.

"What kind is he?" she asked.

"He is part Russian wolfhound," Yuri declared.

"With plenty of traveling salesmen thrown in." The voice came from the kitchen doorway. Sydney looked over her shoulder and saw a striking woman with a sleek cap of raven hair and tawny eyes. "I'm Mikhail's sister, Rachel. You must be Sydney."

"Yes, hello." Sydney straightened, and wondered what miracles in the gene pool had made all the Stanislaskis so blindingly beautiful.

"Dinner'll be ready in ten minutes." Rachel's voice carried only the faintest wisp of an accent and was as dark and smooth as black velvet. "Mikhail, you can set the table."

"I have to take out the trash," he told her, instantly choosing the lesser of two evils.

"I'll do it." Sydney's impulsive offer was greeted with casual acceptance. She was nearly finished when Alex, as dark, exotic and gorgeous as the rest of the family, strolled in.

"Sorry I'm late, Papa. Just finished a double shift. I barely had time to…" He trailed off when he spotted Sydney. His mouth curved and his eyes flickered with definite interest. "Now I'm really sorry I'm late. Hi."

"Hello." Her lips curved in response. That kind of romantic charm could have raised the blood pressure on a corpse. Providing it was female.

"Mine," Mikhail said mildly as he strolled back out of the kitchen.

Alex merely grinned and continued walking toward Sydney. He took her hand, kissed the knuckles. "Just so you know, of the two of us, I'm less moody and have a steadier job."

She had to laugh. "I'll certainly take that into account."

"He thinks he's a cop." Mikhail sent his brother an amused look. "Mama says to wash your hands. Dinner's ready."

Sydney was certain she'd never seen more food at one table. There were mounds of chicken stuffed with rich, herbed butter. It was served with an enormous bowl of lightly browned potatoes and a platter heaped with slices of grilled vegetables that Nadia had picked from her own kitchen garden that morning. There was a tower of biscuits along with a mountain of some flaky stuffed pastries that was Alex's favorite dish.

Sydney sipped the crisp wine that was offered along with vodka and wondered. The amount and variety of food was nothing compared to the conversation.

Rachel and Alex argued over someone named Goose. After a winding explanation, Sydney learned that while Alex was a rookie cop, Rachel was in her first year with the public defender's office. And Goose was a petty thief Rachel was defending.

Yuri and Mikhail argued about baseball. Sydney didn't

need Nadia's affectionate translation to realize that while Yuri was a diehard Yankee fan, Mikhail stood behind the Mets.

There was much gesturing with silverware and Russian exclamations mixed with English. Then laughter, a shouted question, and more arguing.

"Rachel is an idealist," Alex stated. With his elbows on the table and his chin rested on his joined hands, he smiled at Sydney. "What are you?"

She smiled back. "Too smart to be put between a lawyer and a cop."

"Elbows off," Nadia said, and gave her son a quick rap. "Mikhail says you are a businesswoman. And that you are very smart. And fair."

The description surprised her enough that she nearly fumbled. "I try to be."

"Your company was in a sticky situation last week." Rachel downed the last of her vodka with a panache Sydney admired. "You handled it well. It seemed to me that rather than trying to be fair you simply were. Have you known Mikhail long?"

She segued into the question so neatly, Sydney only blinked. "No, actually. We met last month when he barged into my office ready to crush any available Hayward under his work boot."

"I was polite," he corrected.

"You were not polite." Because she could see Yuri was amused, she continued. "He was dirty, angry and ready to fight."

"His temper comes from his mama," Yuri informed Sydney. "She is fierce."

"Only once," Nadia said with a shake of her head. "Only

once did I hit him over the head with a pot. He never forgets."

"I still have the scar. And here." Yuri pointed to his shoulder. "Where you threw the hairbrush at me."

"You should not have said my new dress was ugly."

"It was ugly," he said with a shrug, then tapped a hand on his chest. "And here, where you—"

"Enough." All dignity, she rose. "Or our guest will think I am tyrant."

"She is a tyrant," Yuri told Sydney with a grin.

"And this tyrant says we will clear the table and have dessert."

Sydney was still chuckling over it as Mikhail crossed the bridge back into Manhattan. Sometime during the long, comfortable meal she'd forgotten to be annoyed with him. Perhaps she'd had half a glass too much wine. Certainly she'd eaten entirely too much kissel—the heavenly apricot pudding Nadia had served with cold, rich cream. But she was relaxed and couldn't remember ever having spent a more enjoyable Sunday evening.

"Did your father make that up?" Snuggled back in her seat, Sydney turned her head to study Mikhail's profile. "About your mother throwing things?"

"No, she throws things." He downshifted and cruised into traffic. "Once a whole plate of spaghetti and meatballs at me because my mouth was too quick."

Her laughter came out in a burst of enjoyment. "Oh, I would have loved to have seen that. Did you duck?"

He flicked her a grin. "Not fast enough."

"I've never thrown anything in my life." Her sigh was part wistful, part envious. "I think it must be very liberating. They're wonderful," she said after another moment. "Your family. You're very lucky."

"So you don't mind eating in Brooklyn?"

Frowning, she straightened a bit. "It wasn't that. I told you, I'm not a snob. I just wasn't prepared. You should have told me you were taking me there."

"Would you have gone?"

She opened her mouth then closed it again. After a moment, she let her shoulders rise and fall. "I don't know. Why did you take me?"

"I wanted to see you there. Maybe I wanted you to see me there, too."

Puzzled, she turned to look at him again. They were nearly back now. In a few more minutes he would go his way and she hers. "I don't understand why that should matter to you."

"Then you understand much too little, Sydney."

"I might understand if you'd be more clear." It was suddenly important, vital, that she know. The tips of her fingers were beginning to tingle so that she had to rub them together to stop the sensation.

"I'm better with my hands than with words." Impatient with her, with himself, he pulled into the garage beneath her building. When he yanked off his sunglasses, his eyes were dark and turbulent.

Didn't she know that her damn perfume had his nerve ends sizzling? The way she laughed, the way her hair lifted in the wind. How her eyes had softened and yearned as she'd looked at the silly little mutt of his father's.

It was worse, much worse now that he'd seen her with his family. Now that he'd watched how her initial stiffness melted away under a few kind words. He'd worried that he'd made a mistake, that she would be cold to his family, disdainful of the old house and simple meal.

Instead she'd laughed with his father, dried dishes with his mother. Alex's blatant flirting hadn't offended but rather had amused her. And when Rachel had praised her handling of the accident with Mrs. Wolburg, she'd flushed like a schoolgirl.

How the hell was he supposed to know he'd fall in love with her?

And now that she was alone with him again, all that cool reserve was seeping back. He could see it in the way her spine straightened when she stepped out of the car.

Hell, he could feel it—it surprised him that frost didn't form on his windshield.

"I'll walk you up." He slammed the door of the car.

"That isn't necessary." She didn't know what had spoiled the evening, but was ready to place the blame squarely on his shoulders.

"I'll walk you up," he repeated, and pulled her over to the elevator.

"Fine." She folded her arms and waited.

The moment the doors opened, they entered without speaking. Both of them were sure it was the longest elevator ride on record. Sydney swept out in front of him when they reached her floor. She had her keys out and ready two steps before they hit her door.

"I enjoyed your family," she said, carefully polite. "Be sure to tell your parents again how much I appreciated their hospitality." The lock snapped open. "You can reach me in the office if there are any problems this week."

He slapped his hand on the door before she could shut it in his face. "I'm coming in."

Chapter 7

Sydney considered the chances of shoving the door closed while he had his weight against it, found them slim and opted for shivery reserve.

"It's a bit early for a nightcap and a bit late for coffee."

"I don't want a drink." Mikhail rapped the door closed with enough force to make the foyer mirror rattle.

Though she refused to back up, Sydney felt her stomach muscles experience the same helpless shaking. "Some people might consider it poor manners for a man to bully his way into a woman's apartment."

"I have poor manners," he told her, and, jamming his hands into his pockets, paced into the living room.

"It must be a trial for your parents. Obviously they worked hard to instill a certain code of behavior in their children. It didn't stick with you."

He swung back, and she was reminded of some compact and muscled cat on the prowl. Definitely a man-eater. "You liked them?"

Baffled, she pushed a hand through her disordered hair. "Of course I like them. I've already said so."

While his hands bunched and unbunched in his pockets, he lifted a brow. "I thought perhaps it was just your very perfect manners that made you say so."

As an insult, it was a well-aimed shot. Indignation shivered through the ice. "Well, you were wrong. Now if we've settled everything, you can go."

"We've settled nothing. You tell me why you are so different now from the way you were an hour ago."

She caught herself, tightening her lips before they could move into a pout. "I don't know what you're talking about."

"With my family you were warm and sweet. You smiled so easily. Now with me, you're cold and far away. You don't smile at all."

"That's absurd." Though it was little more than a baring of teeth, she forced her lips to curve. "There, I've smiled at you. Satisfied?"

Temper flickered into his eyes as he began to pace again. "I haven't been satisfied since I walk into your office. You make me suffer and I don't like it."

"Artists are supposed to suffer," she shot back. "And I don't see how I've had anything to do with it. I've given in to every single demand you made. Replaced windows, ripped out plumbing, gotten rid of that tool-and-knot wiring."

"Tube and knob," he corrected, nearly amused.

"Well, it's gone, isn't it? Have you any idea just how much lumber I've authorized?"

"To last two-by-four, I know. This is not point."

She studied him owlishly. "Do you know you drop your articles when you're angry?"

His eyes narrowed. "I drop nothing."

"Your *the*'s and *an*'s and *a*'s," she pointed out. "And your sentence structure suffers. You mix your tenses."

That wounded. "I'd like to hear you speak my language."

She set the purse she still carried onto a table with a snap. "Baryshnikov, glasnost."

His lips curled. "This is Russian. I am Ukrainian. This is a mistake you make, but I overlook."

"It. You overlook *it*," she corrected. "In any case, it's close enough." He took a step forward, she took one back. "I'm sure we can have a fascinating discussion on the subtleties of language, but it will have to wait." He came closer, and she—casually, she hoped—edged away. "As I said before, I enjoyed the evening. Now—" he maneuvered her around a chair "—stop stalking me."

"You imagine things. You're not a *rabbit*, you're a *woman*."

But she felt like a rabbit, one of those poor, frozen creatures caught in a beam of headlights. "I don't know what's put you in this mood—"

"I have many moods. You put me in this one every time I see you, or think about you."

She shifted so that a table was between them. Because she well knew if she kept retreating her back would be against the wall, she took a stand. "All right, damn it. What do you want?"

"You. You know I want you."

Her heart leaped into her throat, then plummeted to her stomach. "You do not." The tremble in her voice irritated her enough to make her force ice into it. "I don't appreciate this game you're playing."

"I play? What is a man to think when a woman blows hot, then cold? When she looks at him with passion one minute and frost the next?" His hands lifted in frustration, then slapped down on the table. "I tell you straight out when you are so upset that I don't want your mama, I want you. And you call me a liar."

"I don't…" She could hardly get her breath. Deliberately she walked away, moving behind a chair and gripping the back hard. It had been a mistake to look into his eyes. There was a ruthlessness there that brought a terrible pitch of excitement to her blood. "You didn't want me before."

"Before? I think I wanted you before I met you. What is this before?"

"In the car." Humiliation washed her cheeks of color. "When I—when we were driving back from Long Island. We were…" Her fingers dug into the back of the chair. "It doesn't matter."

In two strides he was in front of the chair, his hands gripped over hers. "You tell me what you mean."

Pride, she told herself. She would damn well keep her pride. "All right then, to clarify, and to see that we don't have this conversation again. You started something in the car that night. I didn't ask for it, I didn't encourage it, but you started it." She took a deep breath to be certain her voice remained steady. "And you just stopped because… well, because I wasn't what you wanted after all."

For a moment he could only stare, too stunned for speech. Then his face changed, so quickly, Sydney could only blink at the surge of rage. When he acted, she gave a yip of surprise. The chair he yanked from between them landed on its side two feet away.

He swore at her. She didn't need to understand the words to appreciate the sentiment behind them. Before she could make an undignified retreat, his hands were clamped hard on her arms. For an instant she was afraid she was about to take the same flight as the chair. He was strong enough and certainly angry enough. But he only continued to shout.

It took her nearly a full minute to realize her feet were an inch above the floor and that he'd started using English again.

"Idiot. How can so smart a woman have no brains?"

"I'm not going to stand here and be insulted." Of course, she wasn't standing at all, she thought, fighting panic. She was dangling.

"It is not insult to speak truth. For weeks I have tried to be gentleman."

"A *gentleman*," she said furiously. "You've tried to be a *gentleman*. And you've failed miserably."

"I think you need time, you need me to show you how I feel. And I am sorry to have treated you as I did in the car that night. It makes me think you will have…" He trailed off, frustrated that the proper word wasn't in him. "That you will think me…"

"A heathen," she tossed out, with relish. "Barbarian."

"No, that's not so bad. But a man who abuses a woman for pleasure. Who forces and hurts her."

"It wasn't a matter of force," Sydney said coldly. "Now put me down."

He hiked her up another inch. "Do you think I stopped because I don't want you?"

"I'm well aware that my sexuality is under par."

He didn't have a clue what she was talking about, and plowed on. "We were in a car, in the middle of the city, with your driver in the front. And I was ready to rip your clothes away and take you, there. It made me angry with myself, and with you because you could make me forget."

She tried to think of a response. But he had set her back on her feet, and his hands were no longer gripping but caressing. The rage in his eyes had become something else, and it took her breath away.

"Every day since," he murmured. "Every night, I remember how you looked, how you felt. So I want more. And I wait for you to offer what I saw in your eyes that night. But you don't. I can't wait longer."

His fingers streaked into her hair, then fisted there, drawing her head back as his mouth crushed down on hers. The heat seared through her skin, into blood and bone. Her moan wasn't borne of pain but of tormented pleasure. Willing, desperately willing, her mouth parted under his, inviting him, accepting him. This time when her heart rose to her throat, there was a wild glory in it.

On an oath, he tore his mouth from hers and buried it against her throat. She had not asked, she had not encouraged. Those were her words, and he wouldn't ignore the truth of them. Whatever slippery grip he had on control, he clamped tight now, fighting to catch his breath and hold to sanity.

"Damn me to hell or take me to heaven," he muttered. "But do it now."

Her arms locked around his neck. He would leave, she knew, just as he had left that first time. And if he did she might never feel this frenzied stirring again. "I want you." *I'm afraid, I'm afraid.* "Yes, I want you. Make love to me."

And his mouth was on hers again, hard, hot, hungry, while his hands flowed like molten steel down her body. Not a caress now, but a branding. In one long, possessive stroke he staked a claim. It was too late for choices.

Fears and pleasures battered her, rough waves of emotion that had her trembling even as she absorbed delights.

Her fingers dug into his shoulders, took greedy handfuls of his hair. Through the thin layers of cotton, she could feel the urgent drum of his heart and knew it beat for her.

More. He could only think he needed more, even as her scent swam in his head and her taste flooded his mouth. She moved against him, that small, slim body restless and eager. When he touched her, when his artist's hands sculpted her, finding the curves and planes of her already perfect, her low, throaty whimpers pounded in his ears like thunder.

More.

He tugged the straps from her shoulders, snapping one in his hurry to remove even that small obstacle. While his mouth raced over the smooth, bare curve, he dragged at the zipper, yanking and pulling until the dress pooled at her feet.

Beneath it. Oh, Lord, beneath it.

The strapless little fancy frothed over milk-white breasts, flowed down to long, lovely thighs. She lifted a trembling hand as if to cover herself, but he caught it, held it. He didn't see the nerves in her eyes as he filled himself on how she looked, surrounded in the last flames of sunset that warmed the room.

"Mikhail." Because he wasn't quite ready to speak, he only nodded. "I…the bedroom."

He'd been tempted to take her where they stood, or to do no more than drag her to the floor. Checking himself, he had her up in his arms in one glorious sweep. "It better be close."

On an unsteady laugh, she gestured. No man had ever carried her to bed before, and she found it dazzlingly romantic. Unsure of what part she should play, Sydney pressed her lips tentatively to his throat. He trembled. Encouraged, she skimmed them up to his ear. He groaned. On a sigh of pleasure, she continued to nibble while her fingers slipped beneath his shirt to stroke over his shoulder.

His arms tightened around her. When she turned her head, his mouth was there, taking greedily from hers as he tumbled with her onto the bed.

"Shouldn't we close the drapes?" The question ended on a gasp as he began doing things to her, wonderful things, shattering things. There was no room for shyness in this airless, spinning world.

It wasn't supposed to be like this. She'd always thought lovemaking to be either awkwardly mechanical or quietly comforting. It wasn't supposed to be so urgent, so turbulent. So incredible. Those rough, clever hands rushed over flesh, over silk, then back to flesh, leaving her a quivering mass of sensation. His mouth was just as hurried, just as skilled as it made the same erotic journey.

He was lost in her, utterly, irretrievably lost in her. Even the air was full of her, that quiet, restrained, gloriously seductive scent. Her skin seemed to melt, like liquid flowers, under his fingers, his lips. Each quick tremble he brought to her racked through him until he thought he would go mad.

Desire arced and spiked and hummed even as she grew softer, more pliant. More his.

Impatient, he brought his mouth to her breast to suckle through silk while his hands slid up her thighs to find her, wet and burning.

When he touched her, her body arched in shock. Her arm flew back until her fingers locked over one of the rungs of the brass headboard. She shook her head as pleasure shot into her, hot as a bullet. Suddenly fear and desire were so twisted into a single emotion she didn't know whether to beg him to stop or plead with him to go on. On and on.

Helpless, stripped of control, she gasped for breath. It seemed her system had contracted until she was curled into one tight hot ball. Even as she sobbed out his name, the ball imploded and she was left shattered.

A moan shuddered out as her body went limp again.

Unbearably aroused, he watched her, the stunned, glowing pleasure that flushed her cheeks, the dark, dazed desire that turned her eyes to blue smoke. For her, for himself, he took her up again, driving her higher until her breath was ragged and her body on fire.

"Please," she managed when he tugged the silk aside.

"I will please you." He flicked his tongue over her nipple. "And me."

There couldn't be more. But he showed her there was. Even when she began to drag frantically at his clothes, he continued to assault her system and to give her, give her more than she had ever believed she could hold. His hands were never still as he rolled over the bed with her, helping her to rid him of every possible barrier.

He wanted her crazed for him, as crazed as he for her. He could feel the wild need in the way she moved beneath him, in the way her hands searched. And yes, in the way she cried out when he found some secret she'd been keeping just for him.

When he could wait no longer, he plunged inside her, a sword to the hilt.

She was beyond pleasure. There was no name for the edge she trembled on. Her body moved, arching for his, finding their own intimate rhythm as naturally as breath. She knew he was speaking to her, desperate words in a mixture of languages. She understood that wherever she was, he was with her, as much a captive as she.

And when the power pushed her off that last thin edge, he was all there was. All there had to be.

It was dark, and the room was in shadows. Wondering if her mind would ever clear again, Sydney stared at the ceiling and listened to Mikhail breathe. It was foolish, she supposed, but it was such a soothing, intimate sound, that air moving quietly in and out of his lungs. She could have listened for hours.

Perhaps she had.

She had no idea how much time had passed since he'd slapped his hand on her door and barged in after her. It might have been minutes or hours, but it hardly mattered. Her life had been changed. Smiling to herself, she stroked a hand through his hair. He turned his head, just an inch, and pressed his lips to the underside of her jaw.

"I thought you were asleep," she murmured.

"No. I wouldn't fall asleep on top of you." He lifted his head. She could see the gleam of his eyes, the hint of a smile. "There are so many more interesting things to do on top of you."

She felt color rush to her cheeks and was grateful for the dark. "I was…" How could she ask? "It was all right, then?"

"No." Even with his body pressed into hers, he could feel her quick retreat. "Sydney, I may not have so many good words as you, but I think 'all right' is a poor choice. A walk through the park is all right."

"I only meant—" She shifted. Though he braced on his elbows to ease his weight from her, he made sure she couldn't wiggle away.

"I think we'll have a light now."

"No, that's not—" The bedside lamp clicked on. "Necessary."

"I want to see you, because I think I will make love with you again in a minute. And I like to look at you." Casually he brushed his lips over hers. "Don't."

"Don't what?"

"Tense your shoulders. I'd like to think you could relax with me."

"I am relaxed," she said, then blew out a long breath. No, she wasn't. "It's just that whenever I ask a direct question, you give evasions. I only wanted to know if you were, well, satisfied."

She'd been sure before, but now, as the heat had faded to warmth, she wondered if she'd only wished.

"Ah." Wrapping her close, he rolled over until she lay atop him. "This is like a quiz. Multiple choice. They were my favorite in school. You want to know, A, was it all right, B, was it very good or C, was it very wonderful."

"Forget it."

He clamped his arms around her when she tried to pull away. "I'm not finished with you, Hayward. I still have to answer the question, but I find there are not enough choices." He nudged her down until her lips had no choice but to meet his. And the kiss was long and sweet. "Do you understand now?"

His eyes were dark, still heavy from the pleasure they'd shared. The look in them said more than hundreds of silky words. "Yes."

"Good. Come back to me." He nestled her head on his shoulder and began to rub his hand gently up and down her back. "This is nice?"

"Yes." She smiled again. "This is nice." Moments passed in easy silence. "Mikhail."

"Hmm?"

"There weren't enough choices for me, either."

* * *

She was so beautiful when she slept, he could hardly look away. Her hair, a tangled flow of golden fire, curtained part of her face. One hand, small and delicate, curled on the pillow where his head had lain. The sheet, tangled from hours of loving showed the outline of her body to where the linen ended just at the curve of her breast.

She had been greater than any fantasy: generous, open, stunningly sexy and shy all at once. It had been like initiating a virgin and being seduced by a siren. And afterward, the faint embarrassment, the puzzling self-doubt. Where had that come from?

He would have to coax the answer from her. And if coaxing didn't work, he would bully.

But now, when he watched her in the morning light, he felt such an aching tenderness.

He hated to wake her, but he knew women enough to be sure she would be hurt if he left her sleeping.

Gently he brushed the hair from her cheek, bent down and kissed her.

She stirred and so did his desire.

He kissed her again, nibbling a trail to her ear. "Sydney." Her sleepy purr of response had his blood heating. "Wake up and kiss me goodbye."

"'S morning?" Her lashes fluttered up to reveal dark, heavy eyes. She stared at him a moment while she struggled to surface. His face was close and shadowed with stubble. To satisfy an old craving, she lifted her hand to it.

"You have a dangerous face." When he grinned, she propped herself up on an elbow. "You're dressed," she realized.

"I thought it the best way to go downtown."

"Go?"

Amused, he sat on the edge of the bed. "To work. It's nearly seven. I made coffee with your machine and used your shower."

She nodded. She could smell both—the coffee and the scent of her soap on his skin. "You should have waked me."

He twined a lock of her hair around his finger, enjoying the way its subtle fire seemed to lick at his flesh. "I didn't let you sleep very long last night. You will come downtown after work? I will fix you dinner."

Relieved, she smiled. "Yes."

"And you'll stay the night with me, sleep in my bed?"

She sat up so they were face-to-face. "Yes."

"Good." He tugged on the lock of hair. "Now kiss me goodbye."

"All right." Testing herself, she sat up, linked her hands around his neck. The sheet slid away to her waist. Pleased, she watched his gaze skim down, felt the tensing of muscles, saw the heat flash. Slowly, waiting until his eyes had come back to hers, she leaned forward. Her lips brushed his and retreated, brushed and retreated until she felt his quick groan. Satisfied she had his full attention, she flicked open the buttons of his shirt.

"Sydney." On a half laugh, he caught at her hands. "You'll make me late."

"That's the idea." She was smiling as she pushed the shirt off his shoulders. "Don't worry, I'll put in a good word for you with the boss."

Two hours later, Sydney strolled into her offices with an armful of flowers she'd bought on the street. She'd left her hair down, had chosen a sunny yellow suit to match her mood. And she was humming.

Janine looked up from her work station, prepared to

offer her usual morning greeting. The formal words stuck. "Wow. Ms. Hayward, you look fabulous."

"Thank you, Janine. I feel that way. These are for you."

Confused, Janine gathered up the armful of summer blossoms. "Thank you. I...thank you."

"When's my first appointment?"

"Nine-thirty. With Ms. Brinkman, Mr. Lowe and Mr. Keller, to finalize the buy on the housing project in New Jersey."

"That gives me about twenty minutes. I'd like to see you in my office."

"Yes, ma'am." Janine was already reaching for her pad.

"You won't need that," Sydney told her, and strode through the double doors. She seated herself, then gestured for Janine to take a chair.

"How long have you worked for Hayward?"

"Five years last March."

Sydney tipped back in her chair and looked at her secretary, really looked. Janine was attractive, neat, had direct gray eyes that were a trifle puzzled at the moment. Her dark blond hair was worn short and sleek. She held herself well, Sydney noted. Appearance was important, not the most important, but it certainly counted for what she was thinking.

"You must have been very young when you started here."

"Twenty-one," Janine answered with a small smile. "Right out of business college."

"Are you doing what you want to do, Janine?"

"Excuse me?"

"Is secretarial work what you want to do with your life, or do you have other ambitions?"

Janine resisted the urge to squirm in her chair. "I hope to work my way up to department manager. But I enjoy working for you, Miss Hayward."

"You have five years experience with the company, nearly five more than I do, yet you enjoy working for me. Why?"

"Why?" Janine stopped being nervous and went to flat-out baffled. "Being secretary to the president of Hayward is an important job, and I think I'm good at it."

"I agree with both statements." Rising, Sydney walked around the desk to perch on the front corner. "Let's be frank, Janine, no one here at Hayward expected me to stay more than a token month or two, and I'm sure it was generally agreed I'd spend most of that time filing my nails or chatting with friends on the phone." She saw by the faint flush that crept up Janine's cheeks that she'd hit very close to the mark. "They gave me an efficient secretary, not an assistant or an office manager, or executive aide, whatever we choose to call them at Hayward, because it wasn't thought I'd require one. True?"

"That's the office gossip." Janine straightened in her chair and met Sydney's eyes levelly. If she was about to be fired, she'd take it on the chin. "I took the job because it was a good position, a promotion and a raise."

"And I think you were very wise. The door opened, and you walked in. Since you've been working for me, you've been excellent. I can't claim to have a lot of experience in having a secretary, but I know that you're at your desk when I arrive in the morning and often stay after I leave at night. When I ask you for information you have it, or you get it. When I ask, you explain, and when I order, you get the job done."

"I don't believe in doing things halfway, Ms. Hayward."

Sydney smiled, that was exactly what she wanted to hear. "And you want to move up. Contrarily, when my position was tenuous at best last week, you stood behind me.

Breaking into that board meeting was a risk, and putting yourself in my corner at that point certainly lessened your chances of moving up at Hayward had I been asked to step down. And it most certainly earned you a powerful enemy."

"I work for you, not for Mr. Bingham. And even if it wasn't a matter of loyalty, you were doing what was right."

"I feel very strongly about loyalty, Janine, just as strongly as I feel about giving someone who's trying to make something of herself the chance to do so. The flowers were a thank-you for that loyalty, from me to you, personally."

"Thank you, Ms. Hayward." Janine's face relaxed in a smile.

"You're welcome. I consider your promotion to my executive assistant, with the appropriate salary and benefits, to be a good business decision."

Janine's mouth dropped open. "I beg your pardon?"

"I hope you'll accept the position, Janine. I need someone I trust, someone I respect, and someone who knows how the hell to run an office. Agreed?" Sydney offered a hand. Janine stared at it before she managed to rise and grip it firmly in hers.

"Ms. Hayward—"

"Sydney. We're going to be in this together."

Janine gave a quick, dazzled laugh. "Sydney. I hope I'm not dreaming."

"You're wide-awake, and the flak's going to fall before the day's over. Your first job in your new position is to arrange a meeting with Lloyd. Make it a formal request, here in my office before the close of business hours today."

He put her off until four-fifteen, but Sydney was patient. If anything, the extra time gave her the opportunity to examine her feelings and make certain her decision wasn't based on emotion.

When Janine buzzed him in, Sydney was ready, and she was sure.

"You picked a busy day for this," he began.

"Sit down, Lloyd."

He did, and she waited again while he took out a cigarette. "I won't take up much of your time," she told him. "I felt it best to discuss this matter as quickly as possible."

His gaze flicked up, and he smiled confidently through the haze of smoke. "Having problems on one of the projects?"

"No." Her lips curved in a wintry smile. "There's nothing I can't handle. It's the internal strife at Hayward that concerns me, and I've decided to remedy it."

"Office reorganization is a tricky business." He crossed his legs and leaned back. "Do you really think you've been around long enough to attempt it?"

"I'm not going to attempt it, I'm going to do it. I'd like your resignation on my desk by five o'clock tomorrow."

He bolted up. "What the hell are you talking about?"

"Your resignation, Lloyd. Or if necessary, your termination at Hayward. That distinction will be up to you."

He crushed the cigarette into pulp in the ashtray. "You think you can fire me? Walk in here with barely three months under your belt and fire me when I've been at Hayward for twelve years?"

"Here's the point," she said evenly. "Whether it's been three months or three days, I am Hayward. I will not tolerate one of my top executives undermining my position. It's obvious you're not happy with the current status at Hayward, and I can guarantee you, I'm going to remain in charge of this company for a long time. Therefore, I believe it's in your own interest, and certainly in mine, for you to resign."

"The hell I will."

"That's your choice, of course. I will, however, take the matter before the board, and use all the power at my disposal to limit yours."

Going with instinct, she pushed the next button. "Leaking Mrs. Wolburg's accident to the press didn't just put me in a difficult position. It put Hayward in a difficult position. As an executive vice president, your first duty is to the company, not to go off on some vindictive tangent because you dislike working for me."

He stiffened, and she knew she'd guessed correctly. "You have no way of proving the leak came from my office."

"You'd be surprised what I can prove," she bluffed. "I told you I wanted your loyalty or your resignation if the board stood behind me in the Soho project. We both know your loyalty is out of the question."

"I'll tell you what you'll get." There was a sneer in his voice, but beneath the neat gray suit, he was sweating. "I'll be sitting behind that desk when you're back in Europe dancing from shop to shop."

"No, Lloyd. You'll never sit behind this desk. As the major stockholder of Hayward, I'll see to that. Now," she continued quietly, "it wasn't necessary for me to document to the board the many cases in which you've ignored my requests, overlooked complaints from clients, tenants and other associates at the meeting on Friday. I will do so, however, at the next. In the current climate, I believe my wishes will be met."

His fingers curled. He imagined the satisfaction of hooking them around her throat. "You think because you skidded through one mess, because your senile grandfather

Luring a Lady

plopped you down at that desk, you can shoehorn me out? Lady, I'll bury you."

Coolly she inclined her head. "You're welcome to try. If you don't manage it, it may be difficult for you to find a similar position with another company." Her eyes iced over. "If you don't think I have any influence, or the basic guts to carry this off, you're making a mistake. You have twenty-four hours to consider your options. This meeting is over."

"Why you cold-blooded bitch."

She stood, and this time it was she who leaned over her desk. "Take me on," she said in a quiet voice. "Do it."

"This isn't over." Turning on his heel, he marched to the door to swing it open hard enough that it banged against the wall.

After three deep breaths, Sydney sank into her chair. Okay, she was shaking—but only a little. And it was temper, she realized as she pressed a testing hand against her stomach. Not fear. Good, solid temper. She found she didn't need to vent any anger by mangling paper clips or shredding stationery. In fact, she found she felt just wonderful.

Chapter 8

Mikhail stirred the mixture of meats and spices and to-matoes in the old cast-iron skillet and watched the street below through his kitchen window. After a sniff and a taste, he added another splash of red wine to the mixture. Behind him in the living room *The Marriage of Figaro* soared from the stereo.

He wondered how soon Sydney would arrive.

Leaving the meal to simmer, he walked into the living room to study the rosewood block that was slowly becoming her face.

Her mouth. There was a softness about it that was just emerging. Testing, he measured it between his index finger and thumb. And remembered how it had tasted, moving eagerly under his. Hot candy, coated with cool, white wine. Addictive.

Those cheekbones, so aristocratic, so elegant. They could add a regal, haughty look one moment, or that of an

ice-blooded warrior the next. That firm, proud jawline—
he traced a fingertip along it and thought of how sensitive
and smooth her skin was there.

Her eyes, he'd wondered if he'd have problems with her
eyes. Oh, not the shape of them—that was basic to craft,
but the feeling in them, the mysteries behind them.

There was still so much he needed to know.

He leaned closer until he was eye to eye with the half-
formed bust. "You will let me in," he whispered. At the
knock on the door, he stayed where he was, peering into
Sydney's emerging face. "Is open."

"Hey, Mik." Keely breezed in wearing a polka-
dotted T-shirt and shorts in neon green. "Got anything
cold? My fridge finally gave up the ghost."

"Help yourself," he said absently, "I'll put you on top of
the list for the new ones."

"My hero." She paused in the kitchen to sniff at the skillet. "God, this smells sinful." She tipped the spoon in and
took a sample. "It is sinful. Looks like a lot for one."

"It's for two."

"Oh." She gave the word three ascending syllables as she
pulled a soft drink out of the refrigerator. The smell was
making her mouth water, and she glanced wistfully at the
skillet again. "Looks like a lot for two, too."

He glanced over his shoulder and grinned. "Put some in
a bowl. Simmer it a little longer."

"You're a prince, Mik." She rattled in his cupboards.
"So who's the lucky lady?"

"Sydney Hayward."

"Sydney." Her eyes widened. The spoon she held halted
in midair above the pan of bubbling goulash. "Hayward,"
she finished. "You mean the rich and beautiful Hayward
who wears silk to work and carries a six-hundred-dollar

purse, which I personally priced at Saks. She's coming here, to have dinner and everything?"

He was counting on the everything. "Yes."

"Gee." She couldn't think of anything more profound. But she wasn't sure she liked it. No, she wasn't sure at all, Keely thought as she scooped her impromptu dinner into a bowl.

The rich were different. She firmly believed it. And this lady was rich in capital letters. Keely knew Mikhail had earned some pretty big bucks with his art, but she couldn't think of him as rich. He was just Mik, the sexy guy next door who was always willing to unclog a sink or kill a spider or share a beer.

Carrying the bowl, she walked over to him and noticed his latest work in progress. "Oh," she said, but this time it was only a sigh. She would have killed for cheekbones like that.

"You like?"

"Sure, I always like your stuff." But she shifted from foot to foot. She didn't like the way he was looking at the face in the wood. "I, ah, guess you two have more than a business thing going."

"Yes." He hooked his thumbs in his pockets as he looked into Keely's troubled eyes. "This is a problem?"

"Problem? No, no problem." She worried her lower lip. "Well, it's just—boy, Mik, she's so uptown."

He knew she was talking about more than an address, but smiled and ran a hand over her hair. "You're worried for me."

"Well, we're pals, aren't we? I can't stand to see a pal get hurt."

Touched, he kissed her nose. "Like you did with the actor with the skinny legs?"

She moved her shoulders. "Yeah, I guess. But I wasn't in love with him or anything. Or only a little."

"You cried."

"Sure, but I'm a wienie. I tear up during greeting card commercials." Dissatisfied, she looked back at the bust. Definitely uptown. "A woman who looks like that, I figure she could drive a guy to joining the Foreign Legion or something."

He laughed and ruffled her hair. "Don't worry. I'll write."

Before she could think of anything else, there was another knock. Giving Keely a pat on the shoulder, he went to answer it.

"Hi." Sydney's face brightened the moment she saw him. She carried a garment bag in one hand and a bottle of champagne in the other. "Something smells wonderful. My mouth started watering on the third floor, and…" She spotted Keely standing near the worktable with a bowl cupped in her hands. "Hello." After clearing her throat, Sydney told herself she would not be embarrassed to have Mikhail's neighbor see her coming into his apartment with a suitcase.

"Hi. I was just going." Every bit as uncomfortable as Sydney, Keely darted back into the kitchen to grab her soft drink.

"It's nice to see you again." Sydney stood awkwardly beside the open door. "How did your murder go?"

"He strangled me in three takes." With a fleeting smile, she dashed through the door. "Enjoy your dinner. Thanks, Mik."

When the door down the hall slammed shut, Sydney let out a long breath. "Does she always move so fast?"

"Mostly." He circled Sydney's waist with his hands. "She is worried you will seduce me, use me, then toss me aside."

"Oh, well, really."

Chuckling, he nipped at her bottom lip. "I don't mind the first two." As his mouth settled more truly on hers, he slipped the garment bag out of her lax fingers and tossed it aside. Taking the bottle of wine, he used it to push the door closed at her back. "I like your dress. You look like a rose in sunshine."

Freed, her hands could roam along his back, slip under the chambray work shirt he hadn't tucked into his jeans. "I like the way you look, all the time."

His lips were curved as they pressed to her throat. "You're hungry?"

"Mmm. Past hungry. I had to skip lunch."

"Ten minutes," he promised, and reluctantly released her. If he didn't, dinner would be much, much later. "What have you brought us?" He twisted the bottle in his hand to study the label. One dark brow lifted. "This will humble my goulash."

With her eyes shut, Sydney took a long, appreciative sniff. "No, I don't think so." Then she laughed and took the bottle from him. "I wanted to celebrate. I had a really good day."

"You will tell me?"

"Yes."

"Good. Let's find some glasses that won't embarrass this champagne."

She didn't know when she'd been more charmed. He had set a small table and two chairs on the tiny balcony off the bedroom. A single pink peony graced an old green bottle in the center, and music drifted from his radio to lull the sounds of traffic. Thick blue bowls held the spicy stew, and rich black bread was heaped in a wicker basket.

While they ate, she told him about her decision to promote Janine, and her altercation with Lloyd.

"You ask for his resignation. You should fire him."

"It's a little more complicated than that." Flushed with success, Sydney lifted her glass to study the wine in the evening sunlight. "But the result's the same. If he pushes me, I'll have to go before the board. I have memos, other documentation. Take this building, for example." She tapped a finger on the old brick. "My grandfather turned it over to Lloyd more than a year ago with a request that he see to tenant demands and maintenance. You know the rest."

"Then perhaps I am grateful to him." He reached up to tuck her hair behind her ear, placing his lips just beneath the jet drops she wore. "If he had been honest and efficient, I wouldn't have had to be rude in your office. You might not be here with me tonight."

Taking his hand, she pressed it to her cheek. "Maybe I should have given him a raise." She turned her lips into his palm, amazed at how easy it had become for her to show her feelings.

"No. Instead, we'll think this was destiny. I don't like someone that close who would like to hurt you."

"I know he leaked Mrs. Wolburg's story to the press." Worked up again, Sydney broke off a hunk of bread. "His anger toward me caused him to put Hayward in a very unstable position. I won't tolerate that, and neither will the board."

"You'll fix it." He split the last of the champagne between them.

"Yes, I will." She was looking out over the neighborhood, seeing the clothes hung on lines to dry in the sun, the open windows where people could be seen walking by or sitting in front of televisions. There were children on the sidewalk taking advantage of a long summer day. When Mikhail's hand reached for hers, she gripped it tightly.

"Today, for the first time," she said quietly, "I felt in charge. My whole life I went along with what I was told was best or proper or expected." Catching herself, she shook her head. "That doesn't matter. What matters is that sometime over the last few months I started to realize that to be in charge meant you had to take charge. I finally did. I don't know if you can understand how that feels."

"I know what I see. And this is a woman who is beginning to trust herself, and take what is right for her." Smiling, he skimmed a finger down her cheek. "Take me."

She turned to him. He was less than an arm's length away. Those dark, untamed looks would have set any woman's heart leaping. But there was more happening to her than an excited pulse. She was afraid to consider it. There was only now, she reminded herself, and reached for him. He held her, rubbing his cheek against her hair, murmuring lovely words she couldn't understand.

"I'll have to get a phrase book." Her eyes closed on a sigh as his mouth roamed over her face.

"This one is easy." He repeated a phrase between kisses.

She laughed, moving willingly when he drew her to her feet. "Easy for you to say. What does it mean?"

His lips touched hers again. "I love you."

He watched her eyes fly open, saw the race of emotion in them run from shock to hope to panic. "Mikhail, I—"

"Why do the words frighten you?" he interrupted. "Love doesn't threaten."

"I didn't expect this." She put a hand to his chest to insure some distance. Eyes darkening, Mikhail looked down at it, then stepped back.

"What did you expect?"

"I thought you were…" Was there no delicate way? "I assumed that you…"

"Wanted only your body," he finished for her, and his voice heated. He had shown her so much, and she saw so little. "I do want it, but not only. Will you tell me there was nothing last night?"

"Of course not. It was beautiful." She had to sit down, really had to. It felt as though she'd jumped off a cliff and landed on her head. But he was looking at her in such a way that made her realize she'd better stay on her feet.

"The sex was good." He picked up his glass. Though he was tempted to fling it off the balcony, he only sipped. "Good sex is necessary for the body and for the state of mind. But it isn't enough for the heart. The heart needs love, and there was love last night. For both of us."

Her arms fell uselessly to her sides. "I don't know. I've never had good sex before."

He considered her over the rim of his glass. "You were not a virgin. You were married before."

"Yes, I was married before." And the taste of that was still bitter on her tongue. "I don't want to talk about that, Mikhail. Isn't it enough that we're good together, that I feel for you something I've never felt before? I don't want to analyze it. I just can't yet."

"You don't want to know what you feel?" That baffled him. "How can you live without knowing what's inside you?"

"It's different for me. I haven't had what you've had or done what you've done. And your emotions—they're always right there. You can see them in the way you move, the way you talk, in your eyes, in your work. Mine are… mine aren't as volatile. I need time."

He nearly smiled. "Do you think I'm a patient man?"

"No," she said, with feeling.

"Good. Then you'll understand that your time will be very short." He began to gather dishes. "Did this husband of yours hurt you?"

"A failed marriage hurts. Please, don't push me on that now."

"For tonight I won't." With the sky just beginning to deepen at his back, he looked at her. "Because tonight I want you only to think of me." He walked through the door, leaving her to gather the rest of the meal.

He loved her. The words swam in Sydney's mind as she picked up the basket and the flower. It wasn't possible to doubt it. She'd come to understand he was a man who said no more than he meant, and rarely less. But she couldn't know what love meant to him.

To her, it was something sweet and colorful and lasting that happened to other people. Her father had cared for her, in his erratic way. But they had only spent snatches of time together in her early childhood. After the divorce, when she'd been six, they had rarely seen each other.

And her mother. She didn't doubt her mother's affection. But she always realized it ran no deeper than any of Margerite's interests.

There had been Peter, and that had been strong and true and important. Until they had tried to love as husband and wife.

But it wasn't the love of a friend that Mikhail was offering her. Knowing it, feeling it, she was torn by twin forces of giddy happiness and utter terror.

With her mind still whirling, she walked into the kitchen to find him elbow deep in soapsuds. She set basket and bottle aside to pick up a dish towel.

"Are you angry with me?" she ventured after a moment.

"Some. More I'm puzzled by you." And hurt, but he didn't want her guilt or pity. "To be loved should make you happy, warm."

"Part of me is. The other half is afraid of moving too fast and risking spoiling what we've begun." He needed honesty, she thought. Deserved it. She tried to give him what she had. "All day today I looked forward to being here with you, being able to talk to you, to be able to share with you what had happened. To listen to you. I knew you'd make me laugh, that my heart would speed up when you kissed me." She set a dry bowl aside. "Why are you looking at me like that?"

He only shook his head. "You don't even know you're in love with me. But it's all right," he decided, and offered her the next bowl. "You will."

"You're so arrogant," she said, only half-annoyed. "I'm never sure if I admire or detest that."

"You like it very much because it makes you want to fight back."

"I suppose you think I should be flattered because you love me."

"Of course." He grinned at her. "Are you?"

Thinking it over, she stacked the second bowl in the first, then took the skillet. "I suppose. It's human nature. And you're..."

"I'm what?"

She looked up at him again, the cocky grin, the dark amused eyes, the tumble of wild hair. "You're so gorgeous."

His grin vanished when his mouth dropped open. When he managed to close it again, he pulled his hands out of the water and began to mutter.

"Are you swearing at me?" Instead of answering her, he yanked the dishcloth away from her to dry his hands.

"I think I embarrassed you." Delighted, she laughed and cupped his face in her hands. "Yes, I did."

"Stop." Thoroughly frazzled, he pushed her hands away. "I can't think of the word for what I am."

"But you are gorgeous." Before he could shake her off, she wound her arms around his neck. "When I first saw you, I thought you looked like a pirate, all dark and dashing."

This time he swore in English and she only smiled.

"Maybe it's the hair," she considered, combing her fingers through it. "I used to imagine what it would be like to get my hands in it. Or the eyes. So moody, so dangerous."

His hands lowered to her hips. "I'm beginning to feel dangerous."

"Hmm. Or the mouth. It just might be the mouth." She touched hers to it, then slowly, her eyes on his, outlined its shape with her tongue. "I can't imagine there's a woman still breathing who could resist it."

"You're trying to seduce me."

She let her hands slide down, her fingers toying with his buttons. "Somebody has to." She only hoped she could do it right. "Then, of course, there's this wonderful body. The first time I saw you without a shirt, I nearly swallowed my tongue." She parted his shirt to let her hands roam over his chest. His knees nearly buckled. "Your skin was wet and glistening, and there were all these muscles." She forgot the game, seducing herself as completely as him. "So hard, and the skin so smooth. I wanted to touch, like this."

Her breath shuddered out as she pressed her fingers into his shoulders, kneading her way down his arms. When her eyes focused on his again, she saw that they were fiercely intense. Beneath her fingers, his arms were taut as steel. The words dried up in her mouth.

"Do you know what you do to me?" he asked. He reached for the tiny black buttons on her jacket, and his fingers trembled. Beneath the sunny cap-sleeved suit, she wore lace the color of midnight. He could feel the fast dull thud of his heart in his head. "Or how much I need you?"

She could only shake her head. "Just show me. It's enough to show me."

She was caught fast and hard, her mouth fused to his, their bodies molded. When her arms locked around his neck, he lifted her an inch off the floor, circling slowly, his lips tangling with hers.

Dizzy and desperate, she clung to him as he wound his way into the bedroom. She kicked her shoes off, heedless of where they flew. There was such freedom in the simple gesture, she laughed, then held tight as they fell to the bed.

The mattress groaned and sagged, cupping them in the center. He was muttering her name, and she his, when their mouths met again.

It was as hot and reckless as before. Now she knew where they would go and strained to match his speed. The need to have him was as urgent as breath, and she struggled with his jeans, tugging at denim while he peeled away lace.

She could feel the nubs of the bedspread beneath her bare back, and him, hard and restless above her. Through the open window, the heat poured in. And there was a rumble, low and distant, of thunder. She felt the answering power echo in her blood.

He wanted the storm, outside, in her. Never before had he understood what it was to truly crave. He remembered hunger and a miserable wish for warmth. He remembered wanting the curves and softness of a woman. But all that was nothing, nothing like the violent need he felt for her.

His hands hurried over her, wanting to touch every inch,

and everywhere he touched she burned. If she trembled, he drove her further until she shuddered. When she moaned, he took and tormented until she cried out.

And still he hungered.

Thunder stalked closer, like a threat. Following it through the window came the passionate wail of the sax. The sun plunged down in the sky, tossing flame and shadows.

Inside the hot, darkening room, they were aware of no time or sound. Reality had been whittled down to one man and one woman and the ruthless quest to mate.

He filled. She surrounded.

Crazed, he lifted her up until her legs circled his waist and her back arched like a bow. Shuddering from the power they made, he pressed his face to her shoulder and let it take him.

The rain held off until the next afternoon, then came with a full chorus of thunder and lightning. With her phone on speaker, Sydney handled a tricky conference call. Though Janine sat across from her, she took notes of her own. Thanks to a morning of intense work between herself and her new assistant, she had the information needed at her fingertips.

"Yes, Mr. Bernstein, I think the adjustments will be to everyone's benefit." She waited for the confirmation to run from Bernstein, to his lawyer, to his West Coast partner. "We'll have the revised draft faxed to all of you by five, East Coast time, tomorrow." She smiled to herself. "Yes, Hayward Industries believes in moving quickly. Thank you, gentlemen. Goodbye."

After disengaging the speaker, she glanced at Janine. "Well?"

"You never even broke a sweat. Look at me." Janine held out a hand. "My palms are wet. Those three were hoping to bulldoze you under and you came out dead even. Congratulations."

"I think that transaction should please the board." Seven million, she thought. She'd just completed a seven-million-dollar deal. And Janine was right. She was steady as a rock. "Let's get busy on the fine print, Janine."

"Yes, ma'am." Even as she rose, the phone rang. Moving on automatic, she plucked up Sydney's receiver. "Ms. Hayward's office. One moment, please." She clicked to hold. "Mr. Warfield."

The faintest wisp of fatigue clouded her eyes as she nodded. "I'll take it. Thank you, Janine."

She waited until her door closed again before bringing him back on the line. "Hello, Channing."

"Sydney, I've been trying to reach you for a couple of days. Where have you been hiding?"

She thought of Mikhail's lumpy bed and smiled. "I'm sorry, Channing. I've been…involved."

"All work and no play, darling," he said, and set her teeth on edge. "I'm going to take you away from all that. How about lunch tomorrow? Lutece."

As a matter of course, she checked her calendar. "I have a meeting."

"Meetings were made to be rescheduled."

"No, I really can't. As it is, I have a couple of projects coming to a head, and I won't be out of the office much all week."

"Now, Sydney, I promised Margerite I wouldn't let you bury yourself under the desk. I'm a man of my word."

Why was it, she thought, she could handle a multimillion-dollar deal with a cool head, but this personal pressure was making her shoulders tense? "My mother worries unnecessarily. I'm really sorry, Channing, but I can't chat now. I've got—I'm late for an appointment," she improvised.

"Beautiful women are entitled to be late. If I can't get you out to lunch, I have to insist that you come with us on Friday. We have a group going to the theater. Drinks first, of course, and a light supper after."

"I'm booked, Channing. Have a lovely time though. Now, I really must ring off. Ciao." Cursing herself, she settled the receiver on his pipe of protest.

Why hadn't she simply told him she was involved with someone?

Simple question, she thought, simple answer. Channing would go to Margerite, and Sydney didn't want her mother to know. What she had with Mikhail was hers, only hers, and she wanted to keep it that way for a little while longer.

He loved her.

Closing her eyes, she experienced the same quick trickle of pleasure and alarm. Maybe, in time, she would be able to love him back fully, totally, in the full-blooded way she was so afraid she was incapable of.

She'd thought she'd been frigid, too. She'd certainly been wrong there. But that was only one step.

Time, she thought again. She needed time to organize her emotions. And then…then they'd see.

The knock on her office door brought her back to earth. "Yes?"

"Sorry, Sydney." Janine came in carrying a sheet of Hayward stationery. "This just came in from Mr. Bingham's office. I thought you'd want to see it right away."

"Yes, thank you." Sydney scanned the letter. It was carefully worded to disguise the rage and bitterness, but it was a resignation. Effective immediately. Carefully she set the letter aside. It took only a marginal ability to read between the lines to know it wasn't over. "Janine, I'll need some personnel files. We'll want to fill Mr. Bingham's position, and I want to see if we can do it in-house."

"Yes, ma'am." She started toward the door, then stopped. "Sydney, does being your executive assistant mean I can offer advice?"

"It certainly does."

"Watch your back. There's a man who would love to stick a knife in it."

"I know. I don't intend to let him get behind me." She rubbed at the pressure at the back of her neck. "Janine, before we deal with the files, how about some coffee? For both of us."

"Coming right up." She turned and nearly collided with Mikhail as he strode through the door. "Excuse me." The man was soaking wet and wore a plain white T-shirt that clung to every ridge of muscle. Janine entertained a brief fantasy of drying him off herself. "I'm sorry, Ms. Hayward is—"

"It's all right." Sydney was already coming around the desk. "I'll see Mr. Stanislaski."

Noting the look in her boss's eye, Janine managed to fight back the worst of the envy. "Shall I hold your calls?"

"Hmm?"

Mikhail grinned. "Please. You're Janine, with the promotion?"

"Why, yes."

"Sydney tells me you are excellent in your work."

"Thank you." Who would have thought the smell of wet male could be so terrific? "Would you like some coffee?"

"No, thank you."

"Hold mine, too, Janine. And take a break yourself."

"Yes, ma'am." With only a small envious sigh, she shut the door.

"Don't you have an umbrella?" Sydney asked him, and leaned forward for a kiss. He kept his hands to himself.

"I can't touch you, I'll mess up your suit. Do you have a towel?"

"Just a minute." She walked into the adjoining bath. "What are you doing uptown at this time of day?"

"The rain slows things up. I did paperwork and knocked off at four." He took the towel she offered and rubbed it over his head.

"Is it that late?" She glanced at the clock and saw it was nearly five.

"You're busy."

She thought of the resignation on her desk and the files she had to study. "A little."

"When you're not busy, maybe you'd like to go with me to the movies."

"I'd love to." She took the towel back. "I need an hour."

"I'll come back." He reached out to toy with the pearls at her throat. "There's something else."

"What?"

"My family goes to visit my sister this weekend. To have a barbecue. Will you go with me?"

"I'd love to go to a barbecue. When?"

"They leave Friday, after work." He wanted to sketch her in those pearls. Just those pearls. Though he rarely worked in anything but wood, he thought he might carve her in alabaster. "We can go when you're ready."

"I should be able to get home and changed by six. Six-thirty," she corrected. "All right?"

"All right." He took her shoulders, holding her a few

inches away from his damp clothes as he kissed her. "Natasha will like you."

"I hope so."

He kissed her again. "I love you."

Emotion shuddered through her. "I know."

"And you love me," he murmured. "You're just stubborn." He toyed with her lips another moment. "But soon you'll pose for me."

"I...what?"

"Pose for me. I have a show in the fall, and I think I'll use several pieces of you."

"You never told me you had a show coming up." The rest of it hit her. "Of me?"

"Yes, we'll have to work very hard very soon. So now I leave you alone so you can work."

"Oh." She'd forgotten all about files and phone calls. "Yes, I'll see you in an hour."

"And this weekend there will be no work. But next..." He nodded, his mind made up. Definitely in alabaster.

She ran the damp towel through her hands as he walked to the door. "Mikhail."

With the door open, he stood with his hand on the knob. "Yes?"

"Where does your sister live?"

"West Virginia." He grinned and shut the door behind her. Sydney stared at the blank panel for a full ten seconds.

"West Virginia?"

Chapter 9

She'd never be ready in time. Always decisive about her wardrobe, Sydney had packed and unpacked twice. What did one wear for a weekend in West Virginia? A few days in Martinique—no problem. A quick trip to Rome would have been easy. But a weekend, a family weekend in West Virginia, had her searching frantically through her closet.

As she fastened her suitcase a third time, she promised herself she wouldn't open it again. To help herself resist temptation, she carried the bag into the living room, then hurried back to the bedroom to change out of her business suit.

She'd just pulled on thin cotton slacks and a sleeveless top in mint green—and was preparing to tear them off again—when the knock sounded at her door.

It would have to do. It would do, she assured herself as she went to answer. They would be arriving so late at his sister's home, it hardly mattered what she was wearing. With a restless hand she brushed her hair back, wondered if she should secure it with a scarf for the drive, then opened the door.

Sequined and sleek, Margerite stood on the other side.

"Sydney, darling." As she glided inside, she kissed her daughter's cheek.

"Mother. I didn't know you were coming into the city today."

"Of course you did." She settled into a chair, crossed her legs. "Channing told you about our little theater party."

"Yes, he did. I'd forgotten."

"Sydney." The name was a sigh. "You're making me worry about you."

Automatically Sydney crossed to the liquor cabinet to pour Margerite a glass of her favored brand of sherry. "There's no need. I'm fine."

"No need?" Margerite's pretty coral-tipped fingers fluttered. "You turn down dozens of invitations, couldn't even spare an afternoon to shop with your mother last week, bury yourself in that office for positively hours on end. And there's no need for me to worry." She smiled indulgently and she accepted the glass. "Well, we're going to fix all of that. I want you to go in and change into something dashing. We'll meet Channing and the rest of the party at Doubles for a drink before curtain."

The odd thing was, Sydney realized, she'd very nearly murmured an agreement, so ingrained was her habit of doing what was expected of her. Instead, she perched on the arm of the sofa and hoped she could do this without hurting Margerite's feelings.

"Mother, I'm sorry. If I've been turning down invitations, it's because the transition at Hayward is taking up most of my time and energy."

"Darling." Margerite gestured with the glass before she sipped. "That's exactly my point."

But Sydney only shook her head. "And the simple fact is, I don't feel the need to have my social calendar filled every night any longer. As for tonight, I appreciate, I really do, the fact that you'd like me to join you. But, as I explained to Channing, I have plans."

Irritation sparked in Margerite's eyes, but she only tapped a nail on the arm of the chair. "If you think I'm going to leave you here to spend the evening cooped up with some sort of nasty paperwork—"

"I'm not working this weekend," Sydney interrupted. "Actually, I'm going out of town for—" The quick rap at the door relieved her. "Excuse me a minute." The moment she'd opened the door, Sydney reached out a hand for him. "Mikhail, my—"

Obviously he didn't want to talk until he'd kissed her, which he did, thoroughly, in the open doorway. Pale and rigid, Margerite pushed herself to her feet. She understood, as a woman would, that the kiss she was witnessing was the kind exchanged by lovers.

"Mikhail." Sydney managed to draw back an inch.

"I'm not finished yet."

One hand braced against his chest as she gestured helplessly with the other. "My mother..."

He glanced over, caught the white-faced fury and shifted Sydney easily to his side. A subtle gesture of protection. "Margerite."

"Isn't there a rule," she said stiffly, "about mixing business and pleasure?" She lifted her brows as her gaze skimmed over him. "But then, you wouldn't be a rule follower, would you, Mikhail?"

"Some rules are important, some are not." His voice was

gentle, but without regret and without apology. "Honesty is important, Margerite. I was honest with you."

She turned away, refusing to acknowledge the truth of that. "I'd prefer a moment with you, alone, Sydney."

There was a pounding at the base of her skull as she looked at her mother's rigid back. "Mikhail, would you take my bag to the car? I'll be down in a few minutes."

He cupped her chin, troubled by what he read in her eyes. "I'll stay with you."

"No." She put a hand to his wrist. "It would be best if you left us alone. Just a few minutes." Her fingers tightened. "Please."

She left him no choice. Muttering to himself, he picked up her suitcase. The moment the door closed behind him, Margerite whirled. Sydney was already braced. It was rare, very rare for Margerite to go on a tirade. But when she did, it was always an ugly scene with vicious words.

"You fool. You've been sleeping with him."

"I don't see that as your concern. But, yes, I have."

"Do you think you have the sense or skill to handle a man like that?" There was the crack of glass against wood as she slapped the little crystal goblet onto the table. "This sordid little liaison could ruin you, ruin everything I've worked for. God knows you did enough damage by divorcing Peter, but I managed to put that right. Now this. Sneaking off for a weekend at some motel."

Sydney's fists balled at her sides. "There is nothing sordid about my relationship with Mikhail, and I'm not sneaking anywhere. As for Peter, I will not discuss him with you."

Eyes hard, Margerite stepped forward. "From the day you were born, I used everything at my disposal to be certain you had what you deserved as a Hayward. The finest schools, the proper friends, even the right husband. Now, you're tossing it all back at me, all the planning, all the sacrificing. And for what?"

She whirled around the room as Sydney remained stiff and silent.

"Oh, believe me, I understand that man's appeal. I'd even toyed with the idea of having a discreet affair with him myself." The wound to her vanity was raw and throbbing. "A woman's entitled to a wild fling with a magnificent animal now and again. And his artistic talents and reputation are certainly in his favor. But his background is nothing, less than nothing. Gypsies and farmers and peasants. I have the experience to handle him—had I chosen to. I also have no ties at the moment to make an affair awkward. You, however, are on the verge of making a commitment to Channing. Do you think he'd have you if he ever learned you'd been taking that magnificent brute to bed?"

"That's enough." Sydney moved forward to take her mother's arm. "That's past enough. For someone who's so proud of the Hayward lineage, you certainly made no attempt to keep the name yourself. It was always my burden to be a proper Hayward, to do nothing to damage the Hayward name. Well, I've been a proper Hayward, and right now I'm working day and night to be certain the Hayward name remains above reproach. But my personal time, and whom I decide to spend that personal time with, is my business."

Pale with shock, Margerite jerked her hand away. Not once, from the day she'd been born, had Sydney spoken to her in such a manner. "Don't you dare use that tone with me. Are you so blinded with lust that you've forgotten where your loyalties lie?"

"I've never forgotten my loyalties," Sydney tossed back. "And at the moment, this is the most reasonable tone I can summon." It surprised her as well, this fast, torrid venom, but she couldn't stop it. "Listen to me, Mother, as far as Channing goes, I have never been on the verge of making a commitment to him, nor do I ever intend to do so. That's what you intended. And I will never, never, be pressured into making that kind of commitment again. If it would help disabuse Channing of the notion, I'd gladly take out a full-page ad in the *Times* announcing my relationship with Mikhail. As to that, you know nothing about Mikhail's family, you know nothing about him, as a man. You never got beyond his looks."

Margerite's chin lifted. "And you have?"

"Yes, I have, and he's a caring, compassionate man. An honest man who knows what he wants out of life and goes after it. You'd understand that, but the difference is he'd never use or hurt anyone to get it. He loves me. And I..." It flashed through her like light, clear, warm and utterly simple. "I love him."

"Love?" Stunned, Margerite reared back. "Now I know you've taken leave of your senses. My God, Sydney, do you believe everything a man says in bed?"

"I believe what Mikhail says. Now, I'm keeping him waiting, and we have a long trip to make."

Head high, chin set, Margerite streamed toward the door, then tossed a last look over her shoulder. "He'll break your heart, and make a fool of you in the bargain. But perhaps that's what you need to remind you of your responsibilities."

When the door snapped shut, Sydney lowered onto the arm of the sofa. Mikhail would have to wait another moment.

He wasn't waiting; he was prowling. Back and forth in front of the garage elevators he paced, hands jammed into his pockets, thoughts as black as smoke. When the elevator doors slid open, he was on Sydney in a heartbeat.

"Are you all right?" He had her face in his hands. "No, I can see you are not."

"I am, really. It was unpleasant. Family arguments always are."

For him, family arguments were fierce and furious and inventive. They could either leave him enraged or laughing, but never drained as she was now. "Come, we can go upstairs, leave in the morning when you're feeling better."

"No, I'd like to go now."

"I'm sorry." He kissed both of her hands. "I don't like to cause bad feelings between you and your mama."

"It wasn't you. Really." Because she needed it, she rested her head on his chest, soothed when his arms came around her. "It was old business, Mikhail, buried too long. I don't want to talk about it."

"You keep too much from me, Sydney."

"I know. I'm sorry." She closed her eyes, feeling her stomach muscles dance, her throat drying up. It couldn't be so hard to say the words. "I love you, Mikhail."

The hand stroking her back went still, then dived into her hair to draw her head back. His eyes were intense, like two dark suns searching hers. He saw what he wanted to see, what he needed desperately to see. "So, you've stopped being stubborn." His voice was thick with emotion, and his mouth, when it met hers, gave her more than dozens of soft endearments. "You can tell me again while we drive. I like to hear it."

Laughing, she linked an arm through his as they walked to the car. "All right."

"And while you drive, I tell you."

Eyes wide, she stopped. "I drive?"

"Yes." He opened the passenger door for her. "I start, then you have a turn. You have license, yes?"

She glanced dubiously at the gauges on the dash. "Yes."

"You aren't afraid?"

She looked back up to see him grinning. "Not tonight, I'm not."

It was after midnight when Mikhail pulled up at the big brick house in Shepherdstown. It was cooler now. There wasn't a cloud in the star-scattered sky to hold in the heat. Beside him, Sydney slept with her head resting on a curled fist. He remembered that she had taken the wheel on the turnpike, driving from New Jersey into Delaware with verve and enthusiasm. Soon after they'd crossed the border into Maryland and she'd snuggled into the passenger seat again, she'd drifted off.

Always he had known he would love like this. That he would find the one woman who would change the zigzagging course of his life into a smooth circle. She was with him now, dreaming in an open car on a quiet road.

When he looked at her, he could envision how their lives would be. Not perfectly. To see perfectly meant there would be no surprises. But he could imagine waking beside her in the morning, in the big bedroom of the old house they would buy and make into a home together. He could see her coming home at night, wearing one of those pretty suits, her face reflecting the annoyance or the success of the day. And they would sit together and talk, of her work, of his.

One day, her body would grow ripe with child. He would feel their son or daughter move inside her. And they would fill their home with children and watch them grow.

But he was moving too quickly. They had come far already, and he wanted to treasure each moment.

He leaned over to nuzzle his lips over her throat. "I've crossed the states with you, *milaya*." She stirred, murmuring sleepily. "Over rivers and mountains. Kiss me."

She came awake with his mouth warm on hers and her hand resting against his cheek. She felt the flutter of a night breeze on her skin and smelled the fragrance of roses and honeysuckle. And the stir of desire was just as warm, just as sweet.

"Where are we?"

"The sign said, Wild, Wonderful West Virginia." He nipped at her lip. "You will tell me if you think it is so."

Any place, any place at all was wild and wonderful, when he was there, she thought as her arms came around him. He gave a quiet groan, then a grunt as the gearshift pressed into a particularly sensitive portion of his anatomy. "I must be getting old. It is not so easy as it was to seduce a woman in a car."

"I thought you were doing a pretty good job."

He felt the quick excitement stir his blood, fantasized briefly, then shook his head. "I'm intimidated because my mama may peek out the window any minute. Come. We'll find your bed, then I'll sneak into it."

She laughed as he unfolded his long legs out of the open door. "Now I'm intimidated." Pushing her hair back, she turned to look at the house. It was big and brick, with lights glowing gold in the windows of the first floor. Huge leafy trees shaded it, pretty box hedges shielded it from the street.

When Mikhail joined her with their bags, they started up the stone steps that cut through the slope of lawn. And here were the flowers, the roses she had smelled, and dozens of others. No formal garden this, but a splashy display that seemed to grow wild and willfully. She saw the shadow of a tricycle near the porch. In the spill of light from the windows, she noted that a bed of petunias had been recently and ruthlessly dug up.

"I think Ivan has been to work," Mikhail commented, noting the direction of Sydney's gaze. "If he is smart, he hides until it's time to go home again."

Before they had crossed the porch, she heard the laughter and music.

"It sounds as though they're up," Sydney said. "I thought they might have gone to bed."

"We have only two days together. We won't spend much of it sleeping." He opened the screen door and entered without knocking. After setting the bags near the stairs, then taking Sydney's hand, he dragged her down the hall toward the party sounds.

Sydney could feel her reserve settling back into place. She couldn't help it. All the early training, all the years of schooling had drummed into her the proper way to greet strangers. Politely, coolly, giving no more of yourself than a firm handshake and a quiet "how do you do."

She'd hardly made the adjustment when Mikhail burst into the music room, tugging her with him.

"Ha," he said, and swooped down on a small, gorgeous woman in a purple sundress. She laughed when he scooped her up, her black mane of curling hair flying out as he swung her in a circle.

"You're always late," Natasha said. She kissed her brother on both cheeks then the lips. "What did you bring me?"

"Maybe I have something in my bag for you." He set her on her feet, then turned to the man at the piano. "You take good care of her?"

"When she lets me." Spence Kimball rose to clasp hands with Mikhail. "She's been fretting for you for an hour."

"I don't fret," Natasha corrected, turning to Sydney. She smiled—the warmth was automatic—though what she saw concerned her. This cool, distant woman was the one her family insisted Mikhail was in love with? "You haven't introduced me to your friend."

"Sydney Hayward." A little impatient by the way Sydney hung back, he nudged her forward. "My sister, Natasha."

"It's nice to meet you." Sydney offered a hand. "I'm sorry about being so late. It's really my fault."

"I was only teasing. You're welcome here. You already know my family." They were gathering around Mikhail as if it had been years since the last meeting. "And this is my husband, Spence."

But he was stepping forward, puzzlement and pleasure in his eyes. "Sydney? Sydney Hayward?"

She turned, the practiced smile in place. It turned to surprise and genuine delight. "Spence Kimball. I had no idea." Offering both hands, she gripped his. "Mother told me you'd moved south and remarried."

"You've met," Natasha observed, exchanging looks with her own mother as Nadia brought over fresh glasses of wine.

"I've known Sydney since she was Freddie's age," Spence answered, referring to his eldest daughter. "I haven't seen her since…" He trailed off, remembering the last time had been at her wedding. Spence may have been out of touch with New York society in recent years, but he was well aware the marriage hadn't worked out.

"It's been a long time," Sydney murmured, understanding perfectly.

"Is small world," Yuri put in, slapping Spence on the back with fierce affection. "Sydney is owner of building where Mikhail lives. Until she pays attention to him, he sulks."

"I don't sulk." Grumbling a bit, Mikhail took his father's glass and tossed back the remaining vodka in it. "I convince. Now she is crazy for me."

"Back up, everyone," Rachel put in, "his ego's expanding again."

Mikhail merely reached over and twisted his sister's nose. "Tell them you're crazy for me," he ordered Sydney, "so this one eats her words."

Sydney lifted a brow. "How do you manage to speak when your mouth's so full of arrogance?"

Alex hooted and sprawled onto the couch. "She has your number, Mikhail. Come over here, Sydney, and sit beside me. I'm humble."

"You tease her enough for tonight." Nadia shot Alex a daunting look. "You are tired after your drive?" she asked Sydney.

"A little. I—"

"I'm sorry." Instantly Natasha was at her side. "Of course you're tired. I'll show you your room." She was already leading Sydney out. "If you like you can rest, or come back down. We want you to be at home while you're here."

"Thank you," Sydney replied. Before she could reach for her bag, Natasha had hefted it. "It's kind of you to have me."

Natasha merely glanced over her shoulder. "You're my brother's friend, so you're mine." But she certainly intended to grill Spence before the night was over.

At the end of the hall, she took Sydney into a small room with a narrow four-poster. Faded rugs were tossed over a gleaming oak floor. Snapdragons spiked out of an old milk bottle on a table by the window where gauzy Priscillas fluttered in the breeze.

"I hope you're comfortable here." Natasha set the suitcase on a cherrywood trunk at the foot of the bed.

"It's charming." The room smelled of the cedar wardrobe against the wall and the rose petals scattered in a bowl on the nightstand. "I'm very happy to meet Mikhail's sister, and the wife of an old friend. I'd heard Spence was teaching music at a university."

"He teaches at Shepherd College. And he composes again."

"That's wonderful. He's tremendously talented." Feeling awkward, she traced a finger over the wedding ring quilt. "I remember his little girl, Freddie."

"She is ten now." Natasha's smile warmed. "She tried to wait up for Mikhail, but fell asleep on the couch." Her chin angled. "She took Ivan with her to bed, thinking I would not strangle him there. He dug up my petunias. Tomorrow, I think…"

She trailed off, head cocked.

"Is something wrong?"

"No, it's Katie, our baby." Automatically Natasha laid a hand on her breast where her milk waited. "She wakes for a midnight snack. If you'll excuse me."

"Of course."

At the door, Natasha hesitated. She could go with her instincts or her observations. She'd always trusted her instincts. "Would you like to see her?"

After only an instant's hesitation, Sydney's lips curved. "Yes, very much."

Across the hall and three doors down, the sound of the child's restless crying was louder. The room was softly lit by a nightlight in the shape of a pink sea horse.

"There, sweetheart." Natasha murmured in two languages as she lifted her baby from the crib. "Mama's here now." As the crying turned to a soft whimpering, Natasha turned to see Spence at the doorway. "I have her. She's wet and hungry, that's all."

But he had to come in. He never tired of looking at his youngest child, that perfect and beautiful replica of the woman he'd fallen in love with. Bending close, his cheek brushing his wife's, he stroked a finger over Katie's. The whimpering stopped completely, and the gurgling began.

"You're just showing off for Sydney," Natasha said with a laugh.

While Sydney watched, they cuddled the baby. There was a look exchanged over the small dark head, a look of such intimacy and love and power that it brought tears burning in her throat. Unbearably moved, she slipped out silently and left them alone.

She was awakened shortly past seven by high, excited barking, maniacal laughter and giggling shouts coming from outside her window. Moaning a bit, she turned over and found the bed empty.

Mikhail had lived up to his promise to sneak into her room, and she doubted either of them found sleep in the narrow bed much before dawn.

But he was gone now.

Rolling over, she put the pillow over her head to smother the sounds from the yard below. Since it also smothered her, she gave it up. Resigned, she climbed out of bed and pulled on her robe. She just managed to find the doorknob and open the door, when Rachel opened the one across the hall.

The two disheveled women gave each other bleary-eyed stares. Rachel yawned first.

"When I have kids," she began, "they're not going to be allowed out of bed until ten on Saturday mornings. Noon on Sunday. And only if they're bringing me breakfast in bed."

Sydney ran her tongue over her teeth, propping herself on the doorjamb. "Good luck."

"I wish I wasn't such a sucker for them." She yawned again. "Got a quarter?"

Because she was still half-asleep, Sydney automatically searched the pockets of her robe. "No, I'm sorry."

"Hold on." Rachel disappeared into her room, then came back out with a coin. "Call it."

"Excuse me?"

"Heads or tails. Winner gets the shower first. Loser has to go down and get the coffee."

"Oh." Her first inclination was to be polite and offer to get the coffee, then she thought of a nice hot shower. "Tails."

Rachel flipped, caught the coin and held it out. "Damn. Cream and sugar?"

"Black."

"Ten minutes," Rachel promised, then started down the hall. She stopped, glanced around to make sure they were alone. "Since it's just you and me, are you really crazy about Mikhail?"

"Since it's just you and me, yes."

Rachel's grin was quick and she rocked back on her heels. "I guess there's no accounting for taste."

Thirty minutes later, refreshed by the shower and coffee, Sydney wandered downstairs. Following the sounds of activity, she found most of the family had centered in the kitchen for the morning.

Natasha stood at the stove in a pair of shorts and a T-shirt. Yuri sat at the table, shoveling in pancakes and making faces at the giggling baby who was strapped into one of those clever swings that rocked and played music.

Alex slouched with his head in his hands, barely murmuring when his mother shoved a mug of coffee under his nose.

"Ah, Sydney."

Alex winced at his father's booming greeting. "Papa, have some respect for the dying."

He only gave Alex an affectionate punch on the arm. "You come sit beside me," Yuri instructed Sydney. "And try Tash's pancakes."

"Good morning," Natasha said even as her mother refilled Sydney's coffee cup. "I apologize for my barbaric children and the mongrel who woke the entire house so early."

"Children make noise," Yuri said indulgently. Katie expressed agreement by squealing and slamming a rattle onto the tray of the swing.

"Everyone's up then?" Sydney took her seat.

"Spence is showing Mikhail the barbecue pit he built," Natasha told her and set a heaping platter of pancakes on the table. "They'll stand and study and make men noises. You were comfortable in the night?"

Sydney thought of Mikhail and struggled not to blush. "Yes, thank you. Oh, please," she started to protest when Yuri piled pancakes on her plate.

"For energy," he said, and winked.

Before she could think how to respond, a small curly-haired bullet shot through the back door. Yuri caught him on the fly and hauled the wriggling bundle into his arms.

"This is my grandson, Brandon. He is monster. And I eat monsters for breakfast. Chomp, chomp."

The boy of about three was wiry and tough, squirming and squealing on Yuri's lap. "Papa, come watch me ride my bike. Come watch me!"

"You have a guest," Nadia said mildly, "and no manners."

Resting his head against Yuri's chest, Brandon gave Sydney a long, owlish stare. "You can come watch me, too," he invited. "You have pretty hair. Like Lucy."

"That's a very high compliment," Natasha told her. "Lucy is a cat. Miss Hayward can watch you later. She hasn't finished her breakfast."

"You watch, Mama."

Unable to resist, Natasha rubbed a hand over her son's curls. "Soon. Go tell your daddy he has to go to the store for me."

"Papa has to come."

Knowing the game, Yuri huffed and puffed and stuck Brandon on his shoulders. The boy gave a shout of laughter and gripped tight to Yuri's hair as his grandfather rose to his feet.

"Daddy, look! Look how tall I am," Brandon was shouting as they slammed out of the screen door.

"Does the kid ever stop yelling?" Alex wanted to know.

"You didn't stop yelling until you were twelve," Nadia told him, and added a flick with her dishcloth.

Feeling a little sorry for him, Sydney rose to pour more coffee into his mug herself. He snatched her hand and brought it to his lips for a smacking kiss. "You're a queen among women, Sydney. Run away with me."

"Do I have to kill you?" Mikhail asked as he strolled into the kitchen.

Alex only grinned. "We can arm wrestle for her."

"God, men are such pigs," Rachel observed as she walked in from the opposite direction.

"Why?" The question came from a pretty, golden-haired girl who popped through the doorway, behind Mikhail.

"Because, Freddie, they think they can solve everything with muscles and sweat instead of their tiny little brains."

Ignoring his sister, Mikhail pushed plates aside, sat down and braced an elbow on the table. Alex grinned at the muttered Ukrainian challenge. Palms slapped together.

"What are they doing?" Freddie wanted to know.

"Being silly." Natasha sighed and swung an arm around Freddie's shoulder. "Sydney, this is my oldest, Freddie. Freddie, this is Miss Hayward, Mikhail's friend."

Disconcerted, Sydney smiled at Freddie over Mikhail's head. "It's nice to see you again, Freddie. I met you a long time ago when you were just a baby."

"Really?" Intrigued, Freddie was torn between studying Sydney or watching Mikhail and Alex. They were knee to knee, hands clasped, and the muscles in their arms were bulging.

"Yes, I, ah…" Sydney was having a problem herself. Mikhail's eyes flicked up and over her before returning to his brother's. "I knew your father when you lived in New York."

There were a couple of grunts from the men at the table. Rachel sat at the other end and helped herself to pancakes. "Pass me the syrup."

With his free hand, Mikhail shoved it at her.

Smothering a grin, Rachel poured lavishly. "Mama, do you want to take a walk into town after I eat?"

"That would be nice." Ignoring her sons, Nadia began to load the dishwasher. She preferred the arm wrestling to the rolling and kicking they'd treated each other to as boys. "We can take Katie in the stroller if you like, Natasha."

"I'll walk in with you, and check on the shop." Natasha washed her hands. "I own a toy store in town," she told Sydney.

"Oh." Sydney couldn't take her eyes off the two men. Natasha could very well have told her she owned a missile site. "That's nice."

The three Stanislaski women grinned at each other. Sentimental, Nadia began to imagine a fall wedding. "Would you like more coffee?" she asked Sydney.

"Oh, I—"

Mikhail gave a grunt of triumph as he slapped his brother's arm on the table. Dishes jumped. Caught up in the moment, Freddie clapped and had her baby sister mimicking the gesture.

Grinning, Alex flexed his numbed fingers. "Two out of three."

"Get your own woman." Before Sydney could react, Mikhail scooped her up, planted a hard kiss on her mouth that tasted faintly and erotically of sweat, then carried her out the door.

Chapter 10

"You might have lost, you know."

Amused by the lingering annoyance in her voice, Mikhail slid an arm around Sydney's waist and continued to walk down the sloping sidewalk. "I didn't."

"The point—" She sucked in her breath. She'd been trying to get the point through that thick Slavic skull off and on for more than an hour. "The point is that you and Alex arm wrestled for me as if I were a six-pack of beer."

His grin only widened, a six-pack would make him a little drunk, but that was nothing to what he'd felt when he'd looked up and seen the fascination in her eyes as she'd stared at his biceps. He flexed them a little, believing a man had a right to vanity.

"And then," she continued, making sure her voice was low, as his family was wandering along in front and behind them. "You manhandled me—in front of your mother."

"You liked it."

"I certainly—"

"Did," he finished, remembering the hot, helpless way she'd responded to the kiss he'd given her on his sister's back porch. "So did I."

She would not smile. She would not admit for a moment to the spinning excitement she'd felt when he'd scooped her up like some sweaty barbarian carrying off the spoils of war.

"Maybe I was rooting for Alex. It seems to me he got the lion's share of your father's charm."

"All the Stanislaskis have charm," he said, unoffended. He stopped and, bending down, plucked a painted daisy from the slope of the lawn they passed. "See?"

"Hmm." Sydney twirled the flower under her nose. Perhaps it was time to change the subject before she was tempted to try to carry him off. "It's good seeing Spence again. When I was fifteen or so, I had a terrible crush on him."

Narrow eyed, Mikhail studied his brother-in-law's back. "Yes?"

"Yes. Your sister's a lucky woman."

Family pride came first. "He's lucky to have her."

This time she did smile. "I think we're both right."

Brandon, tired of holding his mother's hand, bolted back toward them. "You have to carry me," he told his uncle.

"Have to?"

With an enthusiastic nod, Brandon began to shimmy up Mikhail's leg like a monkey up a tree. "Like Papa does."

Mikhail hauled him up, then to the boy's delight, carried him for a while upside down.

"He'll lose his breakfast," Nadia called out.

"Then we fill him up again." But Mikhail flipped him

over so Brandon could cling to his back. Pink cheeked, the boy grinned over at Sydney.

"I'm three years old," he told her loftily. "And I can dress my own self."

"And very well, too." Amused, she tapped his sneakered foot. "Are you going to be a famous composer like your father?"

"Nah. I'm going to be a water tower. They're the biggest."

"I see." It was the first time she'd heard quite so grand an ambition.

"Do you live with Uncle Mikhail?"

"No," she said quickly.

"Not yet," Mikhail said simultaneously, and grinned at her.

"You were kissing him," Brandon pointed out. "How come you don't have any kids?"

"That's enough questions." Natasha came to the rescue, plucking her son from Mikhail's back as her brother roared with laughter.

"I just wanna know—"

"Everything," Natasha supplied, and gave him a smacking kiss. "But for now it's enough you know you can have one new car from the shop."

He forgot all about babies. His chocolate-brown eyes turned shrewd. "Any car?"

"Any *little car.*"

"You did kiss me," Mikhail reminded Sydney as Brandon began to badger his mother about how little was little. Sydney settled the discussion by ramming her elbow into Mikhail's ribs.

She found the town charming, with its sloping streets and little shops. Natasha's toy store, The Fun House, was impressive, its stock running the range from tiny plastic cars to exquisite porcelain dolls and music boxes.

Mikhail proved to be cooperative when Sydney wandered in and out of antique shops, craft stores and boutiques. Somewhere along the line they'd lost the rest of the family. Or the family had lost them. It wasn't until they'd started back, uphill, with his arms loaded with purchases that he began to complain.

"Why did I think you were a sensible woman?"

"Because I am."

He muttered one of the few Ukrainian phrases she understood. "If you're so sensible, why did you buy all this? How do you expect to get it back to New York?"

Pleased with herself, she fiddled with the new earrings she wore. The pretty enameled stars swung jauntily. "You're so clever, I knew you'd find a way."

"Now you're trying to flatter me, and make me stupid."

She smiled. "You were the one who bought me the porcelain box."

Trapped, he shook his head. She'd studied the oval box, its top decorated with a woman's serene face in bas-relief for ten minutes, obviously in love and just as obviously wondering if she should be extravagant. "You were mooning over it."

"I know." She rose on her toes to kiss his cheek. "Thank you."

"You won't thank me when you have to ride for five hours with all this on your lap."

They climbed to the top of the steps into the yard just as Ivan, tail tucked securely between his legs streaked across the grass. In hot pursuit were a pair of long, lean cats. Mikhail let out a manful sigh.

"He is an embarrassment to the family."

"Poor little thing." Sydney shoved the package she carried at Mikhail. "Ivan!" She clapped her hands and crouched down. "Here, boy."

Spotting salvation, he swung about, scrambled for footing and shot back in her direction. Sydney caught him up, and he buried his trembling head against her neck. The cats, sinuous and smug, sat down a few feet away and began to wash.

"Hiding behind a woman," Mikhail said in disgust.

"He's just a baby. Go arm wrestle with your brother."

Chuckling, he left her to soothe the traumatized pup. A moment later, panting, Freddie rounded the side of the house. "There he is."

"The cats frightened him," Sydney explained, as Freddie came up to stroke Ivan's fur.

"They were just playing. Do you like puppies?" Freddie asked.

"Yes." Unable to resist, Sydney nuzzled. "Yes, I do."

"Me, too. And cats. We've had Lucy and Desi for a long time. Now I'm trying to talk Mama into a puppy." Petting Ivan, she looked back at the mangled petunias. "I thought maybe if I fixed the flowers."

Sydney knew what it was to be a little girl yearning for a pet. "It's a good start. Want some help?"

She spent the next thirty minutes saving what flowers she could or—since she'd never done any gardening—following Freddie's instructions. The pup stayed nearby, shivering when the cats strolled up to wind around legs or be scratched between the ears.

When the job was done, Sydney left Ivan to Freddie's care and went inside to wash up. It occurred to her that it was barely noon and she'd done several things that day for the first time.

She'd been the grand prize in an arm wrestling contest. She'd played with children, been kissed by the man she loved on a public street. She'd gardened and had sat on a sunny lawn with a puppy on her lap.

If the weekend kept going this way, there was no telling what she might experience next.

Attracted by shouts and laughter, she slipped into the music room and looked out the window. A softball game, she realized. Rachel was pitching, one long leg cocking back as she whizzed one by Alex. Obviously displeased by the call, he turned to argue with his mother. She continued to shake her head at him, bouncing Brandon on her knee as she held firm to her authority as umpire.

Mikhail stood spread legged, his hands on his hips, and one heel touching a ripped seat cushion that stood in as second base. He tossed in his own opinion, and Rachel threw him a withering glance over her shoulder, still displeased that he'd caught a piece of her curve ball.

Yuri and Spence stood in the outfield, catcalling as Alex fanned for a second strike. Intrigued, Sydney leaned on the windowsill. How beautiful they were, she thought. She watched as Brandon turned to give Nadia what looked like a very sloppy kiss before he bounded off on sturdy little legs toward a blue-and-white swing set. A screen door slammed, then Freddie zoomed into view, detouring to the swing to give her brother a couple of starter pushes before taking her place in the game.

Alex caught the next pitch, and the ball flew high and wide. Voices erupted into shouts. Surprisingly spry, Yuri danced a few steps to the left and snagged the ball out of the air. Mikhail tagged up, streaked past third and headed for home, where Rachel had raced to wait for the throw.

His long strides ate up the ground, those wonderful muscles bunching as he went into a slide. Rachel crowded the plate, apparently undisturbed by the thought of nearly six feet of solid male hurtling toward her. There was a collision, a tangle of limbs and a great deal of swearing.

"Out." Nadia's voice rang clearly over the din.

In the majors, they called it clearing the benches.

Every member of the family rushed toward the plate— not to fuss over the two forms still nursing bruises, but to shout and gesture. Rachel punched Mikhail in the chest. He responded by covering her face with his hand and shoving her back onto the grass. With a happy shout, Brandon jumped into the fray to climb up his father's back.

Sydney had never envied anything more.

"We can never play without fighting," Natasha said from behind her. She was smiling, looking over Sydney's shoulder at the chaos in her backyard. Her arms still felt the slight weight of the baby she'd just rocked to sleep. "You're wise to watch from a distance."

But when Sydney turned, Natasha saw that her eyes were wet.

"Oh, please." Quickly she moved to Sydney's side to take her hand. "Don't be upset. They don't mean it."

"No. I know." Desperately embarrassed, she blinked the tears back. "I wasn't upset. It was just—it was silly. Watching them was something like looking at a really beautiful painting or hearing some incredibly lovely music. I got carried away."

She didn't need to say more. Natasha understood after Spence's explanation of Sydney's background that there had never been softball games, horseplay or the fun of passionate arguments in her life.

"You love him very much."

Sydney fumbled. That quiet statement wasn't as easy to respond to as Rachel's cocky question had been.

"It's not my business," Natasha continued. "But he is special to me. And I see that you're special to him. You don't find him an easy man."

"No. No, I don't."

Natasha glanced outside again, and her gaze rested on her husband, who was currently wrestling both Freddie and Brandon on the grass. Not so many years before, she thought, she'd been afraid to hope for such things.

"Does he frighten you?"

Sydney started to deny it, then found herself speaking slowly, thoughtfully. "The hugeness of his emotions sometimes frightens me. He has so many, and he finds it so easy to feel them, understand them, express them. I've never been the type to be led by mine, or swept away by them. Sometimes he just overwhelms me, and that's unnerving."

"He is what he feels," Natasha said simply. "Would you like to see some of it?" Without waiting for an answer, she walked over to a wall of shelves.

Lovely carved and painted figures danced across the shelves, some of them so tiny and exquisite it seemed impossible that any hand could have created them.

A miniature house with a gingerbread roof and candy-cane shutters, a high silver tower where a beautiful woman's golden hair streamed from the topmost window, a palm-sized canopy bed where a handsome prince knelt beside a lovely, sleeping princess.

"He brought me this one yesterday." Natasha picked up the painted figure of a woman at a spinning wheel. It sat on a tiny platform scattered with wisps of straw and specks of gold. "The miller's daughter from Rumpelstiltskin." She smiled, tracing the delicate fingertips that rode the spindle.

"They're lovely, all of them. Like a magical world of their own."

"Mikhail has magic," Natasha said. "For me, he carves fairy tales, because I learned English by reading them. Some of his work is more powerful, tragic, erotic, bold, even frightening. But it's always real, because it comes from inside him as much as from the wood or stone."

"I know. What you're trying to show me here is his sensitivity. It's not necessary. I've never known anyone more capable of kindness or compassion."

"I thought perhaps you were afraid he would hurt you."

"No," Sydney said quietly. She thought of the richness of heart it would take to create something as beautiful, as fanciful as the diminutive woman spinning straw into gold. "I'm afraid I'll hurt him."

"Sydney—" But the back door slammed and feet clamored down the hall.

The interruption relieved Sydney. Confiding her feelings was new and far from comfortable. It amazed her that she had done so with a woman she'd known less than a day.

There was something about this family, she realized. Something as magical as the fairy-tale figures Mikhail carved for his sister. Perhaps the magic was as simple as happiness.

As the afternoon wore on, they ebbed and flowed out of the house, noisy, demanding and very often dirty. Nadia eventually cleared the decks by ordering all of the men outside.

"How come they get to go out and sit in the shade with a bottle of beer while we do the cooking," Rachel grumbled as her hands worked quickly, expertly with potatoes and a peeler.

"Because…" Nadia put two dozen eggs on boil. "In here

they will pick at the food, get big feet in my way and make a mess."

"Good point. Still—"

"They'll have to clean the mess we make," Natasha told her.

Satisfied, Rachel attacked another potato. Her complaints were only tokens. She was a woman who loved to cook as much as she loved trying a case. "If Vera was here, they wouldn't even do that."

"Our housekeeper," Natasha explained to Sydney while she sliced and chopped a mountain of vegetables. "She's been with us for years. We gave her the month off to take a trip with her sister. Could you wash those grapes?"

Obediently Sydney followed instructions, scrubbing fruit, fetching ingredients, stirring the occasional pot. But she knew very well that three efficient women were working around her.

"You can make deviled eggs," Nadia said kindly when she noted Sydney was at a loss. "They will be cool soon."

"I, ah…" She stared, marginally horrified, at the shiny white orbs she'd rinsed in the sink. "I don't know how."

"Your mama didn't teach you to cook?" It wasn't annoyance in Nadia's voice, just disbelief. Nadia had considered it her duty to teach every one of her children—whether they'd wanted to learn or not.

As far as Sydney knew, Margerite had never boiled an egg much less deviled one. Sydney offered a weak smile. "No, she taught me how to order in restaurants."

Nadia patted her cheek. "When they cool, I show you how to make them the way Mikhail likes best." She murmured in Ukrainian when Katie's waking wail came through the kitchen intercom. On impulse, Natasha shook her head before Nadia could dry her hands and go up to fetch her granddaughter.

"Sydney, would you mind?" With a guileless smile, Natasha turned to her. "My hands are full."

Sydney blinked and stared. "You want me to go get the baby?"

"Please."

More than a little uneasy, Sydney started out of the kitchen.

"What are you up to, Tash?" Rachel wanted to know.

"She wants family."

With a hoot of laughter, Rachel swung an arm around her sister and mother. "She'll get more than her share with this one."

The baby sounded very upset, Sydney thought as she hurried down the hall. She might be sick. What in the world had Natasha been thinking of not coming up to get Katie herself? Maybe when you were the mother of three, you became casual about such things. Taking a deep breath, she walked into the nursery.

Katie, her hair curling damply around her face, was hanging on to the side of the crib and howling. Unsteady legs dipped and straightened as she struggled to keep her balance. One look at Sydney had her tear-drenched face crumpling. She flung out her arms, tilted and landed on her bottom on the bright pink sheet.

"Oh, poor baby," Sydney crooned, too touched to be nervous. "Did you think no one was coming?" She picked the sniffling baby up, and Katie compensated for Sydney's awkwardness by cuddling trustingly against her body. "You're so little. Such a pretty little thing." On a shuddering sigh, Katie tipped her head back. "You look like your uncle, don't you? He got embarrassed when I said he was gorgeous, but you are."

Downstairs, three women chuckled as Sydney's voice came clearly through the intercom.

"Oh-oh." After giving the little bottom an affectionate pat, Sydney discovered a definite problem. "You're wet, right? Look, I figure your mother could handle this in about thirty seconds flat—that goes for everybody else downstairs. But everybody else isn't here. So what do we do?"

Katie had stopped sniffling and was blowing bubbles with her mouth while she tugged on Sydney's hair. "I guess we'll give it a try. I've never changed a diaper in my life," she began as she glanced around the room. "Or deviled an egg or played softball, or any damn thing. Whoops. No swearing in front of the baby. Here we go." She spotted a diaper bag in bold green stripes. "Oh, God, Katie, they're real ones."

Blowing out a breath, she took one of the neatly folded cotton diapers. "Okay, in for a penny, in for a pound. We'll just put you down on here." Gently she laid Katie on the changing table and prepared to give the operation her best shot.

"Hey." Mikhail bounded into the kitchen and was greeted by three hissing "shhs!"

"What?"

"Sydney's changing Katie," Natasha murmured and smiled at the sounds flowing through the intercom.

"Sydney?" Mikhail forgot the beer he'd been sent to fetch and stayed to listen.

"Okay, we're halfway there." Katie's little butt was dry and powdered. Perhaps a little over powdered, but better to err on the side of caution, Sydney'd figured. Her brow creased as she attempted to make the fresh diaper look like the one she'd removed, sans dampness. "This looks pretty close. What do you think?" Katie kicked her feet and giggled. "You'd be the expert. Okay, this is the tricky part. No wriggling."

Of course, she did. The more she wriggled and kicked, the more Sydney laughed and cuddled. When she'd managed to secure the diaper, Katie looked so cute, smelled so fresh, felt so soft, she had to cuddle some more. Then it seemed only right that she hold Katie up high so the baby could squeal and kick and blow more bubbles.

The diaper sagged but stayed generally where it belonged.

"Okay, gorgeous, now we're set. Want to go down and see Mama?"

"Mama," Katie gurgled, and bounced in Sydney's arms. "Mama."

In the kitchen, four people scattered and tried to look busy or casual.

"Sorry it took so long," she began as she came in. "She was wet." She saw Mikhail and stopped, her cheek pressed against Katie's.

When their eyes met, color washed to her cheeks. The muscles in her thighs went lax. It was no way, no way at all, she thought, for him to be looking at her with his mother and sisters in the room.

"I'll take her." Stepping forward, he held out his arms. Katie stretched into them. Still watching Sydney, he rubbed his cheek over the baby's head and settled her with a natural ease on his hip. "Come here." Before Sydney could respond, he cupped a hand behind her head and pulled her against him for a long, blood-thumping kiss. Well used to such behavior, Katie only bounced and gurgled.

Slowly he slid away, then smiled at her. "I'll come back

for the beer." Juggling Katie, he swaggered out, slamming the screen door behind him.

"Now." Nadia took a dazed Sydney by the hands. "You make deviled eggs."

The sun was just setting on the weekend when Sydney unlocked the door of her apartment. She was laughing— and she was sure she'd laughed more in two days than she had in her entire life. She set the packages she carried on the sofa as Mikhail kicked the door closed.

"You put more in here to come back than you had when you left," he accused, and set her suitcase down.

"One or two things." Smiling, she walked over to slip her arms around his waist. It felt good, wonderfully good, especially knowing that his would circle her in response. *"Dyakuyu,"* she said, sampling *thank you* in his language.

"You mangle it, but you're welcome." He kissed both her cheeks. "This is the traditional greeting or farewell."

She had to bite the tip of her tongue to hold back the grin. "I know." She also knew why he was telling her—again. She'd been kissed warmly by each member of the family. Not the careless touch of cheek to cheek she was accustomed to, but a firm pressure of lips, accompanied by a full-blooded embrace. Only Alex hadn't settled for her cheeks.

"Your brother kisses very well." Eyes as solemn as she could manage, Sydney touched her lips to Mikhail's cheeks in turn. "It must run in the family."

"You liked it?"

"Well…" She shot Mikhail a look from under her lashes. "He did have a certain style."

"He's a boy," Mikhail muttered, though Alex was less than two years his junior.

"Oh, no." This time a quick laugh bubbled out. "He's

definitely not a boy. But I think you have a marginal advantage."

"Marginal."

She linked her hands comfortably behind his neck. "As a carpenter, you'd know that even a fraction of an inch can be vital—for fit."

His hands snagged her hips to settle her against him. "So, I fit you, Hayward?"

"Yes." She smiled as he touched his lips to her brow. "It seems you do."

"And you like my kisses better than Alex's?"

She sighed, enjoying the way his mouth felt skimming down her temples, over her jaw. "Marginally." Her eyes flew open when he pinched her. "Well, really—"

But that was all she managed to get out before his mouth closed over hers. She thought of flash fires, ball lightning and electrical overloads. With a murmur of approval, she tossed heat back at him.

"Now." Instantly aroused, he scooped her up in his arms. "I suppose I must prove myself."

Sydney hooked her arms around his neck. "If you insist."

A dozen long strides and he was in the bedroom, where he dropped her unceremoniously onto the bed. By the time she had her breath back, he'd yanked off his shirt and shoes.

"What are you grinning at?" he demanded.

"It's that pirate look again." Still smiling, she brushed hair out of her eyes. "All you need is a saber and a black patch."

He hooked his thumbs in frayed belt loops. "So, you think I'm a barbarian."

She let her gaze slide up his naked torso, over the wild mane of hair, the stubble that proved he hadn't bothered to pack a razor for the weekend. To his eyes, those dark, dramatic, dangerous eyes. "I think you're dazzling."

He would have winced but she looked so small and pretty, sitting on the bed, her hair tumbled from the wind, her face still flushed from his rough, impatient kiss.

He remembered how she'd looked, walking into the kitchen, carrying Katie. Her eyes had been full of delight and wonder and shyness. She'd flushed when his mother had announced that Sydney had made the eggs herself. And again, when his father had wrapped her in a bear hug. But Mikhail had seen that she'd hung on, that her fingers had curled into Yuri's shirt, just for an instant.

There were dozens of other flashes of memory. How she'd snuggled the puppy or taken Brandon's hand or stroked Freddie's hair.

She needed love. She was strong and smart and sensible. And she needed love.

Frowning, he sat on the edge of the bed and took her hand. Uneasiness skidded down Sydney's spine.

"What is it? What did I do wrong?"

It wasn't the first time he'd heard that strain of insecurity and doubt in her voice. Biting back the questions and the impatience, he shook his head. "Nothing. It's me." Turning her hand over, he pressed a soft kiss in the center of her palm, then to her wrist where her pulse was beating as quickly from fear as from arousal. "I forget to be gentle with you. To be tender."

She'd hurt his feelings. His ego. She hadn't been responsive enough. Too responsive. Oh, God. "Mikhail, I was only teasing about Alex. I wasn't complaining."

"Maybe you should."

"No." Shifting to her knees, she threw her arms around

him and pressed her lips to his. "I want you," she said desperately. "You know how much I want you."

Even as the fire leaped in his gut, he brought his hands lightly to her face, fingers stroking easily. The emotion he poured into the kiss came from the heart only and was filled with sweetness, with kindness, with love.

For a moment, she struggled for the heat, afraid she might never find it. But his mouth was so soft, so patient. As her urgency turned to wonder, his lips rubbed over hers. And the friction sparked not the familiar flash fire, but a warm glow, golden, so quietly beautiful her throat ached with it. Even when he took the kiss deeper, deeper, there was only tenderness. Weakened by it, her body melted like wax. Her hands slid limp and useless from his shoulders in total surrender.

"Beautiful. So beautiful," he murmured as he laid her back on the bed, emptying her mind, stirring her soul with long, drowning kisses. "I should be shot for showing you only one way."

"I can't..." Think, breathe, move.

"Shh." Gently, with an artist's touch, he undressed her. "Tonight is only for you. Only to enjoy." His breath caught as the dying sunlight glowed over her skin. She looked too fragile to touch. Too lovely not to. "Let me show you what you are to me."

Everything. She was everything. After tonight he wanted her to have no doubt of it. With slow, worshipful hands, he showed her that beyond passion, beyond desire, was a merging of spirits. A generosity of the soul.

Love could be peaceful, selfless, enduring.

Her body was a banquet, fragrant, dazzling with erotic flavors. But tonight, he sampled slowly, savoring, sharing.

Each sigh, each shudder filled him with gratitude that she was his.

He wouldn't allow her to race. Helpless to resist, she floated down the long, dark river where he guided her through air the essence of silk. Never, not even during their most passionate joining, had she been so aware of her own body. Her own texture and shape and scent. And his. Oh, Lord, and his.

Those rock-hard muscles and brute strength now channeled into unimagined gentleness. The subtlety of movement elicited new longings, fresh knowledge and a symphony of understanding that was exquisite in its harmony.

Let me give you. Let me show you. Let me take.

Sensitive fingertips traced over her, lingering to arouse, moving on to seek out some new shattering pleasure. And from her pleasure came his own, just as sweet, just as staggering, just as simple.

She could hear her own breathing, a quiet, trembling sound as the room deepened with night. A tribute to beauty, tears dampened her cheeks and thickened her voice when she spoke his name.

His mouth covered hers again as at last he slipped inside her. Enfolded in her, cradled by her, he trembled under the long, sighing sweep of sensation. Her mouth opened beneath his, her arms lifted, circled, held.

More. He remembered that he had once fought desperately for more. Now, with her, he had all.

Even with hot hammers of need pounding at him, he moved slowly, knowing he could take her soaring again and again before that last glorious release.

"I love you, Sydney." His muscles trembled as he felt her rise to meet him. "Only you. Always you."

Chapter 11

When the phone rang, it was pitch-dark and they were sleeping, tangled together like wrestling children. Sydney snuggled closer to Mikhail, squeezing her eyes tighter and muttered a single no, determined to ignore it.

With a grunt, Mikhail rolled over her, seriously considered staying just as he was as her body curved deliciously to his.

"Milaya," he murmured, then with an oath, snatched the shrilling phone off the hook.

"What?" Because Sydney was pounding on his shoulder, he shifted off her. "Alexi?" The sound of his brother's voice had him sitting straight up, firing off in Ukrainian. Only when Alex assured him there was nothing wrong with the family did the sick panic fade. "You'd better be in the hospital or jail. Neither?" He sat back, rapped his head on the brass poles of the headboard and swore again. "Why are you calling in the middle of the night?" Rubbing his hand over his face, Mikhail gave Sydney's clock a vicious stare. The glowing dial read 4:45. "What?" Struggling to tune in, he shifted the phone to his other ear. "Damn it, when? I'll be there."

He slammed the phone down and was already up searching for his clothes when he realized Sydney had turned on the light. Her face was dead pale.

"Your parents."

"No, no, it's not the family." He sat on the bed again to take her hand. "It's the apartment. Vandals."

The sharp edge of fear dulled to puzzlement. "Vandals?"

"One of the cops who answered the call knows Alex, and that I live there, so he called him. There's been some damage."

"To the building." Her heart was beginning to pound, heavy and slow, in her throat.

"Yes, no one was hurt." He watched her eyes close in relief at that before she nodded. "Spray paint, broken windows." He bit off an oath. "Two of the empty apartments were flooded. I'm going to go see what has to be done."

"Give me ten minutes," Sydney said and sprang out of bed.

It hurt. It was only brick and wood and glass, but it hurt her to see it marred. Filthy obscenities were scrawled in bright red paint across the lovely old brownstone. Three of the lower windows were shattered. Inside, someone had used a knife to gouge the railings and hack at the plaster.

In Mrs. Wolburg's apartment water was three inches deep over the old hardwood floor, ruining her rugs, soaking the skirts of her sofa. Her lacy doilies floated like soggy lily pads.

"They clogged up the sinks," Alex explained. "By the

time they broke the windows downstairs and woke anyone up, the damage here was pretty much done."

Yes, the damage was done, Sydney thought. But it wasn't over. "The other unit?"

"Up on two. Empty. They did a lot of painting up there, too." He gave Sydney's arm a squeeze. "I'm sorry. We're getting statements from the tenants, but—"

"It was dark," Sydney finished. "Everyone was asleep, and no one's going to have seen anything."

"Nothing's impossible." Alex turned toward the babble of voices coming from the lobby, where most of the tenants had gathered. "Why don't you go on up to Mikhail's place? It's going to take a while to calm everyone down and clear them out."

"No, it's my building. I'd like to go talk to them."

With a nod, he started to lead her down the hall. "Funny they didn't bother to steal anything—and that they only broke into the two empty apartments."

She slanted him a look. He might not have been wearing his uniform, but he was definitely a cop. "Is this an interrogation, Alex?"

"Just an observation. I guess you'd know who had access to the tenants' list."

"I guess I would," she replied. "I have a pretty fair idea who's responsible, Alex." She touched a hand to the ruined banister. "Oh, not who tossed paint or flooded the rooms, but who arranged it. But I don't know if I'll be able to prove it."

"You leave the proving up to us."

She glanced at the streak of paint along the wall. "Would you?" She shook her head before he could reply. "Once I'm sure, I'll turn everything over to you. That's a promise—if you promise to say nothing to Mikhail."

"That's a tough bargain, Sydney."

"I'm a tough lady," she said steadily, and walked down to talk to her tenants.

By eight o'clock she was in her office poring over every word in Lloyd Bingham's personnel file. By ten, she'd made several phone calls, consumed too many cups of coffee and had a structured plan.

She'd authorized Mikhail to hire more men, had spoken with the insurance investigator personally and was now prepared for a little psychological warfare.

She put the call through to Lloyd Bingham herself and waited three rings.

"Hello."

"Lloyd, Sydney Hayward."

She heard the rasp of a lighter. "Got a problem?"

"Not that can't be fixed. It was really a very pitiful gesture, Lloyd."

"I don't know what you're talking about."

"Of course you don't." The sarcasm was brisk, almost careless. "Next time, I'd suggest you do more thorough research."

"You want to come to the point?"

"The point is my building, my tenants and your mistake."

"It's a little early in the day for puzzles." The smug satisfaction in his voice had her fingers curling.

"It's not a puzzle when the solution is so clear. I don't imagine you were aware of just how many service people live in the building. And how early some of those service people get up in the morning, have their coffee, glance out the window. Or how cooperative those people would be in giving descriptions to the police."

"If something happened to your building, that's your

problem." He drew hard on his cigarette. "I haven't been near it."

"I never thought you had been," she said easily. "You've always been good at delegating. But once certain parties are picked up by the police, I think you'll discover how unsettling it is not to have loyal employees."

She could have sworn she heard him sweat. "I don't have to listen to this."

"No, of course you don't. And I won't keep you. Oh, Lloyd, don't let them talk you into a bonus. They didn't do a very thorough job. Ciao."

She hung up, immensely satisfied. If she knew her quarry, he wouldn't wait long to meet with his hirelings and pay them off. And since the investigator had been very interested in Sydney's theory, she doubted that meeting would go unobserved.

She flicked her intercom. "Janine, I need food before we start interviewing the new secretaries. Order anything the deli says looks good today and double it."

"You got it. I was about to buzz you, Sydney. Your mother's here."

The little bubble of success burst in her throat. "Tell her I'm..." *Coward.* "No, tell her to come in." But she took a deep breath before she rose and walked to the door. "Mother."

"Sydney, dear." Lovely in ivory linen and smelling of Paris, she strolled in and bussed Sydney's cheek. "I'm so sorry."

"I—what?"

"I've had to wait all weekend to contact you and apologize." Margerite took a steadying breath herself, twisting her envelope bag in her hands. "May I sit?"

"Of course. I'm sorry. Would you like anything?"

"To completely erase Friday evening from my life." Seated, Margerite gave her daughter an embarrassed glance. "This isn't easy for me, Sydney. The simple fact is, I was jealous."

"Oh, Mother."

"No, please." Margerite waved her daughter to the chair beside her. "I don't enjoy the taste of crow and hope you'll let me get it done in one large swallow."

As embarrassed as her mother, Sydney sat and reached for her hand. "It isn't necessary that you swallow at all. We'll just forget it."

Margerite shook her head. "I hope I'm big enough to admit my failings. I like thinking I'm still an attractive and desirable woman."

"You are."

Margerite smiled fleetingly. "But certainly not an admirable one when I find myself eaten up with envy to see that a man I'd hoped to, well, enchant, was instead enchanted by my daughter. I regret, very much, my behavior and my words. There," she said on a puff of breath. "Will you forgive me?"

"Of course I will. And I'll apologize, too, for speaking to you the way I did."

Margerite took a little square of lace from her bag and dabbed at her eyes. "You surprised me, I admit. I've never seen you so passionate about anything. He's a beautiful man, dear. I won't say I approve of a relationship between you, but I can certainly understand it." She sighed as she tucked the handkerchief back into her bag. "Your happiness is important to me, Sydney."

"I know that."

Her eyes still glistened when she looked at her daughter.

"I'm so glad we cleared the air. And I want to do something for you, something to make up for all of this."

"You don't have to do anything."

"I want to, really. Have dinner with me tonight."

Sydney thought of the dozens of things she had to do, of the quiet meal she'd hoped for at the end of it all with Mikhail. Then she looked at her mother's anxious eyes. "I'd love to."

"Wonderful." The spring was back in her step as Margerite got to her feet. "Eight o'clock. Le Cirque." She gave Sydney a quick and genuine hug before she strolled out.

By eight, Sydney would have preferred a long, solitary nap, but stepped from her car dressed for the evening in a sleeveless silk jumpsuit of icy blue.

"My mother's driver will take me home, Donald."

"Very good, Ms. Hayward. Enjoy your evening."

"Thank you."

The maître d' recognized her the moment she walked in and gracefully led her to her table himself. As she passed through the elegant restaurant filled with sparkling people and exotic scents, she imagined Mikhail, sitting at his scarred workbench with a bottle of beer and a bowl of goulash.

She tried not to sigh in envy.

When she spotted her mother—with Channing—at the corner table, she tried not to grit her teeth.

"There you are, darling." So certain her surprise was just what her daughter needed, Margerite didn't notice the lights of war in Sydney's eyes. "Isn't this lovely?"

"Lovely." Sydney's voice was flat as Channing rose to pull out her chair. She said nothing when he bent close to kiss her cheek.

"You look beautiful tonight, Sydney."

The champagne was already chilled and open. She waited while hers was poured, but the first sip did nothing to clear the anger from her throat. "Mother didn't mention you'd be joining us tonight."

"That was my surprise," Margerite bubbled like the wine in her glass. "My little make-up present." Following a pre-arranged signal, she set her napkin aside and rose. "I'm sure you two will excuse me while I powder my nose."

Knowing he only had fifteen minutes to complete his mission, Channing immediately took Sydney's hand. "I've missed you, darling. It seems like weeks since I've had a moment alone with you."

Skillfully Sydney slipped her hand from his. "It has been weeks. How have you been, Channing?"

"Desolate without you." He skimmed a fingertip up her bare arm. She really had exquisite skin. "When are we going to stop playing these games, Sydney?"

"I haven't been playing." She took a sip of wine. "I've been working."

A trace of annoyance clouded his eyes then cleared. He was sure Margerite was right. Once they were married, she would be too busy with him to bother with a career. It was best to get right to the point. "Darling, we've been seeing each other for months now. And of course, we've known each other for years. But things have changed."

She met his eyes. "Yes, they have."

Encouraged, he took her hand again. "I haven't wanted to rush you, but I feel it's time we take the next step. I care for you very much, Sydney. I find you lovely and amusing and sweet."

"And suitable," she muttered.

"Of course. I want you to be my wife." He slipped a box

from his pocket, opened the lid so that the round icy diamond could flash in the candlelight.

"Channing—"

"It reminded me of you," he interrupted. "Regal and elegant."

"It's beautiful, Channing," she said carefully. And cold, she thought. So very cold. "And I'm sorry, but I can't accept it. Or you."

Shock came first, then a trickle of annoyance. "Sydney, we're both adults. There's no need to be coy."

"What I'm trying to be is honest." She shifted in her chair, and this time it was she who took his hands. "I can't tell you how sorry I am that my mother led you to believe I'd feel differently. By doing so, she's put us both in an embarrassing position. Let's be candid, Channing. You don't love me, and I don't love you."

Insulted, he pokered up. "I hardly think I'd be offering marriage otherwise."

"You're offering it because you find me attractive, you think I'd make an excellent hostess, and because I come from the same circle as you. Those are reasons for a merger, not a marriage." She closed the lid on the diamond and pressed the box into his hands. "I make a poor wife, Channing, that much I know. And I have no intention of becoming one again."

He relaxed a little. "I understand you might still be a bit raw over what happened between you and Peter."

"No, you don't understand at all what happened between me and Peter. To be honest, that has nothing to do with my refusing you. I don't love you, Channing, and I'm very much in love with someone else."

His fair skin flushed dark red. "Then I find it worse than insulting that you would pretend an affection for me."

"I do have an affection for you," she said wearily. "But that's all I have. I can only apologize if I failed to make that clear before this."

"I don't believe an apology covers it, Sydney." Stiffly he rose to his feet. "Please give my regrets to your mother."

Straight as a poker, he strode out, leaving Sydney alone with a miserable mix of temper and guilt. Five minutes later, Margerite came out of the ladies' room, beaming. "Well now." She leaned conspiratorially toward her daughter, pleased to see that Channing had given them a few moments alone. "Tell me everything."

"Channing's gone, Mother."

"Gone?" Bright eyed, Margerite glanced around. "What do you mean gone?"

"I mean he's left, furious, I might add, because I declined his proposal of marriage."

"Declined?" Margerite blinked. "You— Sydney, how could you?"

"How could I?" Her voice rose and, catching herself, she lowered it to a whisper. "How could you? You set this entire evening up."

"Of course I did." Frazzled, Margerite waved the oncoming waiter away and reached for her wine. "I've planned for months to see you and Channing together. And since it was obvious that Mikhail had brought you out of your shell, the timing was perfect. Channing is exactly what you need. He's eligible, his family is above reproach, he has a beautiful home and excellent bearing."

"I don't love him."

"Sydney, for heaven's sake, be sensible."

"I've never been anything else, and perhaps that's been the problem. I believed you when you came to see me this morning. I believed you were sorry, that you cared, and that you wanted something more than polite words between us."

Margerite's eyes filled. "Everything I said this morning was true. I'd been miserable all weekend, thinking I'd driven you away. You're my daughter, I do care. I want what's best for you."

"You mean it," Sydney murmured, suddenly, unbearably weary. "But you also believe that you know what's best for me. I don't mean to hurt you, but I've come to understand you've never known what's best for me. By doing this tonight, you caused me to hurt Channing in a way I never meant to."

A tear spilled over. "Sydney, I only thought—"

"Don't think for me." She was perilously close to tears herself. "Don't ever think for me again. I let you do that before, and I ruined someone's life."

"I don't want you to be alone," Margerite choked out. "It's hateful being alone."

"Mother." Though she was afraid she might weaken too much, too soon, she took Margerite's hands. "Listen to me, listen carefully. I love you, but I can't be you. I want to know that we can have an honest, caring relationship. It'll take time. But it can't ever happen unless you try to understand me, unless you respect me for who I am, and not for what you want me to be. I can't marry Channing to please you. I can't marry anyone."

"Oh, Sydney."

"There are things you don't know. Things I don't want to talk about. Just please trust me. I know what I'm doing. I've been happier in the last few weeks than I've ever been."

"Stanislaski," Margerite said on a sigh.

"Yes, Stanislaski. And Hayward," she added. "And me.

I'm doing something with my life, Mother. It's making a difference. Now let's go fix your makeup and start over."

At his workbench, Mikhail polished the rosewood bust. He hadn't meant to work so late, but Sydney had simply emerged in his hands. There was no way to explain the way it felt to have her come to life there. It wasn't powerful. It was humbling. He'd barely had to think. Though his fingers were cramped, proving how long he had carved and sanded and polished, he could barely remember the technique he'd used.

The tools didn't matter, only the result. Now she was there with him, beautiful, warm, alive. And he knew it was a piece he would never part with.

Sitting back, he circled his shoulders to relieve the stiffness. It had been a viciously long day, starting before dawn. He'd had to channel the edge of his rage into organizing the cleaning up and repair the worst of the damage. Now that the impetus that had driven him to complete the bust was passed, he was punchy with fatigue. But he didn't want to go to bed. An empty bed.

How could he miss her so much after only hours? Why did it feel as though she were a world away when she was only at the other end of the city? He wasn't going to go through another night without her, he vowed as he stood up to pace. She was going to have to understand that. He would make her understand that. A woman had no right to make herself vital to a man's existence then leave him restless and alone at midnight.

Dragging a hand through his hair, he considered his options. He could go to bed and will himself to sleep. He could call her and satisfy himself with the sound of her voice. Or he could go uptown and beat on her door until she let him in.

He grinned, liking the third choice best. Snatching up a shirt, he tugged it on as he headed for the door. Sydney gave a surprised gasp as he yanked it open just as her hand was poised to knock.

"Oh. What instincts." She pressed the hand to her heart. "I'm sorry to come by so late, but I saw your light was on, so I—"

He didn't let her finish, but pulled her inside and held her until she wondered her ribs didn't crack. "I was coming for you," he muttered.

"Coming for me? I just left the restaurant."

"I wanted you. I wanted to—" He broke off and snapped her back. "It's after midnight. What are you doing coming all the way downtown after midnight?"

"For heaven's sake—"

"It's not safe for a woman alone."

"I was perfectly safe."

He shook his head, cupping her chin. "Next time, you call. I'll come to you." Then his eyes narrowed. An artist's eyes, a lover's eyes saw beyond carefully repaired makeup. "You've been crying."

There was such fury in the accusation, she had to laugh. "No, not really. Mother got a bit emotional, and there was a chain reaction."

"I thought you said you'd made up with her."

"I did. I have. At least I think we've come to a better understanding."

He smiled a little, tracing a finger over Sydney's lips. "She does not approve of me for her daughter."

"That's not really the problem. I'm afraid she's feeling

a little worn down. She had her plans blow up in her face tonight."

"You'll tell me."

"Yes." She walked over, intending to collapse on his badly sprung couch. But she saw the bust. Slowly she moved closer to study it. When she spoke, her voice was low and thick. "You have an incredible talent."

"I carve what I see, what I know, what I feel."

"Is this how you see me?"

"It's how you are." He laid his hands lightly on her shoulders. "For me."

Then she was beautiful for him, Sydney thought. And she was trembling with life and love, for him. "I didn't even pose for you."

"You will." He brushed his lips over her hair. "Talk to me."

"When I met Mother at the restaurant, Channing was with her."

Over Sydney's head, Mikhail's eyes darkened dangerously. "The banker with the silk suits. You let him kiss you before you let me."

"I knew him before I knew you." Amused, Sydney turned and looked jealousy in the eye. "And I didn't let you kiss me, as I recall. You just did."

He did so again, ruthlessly. "You won't let him again."

"No."

"Good." He drew her to the sofa. "Then he can live."

With a laugh, she threw her arms around him for a hug, then settled her head on his shoulder. "None of it's his fault, really. Or my mother's, either. It's more a matter of habit and circumstance. She'd set up the evening after persuading Channing that the time was ripe to propose."

"Propose?" Mikhail spun her around to face him. "He wants to marry you?"

"Not really. He thought he did. He certainly doesn't want to marry me anymore." But he was shoving her out of the way so he could get up and pace. "There's no reason to be angry," Sydney said as she smoothed down her jumpsuit. "I was the one in the awkward position. As it is I doubt he'll speak to me again."

"If he does, I'll cut out his tongue." Slowly, Mikhail thought, working up the rage. "No one marries you but me."

"I've already explained…" She trailed off as breath lodged in a hard ball in her throat. "There's really no need to go into this," she managed as she rose. "It's late."

"You wait," Mikhail ordered and strode into the bedroom. When he came back carrying a small box, Sydney's blood turned to ice. "Sit."

"No, Mikhail, please—"

"Then stand." He flipped open the top of the box to reveal a ring of hammered gold with a small center stone of fiery red. "The grandfather of my father made this for his wife. He was a goldsmith so the work is fine, even though the stone is small. It comes to me because I am the oldest son. If it doesn't please you, I buy you something else."

"No, it's beautiful. Please, don't. I can't." She held her fisted hands behind her back. "Don't ask me."

"I am asking you," he said impatiently. "Give me your hand."

She took a step back. "I can't wear the ring. I can't marry you."

With a shake of his head, he pulled her hand free and pushed the ring on her finger. "See, you can wear it. It's too big, but we'll fix it."

"No." She would have pulled it off again, but he closed his hand over hers. "I don't want to marry you."

His fingers tightened on hers, and a fire darted into his eyes, more brilliant than the shine of the ruby. "Why?"

"I don't want to get married," she said as clearly as she could. "I won't have what we started together spoiled."

"Marriage doesn't spoil love, it nurtures it."

"You don't know," she snapped back. "You've never been married. I have. And I won't go through it again."

"So." Struggling with temper, he rocked back on his heels. "This husband of yours hurt you, makes you unhappy, so you think I'll do the same."

"Damn it, I loved him." Her voice broke, and she covered her face with her hand as the tears began to fall.

Torn between jealousy and misery, he gathered her close, murmuring endearments as he stroked her hair. "I'm sorry."

"You don't understand."

"Let me understand." He tilted her face up to kiss the tears. "I'm sorry," he repeated. "I won't yell at you anymore."

"It's not that." She let out a shuddering breath. "I don't want to hurt you. Please, let this go."

"I can't let this go. Or you. I love you, Sydney. I need you. For my life I need you. Explain to me why you won't take me."

"If there was anyone," she began in a rush, then shook her head before she could even wish it. "Mikhail, I can't consider marriage. Hayward is too much of a responsibility, and I need to focus on my career."

"This is smoke, to hide the real answer."

"All right." Bracing herself, she stepped away from him. "I don't think I could handle failing again, and losing someone I love. Marriage changes people."

"How did it change you?"

"I loved Peter, Mikhail. Not the way I love you, but more than anyone else. He was my best friend. We grew up together. When my parents divorced, he was the only one I could talk to. He cared, really cared, about how I felt, what I thought, what I wanted. We could sit for hours on the beach up at the Hamptons and watch the water, tell each other secrets."

She turned away. Saying it all out loud brought the pain spearing back.

"And you fell in love."

"No," she said miserably. "We just loved each other. I can hardly remember a time without him. And I can't remember when it started to become a given that we'd marry someday. Not that we talked about it ourselves. Everyone else did. Sydney and Peter, what a lovely couple they make. Isn't it nice how well they suit? I suppose we heard it so much, we started to believe it. Anyway, it was expected, and we'd both been raised to do what was expected of us."

She brushed at tears and wandered over to his shelves. "You were right when you gave me that figure of Cinderella. I've always followed the rules. I was expected to go to boarding school and get top grades. So I did. I was expected to behave presentably, never to show unacceptable emotions. So I did. I was expected to marry Peter. So I did."

She whirled back. "There we were, both of us just turned twenty-two—quite an acceptable age for marriage. I suppose we both thought it would be fine. After all, we'd known each other forever, we liked the same things, understood each other. Loved each other. But it wasn't fine. Almost from the beginning. Honeymooning in Greece. We both loved the country. And we both pretended that the physical part of marriage was fine. Of course, it was anything but fine, and the more we pretended, the further apart we became. We moved back to New York so he could take his place in the family business. I decorated the house, gave parties. And dreaded watching the sun go down."

"It was a mistake," Mikhail said gently.

"Yes, it was. One I made, one I was responsible for. I lost my closest friend, and before it was over, all the love was gone. There were only arguments and accusations. I was frigid, why shouldn't he have turned to someone else for a little warmth? But we kept up appearances. That was expected. And when we divorced, we did so in a very cold, very controlled, very civilized manner. I couldn't be a wife to him, Mikhail."

"It's not the same for us." He went to her.

"No, it's not. And I won't let it be."

"You're hurt because of something that happened to you, not something you did." He caught her face in his hands when she shook her head. "Yes. You need to let go of it, and trust what we have. I'll give you time."

"No." Desperate, she clamped her hands on his wrists. "Don't you see it's the same thing? You love me, so you expect me to marry you, because that's what you want—what you think is best."

"Not best," he said, giving her a quick shake. "Right. I need to share my life with you. I want to live with you, make babies with you. Watch them grow. There's a family inside us, Sydney."

She jerked away. He wouldn't listen, she thought. He wouldn't understand. "Marriage and family aren't in my plans," she said, suddenly cold. "You're going to have to accept that."

"Accept? You love me. I'm good enough for that. Good enough for you to take to your bed, but not for changing plans. All because you once followed rules instead of your heart."

"What I'm following now is my common sense." She walked by him to the door. "I'm sorry, I can't give you what you want."

"You will not go home alone."

"I think it'll be better if I leave."

"You want to leave, you leave." He stalked over to wrench the door open. "But I'll take you."

It wasn't until she lay teary and fretful in her bed that she realized she still wore his ring.

Chapter 12

It wasn't that she buried herself in work over the next two days, it was that work buried her. Sydney only wished it had helped. Keeping busy was supposed to be good for the morale. So why was hers flat on its face?

She closed the biggest deal of her career at Hayward, hired a new secretary to take the clerical weight off Janine and handled a full-staff meeting. Hayward stock had climbed three full points in the past ten days. The board was thrilled with her.

And she was miserable.

"An Officer Stanislaski on two, Ms. Hayward," her new secretary said through the intercom.

"Stan—oh." Her spirits did a jig, then settled. *Officer.* "Yes, I'll take it. Thank you." Sydney pasted on a smile for her own peace of mind. "Alex?"

"Hey, pretty lady. Thought you'd want to be the first to

know. They just brought your old pal Lloyd Bingham in for questioning."

Her smiled faded. "I see."

"The insurance investigator took your advice and kept an eye on him. He met with a couple of bad numbers yesterday, passed some bills. Once they were picked up, they sang better than Springsteen."

"Then Lloyd did hire someone to vandalize the building."

"So they say. I don't think you're going to have any trouble from him for a while."

"I'm glad to hear it."

"You were pretty sharp, homing in on him. Brains and beauty," he said with a sigh that nearly made her smile again. "Why don't we take off to Jamaica for a couple of days? Drive Mikhail crazy?"

"I think he's already mad enough."

"Hey, he's giving you a hard time? Just come to Uncle Alex." When she didn't respond, the teasing note dropped out of his voice. "Don't mind Mik, Sydney. He's got moods, that's all. It's the artist. He's nuts about you."

"I know." Her fingers worried the files on her desk. "Maybe you could give him a call, tell him the news."

"Sure. Anything else you want me to pass on?"

"Tell him…no," she decided. "No, I've already told him. Thanks for calling, Alex."

"No problem. Let me know if you change your mind about Jamaica."

She hung up, wishing she felt as young as Alex had sounded. As happy. As easy. But then Alex wasn't in love. And he hadn't punched a hole in his own dreams.

Is that what she'd done? Sydney wondered as she pushed away from her desk. Had she sabotaged her own yearnings? No, she'd stopped herself, and the man she loved from making a mistake. Marriage wasn't always the answer. She had her own example to prove it. And her mother's. Once Mikhail had cooled off, he'd accept her position, and they could go on as they had before.

Who was she kidding?

He was too stubborn, too bullheaded, too damn sure his way was the right way to back down for an instant.

And what if he said all or nothing? What would she do then? Snatching up a paper clip, she began to twist it as she paced the office. If it was a matter of giving him up and losing him, or giving in and risking losing him...

God, she needed someone to talk to. Since it couldn't be Mikhail, she was left with pitifully few choices. Once she would have taken her problems to Peter, but that was...

She stopped, snapping the mangled metal in her fingers. That was the source of the problem. And maybe, just maybe, the solution.

Without giving herself time to think, she rushed out of her office and into Janine's. "I have to leave town for a couple of days," she said without preamble.

Janine was already rising from behind her new desk. "But—"

"I know it's sudden, and inconvenient, but it can't be helped. There's nothing vital pending at the moment, so you should be able to handle whatever comes in. If you can't, then it has to wait."

"Sydney, you have three appointments tomorrow."

"You take them. You have the files, you have my viewpoint. As soon as I get to where I'm going, I'll call in."

"But, Sydney." Janine scurried to the door as Sydney strode away. "Where are you going?"

"To see an old friend."

* * *

Less than an hour after Sydney had rushed from her office, Mikhail stormed in. He'd had it. He'd given the woman two days to come to her senses, and she was out of time. They were going to have this out and have it out now.

He breezed by the new secretary with a curt nod and pushed open Sydney's door.

"Excuse me. Sir, excuse me."

Mikhail whirled on the hapless woman. "Where the hell is she?"

"Ms. Hayward is not in the office," she said primly. "I'm afraid you'll have to—"

"If not here, where?"

"I'll handle this, Carla," Janine murmured from the doorway.

"Yes, ma'am." Carla made her exit quickly and with relief.

"Ms. Hayward's not here, Mr. Stanislaski. Is there something I can do for you?"

"Tell me where she is."

"I'm afraid I can't." The look in his eyes had her backing up a step. "I only know she's out of town for a day or two. She left suddenly and didn't tell me where she was going."

"Out of town?" He scowled at the empty desk, then back at Janine. "She doesn't leave her work like this."

"I admit it's unusual. But I got the impression it was important. I'm sure she'll call in. I'll be happy to give her a message for you."

He said something short and hard in Ukrainian and stormed out again.

"I think I'd better let you tell her that yourself," Janine murmured to the empty room.

* * *

Twenty-four hours after leaving her office, Sydney stood on a shady sidewalk in Georgetown, Washington, D.C. A headlong rush of adrenaline had brought her this far, far enough to have her looking at the home where Peter had settled when he'd relocated after the divorce.

The impulsive drive to the airport, the quick shuttle from city to city had been easy enough. Even the phone call to request an hour of Peter's time hadn't been so difficult. But this, this last step was nearly impossible.

She hadn't seen him in over three years, and then it had been across a wide table in a lawyer's office. Civilized, God, yes, they'd been civilized. And strangers.

It was foolish, ridiculous, taking off on this kind of tangent. Talking to Peter wouldn't change anything. Nothing could. Yet she found herself climbing the stairs to the porch of the lovely old row house, lifting the brass knocker and letting it rap on the door.

He answered himself, looking so much the same that she nearly threw out her hands to him as she would have done once. He was tall and leanly built, elegantly casual in khakis and a linen shirt. His sandy hair was attractively rumpled. But the green eyes didn't light with pleasure, instead remaining steady and cool.

"Sydney," he said, backing up to let her inside.

The foyer was cool and light, speaking subtly in its furnishings and artwork of discreet old money. "I appreciate you seeing me like this, Peter."

"You said it was important."

"To me."

"Well, then." Knowing nothing else to say, he ushered her down the hall and into a sitting room. Manners sat seamlessly on both of them, causing her to make the right comments about the house, and him to parry them while offering her a seat and a drink.

"You're enjoying Washington, then."

"Very much." He sipped his own wine while she simply turned her glass around and around in her hand. She was nervous. He knew her too well not to recognize the signs. And she was as lovely as ever. It hurt. He hated the fact that it hurt just to look at her. And the best way to get past the pain was to get to the point.

"What is it I can do for you, Sydney?"

Strangers, she thought again as she looked down at her glass. They had known each other all of their lives, had been married for nearly three years, and were strangers. "It's difficult to know where to start."

He leaned back in his chair and gestured. "Pick a spot."

"Peter, why did you marry me?"

"I beg your pardon."

"I want to know why you married me."

Whatever he'd been expecting, it hadn't been this. Shifting, he drank again. "For several of the usual reasons, I suppose."

"You loved me?"

His eyes flashed to hers. "You know I loved you."

"I know we loved each other. You were my friend." She pressed her lips together. "My best friend."

He got up to pour more wine. "We were children."

"Not when we married. We were young, but we weren't children. And we were still friends. I don't know how it all went so wrong, Peter, or what I did to ruin it so completely, but—"

"You?" He stared, the bottle in one hand, the glass in the other. "What do you mean *you ruined it*?"

"I made you unhappy, miserably unhappy. I know I

failed in bed, and it all spilled over into the rest until you couldn't even bear to be around me."

"You didn't want me to touch you," he shot back. "Damn it, it was like making love to—"

"An iceberg," she finished flatly. "So you said."

Fighting guilt, he set his glass down. "I said a lot of things, so did you. I thought I'd gotten past most of it until I heard your voice this afternoon."

"I'm sorry." She rose, her body and voice stiff to compensate for shattered pride. "I've just made it worse coming here. I am sorry, Peter, I'll go."

"It was like making love with my sister." The words burst out and stopped her before she crossed the room. "My pal. Damn, Sydney, I couldn't…" The humiliation of it clawed at him again. "I could never get beyond that, and make you, well, a wife. It unmanned me. And I took it out on you."

"I thought you hated me."

He slapped the bottle back on the table. "It was easier to try to hate you than admit I couldn't arouse either one of us. That I was inadequate."

"But I was." Baffled, she took a step toward him. "I know I was useless to you in bed—before you told me, I knew it. And you had to go elsewhere for what I couldn't give you."

"I cheated on you," he said flatly. "I lied and cheated on my closest friend. I hated the way you'd started to look at me, the way I started to look at myself. So I went out to prove my manhood elsewhere, and hurt you. When you found out, I did the manly thing and turned the blame on you. Hell, Sydney, we were barely speaking to each other by that time. Except in public."

"I know. And I remember how I reacted, the hateful things I said to you. I let pride cost me a friend."

"I lost a friend, too. I've never been sorrier for anything in my life." It cost him to walk to her, to take her hand. "You didn't ruin anything, Syd. At least not alone."

"I need a friend, Peter. I very badly need a friend."

He brushed a tear away with his thumb. "Willing to give me another shot?" Smiling a little, he took out his handkerchief. "Here. Blow your nose and sit down."

She did, clinging to his hand. "Was that the only reason it didn't work. Because we couldn't handle the bedroom?"

"That was a big one. Other than that, we're too much alike. It's too easy for us to step behind breeding and let a wound bleed us dry. Hell, Syd, what were we doing getting married?"

"Doing what everyone told us."

"There you go."

Comforted, she brought his hand to her cheek. "Are you happy, Peter?"

"I'm getting there. How about you? President Hayward."

She laughed. "Were you surprised?"

"Flabbergasted. I was so proud of you."

"Don't. You'll make me cry again."

"I've got a better idea." He kissed her forehead. "Come out in the kitchen. I'll fix us a sandwich and you can tell me what you've been up to besides big business."

It was almost easy. There was some awkwardness, little patches of caution, but the bond that had once held them together had stretched instead of broken. Slowly, carefully, they were easing the tension on it.

Over rye bread and coffee, she tried to tell him the rest. "Have you ever been in love, Peter?"

"Marsha Rosenbloom."

"That was when we were fourteen."

"And she'd already given up a training bra," he said with his mouth full. "I was deeply in love." Then he smiled at her. "No, I've escaped that particular madness."

"If you were, if you found yourself in love with someone, would you consider marriage again?"

"I don't know. I'd like to think I'd do a better job of it, but I don't know. Who is he?"

Stalling, she poured more coffee. "He's an artist. A carpenter."

"Which?"

"Both. He sculpts, and he builds. I've only known him a little while, just since June."

"Moving quick, Sydney?"

"I know. That's part of the problem. Everything moves fast with Mikhail. He's so bold and sure and full of emotion. Like his work, I suppose."

As two and two began to make four, his brows shot up. "The Russian?"

"Ukrainian," she corrected automatically.

"Good God, Stanislaski, right? There's a piece of his in the White House."

"Is there?" She gave Peter a bemused smile. "He didn't mention it. He took me home to meet his family, this wonderful family, but he didn't tell me his work's in the White House. It shows you where his priorities lie."

"And you're in love with him."

"Yes. He wants to marry me." She shook her head. "I got two proposals in the same night. One from Mikhail, and one from Channing Warfield."

"Lord, Sydney, not Channing. He's not your type."

She shoved the coffee aside to lean closer. "Why?"

"In the first place he's nearly humorless. He'd bore you

mindless. The only thing he knows about Daddy's business is how to take clients to lunch. And his only true love is his tailor."

She really smiled. "I've missed you, Peter."

He took her hand again. "What about your big, bold artist?"

"He doesn't have a tailor, or take clients to lunch. And he makes me laugh. Peter, I couldn't bear to marry him and have it fall apart on me again."

"I can't tell you if it's right. And if I were you, I wouldn't listen to anyone's good-intentioned advice this time around."

"But you'll give me some anyway?"

"But I'll give you some anyway," he agreed, and felt years drop away. "Don't judge whatever you have with him by the mess we made. Just ask yourself a couple of questions. Does he make you happy? Do you trust him? How do you imagine your life with him? How do you imagine it without him?"

"And when I have the answers?"

"You'll know what to do." He kissed the hand joined with his. "I love you, Sydney."

"I love you, too."

Answer the questions, she thought as she pushed the elevator button in Mikhail's lobby. It was twenty-four hours since Peter had listed them, but she hadn't allowed herself to think of them. Hadn't had to, she corrected as she stepped inside the car. She already knew the answers.

Did he make her happy? Yes, wildly happy.

Did she trust him? Without reservation.

Her life with him? A roller coaster of emotions, demands, arguments, laughter, frustration.

Without him? Blank.

She simply couldn't imagine it. She would have her work, her routine, her ambitions. No, she'd never be without a purpose again. But without him, it would all be straight lines.

So she knew what to do. If it wasn't too late.

There was the scent of drywall dust in the hallway when she stepped out of the elevator. She glanced up to see the ceiling had been replaced, the seams taped, mudded and sanded. All that was left to be done here was the paint and trim.

He did good work, she thought, as she ran her hand along the wall. In a short amount of time, he'd taken a sad old building and turned it into something solid and good. There was still work ahead, weeks before the last nail would be hammered. But what he fixed would last.

Pressing a hand to her stomach, she knocked on his door. And hoped.

There wasn't a sound from inside. No blare of music, no click of work boots on wood. Surely he hadn't gone to bed, she told herself. It was barely ten. She knocked again, louder, and wondered if she should call out his name.

A door opened—not his, but the one just down the hall. Keely poked her head out. After one quick glance at Sydney, the friendliness washed out of her face.

"He's not here," she said. Her champagne voice had gone flat. Keely didn't know the details, but she was sure of one thing. This was the woman who had put Mikhail in a miserable mood for the past few days.

"Oh." Sydney's hand dropped to her side. "Do you know where he is?"

"Out." Keely struggled not to notice that there was misery in Sydney's eyes, as well.

"I see." Sydney willed her shoulders not to slump. "I'll just wait."

"Suit yourself," Keely said with a shrug. What did she care if the woman was obviously in love? This was the woman who'd hurt her pal. As an actress Keely prided herself on recognizing the mood beneath the actions. Mikhail might have been fiercely angry over the past few days, but beneath the short temper had been raw, seeping hurt. And she'd put it there. What did it matter if she was suffering, too?

Of course it mattered. Keely's sentimental heart went gooey in her chest.

"Listen, he'll probably be back soon. Do you want a drink or something?"

"No, really. I'm fine. How's, ah, your apartment coming?"

"New stove works like a champ." Unable to be anything but kind, Keely leaned on the jamb. "They've still got a little of this and that—especially with the damage those idiots did." She brightened. "Hey, did you know they arrested a guy?"

"Yes." Janine had told her about Lloyd's arrest when she'd called in. "I'm sorry. He was only trying to get back at me."

"It's not your fault the guy's a jerk. Anyway, they sucked up the water, and Mik mixed up some stuff to get the paint off the brick. They had to tear out the ceiling in the apartment below that empty place. And the floors buckled up pretty bad." She shrugged again. "You know Mik, he'll fix it up."

Yes, she knew Mik. "Do you know if there was much damage to Mrs. Wolburg's things?"

"The rugs are a loss. A lot of other things were pretty

soggy. They'll dry out." More comfortable, Keely took a bite of the banana she'd been holding behind her back. "Her grandson was by. She's doing real good. Using a walker and everything already, and crabbing about coming home. We're planning on throwing her a welcome-back party next month. Maybe you'd like to come."

"I'd—" They both turned at the whine of the elevator.

The doors opened, and deep voices raised in some robust Ukrainian folk song poured out just ahead of the two men. They were both a little drunk, more than a little grubby, and the way their arms were wrapped around each other, it was impossible to say who was supporting whom. Sydney noticed the blood first. It was smeared on Mikhail's white T-shirt, obviously from the cuts on his lip and over his eye.

"My God."

The sound of her voice had Mikhail's head whipping up like a wolf. His grin faded to a surly stare as he and his brother stumbled to a halt.

"What do you want?" The words were thickened with vodka and not at all welcoming.

"What happened to you?" She was already rushing toward them. "Was there an accident?"

"Hey, pretty lady." Alex smiled charmingly though his left eye was puffy with bruises and nearly swollen shut. "We had a hell'va party. Should've been there. Right, bro?"

Mikhail responded by giving him a sluggish punch in the stomach. Sydney decided it was meant as affection as Mikhail then turned, locked his brother in a bear hug, kissed both his cheeks.

While Mikhail searched his pockets for keys, Sydney turned to Alex. "What happened? Who did this to you?"

"Did what?" He tried to wink at Keely and winced. "Oh, this?" He touched ginger fingers to his eye and grinned.

"He's always had a sneaky left." He shot his brother a look of bleary admiration while Mikhail fought to fit what seemed like a very tiny key in an even tinier lock. "I got a couple good ones in under his guard. Wouldn't have caught him if he hadn't been drunk. Course I was drunk, too." He weaved toward Keely's door. "Hey, Keely, my beautiful gold-haired dream, got a raw steak?"

"No." But having sympathy for the stupid, she took his arm. "Come on, champ, I'll pour you into a cab."

"Let's go dancing," he suggested as she guided him back to the elevator. "Like to dance?"

"I live for it." She glanced over her shoulder as she shoved him into the elevator. "Good luck," she told Sydney.

She was going to need it, Sydney decided, as she walked up behind Mikhail just as he managed to open his own door. He shoved it back, nearly caught her in the nose, but her reflexes were better than his at the moment.

"You've been fighting with your brother," she accused.

"So?" He thought it was a shame, a damn shame, that the sight of her was sobering him up so quickly. "You would rather I fight with strangers?"

"Oh, sit down." Using her temporary advantage, she shoved him into a chair. She strode off into the bathroom, muttering to herself. When she came back with a wet washcloth and antiseptic, he was up again, leaning out the window, trying to clear his head.

"Are you sick?"

He pulled his head in and turned back, disdain clear on his battered face. "Stanislaskis don't get sick from vodka." Maybe a little queasy, he thought, when the vodka was followed by a couple of solid rights to the gut. Then he grinned. His baby brother had a hell of a punch.

"Just drunk then," she said primly, and pointed to the chair. "Sit down. I'll clean your face."

"I don't need nursing." But he sat, because it felt better that way.

"What you need is a keeper." Bending over, she began to dab at the cut above his eye while he tried to resist the urge to lay his cheek against the soft swell of her breast. "Going out and getting drunk, beating up your brother. Why would you do such a stupid thing?"

He scowled at her. "It felt good."

"Oh, I'm sure it feels marvelous to have a naked fist popped in your eye." She tilted his head as she worked. That eye was going to bruise dramatically before morning. "I can't imagine what your mother would say if she knew."

"She would say nothing. She'd smack us both." His breath hissed when she slopped on the antiseptic. "Even when he starts it she smacks us both." Indignation shimmered. "Explain that."

"I'm sure you both deserved it. Pathetic," she muttered, then looked down at his hands. "Idiot!" The skin on the knuckles was bruised and broken. "You're an artist, damn it. You have no business hurting your hands."

It felt good, incredibly good to have her touching and scolding him. Any minute he was going to pull her into his lap and beg.

"I do what I like with my own hands," he said. And thought about what he'd like to be doing with them right now.

"You do what you like, period," she tossed back as she gently cleaned his knuckles. "Shouting at people, punching people. Drinking until you smell like the inside of a vodka bottle."

He wasn't so drunk he didn't know an insult when he

heard one. Nudging her aside, he stood and, staggering only a little, disappeared into the next room. A moment later, she heard the shower running.

This wasn't the way she'd planned it, Sydney thought, wringing the washcloth in her hands. She was supposed to come to him, tell him how much she loved him, ask him to forgive her for being a fool. And he was supposed to be kind and understanding, taking her in his arms, telling her she'd made him the happiest man in the world.

Instead he'd been drunk and surly. And she'd been snappish and critical.

Well, he deserved it. Before she had time to think, she'd heaved the washcloth toward the kitchen, where it slapped wetly against the wall then slid down to the sink. She stared at it for a minute, then down at her own hands.

She'd thrown something. And it felt wonderful. Glancing around, she spotted a paperback book and sent it sailing. A plastic cup gave a nice ring when it hit the wall, but she'd have preferred the crash of glass. Snatching up a battered sneaker, she prepared to heave that, as well. A sound in the doorway had her turning, redirecting aim and shooting it straight into Mikhail's damp, naked chest. His breath woofed out.

"What are you doing?"

"Throwing things." She snatched up the second shoe and let it fly. He caught that one before it beaned him.

"You leave me, go away without a word, and you come to throw things?"

"That's right."

Eyes narrowed, he tested the weight of the shoe he held. It was tempting, very tempting to see if he could land it on the point of that jutting chin. On an oath, he dropped it. However much she deserved it, he just couldn't hit a woman.

"Where did you go?"

She tossed her hair back. "I went to see Peter."

He shoved his bruised hands into the pockets of the jeans he'd tugged on. "You leave me to go see another man, then you come back to throw shoes at my head. Tell me why I shouldn't just toss you out that window and be done with it."

"It was important that I see him, that I talk to him. And I—"

"You hurt me," he blurted out. The words burned on his tongue. He hated to admit it. "Do you think I care about getting a punch in the face? You'd already twisted my heart. This I can fight," he said, touching the back of his hand to his cut lip. "What you do to me inside leaves me helpless. And I hate it."

"I'm sorry." She took a step toward him but saw she wasn't yet welcome. "I was afraid I'd hurt you more if I tried to give you what you wanted. Mikhail, listen, please. Peter was the only person who cared for me. For *me*. My parents…" She could only shake her head. "They're not like yours. They wanted what was best for me, I'm sure, but their way of giving it was to hire nannies and buy me pretty clothes, send me to the best boarding school. You don't know how lonely it was." Impatient, she rubbed her fingers over her eyes to dry them. "I only had Peter, and then I lost him. What I feel for you is so much bigger, so much more, that I don't know what I'd do if I lost you."

He was softening. She could do that to him, as well. No matter how he tried to harden his heart, she could melt it. "You left me, Sydney. I'm not lost."

"I had to see him. I hurt him terribly, Mikhail. I was convinced that I'd ruined the marriage, the friendship, the love. What if I'd done the same with us?" With a little sigh, she walked to the window. "The funny thing was, he was carrying around the same guilt, the same remorse, the same fears. Talking with him, being friends again, made all the difference."

"I'm not angry that you talked to him, but that you went away. I was afraid you wouldn't come back."

She turned from the window. "I'm finished with running. I only went away because I'd hoped I could come back to you. Really come back."

He stared into her eyes, trying to see inside. "Have you?"

"Yes." She let out a shaky breath. "All the answers are yes. We walked through this building once, and I could hear the voices, all the sounds behind the doors. The smells, the laughing. I envied you belonging here. I need to belong. I want to have the chance to belong. To have that family you said was inside us."

She reached up, drawing a chain from around her neck. At the end, the little ruby flashed its flame.

Shaken, he crossed the room to cup the ring in his hand. "You wear it," he murmured.

"I was afraid to keep it on my finger. That I'd lose it. I need you to tell me if you still want me to have it."

His eyes came back to hers and locked. Even as he touched his lips to hers gently, he watched her. "I didn't ask you right the first time."

"I didn't answer right the first time." She took his face in her hands to kiss him again, to feel again. "You were perfect."

"I was clumsy. Angry that the banker had asked you before me."

Eyes wet, she smiled. "What banker? I don't know any bankers."

Unfastening the chain from around her neck, he set it aside. "It was not how I'd planned it. There was no music."

"I hear music."

"No soft words, no pretty light, no flowers."

"There's a moon. I still have the first rose you gave me."

Touched, he kissed her hands. "I told you only what I wanted, not what I'd give. You have my heart, Sydney. As long as it beats. My life is your life." He slipped the ring onto her finger. "Will you belong to me?"

She curled her fingers to keep the ring in place. "I already do."

* * * * *